People Watching

Samantha Lauren

Copyright © 2023 Samantha Lauren

All rights reserved.

ISBN: 979-8-218-20866-0

DEDICATION

To those who can find joy even as the world crashes down around us. To those who can laugh in the midst of the most unimaginable tragedies. To those who keep moving despite it all. The world needs us.

SATURDAY

1
Jess Dawson

Cal has never once been excited about family vacations. He would be perfectly happy taking a staycation and working on projects around the house. He hates the beach, but still, we go every year. I suppose he goes for me.

I'm thirty-five years old, and I've never missed a summer vacation to the coast. Every year of my life, I've buried my toes in the sand at least once, and I'm not about to break that tradition just because my husband doesn't care for it.

Don't worry. I'm not completely selfish. I accepted long ago that Cal would never spend more than a couple of hours on the beach with me. He appeases me for a short time and then retreats to the beach house to read a book or watch one of his television shows that inevitably drives me nuts.

This is why I find it quite odd that my husband is the one excited about our family vacation this year. The car is packed; Cal is wearing his driving-to-the-beach attire (loose shorts, baggy t-shirt, tennis shoes because he swears he can't drive in flip flops); and he's rushing me as I search for the dog's CBD. I don't like to be rushed. It gives me anxiety. Just like the dog. That's why he needs the CBD. Without it, the dog screams all the way to the beach. Literally screams.

"I don't get it. Every year, you want to leave the night before and get a hotel room just so we can check into the house on time. This year, you're hardly ready." Cal runs a hand through his thick, dark, graying hair. I don't mind the gray. I've known Cal since he was a skinny teenager. The gray is keeping things fresh.

"Have you seen Sweeney's CBD? We can't leave until he has his CBD."

"Jess, I think you are the one who needs that CBD." Cal digs around in a drawer by the door, and delivers Sweeney's bottle of salmon-flavored CBD to my hands.

"Thank you," I tell him. I pull a dog treat from the cabinet and drizzle the CBD oil in the core of it. Sweeney is already next to me, ready for his special travel treat. We rescued Sweeney from an older couple who had adopted him as a puppy. They had underestimated his breed and his age. Sweeney was five months old with the blood of a Jack Russell Terrier in his veins. I couldn't believe he hadn't somehow managed to trip one of them, causing them to fall and break a hip. Maybe we rescued him in time.

Now, Sweeney is seven years old. He's no longer a puppy, and he's calmer than he used to be. Every now and then, he'll get a wave of playfulness; but for the most part, Sweeney is a lap dog. *My* lap dog. He knows I'm the alpha. At least, someone in my house understands this.

After much struggle, the dog and I are ready to go. I put Sweeney in his dog car seat and settle into the passenger seat myself, and then Cal backs out of the driveway. I never allow myself to move into vacation mode until we're checked into our beach house for the week. I'm one of those people who expect the worst to happen. For all I know, our beach rental could have burned down overnight, and we're suddenly out of a beach house. Anything could happen.

I'm suspicious of Cal's enthusiasm about our vacation. He's whistling, actually whistling. Cal never whistles—ever. His excitement is sort of getting on my nerves. Cal only acts like this when we're going to see his favorite college football team play.

I plug in my own music through the speakers. I have my own playlist comprised of music from the '60s and '70s. I even threw in a couple of tunes from the '80s and some of my favorites from the '90s. I actually pride myself on the playlists I build. It's not until an old country classic starts playing after a '90s R&B tune that people understand just how diverse my playlists can be.

Cal continues to whistle—this time, with the music, which is mostly annoying, but I've learned to tune it out. Sweeney is slightly calm but chasing cars from the window. I take advantage of the quiet car and begin reading a book that I picked out specifically to read this coming week on vacation.

Three more hours to go until we reach our beach destination: Edisto Island, South Carolina.

2
Drew Clark

I'm slightly confused and trying not to say anything for fear of Lindsey getting offended that I'm bothered by her excitement. Linds has never been this excited for a week of vacation at the beach. When we married ten years ago, we agreed that we'd compromise on vacation destinations by taking turns choosing where we should go. I am a fan of the coast. She's a fan of the mountains. I generally loathe vacation the years she gets to choose the location. However, I wouldn't tell her this, but I have enjoyed a few of the mountain getaways she's planned. The coast is still king, though—at least, for me.

"How long does it take to throw some suitcases in the trunk, Andrew?" Lindsey snaps at me from the passenger seat of our SUV.

"Hurry," our one-year-old daughter adds to her mother's urgency. Lilly speaks in a language only her mom and I understand. Her *hurry* didn't sound like a normal adult's *hurry*. It sounded more like, *huey*, which I know means "hurry" because it's basically the only word Lindsey ever says to me. I'm not sure anyone is capable of being as fast as Linds. She's a superhero. Or so she claims.

I don't respond to Lindsey or Lilly. I throw the last bag in the trunk and then curse to myself because we can't even shut our own trunks anymore. We push a button, and the button closes the trunk. Much like the mobile phone removed the joy of hanging up on someone by slamming the phone down, the "Trunk Close" button has removed the joy of making a statement by slamming the trunk.

Then again, I might be the only one upset with these modern-day advances. Maybe I have anger issues.

"What's your problem?" Linds looks at me as I fall into the driver's seat, an expression of disgust on her face—not worry. Disgust. As though my very existence is obnoxious by itself.

I don't say what I want to say. I don't say anything at all. I put the SUV in reverse and back out. I've known Linds long enough to know she won't care enough to ask what's wrong a second time.

I loved Lindsey when I married her. She was beautiful and vibrant. She saw the world differently, and I loved that about her. Lindsey and I used to stay up until the wee hours of the morning watching World War II documentaries. She was the most unique woman I had ever met, and I couldn't stop myself from falling in love with her.

That was then. Two years ago, she changed. It felt like she had changed overnight, but is that possible? Lindsey became distant and irritable. Everything I did annoyed her. It was like I couldn't even breathe the right way without her getting angry with me. I tried talking to her, but she claimed I was crazy. One time, though, she did blame hormones. But mostly, I was the crazy one. I guess I started to believe her, or maybe I chose to be silent to keep the peace. I thought that's what you're supposed to do in marriage. We all get weird sometimes, right? The spouse just has to dig their toes in and wait for the day they come back.

That's what I'm doing now. That's what I've been doing for the last year and a half. Lindsey hasn't come back yet—not mentally, anyway—which is why I was pretty surprised when she told me she was pregnant more than a year ago. I couldn't even remember the last time we'd had sex. How on earth had she gotten pregnant? In true Lindsey fashion (because she remembers everything), she reminded me.

Her story is that one night, a month before she found out she was pregnant, I had taken her out for her birthday. She said we had gotten a little drunk, and when we came home, we had a little sex. Nine months later, Lilly was born. I remember taking her out for her birthday, but I honestly cannot recall getting drunk or the event that took place once we arrived home. Lindsey assures me that it happened that way and that I just have a terrible memory. I won't argue that. I truly have the worst memory of any thirty-five-year-old man you will ever meet.

I thought that maybe the birth of Lilly would bring Lindsey back to me. I had hoped that since we were officially parents, it would make her want to love me again and be a family like we had always dreamed. And maybe Lilly did that for a little while. I thought things were getting better. They felt better. Then, six months ago, things began to crumble again.

I love Lindsey. I love Lilly. I love our family, but I'm not sure how much longer I can live with them. Most days, I feel like I'm on the outside looking in—like I could walk away one day, and they'd never notice until the toilet needed to be unclogged. Surely, this can't be what marriage is supposed to be? I know that marriage is hard. Sometimes, you're up; and sometimes, you're down. But why would anyone sentence themselves to this—whatever *this* is—between Lindsey and me? I thought marriage was about love—about having that one woman that you know you could never live without again, no matter what she did to drive you crazy. But this? Lindsey? I feel like I will break in half at any moment. At any time, I could spontaneously combust. This cannot be what the rest of my life is supposed to be.

3
Joyce Rose

I'm not sure why we still vacation to the beach. Harold and I have been married for fifty years, and we've always vacationed to the coast. Back in our foundational years, we could only afford to go for a few days at a time, but eventually, we grew to weeklong vacations. We raised our children on beach vacations; and now that our children are grown, we're back to vacationing on our own. Still, our skin is much too old to endure much sun. So, our vacations are spent mostly indoors—either in the beach house we've owned for fifteen years or out antiquing. We do enjoy a few hours in the sun, which is why we're usually the first ones on the beach in the mornings—before the sun gets too brutal.

I have always enjoyed getting to our beach house on Friday evenings. One of my favorite things is sitting on the large front porch on Saturday morning and watching all the vacationers pack their cars to head home. Then, around three or four, I enjoy a midafternoon snack on the deck to watch all the newcomers arrive. I like to see who I'm vacationing with.

Harold doesn't understand this fascination that I have. That's okay. He doesn't have to understand it.

And that's what I'm doing now—sitting on my porch, watching the new families roll into town.

"Joyce, come inside. Stop snooping," Harold calls to me from the kitchen. I can hear him through the screen door.

"Not yet. A new family has just arrived. Oh! They have a dog." I

People Watching

love dogs—all types of dogs. When I see them on the beach, I talk to them and not their humans.

"How do you think that poor family is going to feel when they look up to see you watching them?" Harold retorts.

"I'll just wave." I smile. Having been married to Harold for as long as I have, I've learned how to have an answer for all the points he attempts to make. I think this frustrates him.

The screen door opens and closes behind me. I hear Harold's footfalls, and then he's pulling out the chair next to me to sit. He likes people-watching, too; he just won't admit it.

"Wonder what kind of dog that is?" Harold asks. He takes a sip of beer from the can he's holding.

"Looks like a mutt. But definitely part-Jack Russell," I say. "He's adorable."

"His humans don't look very happy," Harold points out.

I shrug. "They usually never do when they arrive. Whether traveling with a dog or traveling with children, it's exhausting." I remember those days well. For me, vacation didn't begin until Sunday. Arrival on Saturday felt like nothing but exhaustion and grocery shopping. Unpacking, too. Sunday is the day vacation can truly begin.

"Look at that family." Harold nods his head toward the house situated next to the family with the dog. "They're already fighting."

I turn my head to the other family, and he's right. They're already fighting. It looks as though the two females (a baby and an adult) rule the roost in this scenario. I pity the man. He looks like he's been beaten up for quite some time. Even the baby swats at her father in a disrespectful manner as he carries her into the house.

That's one thing about old age. Life has taught me how to be compassionate toward the young families because I've been there. There were many vacations in our past that didn't feel like vacations. They felt like I arrived already emotionally exhausted and left emotionally dead. There were times when our children would argue the entire week of vacation. There were times when Harold and I would argue the entire week. Our vacations weren't always perfect. In fact, more than none went wrong.

Still, we went. We took the children every year for a week. Sometimes, we'd go more than once a year because somewhere in all the fighting, there were memories—good memories. Those are the moments you learn to cling to when everything else seems to be falling apart. One day, when Harold and I are no longer here, I hope my children look back on all our vacations and smile. I hope they smile at the arguments and fights. I hope they smile at the fun, too. That's what life is—a mixture of contention and contentment. The key is in balancing those things.

Harold goes back inside once he's had enough of the people-watching. He's never able to last as long as me in activities such as these. He gets bored. So, I watch the families on my own. The men are unloading their cars. I notice one of the women—the one with the baby—continues to glance in the direction of the man who is with the woman with the dog. He notices her, too, and it appears as though they know each other. Now, Harold would ask how I could possibly know that from this distance. It's in the glance.

Most glances are innocent. I've glanced at a few people in my lifetime, and it's usually because I thought their shoes were pretty. This glance, though—the one being shared by these two strangers—is one of lust. I decide that these two families are the two to watch this week.

People Watching

SUNDAY

People Watching

4
Drew Clark

"I'm going for a run before Lilly wakes." Lindsey pops into the kitchen as I'm pouring my coffee. She's hardly wearing anything—just some tight booty shorts and a sports bra. I realize we're at the beach, but last I checked, it wasn't a nude beach.

I stir the creamer into my coffee and nod my head. Responding would be pointless because as I look up at my wife, she's already bouncing out the door. As soon as the door closes behind her, Lilly begins to cry. I take a very large sip of my coffee and go to my daughter, who has been sharing our bedroom with us.

As I pop my head over the playpen we brought for her, she visibly appears to be disappointed that it's me. She's never happy to see me. I've tried everything to make her like me a little more, but nothing works. Mostly, she looks at me as though there were lobsters crawling out of my ears. Sometimes, I check to see if there are.

How did this happen? Lilly is my daughter, and she hates me. Regardless, I pick her up, hold her on my hip, and carry her to the kitchen for her breakfast.

As I settle Lilly into her highchair, I take a second to glance out the sliding glass doors that face the beach, and I spot Lindsey just before she disappears over the dunes. I really don't like my wife going out in public dressed the way she is; but I'm not her father, and she's not an unruly teenager (even though, sometimes, she acts like one).

I don't think I'd like it if Lindsey started dictating what I wore, but then again, she does. Just last week, we were going to dinner with friends, and she forced me to change my outfit before we left the house. Worse than that, she picked out what she wanted me to wear. I am not a child. Lindsey is not my mother.

"Lilly, don't throw your breakfast on the floor," I warn after watching her chuck one of her banana slices to the tile below her highchair.

Lilly looks at me and takes another banana slice in her chubby, little hand. She holds the banana over the floor for a few seconds before smiling and then dropping it.

I shake my head. I don't have the energy. If she wants to throw her food on the floor, so be it. I sip my coffee and turn my eyes to the television, where the morning news is playing. It's always strange watching the news in another town—mostly strange but also interesting. Funny how we get so accustomed to our own local news reporters and find other news reporters less competent. If I'm being honest, none of the news reporters in our town are very competent. I find myself not even taking the meteorologist seriously. Then again, meteorology is the only job one can have where they can be wrong 95 percent of the time and still keep their job.

I'm a journalist. I'm mostly editing now, but I'll always be a journalist. I've written stories on almost everything, but politics is one topic I won't touch. I actually lost my job once because I wouldn't write on politics. That was right before I moved to Greenville, South Carolina, and met Lindsey.

Now I'm wondering if maybe I should have taken the political assignment. I would have stayed in Georgia and never met Lindsey. What would life have been like then? It makes me sad to think about that.

I don't like to think about things like that. I don't like second-guessing myself. Mostly, I just want to get up every morning and do the best I can. I don't want to worry about things like fate and decisions. I honestly don't want to worry at all, but here I am, worrying. And maybe it's not really worry. Maybe it's concern. Yes, that's it. I'm concerned about the decisions I've made in my past that have led me to this very miserable first day of family vacation.

I grew up in church, and one of the things I remember so vividly from Sunday school is the Bible verse about not worrying. Maybe it's because the verse talks about how the birds just live their lives and God provides for them. I love birds. I love to watch them as they sit and think on telephone wires and the gables of houses. I like to imagine what they're thinking about on those telephone wires when they're just sitting. I guarantee you they're not worrying.

I don't think there's anything wrong with being concerned, though. Concern is good. Concern means you're alert. You're aware. You don't have your head stuck in the sand. I'm concerned about my life, my wife, my marriage, my family. Not worried. Concerned.

5
Jess Dawson

"Jess, I'm going to take an early morning walk on the beach." Cal appears on the balcony of our beach house where Sweeney and I are enjoying our morning coffee. Well, I'm enjoying the coffee. Sweeney is enjoying people-watching. He likes to peer through the rails and watch people below us on the streets. We've always stayed in raised beach houses. When Sweeney was a puppy, I was always so afraid that he would somehow squeeze his little body through the rails and jump, unknowingly, to his death. He's much older now—and a bit chubbier. I'm not sure he could even get his head through a rail now.

"You? Taking a walk on the beach? You don't even like sand." I point out.

"The air feels nice this morning. It's not humid or anything," he says. "I won't be long." Cal kisses the top of my head, pets Sweeney on his head, and then disappears back into the house. A minute or so later, I spot him walking toward the beach access.

I can see the beach access perfectly from our spot on the balcony, and I notice a woman in front of Cal hardly wearing anything, heading out to the beach herself. I know we're at the beach, but last I checked, it wasn't a nude beach. Admittedly, I'm jealous by how amazing she looks in the shorts she's wearing. I could never wear shorts like that.

I'm sure Cal is enjoying the view. I guess I can't be too jealous. I had a short stint with cancer two years ago, and the chemo did a number on my body. Thankfully, my cancer was caught before it progressed too far, and the chemotherapy did the rest. Still, it changed my body. That's been the hardest thing to accept.

Cancer changed Cal and me, too. We haven't been the same since my diagnosis. When my treatments first began, he was there the whole time. He'd sit with me, hold my hand, and read a book to me. But as time continued, he stopped coming along. Cal said it was because the hospital was depressing, and he just couldn't sit there anymore. I never believed that, but I also never felt like pushing it any further. At the time, I was fighting for my life. After that, I was thankful I was alive. I thought Cal and I would find each other again.

I can't have children now. So, we have Sweeney. Sometimes, I think this is why Cal has pulled away from me. He wanted a family—a big family like the one his parents have. It was something we talked about often when we were dating and first married. Having a big family was in the cards for us. Until it wasn't. I wonder if he would have married me at all if he had known that one day, we'd find out I couldn't have children.

I look out at the beach access. Both the woman and Cal have now disappeared out of sight. I wonder if Cal went one way and the woman went the other. I know Cal, though. He probably went in the same direction.

Cal and I have known each other since high school. We didn't date then. He was a band nerd, and I was the one who kept to myself. We did have lunch together most days, though, and high school is where I began to fall in love with him. He was always smiling. Some days, his smile was the only thing that made my day worth anything.

Cal is so intelligent, and he always has been. He's a numbers guy—a CFO by trade—and I'm more of a grammar and literature girl. Numbers confuse me. We seemed to balance each other perfectly.

After high school, we ended up at the same university. I majored in education, and Cal majored in finance. He has since received a master's degree and a Ph.D. in the same field. I was an elementary school teacher before cancer. I think I might return to it someday, but I want to make sure I'm absolutely healthy before I do. Leaving my students behind so suddenly two years ago was not easy.

These days, it's just Sweeney and me. Cal goes to work every morning, comes home late most evenings, and spends minimal time with us on the weekend. I miss him sometimes. I've known him for more than half my life now, and he is part of me, whether he likes it or not. But mostly, we've learned how to live like two ghosts passing each other in the hallway. It can be lonely, though; I will admit to that.

6
Joyce Rose

Well, this isn't good. The man and woman who had been glancing at each other yesterday with lust in their eyes have now disappeared onto the beach together. To be clear, it is not known to me yet if this was planned by either party or if there is any mischief going on. Regardless, the woman might as well have gone out there naked. I sure hope she enjoys that body while it lasts. I can't remember the last time I looked at mine. I prefer not to.

I look for the woman with the dog, but they're nowhere to be seen. Neither is the other man with the baby. I decide I will go on the beach and meet these families today. It's not too hot, and I must know their names and where they're from. I need to see who these neighbors of mine are.

"Harold! We're going on the beach today," I call from the front porch.

I've been married to Harold long enough to know that he is rolling his eyes at me. He may even be mumbling some expletives under his breath. He'll be okay. He likes to watch the women push the lemonade carts up and down the beach. Harold claims he admires their stealth, but I think he admires other things about them. When one becomes my age, it doesn't really matter who their husband is gawking at. Harold is seventy years old, and he is not a rich man. I'm not really worried about some young female coming onto him. Once they find out he hardly has a retirement account, they'll move on.

People Watching

"Joyce, I can't find my swim trunks," Harold hollers to me from the bedroom as I pour the rest of my coffee down the sink.

"I bought you new ones," I tell him. "I washed them last night. Should be dry." I open the door of the dryer and pull out Harold's new swim trunks. We may be old, but I try to make us young. His new swim trunks are short, like the ones men wore in the 1970s, which have curiously come back in style, but I aimed for a solid color instead of the other cute pair I found with pineapples wearing sunglasses printed all over them. Harold would not have put a pinky toe out the door if he thought he'd have to wear pineapple-printed swim trunks.

"Why are these so short? Did you buy them in the kid's section?" Harold holds his new shorts up to me and then lays them against his legs to show me exactly how short they are.

I stifle a giggle. "It's what all the young men are wearing these days!"

"Joyce, I'm a seventy-year-old man. I don't have to wear what the young men are wearing," he says between gritted teeth. "When are you going to accept the fact that we're old?"

"Age is just a number," I say. "And you're not wearing tennis shoes on the beach. That's just embarrassing." With that, I leave our bedroom.

At what point do men stop caring about their looks, the way they dress, the size of their gut? When we were younger, Harold was fashionable. Granted, he basically wore the same outfits over and over again; but at least, they were trendy, and he looked pretty good in them.

Then, sometime after he turned forty-five, he just quit caring. I didn't realize it until one evening when we were going out for dinner, and the man paired white tennis shoes with khaki slacks and a Clemson football sweatshirt. It's important to note that we were not going to a burger joint. No, it was a very nice restaurant—the type where the men wear a suit and tie and the women wear a very nice dress or very expensive slacks. Of course, I wouldn't let him leave the house like that, which inevitably led to an argument, and we ended up staying home to eat frozen pizza.

Harold has always thanked me for not letting myself go after we got married. I worked hard to stay healthy and fit. I kept up with the fashion trends. When my hair began to turn gray, I started seeing a professional hairdresser to have it colored, instead of buying those boxed hair coloring kits one can purchase at the grocery store. I've always tried. But any attempt Harold's made has been due to my incessant nagging.

Regardless, when you've been married to the same person for fifty years, you're really one body with many extensions. We finish each other's sentences. We know what the other is thinking without even having to inquire about it. He knows how I take my coffee, and I know how to cook his eggs. We have become what I can only assume it feels like to have a Siamese twin. Sometimes, I think about how horrible it will be for either myself or Harold when one of us dies. We've always argued about who's going to go first, but when it comes down to it, I really hope we go together. I'm not sure I could live without that man now, and I'm very certain that he could not live without me. Who would wash his underwear?

7
Drew Clark

This is Lilly's first visit to the beach. Before Lilly, Lindsey and I just carried our own chairs and maybe a cooler down to the beach. It was a simple set-up. Nothing extra—just a seat for our butts and something to drink. Now, we have a not-so-normal-sized wagon holding our beach chairs, a cooler, and, basically, Lilly's entire bedroom. I didn't think it was necessary to bring it all, but Lindsey insisted. Lilly is mobile now and could disappear from us in an instant, so it's very important to have enough for her to entertain herself with on the beach. It will keep her from wanting to wander. At least, that's what Lindsey tells me. I personally think Lilly will go wherever Lindsey goes.

"I'm going to take her into the surf while you set up," Lindsey says. She picks up Lilly, holds her on her hip, and carries her to the ocean, pointing out seashells and sea birds along the way.

I roll my eyes at her as they walk away because I know Lindsey isn't paying attention to me anymore—and because it feels good to do that behind her back. Then I begin unpacking the wagon.

"Do you need some help?" a strange voice asks from the other side of the wagon. I'm bent over, pulling all the unnecessary baby equipment out of the canvas-sided junk mobile.

I lift my eyes, surprised to find an older woman standing there. She's got the brightest blue eyes I've ever seen; a big smile; and long, gray hair beneath a straw hat. "I...uh, I think I've got it. Thank you, though."

"You're a new dad," she says, "and you're probably wondering what in the world all this stuff is and why the heck you might need it on a beach."

I gaze back at her, my mouth falling open at the accuracy of her statement. I thought I was at least acting as though I knew what I was doing. Apparently, I really do look like an idiot.

"Let me help," she says. "I've raised three kids and have six grandchildren. I could get this stuff set up with my eyes closed."

I'd be stupid if I denied her support. I don't know what I'm doing. So, I step back from the wagon and gesture with my hands for her to have at it.

She smiles and looks grateful herself. "My name is Joyce." She holds out her hand to shake mine.

"Andrew"—I shake her hand—"or Drew."

"Nice to meet you, Drew." She smiles again, and I notice a sort of sparkle in her eye. It gives me a strange sense of familiarity, like I've known this woman my whole life. It's comforting, which is something I haven't felt since the last time I saw my mother alive.

"So, this one is important." Joyce pulls something that looks like a tent out of the wagon. "It'll keep her from wandering off and protect that precious baby skin from the sun." Joyce pops open the end of the box and pulls the tent from inside. "Oh, your wife picked out the fancy one. You just push this down here, and…" Joyce pushes down a lever, and the tent suddenly expands into a perfectly weighted piece of genius.

Sometimes, I see things like this and wonder why I didn't invent it. What am I doing with my life?

"That's amazing." I gasp. "I can definitely manage that."

Joyce giggles. "I never doubted you could. Sometimes, folks just need it played out in front of them to get it." She leans back over the wagon to look at the rest of the crap we brought down here. "A kiddie pool! That's smart, too. If baby gets too hot, put her in some fresh water out of the sand." Her explanation of a kiddie pool explains why I also had to pack two gallon jugs of water into the wagon. That's the fresh water we'll use to fill in the bottom of the pool. I just thought she was worried about getting thirsty.

Joyce observes the packaging and then pulls the inflatable kiddie pool from its box. She reaches her arm back down into the box and pulls out a small air pump that can be used to manually pump air into the pool. "You think you can handle this one?" Joyce looks at me.

"I've inflated many things in my life," I reply proudly. Then I realize how extremely sleazy that sounded. "Not that kind of infl— I didn't mean that how it sounded."

Joyce is laughing so hard now, she's crying. Her laughter is contagious, and I can't help but join her. The two of us stand there laughing on that hot, sandy beach—me with the inflatable in my hand and her with a sand bucket in hers.

When was the last time I laughed? It feels good. Exhilarating. I'm actually laughing—something that normal human beings do on a daily basis—something that people who live with people like Lindsey don't do—ever—because you're not allowed to make a sound. They only allow you to breathe because it's key to survival, and they only want you to live because who will take out the garbage when the can is full?

"What's so funny?" a voice interrupts, breaking up our laughter. It's a voice I know well—a voice that used to light my world. And now, here she is—the killer of joy. Lilly sits on her hip with a hand clutching the strap of Linds' swimsuit.

I gain my composure and clear my throat. "Uh, Joyce was helping me with some of Lilly's things," I reply. "Joyce, this is my wife, Lindsey. Lindsey, Joyce. And this beauty is Lilly."

"Nice to meet you, Lindsey and Lilly. I was just telling Drew that you picked the best of the best for your daughter. I've got six grandchildren myself, and I know my stuff."

"Andrew," Lindsey replies rather rudely, correcting Joyce's usage of Drew.

Joyce's face doesn't fall the way mine does. I'm embarrassed—and it shows—but Joyce keeps a smile on her face and doesn't even blink.

"I'm sorry," Joyce says. "Andrew." Her blue eyes flash in my direction.

"She's being nice," I tell Lindsey in the same sort of tone a teenager might use when his mother is second-guessing one of his friends.

Lindsey looks back at me. Her green eyes bore into my skull like fangs. Her jaw tenses. I won't cower—not in front of Joyce.

I stare back at her. I pretend that my own eyes are sharp swords, and they're stabbing her eyeballs out. I know it sounds bad, but in this moment, it's how I feel. I wouldn't *really* stab my wife's eyeballs out.

The seconds last forever, and finally, Lindsey blinks. She doesn't say anything to me. She turns on her heels and carries Lilly back to the ocean.

I look at Joyce. "I'm so sorry." I am horrified by my wife. "I don't—"

"Drew, no reason to apologize. You're not responsible for the things that she does or the things that she says. Lindsey makes her own choices."

I'm not generally so vulnerable, but one would have had to live with Lindsey over the last 365 days to understand. I've allowed that woman to shred me of any dignity I had, and now I see myself like Quasimodo. *Yes, Master. What can I do for you, Master? Shall I wipe your butt for you, Master?*

In fact, Joyce may be the first person who has actually done something nice for me in a while. I can't remember the last time someone actually offered to help me with something. Isn't that sad? No, not sad. I'm on the border of completely giving up. I've thought about it a lot. I do still have the slightest bit of fight left in me. But that slight bit of fight is losing power, too. What's a man to do? I feel like a prisoner.

"Thank you for helping me with all of this," I say to Joyce. "Truly."

"It was my pleasure. I'm here all week, and I think we're neighbors. I'm in the little blue house slightly behind yours."

It's only a little weird that she knows which beach house we're staying in, but I can only assume that Lindsey's incessant yelling at me when we arrived yesterday had caught the attention of everyone within earshot.

8
Jess Dawson

Cal is currently trying to set our stuff up on the beach ahead of my arrival. I've not left our beach house yet; but I'm watching him from the balcony, and he seems to be struggling with the umbrella. I giggle, watching his hair toss in the sea breeze.

"You think I should help?" I ask Sweeney, looking down at him as he stares back up at me. I pretend that he shrugs. I sigh.

I've been angry with Cal for a long time. It goes back to his refusal to sit with me at the hospital when I was undergoing chemo. I know he claimed it was because it was depressing, but how does he think I felt sitting there alone in the dark, watching mindless television while chemicals soared through my veins? I'd like to think that it doesn't matter anymore, but I'm still hurt by his actions. He left me. He abandoned me. I know he can't change what he did, but he's also never apologized or try to make up for his negligence.

"I guess I'll go help him," I tell Sweeney. We walk back inside the house. I pet Sweeney's head and tell him to be a good buddy. I've always told him to be a good buddy whenever we depart. I'm not sure why. It just seems to fit.

I slide my feet into flip flops, grab my beach bag, and exit the house. The air is quite warm, but the breeze disguises it well. It's a perfect beach day in my opinion—the right amount of heat, the right amount of sea breeze. I can't wait to nestle in my beach chair and get lost in a book.

"Hey, I was going to help you down," Cal says to me as I

approach him on the beach.

"I can walk, Cal. Besides, it looked like you were struggling a bit."

He doesn't deny either. "I just can't get the umbrella to stay up," Cal says appearing defeated.

"Did you use the twisty thingy?" I ask him. I don't know the real word for it because it's easier to remember "twisty thingy."

"Twisty thingy?" Cal appears confused.

I dig into the bag he brought down and pull out the twisty thingy.

"Ah." Cal takes it from me, drives it into the sand, and then carves out the most perfect little tunnel for the umbrella. He sticks the umbrella into the twisty thingy and then stands proudly when he realizes the umbrella is now secure.

I pull out our chairs and sit them next to each other with our cooler in between. We both sit and let out a sigh because there's really nothing else you can do when your booty finally lands in the beach chair in the sand on the beach in front of the ocean on the first day of vacation.

Cal pulls a beer from his cooler. His eyes scan the beach. He looks anxious, I think—like maybe he's looking for something. *Or someone.* His right leg bounces up and down a bit like a nervous tick. His jaw is tight.

"Are you okay, Cal?" I ask him.

"What?"

"You look like you're up next for a job interview."

Cal shifts in his seat. He drops his shoulders, attempting to visibly relax. "I'm fine."

He's not fine. Something is wrong. I feel it deep in my chest.

And then, when he thinks I'm not looking, I notice he's focused on a woman. By the looks of her butt, it's the woman from the beach access this morning. My stomach turns, and I refuse to let my mind go there. He wouldn't, would he?

I have wondered if Cal stopped coming with me to the hospital because he had found a girlfriend. It made sense then. Even though he wasn't going to the hospital with me, he also avoided me at home. At first, I thought that maybe he was afraid I was going to die, and he didn't know how to act. I thought maybe he didn't know what to do or say, so he withdrew. But as time passed, I began to reconcile that this was not why he had pulled away from me.

I think I could have been happy spending the rest of my life with Cal, but now? I don't know what's going to happen to us. He seems so distant to me. Cal does try to act like he hasn't already left me, but he has. I lost him at some point during my cancer battle, and he's yet to come back. I want this week of vacation to be the week that puts us back together—the week that heals us and reminds us why we love each other and why we married in the first place.

9
Drew Clark

When I finished taking a shower, both Lindsey and Lilly were fast asleep in our bed. I thought I might take advantage of the pause in abuse from Lindsey and head on over to the Jungle Shack. They've got a craft beer that is like no other, and I couldn't think of anything that would make me happier than a cold beer and Jungle Shack fish tacos. They have the best fish tacos.

The waitress led me to a solitary table tucked away into the back of the restaurant, which pleased me immensely. Here, I can sit and drink and people-watch without any interruptions. I enjoy people-watching. I like to imagine the lives of the strangers around me. I wonder what they do for a living, what kind of house they live in, how many times they've been married, and if they have any children. I don't know why I care, and maybe I don't. Maybe it's the storyteller in me. Everyone has a story, and I've always enjoyed writing them.

As I settle back in my chair, enjoying my beer and tacos, I see Joyce, the older woman I met on the beach earlier, come into the restaurant. If I had to take a guess, I'd guess the man with her is her husband.

He doesn't look like someone who could handle a woman like Joyce. He doesn't appear to be weak, but he does have this air about him—like he wants to be Joyce's husband, but he's ready to disclaim her at any minute. Maybe she keeps him on his toes, and that's what keeps them together. Everyone has a little desire to live on the edge like that from time to time. I imagine being with a woman like Joyce would make a man feel caught—in a good way. Lindsey would tell me that statement made zero sense and to stop talking. But Lindsey isn't here now, is she?

Lindsey and I went skydiving once. She forced me onto the plane, strapped my parachute on extra tight, and practically kicked my butt out of the plane when it was time to jump. I was fuming the whole way down. I had begun to initiate a breakup in my head as I floated helplessly to the earth. But then, there was a moment as the earth grew closer and closer. A moment of freedom. Floating. Completely relentless. Defenseless. And I thought if I could just stay like this forever, that would be a good life.

That is the moment I knew without a doubt that I loved Lindsey with my whole heart. I knew then that she would always be there to force me into new things, and that's not always a bad thing. Sometimes, we need people to physically push us out of our comfort zones. When we landed back on earth, we were both laughing—that good type of hearty laugh that sometimes makes you feel like you might explode. I thought that day was the first day of the rest of my life. I asked Lindsey to marry me that night. We were both so high on life—on each other. The skydiving had only added more fuel to the fire. We went everywhere we could afford to go. We did stupid things. We had fun. Admittedly, those were some of the best days of my life.

As I think on these things, something wet rolls down my cheek, and I swat it away. I check the ceiling to make sure it isn't leaking, and it's not. It's my eyes that are leaking. *For Pete's sake, I'm enjoying a beer by myself and crying.*

I cast my eyes to the table, blinking them rapidly to rid myself of any other tears that may still be hanging out, waiting to fall. When I look up again, Joyce is standing next to me.

"Drew, I thought that was you." Joyce smiles at me.

I'm not going to lie, she sneaked up on me, which is startling because I assumed I was alone. Still, I smile back. I glance over at who I think is her husband and then back at Joyce. "I thought that was you when you came in."

"Ah, yes. Harold and I love this place. I should introduce you to my husband. He'd love you," Joyce says. "Do you want to come eat with us?" She gestures her head back to her table.

"Oh, you know, I just... I think I want to eat alone tonight. No offense to you or anything. I'm so grateful to you for your help earlier. My being alone actually has nothing to do with you. I just—"

"Drew, it's okay. You're allowed to want some alone time every now and then."

Lindsey would have told me to grow a set. "Thank you for understanding."

"You must take care of yourself, Drew. You can't care for anyone else unless you care for yourself first." Joyce says this to me now as though this were a conversation between mother and son. She makes me miss my mom. My mom would know exactly what to do about my marriage. I just wish I knew what she would do.

"You can't pour from an empty cup," I say with a bit of a mumble, indicating that I've heard that phrase many times before.

"You're a good man, Drew," Joyce says to me. "Enjoy your alone time." With that, she gives me one last smile and returns to her table with Harold.

I drink my beer. I eat a taco. I enjoy my alone time. I feel a little like a bachelor, even though the wedding band on my finger says otherwise. Thinking about going back to the beach house with Lindsey makes me nauseated, so I decide to return to people-watching. It's like watching T.V., except you've got the dialogue in your own head.

Lindsey would probably be ashamed to know that I sort of enjoy people-watching, but as a writer and journalist, it's the stories I make up that make it an enjoyable activity. People inspire me in positive and negative ways. The things they do, the way they act in certain places, the dynamics of their family while out in public—observing human behavior has inspired so much of my writing as a journalist. I suppose I'll always be a people-watcher. Well, as long as I'm a writer.

10
Joyce Rose

McConkey's Jungle Shack is our favorite place to go for fish tacos. Harold acts like he doesn't like it, but why else would he continue to bring me here? I guess some would say it's because he loves me. Harold does love me. He's always been the best husband, and I'm not just saying that. Strangers look at us now, see us laughing, and assume that we've had an easy life. But it's not always been so easy.

We have three children—a girl and two boys. They're not children anymore. They're fifty, forty-six, and forty-two years old. Each of them has two beautiful children—a boy and girl. That's how I knew how to help Drew on the beach earlier. I've learned more about parenting with all my grandchildren than I did with all three of my own.

Things change, too. Times change. When my kids were growing up, we didn't have fancy beach tents for them to shade themselves under. We slapped some sunscreen on them and reapplied often. Sometimes, I think kids today have it too easy—beach tents; cell phones; unlimited streaming in movies, television, and music. My oldest daughter didn't even have internet for most of her childhood.

The world has progressed at an unprecedented rate. I'm proud of myself for keeping up with it all, but if I'm being honest, I'm exhausted. What I wouldn't give to escape to an island with nothing but a television that played classic movies and shows twenty-four seven. But that's not possible. So, I choose to keep up—because if you don't keep up, you get left behind. I've worked far too hard and been around way too long to get left behind.

That's why I love Edisto. It's as close to an uninhabited island as I can get in reality. Some would say that Edisto is an inherited island. Maybe they're right. The ones who live here have been here since it first became an island. We got lucky. We bought an inherited home that was not wanted. I'll never be more grateful for a break in tradition.

Tonight, the Jungle Shack is quite busy. It usually is on the weekends. Locals and a few tourists will pack out a fourteen-hundred-square-foot restaurant. The waitress spotted Harold and me and waved us over to the table already reserved for us in the corner. They know us. That comes with its own privileges.

"All of those people outside waiting for a seat and we just get to walk in," Harold mumbles as he accepts his beer from the waitress—a beer he didn't even have to order because they already knew he'd order it.

"If you were really that opposed, you wouldn't be popping the top on that can right now," I point out as I take my seat after returning from Drew's table.

He rolls his eyes at me.

"What were you helping that boy with out on the beach earlier today and why did you have to go and bother him while he was eating?" Harold looks at me as he takes a sip from his can.

"I was helping him set up his daughter's toys, and I really don't think there's anything wrong with saying hello to someone I recognize in public. Why do you care anyway?"

"I care because I don't want you meddling in his life. Just leave the boy alone." Harold growls.

"That poor boy is married to the Wicked Witch of the West." It had been everything I had inside of my body not to smack that woman in the face earlier when she had corrected me on the pronunciation of Drew's name. I had only known her husband a couple of minutes, and I knew that he preferred Drew to Andrew. Why else would I have called him Drew?

"I'm not going to say it again, don't go putting your nose into that family. Leave them alone," Harold warns.

I smile back at him. "Oh, Harold, you know I can't do that."

Harold takes a long sip from his can.

Over the years, I've gotten Harold into quite a lot of

embarrassing situations. When we were younger, my shenanigans gave him anxiety. Now, he's learned to just walk away. I don't get upset with him when he leaves me to fend for myself in whatever crazy situation I get myself into. I tend to find myself in the middle of a lot of things that I have a hard time getting myself out of; however, I've always generally found an escape route at the last minute.

Harold calls me an instigator. He has a theory that the world would spin perfectly without any problems if I stopped meddling in folks' lives. The thing is, I want to help; and if I think I can help, then I try. The problem is that sometimes, I think I can help when I actually should run in the other direction.

Harold had to bail me out of jail once. I didn't do anything wrong—not really. I had been shopping at one of our local strip malls when alarms began to ring. I was in the parking lot, but the alarms had been so sudden and loud, I froze instantly. Just then, a man ran right out of the store with a cash drawer from one of the stores. He had on a ski mask, so it was pretty obvious this man had just robbed the store. I don't know what got into me, but I stopped that man in the parking lot to ask him why he had robbed the store. He tried to pull away from me, but I insisted. And before I knew it, we were sitting on the tailgate of his truck, talking about how he was going to lose his house if he didn't pay the bills and how if he lost his house, he would lose his children. The poor man couldn't bear the thought of that, and he had gotten desperate.

As luck would have it, because I was sitting with the robber after he robbed the store, I was arrested. Something about accessory. I don't know. I was just trying to help the poor man. Regardless, Harold forbade me from helping any other thieves after that. Strangely, I've never encountered a situation like that since.

So, if you were to ask my husband what kind of woman I am, I think he would tell you I'm a fighter. I do what's right, even when it's wrong. I help people in the most unusual ways. In my defense, the most unusual circumstances seem to find me. Maybe it's my superpower. Yes, that's it. I have superpowers!

11
Jess Dawson

Naps after a day on the beach are the best naps. There's something about the way the air conditioner hits the skin after coming in from a day on the beach, the way the hot shower feels as the salt and sand are washed away, how a cotton t-shirt on clean skin is the actual secret ingredient to the post-beach nap, how the roar of the ocean can still be heard as the body falls into relaxation, and the way the conscious slips so gently into sleep.

When I awaken from my nap, I realize Cal is gone. He's left a note for me next to my pillow.

Went to dinner. You were sleeping so well, I couldn't wake you. I'll bring you something home.

Love—Who Else?

I sigh. I feel like I've barely seen my husband since we arrived. Sure, we sat on the beach together this afternoon, but he was in another universe. I nearly finished reading my book because of the lack of conversation. True, I had come in and taken a nap, but that hadn't been my intention. Not completely. I only wanted to rest my eyes while Cal showered. And now, it looks like a night in with Sweeney. So, we order pizza.

People Watching

At eight o'clock, Cal comes home. I'm not sure why he thought I'd wait to eat until then, but as promised, he did bring home a cold fast-food burger. I smile and take it, anyway. I tuck it into the refrigerator and tell him I ordered pizza three hours before.

"I'm sorry," he says. "I met some guys at the restaurant. We were talking, and time got away."

I can't help but notice how feral he appears. He's wearing the look of someone who has just exited a roller coaster ride: feet still adjusting to gravity, eyes wide, hair a little wild from the ride itself. Except I know that Cal hasn't been on any roller coasters. There aren't any on this island.

I want to ask where he really was. I want to prod. But I won't. Because if I do, this vacation will begin in an argument which will inevitably ruin the entire thing before it even has a chance to start. And I won't do that. I won't start our vacation with an argument. He hates accusations; I've got zero proof he's up to no good; and I need this week. I need the salty air and the ocean water and the sea breeze. This is the first year in a few years that I haven't been sick, and I finally feel like myself again.

Last summer, I had just completed my treatments. I was weak, thin, and frail. Most of our vacation was spent inside. But this summer, I'm a new woman. I won't ruin it by accusing my husband of cheating on me. Like I said, he doesn't like accusations; I have no proof, and he wouldn't take it well—even if it's true. I'll do what I've always done. I'll catch him. And that will be it. That will be the end of us. I guess I just hope that there's nothing to catch and that I'm paranoid. This is all in my head.

But when you've knocked on Death's door and have come awfully close to entering, life takes on new meaning. Things look different. Time looks different.

I love Cal. I always have. But things are not what they were. He is not who he was. He is not my Cal anymore. I'm not even sure our marriage can be saved at this point, even if he isn't cheating on me. He left me in sickness, when I needed him the most. I'm not sure that's something I can forgive.

But I want to try. That's what this week is for. Trying.

"I think I'm going to bed," Cal announces after taking his medications. The man has high blood pressure, high cholesterol, and a stomach ulcer. It's all stress related and due to his job. I tried to talk him into switching careers years ago, but he won't even ponder that thought.

I look up at him from the couch. "Okay. I'm going to finish this movie."

"Don't stay up too late," he says and then kisses the top of my head before turning for the bedroom.

Sweeney looks up at me with his beautiful, brown doggy eyes. His eyes tell me he loves me. His eyes tell me that if he had been allowed, he would have sat with me at the hospital through all of my chemo treatments, even though I know he would have much rather been at home on the back of the couch snuggled in his blanket. Sometimes, dogs love harder than humans.

When you've been married to the same person for more than a decade, you tend to know them better than they know themselves. Cal isn't a very good liar. He thinks he is, and for that reason, I allow him to continue. It's easier to remember all the details when it's the truth; but when you've spent the last two years lying to your wife, eventually you slip up. Cal has nearly slipped a few times, but he's always been able to tell just enough lies to cover it up and keep me from prodding further. Sometimes, I believe him. Sometimes, I don't.

One time, when he picked me up from the hospital after one of my treatments, the entire car smelled like women's perfume. His lips were lightly stained red, too, which he blamed on a glass of red wine he'd had while out for lunch with a colleague. Even if the story he told me was true, it still felt pretty heartless. Your wife is undergoing chemotherapy, and you're out having red wine with a colleague for lunch?

I'm not a fan of phrases like, "I'll cross that bridge when it gets here" because eventually, the bridge arrives, and you've done nothing to prepare for it. The same can be said for tucking important issues into the "To Be Dealt With Later" section of your mind. This is what I've done with Cal, and now that *later* has arrived, I've technically done absolutely nothing to prepare for the reality that I must face.

How do you start a conversation with your husband and accuse him of cheating? Better yet, how do you tell your husband that his absence while you were dying of cancer actually really hurt you, even if you spent the entire time telling him you understood?

A lot of this is my own fault. I dug this grave, but I will not die in it. I know that much—especially after seeing my husband on the beach this afternoon watch that woman and her little girl. He watched with a longing, of sorts. I can't really explain it, but I may as well have not even been sitting next to him. I may as well have not even existed.

MONDAY

People Watching

12
Drew Clark

It's hot today. Stifling. There's a very large part of me that wants to crawl into Lilly's tent to shade myself. There's absolutely no breeze on this beach; the sun is high; and the ocean hardly provides any relief. Still, I prefer this over a mountain vacation any day.

It seems that Lindsey has made friends with one of our beach house neighbors. Not a female friend, though. The friend is a man—a husband (I assume) to another woman I've watched him completely ignore. This man has been in the surf with my wife and daughter for the last hour. I've thought about getting up and doing something about it. Regardless of how I feel about my wife right now, I don't particularly enjoy seeing another man come onto her. But there's a larger part of me that is enjoying not being bossed around.

I'd be horrified if anything happened to Lindsey or Lilly, but if I'm being honest, I don't look forward to coming home to be with them after a day at work. Sometimes, I do find myself taking the long way home. Sometimes, I stop off at the grocery store, or I'll park down the street a little ways until I'm ready to go home. Sometimes, I go to the gym.

What am I doing? What have I done to my wife to deserve these feelings I have toward her? What did I do wrong?

I feel like my marriage is over. Maybe I know it is subconsciously. But how could I abandon them? My wife? My daughter? What kind of man does that make me?

I don't take making promises or vows lightly. My marriage vows were written straight from my heart, and I meant every word. But Lindsey hasn't kept her vows. I feel certain she's had an affair. A couple of times. Maybe three. At least twice that I'm sure of. Does that not make my vows null and void?

Once, I was leaving a hotel where I had just finished interviewing a bellboy about a prostitution ring that had been discovered there. On my way out, I spotted Lindsey crossing the street and walking straight toward the same hotel. I ducked around the corner, out of sight, so she wouldn't see me. As I watched her approach, I kept trying to come up with an explanation as to why she was there, but I couldn't think of a single reason. It was the nicest hotel in town, despite the prostitution ring, but it didn't even have a restaurant. The only reason anyone would visit that hotel would be to get a room.

At the exact moment Lindsey approached the front door of the hotel, another man arrived as well; and even though they acted as if they didn't know each other, I saw it in their eyes. As they both reached for the door at the same time, their eyes locked for just a few seconds before they entered. The moment was long enough for me to see the look of familiarity in their eyes and in the expression on their faces. I had no doubt that they absolutely knew each other. I could have cut the sexual tension with a knife from where I was standing. I froze where I was, completely dumbfounded, for a minute or so and then spent the afternoon driving in circles around town trying to figure out what I had just seen and trying to talk myself out of what I knew was happening. She wouldn't, would she? No. We made vows. She loves me. I love her.

I didn't say anything to her—probably because I didn't know what to say. How do you accuse your beautiful wife of having an affair without any legitimate evidence? The only thing I had was seeing her walk into the hotel. I had no way of proving she had arrived with the strange man. So, I let it slide.

Sometimes, I wish I hadn't. I wish I had confronted the situation then. I probably could have spared myself a lot of pain. But I'm passive, I suppose. I haven't always been passive, but being married to Lindsey for the length of time I have will make any man passive. It's easier to not have an opinion. It's easier to cater all my likes and dislikes to hers. I have made myself into who she wanted me to be.

I sort of miss my old self. I think I used to be a fun guy. I went to parties and football games. I loved live music. I don't know how

Lindsey did it, but she stripped all that away from me. It must have been gradual because I can't think of a single moment in our lives where she told me I wasn't allowed to go to football games anymore. I just stopped.

I did question Lindsey when she found out she was pregnant with Lilly. I knew for a fact that we hadn't had sex in quite some time; but then she told me that story about her birthday and how we got drunk, and I couldn't argue with that. She had the details of that night memorized. Clearly, I was the one suffering from amnesia.

Now, I wonder if that story was even true. I don't normally get drunk. I drink, but I don't drink until I'm drunk. And the times I have been drunk, I still remembered everything. I think I knew she was lying to me when she told me that story, but I think I also wanted to hope that my wife wouldn't do that—she wouldn't cheat on me, get pregnant, and then lead me to believe the baby is mine.

I'm still not sure she's that heartless. She's cold and manipulative, but even lying about who Lilly belongs to would be a new low for her.

13
Joyce Rose

"Oh, I can't bear to watch this," I exclaim, watching poor Drew slumped in his beach chair while his wife fraternizes with another man.

"Then stop watching," Harold mumbles. He's got his straw hat pulled over his face as he's laid back, tanning the rest of his old body. He's not happy that we also made today a beach day. Monday is generally the day we go antiquing when vacationing.

"There's something going on here, Harold—something horrible. I've been watching those two, and something tells me they know each other—quite well."

Harold lifts his hat from his face, raises his head slightly, and casts his eyes in the direction of the two people I've been watching. "Hell, Joyce. They probably do know each other. No one stands that close together unless they do know each other, or they're drunk. Either is possible out here. I just watched the guy two spots down from us finish a six-pack in five minutes. And yes, I timed it. But what do their lives have to do with our own? You're getting obsessed, Joyce. You need to stop." With that, Harold puts his hat back over his face and retreats to corpse pose.

I don't know what their lives have to do with my own. I don't know why I'm beginning to get obsessed. Harold's not wrong. Last night, I had a hard time falling asleep because I couldn't get Drew and his sad eyes out of my mind. I don't have an explanation, except that maybe I feel drawn to Drew in the same way I'm drawn to puppies. He appears to be soft and loving—like a sweet boy, a sweet man. Like Harold used to be before he got old and crotchety.

I won't bother Drew. He does look somewhat relaxed. Drew needs the quiet, I suppose. Just like last night. When she's not nagging him—which I'm sure is every waking hour, judging by the looks of her—it's the only time he's at peace.

I can't even look at the poor woman whose husband (I assume) is with Drew's wife. She's been sitting in that beach chair all by herself today. Yesterday, he hardly even spoke to her. That woman just sat there with a book in her hand, looking as though she could cry at any second. He never even noticed.

Still, it's everything inside of me not to invite Drew over to our spot. Harold is obviously not a ray of sunshine, and I could use some joy. Drew seems like a good man.

I've never worried about Harold cheating on me—I mean, maybe when we were a lot younger, but these days, it's not a concern. If some other woman wants to take a chance with his wrinkly, grumpy self, then have at it. She'll send him back. I'm sure of it. I've never been interested in cheating on Harold either. We've had a lot of arguments over the years. I even left him for a whole weekend once. I went back that following Monday, though, because I missed him. We fought a little more and then made up.

One time, I went to counseling because I thought I wanted to divorce Harold. I was certain he was the problem. He had to be the problem because it certainly wasn't me. Turns out it was me and all my baggage.

Things should have gotten easier after that realization, but they got a lot harder. I shifted from wanting to divorce him to being completely and utterly afraid that he only married me because I was pregnant—because Harold is that kind of man. He's loving and caring, even when he's being grumpy. I had watched him do things for people just because it appeased them, not because it made him happy, and I feared that this was what our marriage had been about—appeasing me.

Having a baby within the first months of getting married didn't make things easier either. We were children ourselves. We didn't know what we were doing. It's a miracle our firstborn survived childhood.

I can't think of a single reason why we should still be together, except hard work, determination, and love. Really, when I think about life without Harold, my heart shatters. So many young people these days give up on their marriages a little too quickly. First little bump in the road, they're ready to call it quits.

Divorce costs money—money we didn't have when we were younger. It was yet another reason we decided to fight for each other. It was the only route we could afford. Still, I do wish more couples fought a little harder to stay together. It is worth it in the end.

In the case of cheating, though, I don't believe in second chances. Over the years, I've watched so many of my friends lose their spouses to an affair. Some of them forgave their spouse and tried to make the marriage work. All of them failed, and the marriage ultimately ended. It breaks my heart. I can't imagine what that must feel like. I don't want to imagine.

14
Jess Dawson

I'm mostly mortified that he would even do this to me, on this beach, in front of all these people. I see the eyes. There's not a lot to do on a beach except people-watch. They've been watching us because I've been watching them. Regardless, I've never been more confident of anything than I am right now—my husband is cheating on me with the woman who has the nice butt. They know each other. I can see it, feel it.

How did they meet? When did they get together? I don't have those answers yet, but I'll find out.

I won't get obsessed. I don't intend on stalking him and recording his every move or even hiring a private investigator. In time, what I believe to now be true will come to light.

Until then, I won't let on. I won't change. I'll remain the same fragile but cancer-free woman that he thinks I am. I'll play the part. I'll keep a smile on my face. I'll kiss his lips when he kisses mine. He thinks cancer made me stupid, but he's wrong. It cleared my head. It changed my perspective. I understand completely now that Cal left me a long time ago. He just still comes home at night. I can part with that.

The pier calls me out of the heat for a drink. The pavilion of the pier is crowded—likely for the same reasons I'm here now—to escape the heat. Though, I can't say it feels much better in here with all of these bodies.

I head over to the bar inside the pavilion and order my usual Long Island iced tea. When the bartender hands me my drink, I turn away from the bar only to bump right into a familiar face from the beach—the man whose wife has spent most of the day frolicking in the surf with my husband. He's holding the little girl I assume is his daughter. I've only really seen her with her mom and my husband in the surf.

"Oh, I'm sorry!" I apologize quickly, wiping some of the Long Island iced tea from my arm that spilled during the collision.

His eyes meet mine, and I can't help but be immediately taken by them. He smirks, causing the corner of his eyes to squint upward. "How many of those have you already had?"

I laugh at his joke. "First one of the day! I recognize you from the beach. I think you're sitting a couple of spots down from me. My name is Jess."

"It's nice to meet you, Jess. My name is Drew, and this is my daughter, Lilly." He starts to shake my hand, but then he realizes the ice cream cone he's holding in his free hand is now melting and running down the back of his hand and arm.

"We can shake hands later." I smile. "It's nice to meet you both. I think Lilly here has already met my husband, Cal." I'm admittedly prodding, trying to see if he's noticed this connection between my husband and his family, too.

Drew shifts on his feet, appearing uncomfortable. I'm hoping he doesn't think I'm going to attack him for his wife's shenanigans, but then as I'm thinking this, Drew's expression goes soft. He gives a gentle nod of his head and there's something that looks like sadness in his green eyes. He doesn't say anything though.

I nod, understanding his silence on the topic, "You are beautiful, Lilly." I say, taking my attention from Drew while attempting to change the subject I started.

"She's just over a year old and already a total diva." He smiles, removing the sadness from his eyes. "And she's obsessed with her mother."

"I think she's going to be trouble when she's older. Those beautiful blue eyes of hers will have all of the boys begging for her phone number." I laugh. Lilly has chubby, little, pasty legs; bouncy, blonde curls; and the most exhilarating blue eyes—so blue, I noticed them from my chair on the beach. Now, up close, they're even bluer than I had originally thought.

"Thank you," Drew replies. "Well, I better get Lilly back to the beach. Lindsey will be worried if she's gone too long."

"Maybe I'll see you around," I call as he hurries down the pier steps back to the beach. He looks back once, waves with a smile, and then disappears.

I stand there for a moment, registering our conversation, then sigh and find a seat in the shade of the pavilion. I sip my drink, watching the various types of people come in and out—mostly teenagers with skateboards. They're not allowed to ride their skateboards inside the pavilion, which is why a manager wearing flips flops, shorts, and a tank top pokes his head out from one of the concession counters and yells, "There's a whole park two minutes from here. Go skateboard there." The teenagers fuss a little but, in the end, concede. I laugh to myself as they pick up their skateboards and shrug back outside into the heat.

My mind goes back to Drew and his wife and their little girl—my Cal standing next to Drew's wife like they've been together this whole time. There's also the way Cal smiles at the little girl. Am I jealous? He's my husband, and we can't have children. Of course, I'm jealous.

I didn't expect this on our vacation. I had hoped for a week together to maybe try and repair our marriage. Anytime I've tried to broach the subject, Cal acts like nothing is wrong with us and tries to change the subject. But he'd have to know that something is wrong with us. These days, we feel a lot more like roommates than husband and wife. I used to be angry with cancer. I blamed it for destroying our marriage, our plans for a family, our goals. But when we said our vows so many years ago, did we not vow "for better or for worse"?

Cancer was definitely our "worse," but I survived. And I had hoped that it would bring us closer together. The only thing it did to Cal and me was drive us apart. I became a defective human. Cal cannot be with a defective human. He requires perfection in most everything. I assume that comes with his chosen career. However, people aren't numbers. People are people. We can't be perfect. We get sick. We get ill. We get angry. We cry. We make mistakes. We don't always amount to what we should. Sometimes, the formula is wrong. Cal seeks something in others that doesn't exist.

15
Joyce Rose

I would be lying if I said I didn't plan our vacations around the full moon. On the East Coast, the moon always settles over the ocean for the night. All phases of the moon are beautiful, but it's when it's at its fullest—hanging there, suspended over the ocean, a perfect circle completely illuminated and reflecting across the ocean water— that it's absolutely perfect. I always wait for Harold to go to bed before I venture out to the beach to admire the moon. I don't have to wait long—he goes to bed at eight o'clock most evenings. And at the sound of his first snore, I sneak out into the salty air, pad across the sand in bare feet, and plop down in the soft sand to gaze at the full moon. That's all I do—gaze. No thinking allowed. Nothing but complete and utter adoration for the miracle that the moon is.

So, tonight, I wait to hear Harold's first of many snores for the evening, and then I head out to the beach. The air is absolutely perfect. It has the right balance of heat, humidity, and breeze. Spend time with me on the beach, and you'll notice the addiction I have to inhaling the salty air and closing my eyes to process—the way a person does when they walk by a Cinnabon store at the mall.

The beach isn't empty. In fact, sometimes I think it's more alive at night than in the day. Children can be seen running up and down the beach, collecting shells, their parents holding flashlights for them, so they don't step on a hermit crab or a washed-up jellyfish. Tonight, some folks are walking their dogs. Others are sitting in the sand just as I am about to do. Obviously, I don't sit with the other people in the sand. This is my ritual. It doesn't belong to anyone else.

The sand is cool beneath my feet and bum. I hear the distant laughing of children frolicking along the beach, but for the most part, the ocean makes everything silent. The roar of the waves demands the respect of silence. There's not much that can penetrate that sound—well, except the high shrill of a child screaming. There's not a lot that can be heard over the sound of a devastated child. But there aren't any screaming children on the beach tonight, and so I turn my eyes to the sky and relax into the gentle sea breeze.

"Joyce?" a familiar voice comes from my left, giving me a start. I look up quickly and am relieved to see Drew standing there, smiling.

"Oh, hi, Drew!" I exclaim. "Here for the moon, too?"

"They disappeared again." He shrugs and then sits down next to me. He brings his knees to his chest and wraps his arms around them.

Though this ritual of beach-sitting and full-moon-viewing is mine, I suppose I will have to share the full moon with Drew tonight.

I smile. "Good day?"

Drew cuts his eyes at me. "Good enough, I suppose. I tried to get a little time with my family today, but I really only managed some time with Lilly. Lindsey didn't seem interested in coming with us." He shakes his head. "I don't know what I'm doing anymore. Trying to be whatever Lindsey needs me to be feels a lot like trying to learn a second language without a teacher."

"Women are…complicated," I say. "We're always changing. Some days, we really do like the color purple. Other days, we really do despise it. I do pity men. I doubt we're easy to get along with or understand."

"I thought I knew everything about Lindsey. Now, I can't even take a guess at what she might be thinking. At this point in our marriage, I thought we'd be finishing each other's sentences."

"Everything happens just as it's meant to. Every circumstance we are dealt has a purpose. Where most people fail is in finding that purpose; they give up and succumb to the circumstance. You've heard the stories from the Great Depression. A lot of people killed themselves because they lost everything they owned. But don't you think it could have been a good opportunity to start over new? Be someone new? You're at a crossroads in your marriage. You know there's a problem. So, what are you going to do about it? Confront it or sink with it?"

Drew considers this.

"Listen, I'm not saying my life has been perfect. Harold and I have been through a lot over the years, together and individually—things that should have destroyed us. But you just…hang on—whatever that looks like. Don't let go of the life you want, Drew."

Drew casts his eyes out across the ocean. His eyes drop, but he doesn't say anything.

"You're still young, Drew." I tell him. "Your life isn't over."

He nods softly. "Earlier today on the pier, I met the woman whose husband is likely banging my wife. Her eyes were so sad."

"Like yours?"

"I guess." He shrugs.

We sit silently for a moment, and then I repeat something I had said just a few minutes earlier. "Your life isn't over."

Drew nods his head once more. "I don't think I know how to move forward," he confesses. "And I guess I keep hearing my dad's voice in my head. 'Son, you do what you have to do. Divorce is an abomination.'"

I giggle at Drew's impersonation of his dad—a big, deep, booming voice. I can only assume his father was a preacher in a Southern Baptist church somewhere. "Sounds like your father should have been a pastor."

"He was." Drew rolls his eyes.

"Well, I know something about the Bible, too, and divorce is not something God particularly cares for. But there are exceptions. Abuse being one. Infidelity being another."

"I'm almost 100 percent sure that Lindsey has had an affair. More than once. I don't know if they were with the same man, but I can't even think of a way to confront her about it. She'd be so angry of the accusation, there'd be a fight. I'm tired of fighting. And yet divorce is such a scary word. When I said, 'I do,' I meant it. I never thought I'd ever have to say, 'I don't.'"

"We can never know what kind of curveballs life is going to throw at us. Most of us never live the life we thought we would. You must forgive yourself, Drew. Even if you did nothing wrong, you still must forgive yourself and then do what is best for you."

"My mom died when I was fourteen," he says after a few

moments of quiet. "I miss her. I've needed her for so long. She would have known exactly what to do." Drew turns his eyes to mine. "I know we just met, but there's something about talking to you that makes me feel as though I'm speaking to my mom."

I smile at him and pat his hand. "It's because I am a mom. We tend to think alike. Except for Lindsey. I don't know what she's thinking."

At this, Drew laughs. "I'm not sure if this explains anything, but she was a cheerleader in high school."

I burst out in a fit of laughter. "That explains her really nice ass!"

Now, Drew is laughing harder. "You said 'ass'!"

"Old ladies can cuss, too."

And then we sit there, both rolling in our own tears from laughter.

16
Jess Dawson

Cal is missing again.
He left a note.

Out for dinner, didn't want to wake you.

It's no coincidence that he happens to get hungry about the same time I decide to take a cat nap. He thinks he's sneaky. I won't stay in tonight. Nope, Sweeney and I shall go out for dinner, too.
    I get dressed, brush my hair, spread a little makeup across my face, and toss on a tank top and some linen shorts. I slide my feet into some sandals, grab Sweeney's leash and my purse, and head out the door. Something about this feels rebellious, but mostly, I feel like an empowered woman. I'm not sure why, other than the fact that Cal would have expected me to stay in again tonight and I'm rebelling against his thought process. It feels good! Empowering.
    The pier has a wonderful, little restaurant at the far end of its structure. Burgers are their specialty, and it just so happens that burgers are my favorite food. I love all sorts of hamburgers. Blue cheese burgers, regular cheeseburgers, burgers with gouda, burgers with bacon—you name it, I'll probably eat it. The only burger I've never been able to stomach is one that might be adorned with

avocado between its buns. I do not like avocado. Apparently, that's a cardinal sin.

I order a blue cheese burger, some onion rings, and a Long Island iced tea. Sweeney sits on the floor next to me with his own doggy burger. It means a lot to me when restaurants have food for the guests' doggies. Sweeney feels very lucky as he scarfs down his dinner, and I can't help but smile. Who needs a man when you've got a dog?

After we finish our burgers, we decide a walk on the beach sounds nice. I always enjoy walks on the beach at night. It's not too hot, and it always feels like a different beach—not the same beach you just spent all afternoon sitting on, basking in the sun. No, the beach at night feels a bit more forgiving. The cool sand envelopes your bare feet. The breeze is calm. Even the horizon looks a bit different than in the sunlight, with a big moon hanging so perfectly over the sea.

Sweeney sniffs the sand as we walk. He sneezes as he does, but he can't help it. Sweeney uses his nose a bit more than his sight when we're out walking. I've tried to teach him not to snort the sand, but what can you do?

The beach is mostly dark, but the lights from people's cell phones and old school flashlights illuminate enough. That's how I notice Drew and an older woman that I recognize from the beach sitting next to each other, laughing so hard I thought they were crying at first. I wonder if I should stop to say hello. I've at least already introduced myself to Drew, but I've not yet spoken to the older woman. I've only caught her casting pitying glances in my direction on the beach in the day.

I don't like to be pitied. I'm fairly certain I know what my husband is doing, but I don't want anyone to feel sorry for me. I actually feel sort of fortunate. Wouldn't it be terrible to be married to a man for sixty years, only to have them leave you for a sexier old lady in the room down the hall in your assisted living facility? I'd rather know now that my husband is a jerk.

I don't think I'm in the mood for conversation with strangers this evening, so I decide to pretend not to notice them. They look like they're having a lot of fun, anyway, and I wouldn't want to interrupt. As I approach them, I keep my eyes forward, and Sweeney pads across the sand next to me.

"Jess?" His voice stops me dead in my tracks. There's something about the sound of Drew's voice and the way it seems to instantly soothe the corners of my heart—corners I didn't even know could be soothed or needed soothing.

Sweeney stops when I stop, and then I turn toward the calming voice. I fake recognition, like I hadn't just recognized him moments before I decided I would ignore him. I've perfected this act. It serves me well when I spot someone I know in the grocery store I don't feeling like talking to.

"Oh, hi!" I exclaim, and my voice sounds nothing like itself. It's squeaky and pubescent. Geez, I think this man makes me nervous—but good nervous—the kind of nervous I felt as a teenager in the halls at school when the cutest boy in school passed by me in the hallway.

Drew hops up out of the sand and stands next to me as he introduces me to his older female companion. "Joyce, this is Jess." And then he looks at me. "We're all neighbors, actually. Hey, where's—"

I shake my head before he finishes his sentence. "I'm on a date with my dog," I say with a smile. I almost ask him where his wife and daughter are, too, but I don't.

It's then that Drew notices Sweeney. His smile grows wider, and he squats to give Sweeney a pat on his head, and I almost stop him. Sweeney is generally pretty protective of me. Other men aren't allowed to come near me, which is why no one is more surprised than I am when Sweeney begins to wag his tail and let Drew pet him.

"He never likes anyone," I say, surprised.

Joyce pets Sweeney, too, without any disapproving growls or stares from Sweeney. She looks up at me and smiles. "It's nice to meet you, Jess. Do you want to sit with us? We're just watching the full moon settle over the ocean."

I look down at Sweeney and then the stretch of beach before us. I look back at Drew and then Joyce. Both of them look back at me like they'd love nothing more than for me to join them. I can't remember the last time someone looked at me like they wanted my presence.

"Okay." I lead Sweeney to a spot in the sand. Drew sits between Joyce and me; Sweeney lays in the cool sand next to me.

"Where are you from, Jess?" Joyce asks me. Her voice is so kind, and now I understand why I've seen Drew and Joyce together a few times this week. She's motherly in how she speaks—like she's loved me my entire life, even though we've only just met each other.

"I'm from Greenville, South Carolina," I reply. "Not too far from here."

"Ah, born and raised?" Drew asks me.

"Born and raised. What about you two?"

Joyce speaks first. "Harold and I have lived in Greenville for the last twenty years, but we're originally from Atlanta."

"I'm originally from Georgia, but I also currently reside in Greenville. That's where I met my wife," Drew says.

"You're not serious. Greenville? Both of you?" I ask.

"I can't believe we haven't run into each other at some point," he says.

"Maybe we have and just didn't know it," I suggest.

"No, I think I'd remember bumping into you." He smiles at me.

I feel my face grow hot at that comment. Is he hitting on me?

"Greenville is a big city. It's quite possible none of us have ever crossed paths," Joyce adds.

As we continue to sit and talk about different things, I'm thankful Drew called my name and Joyce asked me to sit with them. I didn't want to be alone tonight, but if I were, I'd probably be reflecting on my marriage. I'd probably cry some. It's an odd feeling, having good memories that I no longer wish I had. That's what breaks the heart— the memories we made together, the trips we took together, the meals we burned together—laughing together through it all.

Cal and I haven't had that in quite a while. We don't laugh together. Not anymore. Not since cancer. I suppose if you promise to love someone through sickness and in health and they leave you in the sickness, they probably weren't great to have around, anyway. But even that is a hard pill to swallow. It would have been nice to know that about him before I agreed to marry him so many years ago.

"Do you think our spouses are cheating on us?" Drew asks me rather bluntly and seemingly out of the blue.

I look at him, gazing into his green eyes—eyes that I think I could get lost in for a few hours if I stared into them long enough. "What do you think?" I counter with a hint of sarcasm.

Joyce clears her throat, and I wonder if she's feeling uncomfortable. But Joyce doesn't really strike me as the type of person who ever feels uncomfortable. She's the kind of woman that's ready to spring into action at any moment.

Drew doesn't answer my question. He throws his eyes to the sand, and I watch as his face drops. "I guess people get divorced every day, don't they?"

I shrug my shoulders. Joyce responds, "I think some couples give up on their marriages a bit too quickly. But you two? I think you've got reason."

Drew and I are both looking at Joyce now. Even Sweeney seems to be listening to her words.

"All I'm saying is living with people is hard. We're all so different. We think differently. Make different decisions. See things differently. A lot of married couples these days seem to throw in the towel at the very first sign of a rough patch. Maybe it's finances or an addiction or whatever it may be. Some of those things can be worked out and forgiven, and in the end, that work is worth it. Couples who fight to save their marriages try things like counseling and dating each other again. But I think extramarital affairs are different. I've never understood how the faithful spouse could ever trust the unfaithful spouse ever again. And what's a relationship if there is no trust?"

"If I tried to date my wife now, she'd have me castrated," Drew jokes.

"I'm not telling you to go ask your wife out on a date. I'm telling you that some relationships are worth fighting for. Others are not."

I consider Joyce's words. I know they're true. Some things are worth fighting for. I fought for my life and won. That was worth fighting for. Cal didn't fight *with* me, so why would I want to fight *for* him?

The four of us (Sweeney included) sit there in the sand quietly for a few minutes, observing the moon, transfixed by the words of Joyce and the rhythm of the ocean. I'm somewhere in my head, Drew in his. Joyce seems to be the only one at peace.

"Well, I guess I should be off to bed," Joyce says, breaking the silence between us.

Drew is on his feet in seconds to help Joyce up from the sand. She thanks him, winks at both of us, and then tells us that she'll see us tomorrow. I can't help but feel as though I've made a friend in Joyce. But not like a "let's-go-get-our-nails-done" type of friend. More like the kind of friend you call when you need them to kick someone's butt for you.

When Joyce has disappeared over the dunes and into the

darkness, Drew settles back in the sand next to me. He draws circles in the sand with a stick that the ocean spit out at some point during high tide. He's quiet, but I don't feel as though he wishes I would leave.

"I had cancer," I say suddenly. I don't do well with awkward silences. They make me feel weird. I realize I could have said anything but this. I could have said, "I love blue cheese burgers" or "my favorite color is orange," but instead, I lead with the single most horrifying thing I've ever had happen to me.

Drew looks up quickly. "What?" His expression is a mix of sorrow and surprise.

"That's when I lost Cal," I say. "When I had cancer, he came to my first couple of treatments, but then he stopped coming to the hospital with me altogether. At first, it was stupid excuses like a lunch meeting with a colleague that he couldn't get out of. Finally, he admitted he couldn't stand the smell of the hospital and that the mood of the place really brought him down. Basically, his feelings were more important than mine. He never once cared that I had to sit there in that dark room with chemo running through my veins, cold and lonely. I think...I think that's when he started having an affair."

"If that's true—if that's what he did—he deserves to burn in Hell," Drew says without any hint of sympathy toward the man I'm married to. I obviously don't know Drew very well, but I can hear the anger in his tone.

I don't disagree with the statement, though. "It took about a year for my body to bounce back after chemo. It's still not the same, obviously, but I feel better than I did last summer. I feel like a new person altogether. Cal sometimes struggles to even look at me."

"I think you're beautiful," Drew says to me. "I'm not just saying that."

At that, I blush, and Sweeney stands from his sitting position to give Drew a friendly lick on his knee. It's Sweeney's mark of approval. It sounds gross, but a lick is better than the way Sweeney marks his territory.

"He likes you." I smile.

Drew smiles and pets Sweeney's head. "I kinda like the guy, too." Sweeney wags his tail.

"We're going to be okay, Drew. I know it doesn't feel like it right now, but I think it will be. Good things are coming our way."

Drew sighs and then nods his head. "I hope so. Want to walk a little?"

The beach is beginning to thin out. It's getting late now. The children that were once hunting for hermit crabs are now crying tired tears while their parents carry them off the beach. I have no idea when Cal will return, but for once, wouldn't it feel nice for him to arrive back at the beach house while I'm out?

"Let's walk," I say.

Drew helps me up from the sand as I take hold of Sweeney's leash, and then we walk, side by side, down the beach.

"Lindsey hates the beach. She prefers mountains," Drew confides. "I think I'll move here one day."

"Cal doesn't like the beach either." I laugh. "He hates the sand. I don't get it. I could live here forever and never get tired of it."

"Right? People always tell me that I'd eventually get sick of living on the coast—that it won't feel like a vacation. I understand that living on the coast wouldn't be like a vacation every day, but you know what you can do? You have a bad day, you can end it on the beach in a chair with a beer. That beats a bar any day."

"I hope this week doesn't ruin my feelings for this island."

"It shouldn't," Drew says. "We met Joyce, and now, we've met. It's been a while since I met some strangers I like."

"You've known me less than twenty-four hours; I'm not sure you could know whether or not you like me," I point out.

He smirks. "I guess that's true. But actually, I had already spotted you before we officially met on the pier earlier."

"Oh? You've been watching me?"

"People-watching is sort of a hobby of mine," he admits with a sheepish grin.

"I enjoy people-watching, too. Even Sweeney people-watches."

"Really?"

"His favorite thing is standing on the balcony of our beach house and watching the people go to and from the beach. He could stand there for hours, never moving. He doesn't even bark. He just...watches."

"I bet everyone people-watches. How could you not?"

"Humans are rather interesting," I say. "They do some of the craziest things."

"I went to a college football game once. Well, I've been more than once; but this one particular time, I watched a very overweight man, who had clearly had too much to drink, just topple over the wall of the stands right into the bushes beneath him—standing one second, in the bushes the next."

"I once watched a man at a college football game pass out from being intoxicated and from the heat. It was so hot that day. Anyway, he was heavyset himself, and his friends started lifting his shirt to fan his belly to cool him down. They even poured their bottled waters on his belly. My friends and I made a pact, then, that if any of us were to pass out, no one—and we meant no one—was allowed to lift our shirts!"

Drew laughs, and I can't remember the last time I made someone else laugh. When was the last time *I* had laughed?

"We should go to a game together one day," Drew says. "Now that we know we live in the same location."

"As long as you're not a South Carolina Gamecock," I say, cutting my eyes at him.

"Oh, definitely not. My blood runneth orange."

"A Clemson Tiger! My kinda guy." I'm a bit too excited. "Sorry, I didn't mean that last part. I mean, I did, but not—"

"I was just going to say, you're my kinda gal." Drew smiles, interrupting me.

My heart begins to race, and my cheeks feel hot again like I'm blushing. I've not flirted or been flirted with in so long, I can't even be sure that's what we're doing. But it feels like that. I feel a little guilty about it, but if I allow my mind to wander to wherever Cal may be at this very moment, I realize there's not a whole lot I should feel guilty about. I am actually laughing this evening, and I can't remember the last time I did that.

"I still can't believe that we live in the same town but have never bumped into each other," I say.

"Well, we do live in the fastest growing city in South Carolina—a lot more of us now than there were. But I don't get out as much anymore. I work, go home, work a bit more."

"I don't really get out either. I even have my groceries delivered to me."

"I wish Lindsey would do that. She insists on going to Target for groceries. She comes home with everything *except* groceries."

I laugh. "That's understandable, though. Target is notorious for showing you all the things you don't need but definitely want."

"We should probably turn back before we walk too far. That's easy to do on a beach." Drew slows his pace before coming to a stop.

"I was just about to say the same thing." Sweeney turns around with us, and we begin the walk back to where we started.

We're quiet for a bit. No words are exchanged between us; but the ocean continues to roar its gentle roar, and the sound of the wet sand beneath our bare feet permeates the air.

When we arrive back to where we started, Drew turns toward me. "I don't know what's going on between your husband and my wife, but I'm thankful to have met you. I feel a little less alone in this."

I smile gently. "I think we both know what's going on between our spouses; but you're right—we're not alone. And we have Joyce now, too. Something about that woman motivates me."

"I thought it was just me!" Drew exclaims. "She reminds me of my mom. I've never met anyone who reminds me of my mom."

"She seems like an amazing woman. I know your mom must be, too."

"She was. My mom died when I was fourteen. She had…cancer."

My eyes fall, and my heart shatters. We don't all win the fight. I know I'm fortunate. I also know that I'll never take my life for granted again. "I'm sorry, Drew."

Drew drops his own eyes to mine and then lifts my chin with his thumb. He's wearing a sweet smirk on his face. His green eyes seem to shine in the moonlight, and I feel pretty certain that I could sit and stare at him for the rest of my life. There's something in his smile that puts me at ease—something I can't explain.

"She would be happy that you beat it," he says to me.

At that, a tear forms in my eye and escapes down my cheek. "I met so many incredible women on my journey. Some of them lost their fight. Some of us didn't. Sometimes, I do wonder why I was allowed to win mine. There are others who deserved life more. Your mom, for instance. She had a son to raise."

"I think you can't ask questions like that, Jess. I don't think we're meant to question life. We're supposed to do something with it. My mom had fulfilled her purpose here."

I think it's his instincts, but as he finishes that last sentence, he reaches up and wipes away my tears with his thumb. The act surprises me. It feels intimate, and yet, we only met each other today. I stare into those green eyes of his for a second too long, and fear begins to build in my chest. There are feelings that I'm feeling that I'm not sure I want or should be feeling. And maybe it's the want-to that's scaring me. I want to feel these things more than I don't want to.

"I should get back to the house," I say quietly, retreating because that's what we should do at this point.

Drew steps back slightly and nods his head. "I should, too, I guess."

My stomach is in knots. My heart is pounding. I have an urge that I can't act on. I'm married!

"See you tomorrow?" Drew asks when I don't say anything else.

I nod. "Tomorrow."

People Watching

TUESDAY

People Watching

17
Joyce Rose

"Where were you last night?" Harold eyes me from across the breakfast table looking like he's suspicious.

I roll my eyes at him. "Harold, if I were going to cheat on you, I would have done it thirty years ago." I sip my coffee and divert my eyes back to the morning news that's playing on the television.

"I didn't say you were cheating."

"Your tone implied it."

"You're meddling in that boy's life again, aren't you? That Drew kid. Joyce, I told you to leave it alone."

"Harold, if I were going to start listening to everything you tell me not to do, I would have done it thirty years ago." I'm not sure why I think that if I were going to do anything bad, it would have been thirty years ago, but I'm going with it.

"Joyce, leave them alone. It's not your business." He's annoyed with me. "Honestly, you're going to end up messing with the wrong people one day, and I'm going to find you dead in an alley somewhere."

"You're ridiculous," I tell him. "Besides, I still remember my martial arts training."

"Joyce, you were sixteen the last time you qualified to be a black belt. You're a bit older than that now."

"Is that a challenge?" I'm always up for a challenge. I still remember the moves. I still remember how to take a full-grown man down with one pressure-point pinch."

Harold glares at me. "You forget you're an old lady now."

"You forget you're an old man."

"Stop repeating everything I say back to me."

"Stop telling me what to do."

Harold huffs at me one more time, chugs his coffee, and then opens the newspaper with great force. I chuckle at him because I can see that his eyes are watering from chugging the hot coffee, and who the heck even reads a newspaper anymore? I don't even know where he went to get that newspaper.

Harold has always worked hard at never changing. He still thinks life should be as it was in the '70s, but—news flash—it's not the '70s. In fact, we're closer to 2050. He never understood social media or the internet. I had to beg for Netflix. If resisting change were a sport, Harold would be an all-star.

Change isn't always a bad thing. Yes, I do believe there are some things that should remain a tradition, but there are a lot of other things that shouldn't. Society evolves and with it, technology, culture, the way we speak, and so forth.

I read this book once that presented the idea of getting left behind—not being left behind when Jesus comes back, but more along the lines of getting left behind in life by not staying up-to-date on the latest and greatest.

So, I've spent most of my marriage with Harold, trying to keep him up to speed with the current happenings of the world. I've tried to keep us fashionable and in the know about all of the newest technology. We both have smartphones, but Harold doesn't know how to use his. I've tried to teach him. He doesn't listen.

"I met the woman whose husband has been fraternizing with Drew's wife," I tell Harold. "She's very kind."

"Must not be too kind if her husband is cheating on her," Harold mumbles without looking away from his newspaper.

"Why would you assume it's the woman's fault the man is cheating?" I snap at him.

Harold peers over the top of the newspaper to evaluate me. Am I really angry or just pulling his leg?

"I'm serious!" I say a little louder.

"Geez, Joyce. I was just adding to the conversation. I don't care who is cheating on whom. I just want to vacation with my wife!"

"We are vacationing together, Harold."

"Can you do me a favor? Can you just drop it? Let those two families sort out their own issues."

I won't agree to drop it. I just won't answer his question.

Harold peers at me again from over the top of the newspaper. "Can we at least go to the antique store today? You threw off the whole week by making it a beach day yesterday. We were supposed to go to the antique stores."

"Harold, sometimes we have to do things differently than we're used to. There's nothing wrong with a little change."

"I don't see why our vacation routine has to change. It's something we discovered we enjoy—antiquing on a Monday. Remember when we established the tradition? It was because no one goes antiquing on a Monday—especially at the beach. It's different!"

"We've been doing that for the last fifteen years now, Harold. Maybe it's time to start a new tradition."

"But I enjoy antiquing on a Monday at the beach while on vacation." Harold looks sad now. His old, blue eyes droop like a sad cartoon character.

This look pulls at my heart strings. It's the only look Harold is capable of giving me that forces me to bend in his favor. When he wins an argument, it's because he's given me this look.

I think about it for a second and come up with a compromise. "We'll go antiquing this morning. Get some lunch. Then we can spend the afternoon on the beach."

Harold considers this for a few seconds and then says, "Deal." Harold's hand comes from around the newspaper to shake mine.

"Sometimes, I think you never grew up at all." I giggle at him and shake his hand.

18
Drew Clark

"Where were you last night?" Linds glares at me from across the kitchen as she prepares Lilly's breakfast.

"Oh, you noticed," I quip. "I was on the beach. There was a full moon. It was quite lovely." I go back to my coffee and the sports update on the television.

"Quite lovely?" she mocks me. "What has gotten into you?"

I shrug because there's nothing I could tell her that would make a difference. "What did you do last night?"

Lindsey puts Lilly in her highchair. "We went out for ice cream. When you weren't here when we got back, I was a bit concerned."

"Why? No one here to fix your problems?"

"What has gotten into you, Drew? Are you angry with me?" Lindsey appears shocked by my new attitude. I'm actually a fan of this new attitude. I think I might keep it. Maybe if I stop being a push-over, she'll stop being…whatever it is she's being.

"No, I'm not angry." And I'm not. I'm exhausted.

"Is this about that man I've been spending so much time with on the beach?" She now stands with her hands on her hips, staring at me from Lilly's highchair; and I feel certain there's a slight look of fear in her eyes.

"What man?" I ask as though I've not noticed, but really, it's because Jess' husband is no man. If he were, he could have sucked up his pride and sat with his wife while she underwent her chemo treatments.

"You're impossible."

Maybe it's Joyce. Maybe it's Jess. Maybe it's both of them. Regardless, I feel like I've found my balls again. Pardon my language, but I'm not sure how else to explain it. It felt easier to submit to my wife, but in reality, my passivity caused me to lose myself. I'm not motivated by anything anymore. It's like I resolved myself to living like this for the rest of my life. We're supposed to help, support, and do things for our spouses—I get that. I wanted that. When I married Lindsey, I wanted nothing more than to take care of her, give her things, and make her happy. But Lindsey sort of grew into something like an evil dictator. Our relationship now is so one-sided.

"Anyway, I don't think I'm going to the beach today." I tell her. "I'm going to head out to Botany Bay in a bit, do a little exploring there."

"But we're on vacation—a *family* vacation." Ah, the guilt trip. She's good at that.

"Really? Because this is pretty much the first conversation we've had since we arrived on Saturday. You and Lilly have spent the last two days with that man. I've hardly seen either of you since we rolled into town." I won't fall for her little guilt trips. This is how she manipulates me.

Lindsey stares back at me, and for the first time in her life, she's speechless. I have rendered my wife speechless. I feel like I need an award or something.

"I would like to know one thing," I continue. "How did you think it would make me feel to watch you and our daughter spend *our* family vacation with a stranger? You've left me in that beach chair by myself, only coming to talk to me when you want something. I took Lilly to the pier for ice cream, and you yelled at me for being gone too long. I want to spend time with you and Lilly."

"It's only Tuesday, Drew. You're being so dramatic." Lindsey turns away from me. I can only assume she's hiding the red in her cheeks.

"Tuesday—and we haven't done a single thing together. We've not even had dinner together. Not once!" I don't want to fight. I don't want to yell at my wife in front of Lilly, but at the same time, I won't sit here and have my wife make me feel a little guilty about not being home when she and Lilly got back last night. What was I supposed to do? Sit here and wait on them like a sad puppy?

"Where is this coming from?" Lindsey is uncomfortable now. I can see it in the way she's holding her shoulders.

"Where is this coming from? Seriously?"

"You never talk to me like this, Drew. I'm concerned." She turns to face me again.

The gaslighting is unbelievable. And so, I start laughing uncontrollably at the idiocy of it all. And I can't stop. I'm laughing at her so hard, tears stream down my face, and my breath is uncatchable. I feel like a lunatic. Something inside of me is coming unraveled.

Lindsey watches me as though I've lost it completely. I wonder if she's contemplating calling a mental hospital. I almost think she should. But she's right: I never do this. I never talk to her the way I just did, and I can't even remember the last time I laughed manically like this.

I think it's mainly because I'm basically out of oxygen now, but I come to my senses and wipe my face dry from my laughing tears.

"Feel better?" She looks annoyed.

"Actually, yeah. I do." I feel a lot better. I read somewhere once that laughing actually releases endorphins. Your body gets a sort of high from it. In fact, one good bout of laughter has proven to help postpartum depression in women after childbirth in ways a prescription never could. Laughter is medicine, and apparently, that applies to the condescending type of laughter as well.

19
Jess Dawson

"Where were you last night?" Cal meets me on the front porch of the beach house with a coffee in hand. Sweeney doesn't even lift his head to greet him.

I look up from my phone, where I've been catching up on the latest from friends and family on social media. "Out," I tell him, albeit a bit short.

"Out where? I came home, and you weren't here. You didn't even leave a note." He's accusing, maybe even a little angry.

"You went out, so Sweeney and I went out. Grabbed dinner from the pier and took a stroll on the beach."

"By yourself?" Cal looks like an overbearing father drilling his teenager for missing curfew by a couple of minutes.

"No, I had Sweeney." I divert my eyes back to my phone. My aunt just returned from a six-week hiking trip on the Appalachian Trail, and her photos are exquisite!

"What's this attitude?" Cal stands at the table, one hand on his hip, appearing exasperated.

I look up at Cal again, surprised to find him so upset over this, but I play dumb. "What attitude?"

"The one you have right now. Like you don't care that I was worried sick about you. You wouldn't answer your phone."

"You must not have been too worried, Cal. When we came home, you were snoring."

"I was worried." He bites his bottom lip and adds, "I was exhausted, too."

"Why do you leave every time I take a cat nap?"

"What?"

"Every time I take a little nap after we come in from the beach, you take the opportunity to sneak out for dinner. We've not had dinner together once this week. I waited for you, but last night, I wasn't waiting for you again. We're supposed to be on vacation together, but it feels a lot like a Sweeney-and-Jess vacation. Not to mention that woman you've been spending so much time with on the beach."

"That's because her loser husband doesn't know the first thing about what it means to be a husband or even a father."

"So, you're trying to show him how to be a husband by leaving your actual wife to spend her vacation alone?"

"You're being a little dramatic here, Jess. It's only Tuesday."

"And I've yet to have dinner with you. We've not even had one of those really good beach conversations we usually have before you generally head back to the beach house to read a book. In fact, you've spent more time on the beach in the last two days with two total strangers than you ever have with me in all the years we've been married and vacationing together!"

Cal stares at me, hard. His jaw is clenched. He's somewhere between angry and afraid. I've known the man long enough to know what each of his expressions mean, and this is one I'm not sure I've ever seen. The closest interpretation I have is fear and anger.

"I'm going to get our spot on the beach set up," Cal finally says after too many seconds of tense silence. Then he turns and disappears into the house.

A few minutes later, I spot him approaching the beach access. His shoulders are tense, and his stride is more of a stomp. If there had been fear in his expression before he left, he's now completely enveloped with anger. I wonder with whom, though? Is he angry with me or himself?

Today is hot again. There's hardly an ocean breeze, and the sun feels like it's a bit closer to earth than it has been in the past. There's not a big enough umbrella or a cold enough drink to quench this heat.

I spot Drew a few umbrellas down from me. He catches my eye

People Watching

and gives me a wave with a grin on his face. My heart then does this weird thing in my chest that I haven't felt it do in a long time: it flutters. The flutter startles me. One, it's a foreign feeling. Two, I can't have my heart fluttering over another man while I'm still married because then that doesn't make me any better than Cal.

I can't forget that moment on the beach last night though—his wiping my tears with his thumb, his smile, his eyes, the undeniable urge to lift myself on my tiptoes and kiss his perfect lips. It was the intimacy of it all that I was wrapped in. It was a feeling of closeness that I've not had with another human in quite some time.

When was the last time Cal was intimate toward me? When was the last time he wiped my tears away? It's not that I'm desperate for attention and willing to throw myself at anyone who gives that to me, but I think I forgot what it felt like for another human to actually see me.

Sure, I see Cal every day, but he doesn't *see* me anymore. I have often wondered if maybe cancer really did kill me and now I'm actually a ghost who doesn't know she's a ghost—like that movie with the kid who could see dead people. The therapist had no clue he himself was actually dead. From his perspective, he was still living and breathing and wondering why his marriage was falling apart. What if that's what happened here? What if I'm actually dead?

I smile at Drew and wave back to him, wondering if maybe we're actually both dead. Maybe that's why our spouses seem to be ignoring us. I can't dwell on this thought too long because I find myself finding it sort of appealing. If I'm really dead, none of this is happening.

Then, I notice Joyce stopping by Drew's umbrella before they both start toward me.

"Hi, Jess!" Joyce waves big and vibrant as they approach. She's wearing red lipstick and a giant straw hat today. She's definitely got the coastal grandmother-style down, and there's something about her that I envy in a good way. I wish I could be Joyce—fearless, powerful, strong. Maybe I will be one day.

"Hi, Joyce! Hi, Drew!" I say, pushing myself up from my beach chair to greet them.

"It's a hot one today, isn't it?" Joyce smiles at me. "Drew and I were heading up to grab some cold lemonade from the pier. Do you want us to grab you one?"

"How about I come with you?" I never invite myself anywhere, but I don't know how long I can sit here watching my husband with that woman.

"Even better," Drew says with his brilliant smile.

"Should we see if your significant others want anything?" Joyce sarcastically suggests.

Drew and I laugh at the suggestion, shake our heads, and say in unison, "No."

"I was just messing with you," Joyce says. "They look hydrated enough."

Drew, Joyce, and I walk through the surf toward the pier. The water feels good as it laps at our ankles; and if I turn my head just the right way, I can feel some semblance of an ocean breeze. Joyce puts Drew in the middle of us as we walk, and my heart flutters again when he accidentally brushes my hand with his. He tries to act as though he didn't notice, but I catch his eyes cut toward me from beneath his sunglasses.

"Joyce, does your husband ever miss you when you befriend people like us at the beach?" I ask her.

Joyce laughs. "Oh no. He gave up trying to stop me a long time ago. And, well, I don't do this all the time. There's just something I like about the two of you."

"The week is almost halfway over now. What happens next week?" Drew asks both of us.

I don't really care to think about next week yet. I've even avoided thinking about the drive home. The thought of going home with Cal makes my skin crawl. "I think we shouldn't think about next week," I suggest. "I'm a big believer in living moment by moment, and for now, we're in this moment together."

"I think Jess is right. You'll figure out the rest soon enough. For now, enjoy your vacation. We can have fun. This can still be the best vacation ever!" Joyce says enthusiastically.

I admire her optimism, but I still highly doubt this week is going down as the best vacation ever, even if I have met two strangers I could envision seeing myself remaining friends with long after this week is over. It would be a pity for us all to go back to Greenville only never to see each other again.

The lemonade is just as heavenly as Joyce described it. It's not too sweet, slightly tart, and immediately refreshing. I was thirstier than I had realized. Because I sucked down the first cup of lemonade so quickly, Drew purchased a second cup for me. I told him he shouldn't be buying other women lemonade. He smiled and told me that he wasn't buying other women lemonade—just me.

The pavilion in the pier is a lot busier than it was yesterday. Everyone is trying to escape the heat, but all they've managed to do is heat up the entire pavilion with their bodies. It's so stuffy, it's nearly impossible to breathe. Even still, we find a small table in the corner of the pavilion that no one seems to have noticed yet. We move quickly toward the table to claim our seats, and we manage to slide in just before a group of teenage boys do.

"I hadn't expected to meet new friends on this vacation, but I'm thankful to have met you both. This would have ended up being quite a lonely week without you." I smile and sip my lemonade. "I do have one request, though." I look at Joyce. "No more pitying me."

"I don't want anyone feeling sorry for me either," Drew chimes in. He and I both look at Joyce.

Joyce looks back at both of us for a few seconds before she realizes we're asking her not to feel sorry for us. Her eyes grow wide, and she jumps slightly in shock. "Honey, I do not feel sorry for you. I told you; I like both of you. I think you are good people in a confusing situation." She shrugs. "I guess I miss my kids, too. Meeting you has sort of filled that space in my heart this week. You know, you spend most of your young adult life starting a family and then carrying said family off on vacation every year. They grow so quickly, though. One year, they need the life jackets; the next, they're Olympic swimmers.

"I remember when my kids were nearing the age of sixteen. I was very cognizant of how many weeks of vacation at the beach I had left with them. I tried to enjoy every moment of those final years. Even still, when they stopped coming with Harold and me to the beach either for school or work or because they wanted to go on vacation with their own families, it was a shock to the system.

"That first year Harold and I vacationed without the kids, I think I cried the entire week on the beach. Harold didn't express any emotion, but I think he missed them, too. We sort of just sat around all week and stared at each other. Harold and I had never really vacationed alone, just the two of us. We didn't know what to do. Eventually, we figured it out. We kept moving, and I think that's the most important thing we as humans can do—to keep moving even in the face of adversity."

I don't disagree with Joyce. When I received my cancer diagnosis, Cal hovered over me like I would croak at any second. He wouldn't even let me take out the garbage. He took away all of my freedoms and rights. I couldn't even go to the bathroom alone. Did I need a partner to stand by me? Support me? Help me? Yes. Did I need someone to wipe my own butt for me? No. I wanted to keep moving despite the cancer and despite how the chemo made me feel. I had to keep moving. If I stopped, succumbed to my bed, and only left it for chemo treatments, well, I think that would have killed me—not the cancer. The loss of everyday life would have certainly sent me to the grave.

We're quiet for a few moments, sipping our lemonade, thinking about the brevity of life when Drew suddenly speaks up. "I don't think Lilly is my daughter."

Joyce and I look at him in silence. It's a thought I have had, and it looks like Joyce may have had it as well. But none of us has had the gall to say it out loud. Speaking for myself, I've definitely had the thought, but it's not one I wanted to sit on too long. If Lilly isn't Drew's daughter, whose daughter is she? I can't seem to force myself to answer that last question.

Drew's eyes meet ours, and he realizes he's startled us both with his admission. "I'm sorry. I know that was sort of out of the blue there. It's just...I needed to say that out loud."

In a quick attempt to ease his embarrassment, I say, "Why do you think Lilly isn't yours?"

Drew spins his empty plastic lemonade cup in circles around his index finger. He shrugs, but his eyes do not meet mine or Joyce. He's suddenly distant, lost somewhere in his mind, transfixed on the spinning plastic cup around his index finger. "Linds and I haven't really been great in a couple of years. This is probably too much, but we stopped having sex, like, two years ago. I mean, maybe a few times here and there just to relieve the tension, if you know what I'm saying..."

I really do not want to hear the details of Drew's sex life. Not because I'm a prude and find this type of conversation inappropriate, but for some reason, the thought of it makes me angry.

"Anyway," Drew continues, "Linds popped up pregnant, and I've spent the last year and nine months wondering when it happened. You know how men are. We keep a running ledger of the last time we had sex, and it wasn't registering."

"Have you asked her about it?" Joyce asks.

"When she told me she was pregnant, I think the first question out of my mouth was 'when?'" he says. "She says we went out one night for her birthday; I got drunk, and we fooled around a bit. I remember going out that night. But I don't typically get hammered, so the story never really made sense to me." Drew goes quiet again. Joyce and I doing the same, and then he looks at me. "It wouldn't make sense, right? If our spouses had cheated on us with each other? When would they have even met?"

This is the one piece of the puzzle that I've not been able to wrap my mind around. I've spent much of my alone time on the beach this week, reflecting on exactly when Cal and I began to fall apart, and it doesn't make sense. Cal always came home at night—though, late sometimes. He's in finance, and Lindsey is a stay-at-home mom, from the sound of it. There aren't really any common interests there. Lindsey doesn't even look like Cal's type, but then, what do I know about Cal's type? I thought I was his type.

Joyce and Drew stare into their empty lemonade cups. Joyce appears to be unsure of what she should say.

"But if not with each other, then with whom?" Joyce asks.

It only mostly makes sense that my husband and Drew's wife would be having an affair together. The way they've been on the beach together this week, they have looked like husband and wife. But it's the when, where, and why that stumps me. I was happily married. Even with the cancer diagnosis, I was happy because I had a husband who I knew would take care of me no matter what. Now I realize that I actually know very little about Cal these days. He's not my Cal anymore.

Drew sighs and shoots his plastic cup into a trash can a few feet away as though he were an all-star on a basketball team. "This feels like some horrible movie when you know something bad is coming up but you're just not sure what it is yet. I wish I could change the channel."

"I thought we were supposed to be enjoying our vacation," Joyce says. "This conversation is quickly getting depressing."

"Joyce is right," I say. "There's no use in sitting here going over the situation in our heads. We're speculating, and we'll only drive ourselves crazy." I try to toss my lemonade cup into the trash the way Drew did, but it bounces off the side of the trash can and hits a kid in the head instead. The kid looks around confused, rubbing his head where the cup hit him. Drew quickly apologizes for the mishap and picks the cup from the ground, placing it into the garbage again.

"Sorry." I stifle a giggle as Drew looks at me, trying not to laugh himself.

"When we get back to Greenville, I'm teaching you how to shoot a basketball. No way you should have missed that big opening on that giant garbage can."

"Listen, sir," I joke, "I know how to shoot a basketball. That kid's head just got in the way."

"He wasn't anywhere near that garbage can!" Drew laughs at me.

Joyce, laughing at both of us now, stands from the table. "Come on, children. Looks like I can't take you out anywhere."

"Are we embarrassing you?" Drew teases.

"Only slightly." Joyce winks.

20
Joyce Rose

"How's your infatuation going?" Harold asks me over dinner. He's talking about Drew and Jess and their presumably cheating spouses. I suppose it has become a slight infatuation, but mostly, I've enjoyed their company. I don't feel as useless. I have a project—someone to help. Though, I'm not sure how I'm helping them really. Other than keeping them company, I suppose.

"It's not an infatuation as much as it's my innate need to help people. Those two people need help, Harold."

"You need help," he mumbles.

I ignore him. Harold has always mumbled insults like that under his breath; but I also know that he would crawl into a burning building to save my old wrinkly butt from death, so I forgive him.

"Let me ask you something, Harold. You're a man. You've been married to me a long time…"

"Too long," Harold interrupts, and then a little smirk spreads across his gray-bearded face.

I ignore him again and continue, "When you've entertained the thought of cheating on me—"

"Whoa! Wait a minute. Just one second there! Don't pull me into this 'all men are cheaters' crap."

"Would you shut your mouth long enough to hear what I have to say?" I quip, a little frustrated.

Harold clears his throat and motions for me to proceed.

"As I was saying, when you've entertained the thought of cheating on me—even though I know you never have—did you connive a scheme together to make it work? Something that would keep me in the dark?"

"Joyce, I never got that far in the thought process because I'm scared to death of you. If I cheated on you and you found out, I'd go ahead and plan my own funeral."

"Harold, I'm being serious."

"So am I. Any man who's looking to cheat on his wife isn't a man at all. It takes a real man to put up with the same woman's crap until one of them dies."

"You've always had such a way with words." I close my eyes briefly, annoyed. "Just forget I asked."

"You should be happy I can't answer your question. It means I've never thought about cheating on you." Harold looks proud.

Sometimes, he's so obnoxious, it's lovable. I'm still not sure I believe him. I feel like every married man (and probably woman) has at least thought about it.

"What am I supposed to do?" I ask him seriously.

Harold puts on his serious face. "Joyce, you don't know these people. You don't owe them anything. You can't fix everyone's problems."

I sigh. I can't explain why I feel the need to help Drew and Jess. I don't know what I'm going to do, but I'm going to help them. The young ones tend to get a bad reputation among us older folks, but Drew and Jess are different. Yes, they're young. But they happen to be pretty wise for a couple of kids in their mid-thirties. I thought my children were intelligent, but Drew and Jess could have them beat. Maybe it's because they experienced adult problems as a child. I worked to keep my children's lives trauma-free, though some circumstances are impossible to avoid. We can't protect our children from everything, but I tried.

My mother was diagnosed as bipolar when I was in high school. By then, the damage had already been done to me, but the diagnosis seemed to make everything my mother had ever done make sense. She would start fights with women she thought were hitting on my dad. She would absolutely lose it sometimes, crying and screaming. The smallest thing could set her off. Sometimes, she'd start trouble that would eventually get us all into trouble.

One night, she got so out of hand, my dad had to call the police.

Before the police arrived, my dad told my brother and me to run to our grandparents' house. They only lived a few houses down, but he didn't want us home if things got worse. So, my brother and I ran. I couldn't have been more than three or four years old, but I vividly remember running through the grass in my socked feet. The rain from that afternoon still lay in droplets across the grass, and it soaked through my socks. It's really the last thing I remember about that evening. I can't recall how it ended.

I had counseling later in life that helped me to resolve some issues that had happened in my childhood. I learned a lot in counseling, and those lessons are how I chose to raise our kids. Of course, I'm not a perfect mother. I failed many times, but I tried.

I wonder what sort of childhood trauma Drew and Jess encountered. It breaks my heart when I think of all of the things some people go through in a single lifetime. It really does seem as though some people get all the luck, while others don't. I'm not really sure why life is like that sometimes.

I can recall times in my adult life when Harold and I were struggling financially, and it felt like everyone around us was buying houses and cars. They were going on extravagant vacations and installing in-ground swimming pools. Meanwhile, it was all we could do to keep a nail in the floor. It would be easy to get caught up in what looks like a lot of good things happening to other people, but the reality is that life is an ebb and flow. When it feels like everyone else is on top, the script flips; and suddenly, you're the one on top, while everyone else is on the bottom. I don't think a single person makes it through this life without having a few hard times in the mix.

I had an uncle I only knew to be wealthy. It would have been natural to assume that he had been born wealthy, but the reality is that when my aunt and uncle first married, they were poor. They were poorer than poor. While normal folks were having a meat-and-three dinner, my aunt and uncle were heating up a can of beans because that's all they could afford. I never knew this side of my aunt and uncle. I only knew the wealthy side. I think sometimes, we forget that others have lived a whole life before we meet them. We can never truly know what sort of circumstances shape others into who they become.

21
Drew Clark

"Let's go do something fun. Just the three of us." Lindsey crawls up next to me on the couch. I resist the urge to pull away. She's not been this close to me in quite some time. Even when we sleep at night, Lindsey is clinging to the side of the bed as though she's having to bunk with the Incredible Hulk. Now I'm wondering if she's getting close to me just to slit my throat.

"Like what?" I don't take my eyes from the television, though, if I'm being honest, I've only been mindlessly watching whatever is on the screen. My mind is elsewhere.

"Let's take Lilly to an amusement park."

"Linds, she can't ride anything except maybe the carousel." The only amusement park on this island consists of nothing but roller coasters and big kid rides. I don't even know if they have a carousel.

She sighs. "Maybe we just go, anyway. We can just walk around and get a funnel cake or something. We've not done anything together this week; and now it's Tuesday night, and the week is half over."

"Whose fault is that? You and Lilly have spent nearly every moment on the beach this week with a stranger. You sneak off in the evening for ice cream without me. I'm just an innocent bystander on this so-called family vacation."

"Andrew, what is going on with you?" Linds appears to be shocked again. She probably is. I've never really talked back to her the entire time we've been together. I've always just nodded my head and done whatever she's asked of me. I'm always the person to concede. I always roll over and do what she wants. But when was the last time I did what I wanted?

Even taking turns on choosing where we go on vacation doesn't seem like an independent decision. It was Lindsey's idea to alternate the mountains and the beach. I thought it felt like a good compromise at the time, and maybe it still is. I'm not sure what I'm thinking right now—or feeling, for that matter.

"If you want to take Lilly to an amusement park, go ahead. I'm sure the man from the beach is available this evening. Maybe you can go together." I know I'm being a jerk in this moment, but I can't seem to stop myself. It's all this pent-up rage I've been harboring for so long.

"Andrew, there's nothing going on between that man and me. His name is Cal, by the way. He's just been very kind. I've enjoyed his company."

"And what about mine?"

"Your what?"

"My company? You don't enjoy mine?"

"Not with this new attitude you've developed," she says with a slight snarl.

I shake my head but don't offer any other words. Lindsey sighs, gives up, and goes to Lilly, who is playing quietly in her playpen. She picks up Lilly, gives me one more glance, and then grabs the diaper bag and her purse before heading out the door. The beach house goes quiet, and I'm not sure if I'm supposed to relax in the silence or go after my wife.

I know what you're thinking: *go to the amusement park with your wife and daughter.* But had I agreed to the amusement park, I wouldn't have been allowed to have the fun that Lilly and Lindsey would inevitably have. No, that's not my role in this family. My role in this family is to do everything Lindsey asks me to do while she has all the fun. I wouldn't be allowed to ride with Lilly on the carousel because someone has to take her picture, and it certainly can't be Lindsey because Lindsey must also be in the picture. There have been so many times I've wanted to take Lilly to baseball games or the circus, and Lindsey opposes every single time. She claims she's worried I'll lose our baby if she's not with us; but sometimes, I wonder if she really doesn't want me to get close to Lilly and form a bond with her.

People Watching

I lean back into the couch, only feeling slightly guilty that I did not take my wife and daughter to an amusement park. But I'm not wrong about how the event would go down, and for that reason, I decide to find something to watch on television. I can't remember the last time I watched something other than the news.

Just as I begin to relax, the door bursts open, and Lindsey is standing there. She doesn't have Lilly anymore, though, and I can only assume she's still buckled into her car seat.

"We're going out tonight," Lindsey says sternly. "Just you and me. We're going out for dinner."

"Where's Lilly?"

"She's with your old lady friend from the beach."

"You trusted our child with a stranger?" I find this incredulous. Lindsey has yet to find a babysitter back home so that we can go out more. She always insists that Lilly isn't ready to be left with someone else.

"I could use the break, too." Lindsey sighs. "And besides, I just want to be with you tonight." Her voice transitions to one of gentleness. Her eyes are big and hopeful. In this moment, she reminds me of the Lindsey I fell in love with.

I want to resist her, but I do need to eat. Maybe we should go out. Maybe we can talk. "Let me change into something besides basketball shorts."

Lindsey appears relieved as she smiles at me. "Okay."

I disappear into our bedroom, throw on some slacks and a button down, slide my feet into my sandals, and reappear a few minutes later.

"You look nice," Linds says to me. "Where are we going?"

"Our usual," I reply dryly. "And then maybe some ice cream."

"Sounds like a perfect date night." She beams at me, and my stomach turns.

She's pure evil, and yet tonight, she's looking at me the way she did on our wedding night. It's confusing. And because I'm confused by her in this moment, I'm also suspicious. What if she's trying to get me to take her out so she can poison me? Murder me right here on my favorite island? I mean, if I am going to be murdered, I wouldn't mind being murdered on Edisto, but I don't think I'm ready to die yet.

22
Jess Dawson

"Let's go out tonight," Cal says to me, coming up behind me and wrapping his arms around my waist as I wash the few dishes left over from lunch.

I smile briefly. I have missed how his arms feel around my body. He used to hold me so tightly, his arms strong around me. "And where would we go?"

"To dinner. I've not taken you to dinner in quite some time. I feel like I haven't seen you much this week either."

"I've been here all week. Where have you been?"

"I know, and I'm sorry. I just feel terrible about the time I've spent on the beach with Linds and her little girl, Lilly. I'm just drawn to that little girl. I wish we had been able to have a child of our own. I wish we had our own family to show the beach to."

"I'm sorry I can't give you that," I tell him softly.

"Jess, come on. I didn't say that I'm miserable without a family of our own. I know your illness took a lot away from us. That's not your fault."

"Then how do you think it makes me feel to see you spending your vacation with two strangers? It feels like it's my fault. It feels like you've found someone else to replace the family you thought you'd have with me."

Cal's arms fall from my body. He leans against the counter next to the sink. I feel his eyes boring into the side of my head. "What is that supposed to mean?"

I shrug, not looking up at him. "It means, Cal, that I'm asking you if you have found another family to replace the one you thought you'd have with me." I feel the tears in the back of my throat. It's the tightness one feels when attempting to not cry. My heart aches inside my chest though. This is the closest I've come to asking him if he's having an affair, the closest I've come to verbally acknowledging that there is something terribly wrong going on here.

"I think that's a ridiculous thing to ask me, Jess. Ridiculous that you could even think that I would do something like that to you."

My heart starts pounding as I feel the anger build up in my chest. I tell myself I won't explode, and I won't. I have to stay calm, even though I know with everything in my being that he's running around on me.

I choke down my anger and say, "I can't think of another woman in the world that would be giddy over her husband spending their entire vacation with another woman and her child."

"Tell you what—tomorrow, I'll spend the whole day with you." He says this as though he would be doing me a favor.

"How nice. A whole day with my husband who I'm VACATIONING WITH!" I was really trying not to shout. I was trying to be calm.

"Why are you yelling?" He steps away now, holding his hands up in surrender.

"Are you serious?" I'm seething.

The kitchen is quiet for a few moments. He stares at me while I stare back at him. There's anger between us, but there's something else between us, too. It's a feeling or an emotion—I can't quite pinpoint it—coming off of Cal—a secret or something else that's so big, he's having a hard time hiding it. Fear grows inside my chest because now I realize that whatever he's hiding, it's a lot worse than an affair.

"Do you still want to go to dinner?" Cal asks after the most intense staring contest I've ever experienced.

I honestly can't believe he still wants to go to dinner. I really don't want to go to dinner with him; but at the same time, I don't really see a reason to say no—other than the fact that I'd like to punch him in the face. But what's the saying? Kill them with kindness? I'm going in for the kill.

"I guess I wouldn't mind a meal from somewhere else other than the pier," I mumble, drying my hands on a dish towel.

"I think a night out is everything you need to help you out of this mood you're in." Cal winks at me and smiles that dashing smile of his. Both actions used to make my heart flutter; now, I'm repulsed.

"Just let me freshen up a bit." I say, biting my tongue to refrain from responding with anything else that might not be considered kind. With that, I turn on my heels and head for the bedroom.

Cal opens the door to our SUV for me; and as I step in, I notice Drew and Linds heading out from their beach house as well. Drew only locks eyes with me, but Linds and Cal both wave at each other.

When both of our vehicles get to the main road, Drew goes one way, and we go the other. I'm relieved. I don't think I could have dealt with dinner in the same place as Drew and Lindsey. Seeing the two of them get in the car together did something to my heart that I've not quite figured out yet. It felt like jealousy. But what am I jealous of?

Cal drives to one of our favorite restaurants on this small, shabby, little island. One could never find fish and chips that tastes better anywhere in the continental U.S. than the fish and chips they serve here at Ella's. My mouth is watering just thinking about it. Oh! And I can't forget the Long Island iced tea the bar serves. One year while vacationing, one of my wisdom teeth thought it would be a fabulous idea to go ahead and come on through. I had taken a lot of Tylenol, and I even tried a painkiller. Nothing eased the pain. But then I ordered a Long Island iced tea from Ella's. It was a miracle!

"When we're finished with dinner, I want to take you to this new ice cream place I found," Cal informs me as he scans the menu. I'm not sure why he scans the menu. He gets the same thing every time we eat here.

"Sounds fine."

"I love bringing you here," Cal says to me.

I instinctively look up at him from the menu, and he's gazing at me. The look sort of surprises me. My husband hasn't gazed at me like this in years—not since before the cancer diagnosis. "Why are you looking at me like that?"

Cal's expression turns to confusion. "I'm sorry. I didn't know I couldn't look at my wife like that."

I want to roll my eyes. I want to tell him that I see him looking at that woman on the beach like that all day long. I want to start a fight. Honestly, I wouldn't mind picking up the knife that's so tenderly wrapped in this white cloth napkin and stabbing him in the eyeball with it. Of course, I won't do any of these things. It's not time to make a scene just yet. I still have a Long Island iced tea and fish and chips to eat.

"You just don't really look at me like that anymore," I say softly. I decide the victim card is my best move in this instance. If I can force him into feeling some sort of shame, my night will be made.

Cal's eyes fall to the table. He nods his head. "I'm sorry I've been so distant. Work has been so busy lately, and when we got to the beach, I think I just wanted to be on my own for a while. Breathe. Not have to think about anyone or anything."

"But, Cal, you haven't been alone." I can't help it. I must point it out to him again.

"Why do you keep bringing that up?" His eyes aren't soft anymore, and I realize it's time to retreat. I am still very adamant about not causing a scene until after I've had my Long Island iced tea and fish and chips.

"Let's not fight," I say softly. "Let's just eat. And drink. Let's have a great night."

Cal appears as though he wants to say something else, but he thinks better of it and nibbles on a roll from the basket on the table. I can't help but notice how nervous he appears. Why is he nervous?

We're quiet for a few minutes after the waitress takes our order, and we sip our drinks. The air feels thick between us. It's hard to talk. Hard to think, really. I watch him from across the table, and I realize I have no idea who this man is. I can't remember the last time I really looked at my husband, but as I do now, he really doesn't look like himself at all. Certainly not like my Cal, the one I married. When did he change? Have I been negligent in our marriage, too? Shouldn't I have noticed the change?

Still, he's attractive—more than attractive. I remember feeling so incredibly fortunate that he was even interested in me when we were in school. It's not like he was popular or anything, but he was so handsome. He had a swagger about him that would have normally not been a turn-on for me, but it worked for him.

Now, I wish Cal had never happened. I wish I had said no when he had asked me out on our first date. And I wish I had said *hell no* when he had asked me to marry him.

But I didn't. And here we are—both of us pretending that we're but turn my eyes to him. "Joyce is watching her tonight."

"I'm glad you two could get out for a little date night." This is something I would say. I did say it. But the sound of my voice didn't sound like my voice at all as the words fell off my tongue. The words were stiff, my tone flat. Drew's eyes change as he looks at me. Even he picked up on the oddity of my voice.

Lindsey and Cal continue to chat, leaving Drew and me to look at each other. And when I'm certain I can't handle the small talk any longer, I turn toward the counter to order my ice cream. Once Cal notices I'm walking away from him, he starts toward me in a jog.

When we arrive at the counter, Cal orders for me. It is mostly flattering he remembers my favorite flavor of ice cream. He is good about things like that. I have never had to tell him my preferences more than once. Cal remembers. He always remembers, which is one trait I've always loved about him.

With our ice cream in hand, we find our own table and sit. The table is within Drew's line of sight, but thankfully, I can't see them without being obvious about it. It still feels like a strange situation, no matter the distance between us. Knowing they're here is awkward enough, but every now and then, I feel Drew's eyes on me, too. I ignore them, engaging in conversation with Cal instead.

It's not easy to focus on my husband, though—not with Drew's green eyes burning holes into the back of head. Still, we discuss post-vacation plans, Cal's company, and the goals he has for the rest of the year. We talk about our home and the renovations we've been wanting to do. We talk about things as though there is a future for Cal and me. I want there to be a future for us, but deep down, I know there isn't. There is still something bad on the horizon. I can feel it.

Still, I'm enjoying this night, enjoying my husband despite the almost argument in the kitchen earlier, despite the things he said. Even if this isn't real anymore—and it's not—I want to enjoy this evening, humor Cal for a bit before everything hits the fan.

The sunset is beautiful as it falls across the sea. Cal and I have pushed our chairs together now, and we watch as the colors fade into the rolling water. The sea breeze is warm, but I feel a slight chill. Cal instinctively puts his arm around me. His lips kiss my cheek gently, and I rest my head on his shoulder as we sit quietly, content.

I wish I could look forward to many nights like this with Cal until myself less interested in my ice cream as I watch them together. I feel like such a creep, and yet, I can't look away. I'm trying not to be obvious, but watching Cal touch Jess—his fingers grazing the bare skin of her arms, his lips gliding across her cheek—makes my stomach turn. There's a heaviness in my heart that I can't quite interpret. My face feels like it's on fire as I watch them, some sort of emotion bubbling up inside of my chest. In this moment, Linds is just background noise as she goes on and on about our daughter and the new Mommy's Day Out program she's enrolled her in and all of the things she plans to do while Lilly is in the program. She had mentioned this program to me sometime last week, too, and it surprised me. I assumed Lindsey would keep Lilly glued to her hip until Lilly went off to college.

"Drew, are you even listening?" Linds may be heartless, but she isn't dumb.

I snap out of it, only briefly. "Yeah, totally listening." I take a bite of my ice cream that's already melting in this summer night air.

Linds continues talking.

I slide my phone from my pocket and pull up my text messages. I find Jess' number that she had just given me earlier in the day and, against my better judgment, type out a message.

Me: Are you being held against your will?

It's mostly a joke.

I watch as Jess pulls her phone out in response to what I can only assume was the notification that my text had been delivered to her. She glances at the screen, and her brown eyes dart toward me and then back to Cal almost immediately. She shoves the phone back in her pocket, shifting in her chair.

I'm disappointed she doesn't text back; but I also understand it was the mature thing for her to do, and I can't be upset with her. Besides, what if Cal had seen the message? He strikes me as a hothead—someone who would see a message like that and assume I'm flirting with his wife. He'd probably storm over to give me a piece of his mind.

I'm sure I'll hear about that text later from Jess, but for now, I can't watch this any longer. I feel like I'm going to be sick. Maybe we should go home, play a board game or something. Maybe we'll find a movie. I do miss watching movies with my wife.

"Let's head back. Maybe we can find a good movie to watch," I say to Linds, cutting her off mid-sentence and not even giving her an opportunity to protest. I stand and gather our mostly melted ice cream cups and toss them in the garbage nearby. Then I take Linds' hand, only glancing back at Jess long enough for her to see me leave. Jess' eyes capture mine, and the expression on her face shatters everything inside of me. I'm not sure what her expression means, but it triggers a series of emotions within me. I have to get away from her before I do something stupid. I have to focus on Lindsey. On Lilly. My family. The one I want to try and save and not abandon.

When we get back to the beach house, Linds decides she doesn't want to watch a movie. She doesn't even want to play a board game with me.

"I'll just get Lilly. It's getting late, anyway," Lindsey says to me when I half-heartedly protest.

"I guess I just thought we were out on a date tonight."

"Well, we were. But now, we're not out anymore. And Lilly probably misses me. You know she never stays with anyone for long."

"So, that's it? That's our night?"

Lindsey looks at me for a few quiet seconds. It appears as though she may be weighing some options in her mind. Maybe she'll stay and play a game with me.

"I should get Lilly." Then she disappears out the door.

I stand there for a moment, sort of shocked that she couldn't just play one board game with me or watch one movie with me. I don't resent Lilly even in the slightest, but shouldn't a mother also exist outside of her children? For her own sake and sanity, at least? Maybe we could work on our marriage if Lindsey allowed herself a little time for her (and me) instead of making all of her time about Lilly.

I grab a beer from the refrigerator and decide I'll head out to the beach for a little while. Maybe Lindsey doesn't need time to herself, but I think I do.

The sun has set. Darkness envelops the sand, but dots of light from flashlights of seashell hunters speckle the beach. There's a gentle sea breeze—one that is hardly noticeable, but I would miss it if it weren't there. I find a spot in the sand and sit down, my knees to my chest as I sip from the amber beer bottle.

My mind is in a thousand different places. There are emotions building inside of me that I'm not sure I've ever felt in my life, and I have no idea what to do with them. I'm angry, but happy. Broken, but complete. How is it possible to feel contradicting emotions all at the same time? I need a therapist.

Mostly, I'm somewhere between wanting to save my marriage and wanting to end my marriage. The addition of Jess in my already very confusing situation has really only worsened things. And maybe it's not only Jess herself but also her husband who has really put a kink in the hose of my thought process.

My phone begins to buzz from my pocket. I go for it, quickly recognizing the steady stream of vibrations as a phone call instead of a text message. Jess' name is there on the screen. My heart stops. I take a deep breath and then answer, "Jess?"

"You can't text me like that," she says, her voice cracking.

"I'm sorry," I apologize quickly. "It was mostly a joke."

"What's going on, Drew?" she asks me gently now.

"I don't know," I whisper, relenting. "I don't know. I don't—"

"Where are you? We should talk." Jess sounds timid and confident all at the same time.

We should talk is never anything any man ever wants to hear from a woman. It never ends well—even in friendships.

"On the beach," I tell her. "We can talk tomorrow. I don't want to get you in trouble with Cal." I'm mostly a coward. I don't think I can face her tonight.

"I'll be out there in a few minutes," Jess says, and then she ends the call.

I sit in the sand, staring at the star-studded sky, listening to the waves roll in and out. Children laugh in the distance. A dog barks. I don't even know what there is to talk about with Jess. My mind is a cluttered sea of debris at the moment. I can't imagine having anything to say that doesn't sound like gibberish.

"Drew?" Jess' sweet and gentle voice comes from behind me.

I spin around on my butt, standing as I do. "Jess, I'm sorry. You didn't have to come down here."

"Stop apologizing," she replies and gestures for me to sit back down as she crosses her legs and lowers herself to the ground.

I do as she says because who am I to argue?

"What's going on, Drew?" She looks at me in such a way it takes my breath away.

I look back out across the ocean, hoping to refocus. A boy with a flashlight runs right in front of us, screaming that he found a crab. I can't help but feel annoyed with the interruption. Can't the kid see that there's something wrong here? And why did it never cross the boy's mind that a beach is about the only place one can find a crab? Well, besides the hermit crabs they sell in those beachside stores. I've always felt sorry for those little crabs. They didn't know they were born to live in a plastic container with some tacky décor inside.

"I don't know," I mumble. "I just…watching him touch you like that tonight. His lips on you. I wasn't expecting you and Cal to show up. I was trying—actually trying—to enjoy the evening with Lindsey."

"I wasn't expecting to walk up on you and Lindsey either," she admits. "But I also wasn't expecting you to send a text like that either. What if he had seen the message? He wouldn't have taken it as a joke! Are you jealous, Drew?"

"J-jealous?" I stammer. "I'm not… I mean… I… I don't…"

Jess laughs. "Okay. Well, you literally just answered my question. Why?"

I sigh heavily. "I don't know why. That's why I'm sitting down here, hoping for an answer. But all I'm getting is annoyed at these damn kids down here. Why are they so excited to find crabs? It's a beach! What did they expect to find?"

"Drew, are you having a nervous breakdown?" She's looking at me strangely now.

I suppose it does seem that way. I'm screaming at children to stop being excited about seashells and crabs.

"I didn't know it would make me crazy to see you so close with your husband tonight," I finally admit. I push the words out of my mouth with force. "I felt so angry."

Jess sits quietly for a few moments. I do the same. Then she says, "We're still married, Drew. Both of us, to our spouses. I know things are awry for both of us, but we can't do what they've likely done to us. It makes us no better than they, and I refuse to be placed in the same category with Cal Dawson. I'm thankful to have met you—to have found a friend in you."

My heart sinks inside my chest at the mention of *friend*. I hadn't been thinking of having my own affair with Jess, but I also can't be completely sure of anything I've been thinking since we arrived on this island. Jess confuses me. My wife confuses me. Cal confuses me.

People Watching

"I don't want to lose you, though," Jess adds. "When we go home, I want to stay in touch with you."

"We don't even know what's going to happen when we get home," I mumble.

We're quiet again. The tension between us is strong, and I hate myself for putting it there. I turn toward Jess, and she looks at me, her curly, dark hair caressing her jawline in the sea breeze. I've never seen anyone more beautiful in all my life. The sight of her catches my breath, and now I understand why I've felt breathless since I first laid eyes on her.

"Promise me something, Jess," I say to her with every ounce of seriousness that I can muster.

"Anything," she says, and I believe her.

"I obviously don't know the whole story within your marriage, but when you do finally leave him, don't settle. You deserve the world, Jess. I've only known you for a short time, but of that, I'm certain. You deserve the world."

Jess' eyes soften. The palm of her hand comes up and rests gently on my cheek. "Only if you promise me that you'll find someone who loves you the way you deserve."

"I'm sorry he abandoned you," I whisper.

"I'm sorry she abandoned you."

Then, we sit there—two neglected but married adults. Two people who started their adult life with love and enthusiasm. Two people who are broken.

I wasn't sure how I was going to fix my marriage in one week on this vacation, but I'm beginning to realize that maybe that shouldn't have been the goal to begin with. Some things are beyond repair. This is true with anything. And I think, maybe my marriage is beyond repair. Maybe my family is beyond repair. I can't dance around how I feel anymore. It's time to confront Lindsey. It's time to find out the truth. I don't want to live in this lie anymore.

I walk Jess back to her house before returning to mine. Her house is dark, just like mine. Our families are asleep while the two of us are left wrestling with our own thoughts and feelings in the moonlight.

"Focus on you, Drew," Jess tells me with a smile before closing the door to her beach house.

I feel a smirk cross my face, and then I turn and head back to my own beach house.

People Watching

WEDNESDAY

People Watching

24
Jess Dawson

The morning sun breaks through the drawn curtains of our bedroom. My eyes slide open, and every memory of the night before rushes back into my mind. In an attempt to divert my thoughts from Drew, I roll over toward Cal, only to find that he isn't there. I'm not surprised. When we got home last night, he went straight to bed, which was why I was able to sneak out to the beach. I hadn't expected to be taken out for dinner and then left to navigate the rest of the evening on my own. Cal was snoring by 9:00 p.m. I had hoped we would at least play a card game or something. We used to play card games all the time. And checkers. I like to play checkers.

On the nightstand, my phone vibrates once—a text message, apparently. I roll back in the direction I had been facing and pick up my device from the nightstand. Drew.

Drew: *Want to meet for breakfast?*

I think I'll have to be careful with Drew now, since it seems he may have developed some sort of feelings for me. And maybe I've developed some sort of feelings for him, too, but I have no way of really knowing if my feelings are a derivative of what I'm lacking in my relationship with Cal or not.

Me: *It's not a date.*

Drew: *Of course not.*
Me: *Pier?*
Drew: *See you there in fifteen minutes.*

I roll out of bed and stumble into the bathroom. I splash some water on my face, run my fingers through my curly locks before deciding on pulling it up, and then throw a little color on my face. It's the beach, so makeup isn't always required; but when I wake in the mornings, I look like a cancer patient again. My skin is pale. The skin around my eyes is dark. I'm like something out of a horror movie. No wonder Cal wasn't in bed when I woke up this morning. I'm too scary of a thing to encounter.

The pier serves up a good breakfast. Biscuits, waffles, coffee—you name it, they can probably make it. The smell of bacon frying is what gets my mouth watering, though, as I walk into the pavilion of the pier where Drew is waiting patiently by the coffeepots.

"Good morning," he says to me with a smile.

"Good morning." I smile back. He looks different this morning. His eyes are clearer or something. Brighter. Hopeful, maybe. "You must have gotten lucky this morning."

Drew's face twists into a disgusted expression. "Why would you say that?"

"You look…happy." I take a Styrofoam cup from the coffee bar and begin pouring that hot liquid gold from the coffee carafe into the cup. It's fresh coffee. I can tell by its smell, and I nearly melt.

"Never equate my happiness with 'getting lucky,'" Drew says, offended. He still appears to be disgusted, and I wonder if I've ruined his appetite.

"Lesson learned." I smile. "I'm glad you're happy." I can't think of a single thing that might have changed between last night on the beach and this morning on the pier. Drew appeared to be coming unraveled last night. Today, he's got the look of a man who knows exactly what he's doing, thinking, feeling.

"Ready to order breakfast?" he asks me. "I almost ordered for you, but then I realized I had no idea what your favorite breakfast food is. Hell, you could be one of those girls who doesn't eat breakfast at all."

At that, I laugh. "I eat breakfast. And second breakfast. Oh, and then brunch. Of course, lunch, too, but then there's got to be second

People Watching

lunch. Dinner is the only meal that doesn't require a second dinner, unless the first dinner failed."

"A girl who eats! Finally. I think I just assumed all of you women skip out on a good, wholesome meal."

"I exercise so I can eat what I want." I smile.

"I'm paying, by the way, and don't argue," Drew says as we approach the counter to order our breakfast.

I want to protest, but I don't. I did tell him this wasn't a date. So, at least the expectation is set. "I'll have a stack of waffles—extra butter and syrup—two bacon strips, and a bowl of grits."

Drew is quietly laughing at me as I order, and when it's his turn, he orders the same. We find a seat in the pavilion and wait for our food.

"Why did you order the same thing I did?" I ask him as I sip my coffee.

"To see if I could eat it all in one setting," he says honestly. "I like a good competition. Especially when it comes to food."

I laugh. "I won a hotdog-eating contest when I was twelve. The funny thing is that I was up against this giant of a man. He had to have weighed, like, three hundred pounds. No one believed that I could eat that many hotdogs."

"How many was it?"

"Fifty-five hotdogs in ten minutes. I hear the record is seventy-five, but after I swallowed that fifty-fifth hotdog… I've yet to touch another one to this day. Lost my taste for hotdogs but beat a three-hundred-pound man in a hotdog-eating contest. I'm quite proud."

"Please tell me that this will be engraved somewhere on your tombstone when you die an old lady."

I laugh. "Beat Cancer and Hotdog Eating Contest Champ."

Drew laughs, too, and for a moment, we're both laughing. Laughter—it feels good.

The stack of waffles is higher than I could have imagined. The bowl of grits might as well have been a pot of grits, and I swear the two strips of bacon came from the entire length of the largest pig in the world. Still, my mouth waters, and my stomach growls with anticipation. I wake up starving most mornings, as though I've not had a meal in days. Sometimes, it's embarrassing.

The butter is already melting across the top of the waffles, draining into each square of that yummy, toasted bread. I sandwich my bacon between the stack of waffles and then drizzle the syrup over the top, lifting each layer to douse in syrup as well.

"You've done this before, haven't you?" Drew asks me as I take my first big bite of waffles and bacon after I drag the waffle through my grits.

"Stop watching me eat!" I cover my mouth, halfway embarrassed.

"I've got to try this." Drew does exactly as I did—sandwiches his bacon within the stack of waffles, dunks the bite into grits, and then shoves it in his mouth.

"What do you think?" I watch him with anticipation.

He thinks for a moment as he continues to chew. Then, he begins to slowly nod, and as he swallows his first bite, he says, "Good. Rich. But good. I'll be eating the rest of this like a normal human being, though." Drew laughs and pulls the bacon out of his waffles, reconstructing his plate to look exactly as it did when it was brought out.

"I was an elementary school teacher for a few years," I tell him. "Before cancer. Anyway, I had to learn how to eat quickly. I basically turn every meal into a sandwich. One can eat faster that way."

"I didn't know you were a teacher," Drew says to me.

"For a few years, I taught second grade. I've taught first grade as well. I loved those kiddos so much." I smile, reflecting on my time teaching. I haven't thought of it in a while.

"How come you didn't go back?"

"It's a whole thing. I'd have to renew my teaching license and such. Really, after chemo was done, it took a long time to get back to myself. This is the first year I've actually felt like me. My hair came back thicker than ever. I put some weight back on. Energy is better. Maybe I'll go back soon. I just… I haven't felt like I was in a great place mentally to submerse myself into teaching again."

"You should do it again. One day, when you're feeling up to it. I know I've never seen you teach, but I can imagine you're one of those teachers kids never forget."

I smile, blushing a little. "I do miss them—the kids. They're always so happy, even when their home life is in shambles. Kids are so resilient. So hopeful. I do wonder when we lose that as adults—the happiness and hope, I mean."

"Probably about the time we get that first notice that our bank account has fallen below one hundred dollars."

"Ugh. That's the worst notification."

"Nothing like feeling on top of the world and then suddenly not even being able to afford to walk to the living room."

I laugh. "But those are good times, too—when you're broke. You kind of learn how to have fun at home."

"There's no more fun at home now. It used to be fun, though. I don't know what happened."

"Cal just acts like everything is normal," I say going back for another bite of my bacon and waffle sandwich. "I hate it, and anytime I've tried to talk to him, he just denies everything. *No, I'm not having an affair. No, I'm not out of love with you. No, everything is just fine.*" I sigh. "It's a bunch of hogwash. Nothing has been normal since I was diagnosed with cancer. In the moments that I needed him most, he just left me to sit there in that hospital for hours on end—alone, cold, and bored. The hospital tries to give you things like books and magazines to help pass the time, but when you've got chemicals being pumped into your body to kill an intruder that's trying to kill you, books and magazines aren't appealing."

"I don't know how he, as a man, can sleep at night knowing that he left his wife in quite possibly her greatest moment of need. You needed him there, regardless of how he felt about the situation. You should have been the only person to matter."

"He's such a passive man. He'll say and do anything that keeps him comfortable." I roll my eyes. "I have no idea what I'm going to do when we get home after this vacation, but I know that I'm not wasting another second with him. I have a whole life ahead of me, and after nearly losing it completely, I just want to live."

"You're a survivor through and through." Drew beams at me.

"I'm glad I met you," I tell him. "And Joyce, too. I don't know how I would have managed this far into the week without you."

"Well, it helps that our spouses seem to be infatuated with each other."

"It's so weird. And they act like it's normal."

"Right?" Drew quips. "What is that? And then you try to mention it, and they attack you like you're the one who's been ignoring them the entire week!"

"And I know we've already asked this question, but again, how do they know each other?"

"I've been trying to figure that one out all week. Lindsey doesn't have a job outside of being a mom. You said that Cal is in finance. I can't imagine they have common interests. How would they have met?"

"Maybe they know people in the same circle," I suggest. Cal is a very talented CFO, highly sought after; and for this reason, he never stays employed in one place long. He continues to climb the financial ladder. Bouncing from firm to firm, chasing the next highest dollar amount. Good news for me when I divorce him for infidelity. I should get a pretty decent payout.

"Linds does spend a lot of time at the gym. I mean, Cal isn't a bad-looking man, but he doesn't appear as though fitness is high on his list of priorities."

I laugh again. "He's gotten a bit pudgy! He used to be thin."

"Maybe cheaters are like Jeep-owners. They just know each other without knowing each other. Cheaters pass each other in the street and wave with a couple of fingers, just like Jeep-owners passing each other on the road." Drew shrugs. "I've got to do something, though. I'm not doing a great job at work these days, and I know it."

"What do you do for work?"

"I'm a journalist—well, sort of. I started out as a journalist, but I'm mostly editing now. Part of the promotion was that I would still write five articles a month on the political situation across the country. I can't seem to get into it much. I hate writing politics. I actually lost a job once because I wouldn't write anything political, which prompted my move to Greenville. That's how I met Lindsey. Now, I can't help but wonder what might have happened if I had just written the political columns and stayed in Georgia. I was a different person back then. Willing to lose a job to stand up for something I didn't want to do, and now my entire being feels like it's been taken away from me by my wife."

"She didn't take it away. You gave it away." I've had years of therapy. No one can take something like your identity away without you giving it to them first.

"What, you're a psychologist, too?"

"Just a patient." I wink.

"I think I *gave* it away to keep peace," Drew admits.

"We do a lot of neglecting of ourselves to create or maintain peace. It's not true peace, though. It's fake peace."

"I'd like to find myself again. I liked myself, for the most part. I mean, I always wished I could play basketball a bit better. But other than that, I was an okay dude."

I smirk. "You're still an okay dude."

"And you're a female superhero. I admire you in so many ways already, and I hardly know you."

I blush. "You don't have to say things like that. I'm really not that amazing. I'm just… I'm a survivor. Plain and simple."

"You're more than a survivor, Jess," Drew says with a bit more seriousness in his tone.

I consider this, reflecting on the last few years of my life. Perhaps I found myself through the cancer and spousal neglect. I think I did. Part of me feels as though I came out of the venture like a phoenix from the ashes—a new woman, a warrior. I wish I had obtained these attributes some other way, but sometimes, it has to be tragedy. Most of the time, it is tragedy that makes us new and builds us into someone we never believed we could be. Surviving is a superpower by itself.

25
Drew Clark

I'm not sure why I feel a bit differently today than I did last night. I'm actually trying not to think about last night. It's embarrassing the way I acted. But there was something Jess said to me on the beach last night that sort of changed my perspective on the current situation. I've been blaming Lindsey for taking who I was away. Jess was right. Lindsey didn't shred me of my identity. I gave it away willingly—to keep peace, really.

I didn't realize until last night that the peace I have been receiving hasn't been peace at all. Inside, my mind and soul have been at war with who I really am and who Lindsey wants me to be. So, I decided before I drifted off to sleep that I'm getting me back. I'm going to find the Drew I used to be and be him again. I liked him. My mother liked him.

After breakfast, we departed to our homes and readied ourselves for a day on the beach. We came down together and situated our chairs as though we would sit together. Then Lindsey and Lilly left me to play with Cal. At one point, I did try to take Lilly to the pier for lemonade, but Lindsey insisted that she was perfectly happy in the surf with them. She reminded me that no one should ever disturb a happy baby. So, I conceded and went back to my beach chair.

Now, Lindsey and Lilly have disappeared again—probably with Cal, although I didn't see either of them leave the beach. I glance over at Jess, sitting alone in her beach chair. She holds a book in her hand, reading, but I can't help but think she's lost in thought instead. Maybe we should walk. I can't bear to watch her sit there alone anymore, and I'm rather bored on my own, too. I'm still getting to know Jess, but I have a feeling she doesn't really take well to someone pitying her. I don't pity her; I just wish Cal could see how amazing his wife is.

"Hey, Jess," I say as I near her and her beach chair.

Jess lays the book across her chest and looks up at me, shielding her eyes from the sun with her hand. "Hey." She smiles. My knees grow a little weak at that smile. It's intoxicating.

"Want to walk? I have a secret hiding spot on the beach that I discovered a few years ago. It's about a mile that way. I think you might enjoy it." I offer my hand to help her out of the beach chair.

Jess looks behind her and then on either side of us down the beach, looking for Cal, I assume.

"All three of them disappeared about twenty minutes ago," I inform her with a shrug. Something that appears like pain crosses Jess' eyes. "I'm sick of watching you sit here alone, and I'm sick of being along. Come on, Jess."

She looks at me for a few moments, and then she nods her head. "Let's walk," Jess says with confidence and determination.

I continue to hold out my hand to help her out of the chair, but she springs up like she's twenty-two years old and smiles at me. "I'm not a cancer patient anymore."

"Of course not," I say. "I don't know what I was thinking, trying to help a lady out of her chair."

Jess laughs at my sarcasm, which then causes me to realize I'm addicted to that laugh, too. Her laugh seems to charge my internal battery. It gives me a little pep in my step. In the workplace, they would call this feeling "boosting morale." I think I'll do anything to make her laugh, just so I can selfishly indulge in the joy that each of her laughs provide for me.

We set off down the beach, not saying a lot at first. I like that Jess doesn't always feel the need to talk. I'm not really much of a talker. I mean, once you get me started, it's hard to get me to stop. But for the most part, I can survive in silence.

"What on earth could you have possibly found on the beach that's worth the mile-hike to get there?" she asks.

"You'll see." I smile. "It's my secret hiding place. Not even Lindsey knows where it is. It's my fortress of solitude."

"I knew it! You're Clark Kent. You're even a journalist."

"You caught me." I laugh. "Finally, someone knows my secret."

"I knew there was something off about you." She winks at me.

We walk a bit more, quiet again. I'm not sure what she's thinking, but I'm thinking how I could actually be Superman. I know I'm not, obviously, but it's been decades since I last dreamed of being Superman. I'm surprised to find that it's still fun to imagine myself flying high in the sky with my red cape flying in the wind. Maybe if I really were Superman, Lilly might like me a little more.

"I've not even seen Cal today," Jess says with a sigh. "Briefly, after breakfast, but that's it."

"Let's leave this place together," I say to her, disposing of my Superman dreams. "On Saturday morning, when they're packing the car, we put our stuff in a rental and head home together."

"Drew, do you understand how ridiculous that sounds?" Jess points out.

"Do you honestly want to make the five-hour drive home with Cal?" I counter but only because I've already thought about the five-hour drive home with Linds, and I don't think I've got it in me to do it.

"No. No, I don't." She sighs. "But we can't just leave together. Besides, what if you're actually a serial killer, and you've been acting nice to me all week just to get me to go with you somewhere in the car?"

This time, I laugh.

"I'm serious. Well, maybe not about the serial killer part. But, Drew, we've only just met each other. I don't know. I don't think we can just hop in the car together and drive away into the sunset."

"Why not?"

"Are you serious? This is not a novel or a movie—or a television show, for that matter. This is real life. Our life."

"Hear me out. We're likely both going home to file for divorce. You don't want to be with Cal, and I think I'll vomit if I have to crawl into bed next to Lindsey again. We only have two days left here to pretend, and then it's back to reality."

"You cannot come home with me, and I cannot go home with you," Jess says a bit more sternly. "This is crazy, Drew."

She's not wrong. I know she's not, but maybe I've lived in such restrictive conditions for so long, I want to do something crazy and sporadic. I'd be okay if I never went back home again. I've got enough money in the bank. I can move and start over new somewhere else. I'm Superman, for Pete's sake.

"I'm sorry," she says in response to my silence. "I guess, I'm afraid. I don't know how to divorce someone. I've never had to. And really, outside of the way he acted when I had cancer, what has he done that I have proof of that gives reason to divorce him? I loved him, Drew. I know that I *think* he's been unfaithful. I know that. But I loved him. I still love him. Divorce is not going to go as easy for me as it sounds like it will for you. I've known Cal since I was kid. I've loved him that long."

I suppose that's fair. Maybe I've already mourned what I thought would be a lifetime marriage. It's easy to do that when you're married to the most hateful woman in the world. Cal, though—Cal is smart about it. He balances things just so to keep Jess happy and unsuspecting. It's obviously not working anymore, but Jess hasn't had the time I've had. I've had a lot of time—more time than I wish I had. I wish none of this was happening—that Lindsey was still my Lindsey, we were happy, and this first vacation with Lilly was the first of many with our daughter. Those are the things I want. They're not attainable. Not anymore. Maybe they were never attainable.

"You see the bend in the beach there?" I point out, changing the subject. "Just around that bend is the surprise."

"I didn't know it was a surprise." She smiles.

"I didn't tell you what I found; I only told you it was a secret. So yes, it's a surprise."

Jess loops an arm in mine. "I'm sorry you can't come home with me."

"I'm a writer. Sometimes, my ideas can get a little out of hand."

"You're a romantic."

"Close your eyes," I tell her, ignoring how close she is to me, ignoring the way her skin feels against mine, ignoring how she makes me feel. "Take my hand."

"What?"

"Trust me, okay? It's a surprise. Remember?"

Jess looks intently into my eyes. I try not to blink. I want her to trust me. My hand is out for her to take, but her hands are still by her side. Then, slowly, she raises a hand to meet mine and closes her eyes.

"No peeking," I instruct, "and I'll tell you when to open your eyes. Just follow me." I turn with Jess' hand in mine and lead her around the bend in the beach and to my secret hiding spot. I smile as the spot comes into view. There's not a single soul around, which is quite odd because the beach itself is full today. But alas! It remains my secret.

"Okay," I say, turning to face her again. "Open your eyes."

Jess' eyelids flutter slightly and then open slowly. As they do, I step to her side and allow her to see the beauty of this place I found.

Her eyes go wide as she surveys the scene in front of her. There's a cluster of about six or seven oak trees that have been taken up by the sea but still lie in perfect harmony across the sand. The root systems of the oak trees are exposed, as though someone has only just walked through this spot and pushed the trees over with their bare hands. The trunks of the trees are smooth from the wear of the water that engulfs them at high tide. One of the trees is bent in such a way that it's created a sort of cave. It looks like the most perfect place for a beach picnic.

"This is beautiful," Jess marvels. "I've been coming to this island my entire life, and I've never known this was here."

"See? I told you." I beam. "I found it one night a few years ago after a fight with Linds. It's like no one knows it's here. Every time I come back, it looks exactly the same. I'm glad you can actually see it. I was beginning to wonder if I was imagining things."

Jess laughs again. "It's like our own little, devastated piece of Edisto Island. These massive trees all uprooted and corroded by the tides—I've never related to anything more."

I take Jess' hand again, leading her into the tangled mess of fallen oaks. "I checked the tide chart. High tide isn't for another four hours. I thought maybe we could hike over the dunes and grab a couple of sandwiches from the store. Have a picnic."

"The store?"

"The main road is just right there." I point over the dunes. "There's a trail. I'm telling you, I've explored this. I've even considered just moving out here. But there's the whole high tide thing, and I don't really want to drown in my sleep."

"I am hungry," she admits.

"Come on. Lunch is on me."

"Drew, you already bought breakfast."

"It's okay. And it's not a date. Just a friend buying a friend lunch."

"And breakfast."

"And breakfast. And maybe dinner, too. Haven't crossed that

bridge yet."

Jess laughs. "Okay, I'll let you buy me lunch."

"Come on." I take her hand again, instinctively. "I'm sorry." I drop her hand. "It's not a date."

"Stop apologizing. You apologize for everything when there's no reason for apologies."

"Sorry."

"Drew."

"Geez. I'll stop. I promise." I do have an issue with apologizing for literally everything. That's not something Lindsey did. I've always been that way.

We walk across the boardwalk that has been built into the dunes and head to the store for some premade sandwiches. Once inside the store, we select our sandwiches and some chips and grab some bottled waters before setting back out to our new secret hiding place.

The heat isn't so bad today, and there's a nice sea breeze. In this secret hiding place, all the noise from the beach is completely drowned out by the roar of the ocean waves. If I didn't know any better, I'd think it's a portal to a quiet beach—one where you can sit and just be you for however long you want. A place where no one can find you—not even life. Part of me wants to pack up this little spot on Saturday morning and take it home with me. But then, maybe it's better left here, waiting on us to come back.

"I've not seen Joyce today," Jess says as she bites into her sandwich.

"She and Harold were going to spend some time together," I reply. "At least, that's what Lindsey told me."

"It gives me hope when I meet people like Joyce. She's older but spunkier than ever. Like a grandmother I could get in trouble with."

"She's definitely a grandma we could get in trouble with. I feel like she's probably been to jail before."

"Really? She looks too happy to have previously been an inmate." Jess nibbles on her sandwich, and we fall quiet again.

"What makes you happy, Jess?" I speak suddenly, breaking the quiet and changing the subject, asking this question seriously. I do wonder what makes Jess happy. She deserves happiness.

Jess thinks for a few moments. I watch her think, watch the way she moves her mouth to the right as the gears in her mind turn. Her eyes are bright and wide with furious curiosity. The sea breeze catches her hair, and she catches my breath. I control the pounding in my chest, though, and the desire to lean forward and kiss her, touch her skin, and take her into my arms and hold her the way she deserves to be held.

"Dogs. Dogs make me happy." She smiles. "I've been thinking about it for a while, but I think I want to foster dogs until they find a new home. So many of the shelters back home are overcrowded. Perfectly healthy animals are having to be put to sleep because there's not any space left. I want to help dogs—and cats, if I must—but there's just something about a doggy."

"I was hoping you wouldn't say money." I laugh.

"Oh, money doesn't make anyone happy. I have a ton of it because of Cal, and I'm still miserable."

"I can see it now. Jess on a farm with pastures for the dogs to run and play in—a kind of heaven for all misplaced doggies."

"A farm would be perfect! And I don't need a big, fancy farmhouse. A small cottage would be enough for Sweeney and me."

I noticed a good bit of farmland for sale on the drive to Edisto. It was about an hour outside of the island—four acres and a house. I make a mental note to check it out online later.

"Lindsey never liked animals. I miss having a dog. When I was a kid, I got a black lab puppy for Christmas one year. He was the best dog. Went everywhere with me. I thought I was going to die the day he died. I was seventeen years old, and he had been by my side since I was six years old."

"That's so sad."

"I've never been successful at talking Lindsey into getting a dog. She thinks they stink and shed."

"They do, but that doesn't matter." Jess shrugs. "Their love is unmatched."

My cellphone begins to buzz in my shorts. I pull out my phone and see Lindsey's name flash across the screen. I decide not to answer. I'm on a date. Okay, not really, but regardless.

"Who is it?"

"Lindsey. She can wait. She probably just discovered I'm not there for her to boss around."

As soon as I slide the phone back into my pocket, it begins to ring again. Lindsey's name is on the screen, and again, I ignore it. Still, it continues to ring; and now, I'm beginning to think something is wrong.

"Maybe you should answer it," Jess says as she notices my

expression change from being annoyed to worried.

"I don't want to," I complain. In my head, I'm thinking that nothing could be wrong. What could possibly go wrong on the beach? Then I begin to think of all the things that can actually go wrong on the beach. Shark attacks, drowning, impaled by a rogue beach umbrella (that really does happen).

"She's not going to stop calling."

I stare at the buzzing phone in my hand. I give in and answer.

"Where are you?" Lindsey is screaming through the phone before I even have an opportunity to say hello. "She's gone! Lilly is gone. She was here, and then she was gone."

"Lindsey, calm down." I fight the urge to panic myself. There's something about the shrill of Lindsey's voice when she's in hysterics that triggers panic in even the calmest of people.

"Don't tell me to calm down, Drew. Our daughter is missing!" she screams at me as she enunciates the word *our*.

I'm 95 percent sure that Lilly is not my daughter, but I do love her. I mean, once you change a baby's diaper or hold them while they cry uncontrollably, you're connected to them in a way that can't be explained. The thought of her in the arms of a kidnapper makes my chest ache. And I can't discount the way her big, blue eyes make me feel when she looks up at me from her crib in the mornings or the way her finger wrapped around mine on the day she was born.

"Okay, call the police and alert the lifeguards. I'll head back in that direction," I tell her. "Calm down. You're not going to accomplish anything being hysterical." With that, I hang up the phone and look at Jess, who is looking back at me.

"What's wrong?"

"Lilly is missing," I say calmly. "We better head back."

"Missing?"

"I don't know. Linds was screaming. Not the best time to ask a lot of questions." I start gathering our trash from lunch and shove it all in the plastic bag from the store. Jess helps, and then I help her up from the sand. "We should probably walk fast. Up to it?"

"I'm not a cancer patient, Drew," she says to me again. "I walk; I run; sometimes, I lift weights!"

"I almost apologized for underestimating you again."

"I'm glad you didn't. Come on, your daughter is missing!"

Jess takes off down the beach at such a quick sprint, I have trouble catching up at first. She had been calm, but now, she sprints with purpose.

"I ran cross-country in high school," she says proudly, and I can appreciate that she's keeping me distracted with conversation that has nothing to do with the fact that my daughter may have been kidnapped. It's like when a nurse is about to give you a shot and asks you a question right when she jabs the needle in your arm so that you aren't anticipating the pain.

"I can tell. I played football."

"You look like you probably played football in high school. Got that jock look about you."

"I do not."

"You do so."

I follow her lead and keep my mind away from why we're running. Instead, I remind myself that I used to run a whole mile in less than three minutes in high school. If I could do it then, I can do it now.

My run is slow at first as my legs begin to realize that I intend to push them harder than I have in a while; but as my heart rate rises and my legs catch up, I find that adrenaline is now pushing me forward.

"Hey, he runs!" Jess announces. "Mr. Football runs!"

"Stop making fun of me!" Soon, we're running side by side, jumping over stray sand buckets, empty beach chairs, and random holes dug by children. Our speed increases as we near our places on the beach because the scene beginning to build before us is like something from a movie.

The beach is practically a crime scene when we arrive. We're both out of breath from the run, each of us seeking out our spouses in the mass of people gathered. There's police and lifeguards and tons of strangers all hovering around my wife. When I break through the crowd to get to Lindsey, the first thing she does is scream at me for not being there. If I wanted to be a jerk, I could tell her she wasn't there either, apparently; and now, our daughter is missing. But I won't. Now is not the time to be a jerk.

"They're forming a search party," Lindsey tells me. That's when I notice Cal. He's just outside the crowded circle, on the phone, pacing the sand and pleading with whomever he's talking to. I look for Jess, and she's avoiding the crowd but looking after me.

"How long has she been missing?" I ask Lindsey.

"Thirty minutes, at least. I don't know. She was right next to me, and then she wasn't. She just disappeared. You've seen her walk. She's not that great at it. Someone took her."

"Let's not jump to any conclusions. Lilly could have wandered off just as easily as she could have been snatched up. It's a big place with a lot of people." I look at the scene around us and decide that I can't stay here. I'll go look for the kid before I stand here in the midst of this chaos. "I'm going to go look for her."

"They're organizing a search party," she snaps.

"I don't need a search party. I'll get a head start. You lost her here? Or were you elsewhere?"

"I didn't lose her, Drew. She disappeared!" Lindsey screams at me again.

"Just answer the question."

"We had just come back to the beach after lunch. So yes, we were right here."

"I've got my phone. Call me if they find her." With that, I break back through the crowd and go straight to Jess. "I'm going to go look for her."

"I'll go with you."

"You don't have to, Jess."

"I know I don't have to. I want to. Come on, let's go. I was a teacher, remember? I'm familiar with where kids go to hide."

"What makes you think she's hiding?"

Jess shrugs. "I don't know."

We start out up the beach in the opposite direction from which we just came. I pull up a photo on my phone of Lilly and ask people we pass if they've seen her. Everyone responds with a shaking head. Jess scans the beach with her eyes, looking intently at each child to make sure they're not Lilly.

"Do you remember what her swimsuit looked like today?" Jess asks me.

I think for a moment. I don't. I'm instantly ashamed.

"It was a yellow and white polka dotted two-piece," she tells me. "I remember because I started singing in my head that song about the yellow polka dot bikini."

I chuckle and then immediately feel ashamed. I shouldn't be laughing; my daughter is missing. "We really shouldn't be making jokes."

"I can't help it. It's what I do when there's a crisis. You do not want to sit next to me at a funeral. I will laugh."

People Watching

I don't say anything, instead focusing my eyes on the beach and looking desperately for the color yellow.

"I'm sure she's okay," Jess responds to my silence. "I doubt she wandered into the water or anything." Most children are terrified of the ocean. A pool is a different story, though.

"I'm sure she's fine, too," I say absently.

"I'm not seeing any yellow polka dot bikinis, though," Jess says sadly.

"Or little girls with big, bouncy curls." Those big, blue eyes of hers will help her get away with murder when she's older.

"We'll find her," Jess says with confidence, and she looks at me with a smile. "I know I've spent enough time watching her and my husband play together in the surf this week. I've memorized her every attribute."

I'm not quite sure what to say to that. I've watched the same scene play out this week, and I still haven't been able to form a feeling or emotion around it. Sure, if I were any kind of a man, I would have put an end to this whole thing earlier in the week. But for the life of me, I can't find it anywhere in my being to stop it. We're not above doing a lot of things as humans, but I suppose divorce is one of those things that some people would do anything to avoid. Even if it means living in misery.

"There's no way her little legs made it up this far, though," Jess says, stopping abruptly. "Maybe we missed her?"

I turn to look back in the direction we just walked. "I don't think so."

"Keep walking?"

"Another five minutes, then we'll turn around. Just to be absolutely sure."

"You don't think we missed her when we were running back from our picnic?" Jess sounds as though she may panic now, and that's something I've not seen in her yet.

"No, no, I don't think so. I think I would have seen her. You would have seen her." I can't have another hysterical woman on my hands. I can't function.

"Yeah, I think so, too," she says. "I'm sorry. I don't mean to be a little panicked; it's just that most kids are found pretty quickly after they go missing. She's nowhere out here. We would have found her already."

"Listen, kids wander off all the time. I'm sure it will be fine. We'll find her," I assure her, although every missing kid article I've ever written flashes before my eyes.

Jess' pace picks up, and I follow suit. We drop conversation, cutting off all senses except sight and sound. I'd know Lilly's voice anywhere. She screams my name enough times in a day. I know I should blame myself for this, but honestly, Cal should have been watching my daughter. He's spent enough time with her this week. What was he doing? What were they doing?

"It's been five minutes," Jess says, checking the sports watch on her wrist.

We stand there in the sand for a few moments, making slow turns, looking for that yellow polka dot bikini.

"I don't... I don't see her." I say, and I'm surprised to find myself out of breath and sounding a bit panicked myself now. When people set out searching for a missing child or pet, it's always assumed the search will end sooner rather than later. *They couldn't have gotten far.* But when the search doesn't end when it should—when the missing person or pet isn't where they should be—that's when things get scary. That's when they're officially lost.

Jess is still scanning the beach, her hand just above her eyes, shielding the sun. She shakes her head. "I don't either."

"Come on. Let's head back," I tell her, and I almost reach for her hand.

Our eyes scan all sides of the beach, searching for that little girl with the big, blonde curls. My little girl. I've known her every single day of her entire life. Sure, she's difficult like her mom, but she's a baby. She doesn't deserve to be missing. Regardless of paternity results.

We make it back to the scene empty-handed. Lilly is nowhere to be found in that direction. Lindsey is still hysterical, hunkered in a beach chair with a blanket wrapped around her. No doubt, she's broken. Lindsey has made Lilly her entire world, her whole heart.

"I'm sorry," I tell Lindsey, squatting down next to her in the beach chair. "We looked. I looked. She's not out there."

"Don't tell me that, Drew. If she's not on the beach, there's only one place she could be, and we may never find her there." Lindsey cries.

"Linds, Lilly hates bath time. What makes you think she'd go straight for the ocean?"

Lindsey lifts her eyes to mine, acknowledging the logic behind my statement. "That's true."

"We'll find her. I promise." I realize that's a mighty large promise. I have no idea where Lilly is or if we'll find her before someone else does. But there's still a piece of my heart that loves Lindsey, too, I realize. I've never liked seeing her cry. I'd do almost anything not to see Lindsey cry.

Lindsey wraps her arms around my neck, and I reluctantly put my arms around my wife. I want to love her fully in this moment, but the only person I can seem to think about is Lilly. My eyes meet Jess' as Lindsey hangs from my body. Jess looks away from us and glances at Cal, who is still pacing the beach with his phone to his ear. And then she walks off the beach alone. There's a part of me that wants to go after her, but I know that this is where I should be— where I *need* to be.

one of us dies. I wanted to grow old with him. We have known each other since we were children, and perhaps that's my greatest hurdle. How can someone treat another person this way, especially with so much history between them? We've been through some hard stuff. Yet everything I thought I knew about us was wrong.

This much is clear: while I was fighting for my life, he was building a new family.

23
Drew Clark

Cal and Jess had been two people I least expected to see out for ice cream. When we left our homes in opposite directions, I was relieved. But now, here they are. There's a part of me wondering if Cal and Lindsey had planned this.

I can't help but notice that Jess is beautiful this evening. It feels wrong to notice, but she's the kind of woman who will silence a room when she walks in. If I hadn't known, I would have never guessed that she had battled cancer. She's radiant. Her brown eyes glisten; her face glows. She's funny, too. Jess makes me laugh, and that's something no one has been able to do in quite some time.

I don't want to fall for her for many reasons, but the most important is that I am married. I have a family, regardless of how I feel about that at the moment. But I can't get Jess off my mind either. She's a breath of fresh air. Up until now, I hadn't realized how much stagnant air I was actually breathing.

I'm relieved when Jess turns off toward the counter to order her ice cream. The move got Cal to stop talking to my wife and led him back to his own. I don't know what it is about Cal—other than the fact that he's been trying to move in on my family since we got here—but he has a face I'd like to punch. I'm not normally a violent person, but I could see myself punching this man in his almost perfectly chiseled jaw.

Now, the two of them sit within my line of sight, and I'm finding

26
Jess Dawson

I did not want the sun to set and Lilly still remain missing. There were at least one hundred people on the beach this afternoon and evening looking for Lilly, and we all came up empty-handed. Regardless of how horrible Lindsey seems to be as a person, I can't imagine how she must feel with her daughter missing. Sweeney was missing one time, and I nearly lost my mind. Granted, it was just a couple of hours, but a dog could end up anywhere! That's not to say a dog and a child are the same.

Regardless, I didn't feel that my presence was needed on the beach any longer. Drew and Lindsey need each other in this moment, and I understand that. Cal, apparently, needs to be part of this as well. I guess I can understand why. He has grown quite close with Lilly since our vacation began.

Currently, Cal is still out on the beach with the search party. It's dark out now, but when I left the beach, everyone still seemed hopeful. But Cal? I've never seen Cal quite so determined, especially with something like this. I'm not saying he hates children—quite the opposite, really—but this is a child he had no idea existed until this week. Why does he care so much?

Sweeney and I sit on the couch together, mindlessly watching whatever is on television. I find myself unable to stop thinking about Drew. He does love that little girl, regardless of how he feels about whether or not she's actually his. Even his distaste for his wife seems to have been placed on the backburner while they face this situation together. I admire that. Cal isn't really capable of setting his selfishness aside for anything. Drew wouldn't have left me the way Cal has. Drew is still committed to his family, regardless of how he feels.

I can't start falling for Drew, but it would be so easy to allow myself to do so. From what I've learned of Drew so far this week is that overall, he just wants to do what is right. Really. When it comes down to it, he wants to do the right thing, whatever that may be.

My mother never really warmed up to Cal. She's always claimed to be an empath, and she's been warning me about Cal since we first started seeing each other. I suppose I will have to swallow my pride and tell her about Cal. Even if he hasn't had an affair, I do believe our marriage is over. I won't chase after him any longer—not after this week, not after what he's done to me in the past. My mother won't be surprised. She'll probably even gloat a little.

Maybe I haven't really been able to wrap my mind around what he's done to me this week. But then, what does it say about me that I haven't done much to stop it? A couple of confrontations here and there, but I've yet to storm up to those two people and demand the relationship end. I've just let them continue. Drew hasn't done anything either. Not really. We've just sat back and watched, for the most part. What's wrong with us?

I think we don't know what to do or say. This is an odd situation that I'm fairly certain no other human being has ever experienced in a relationship. I, for one, have never seen this type of circumstance in movies. Generally, the offending partners are sneaking around and having an affair. Never have they ever been blatantly obvious about it, which leads me to my next point: what are we even watching happen? I've not seen Cal kiss Lindsey or vice versa. Really, all I've seen is my husband being friendly with a couple of strangers. I can't help but feel a little crazy understanding what my gut is telling me while also trying to believe the opposite.

Mostly, I'm disappointed in Cal. I thought he was different. But we must give Cal some credit; he isn't the sort of man who would divorce his wife over an illness. No, he's the kind of man who creates another world separate from the one he's in because he'd like to come and go as he pleases. When things get a little rough with me, he visits the other world he's created. I feel like an idiot. I have loved this man for more than half my life. I believed him when he promised to love me forever, when he promised "in sickness and in health," when he promised "'til death do us part." I believed him. And now, I'm sitting in our beach house alone while he paces a beach, making phone calls, and obsessing over this missing little girl. This is not how I expected our vacation would go.

My phone rings next to me. I glance at the screen. Drew's name appears across the top. I notice that ridiculous flutter my heart keeps doing every time I see his name on my phone or his face in person, but I ignore it this time.

"Hey, Drew," I answer hoping for good news. "Any luck with Lilly?"

"No, but you might want to get down to the beach. Cal is sort of falling apart. I don't know what's wrong with him, but… I think he needs you."

"What do you mean he's falling apart?" This is not what I expected to hear. Besides, Cal has never needed me a day in his life—not really—not when I think back on it all. Cal doesn't fall apart. He's always put together, even when he isn't.

"Just get down here as soon as you can." Drew ends the call.

I sit for a moment, collecting my thoughts. I don't want to care. I want to let him fall apart. But then, I suppose he is still my husband, and it's my responsibility to at least get him away from the beach and all of its innocent bystanders.

"I'll be right back, Sweeney." I pull my hair up into a scrunchie and throw a hoodie on top of my t-shirt. My sweatpants will be fine.

I start out in a casual walk to the beach; but then I begin to hear the commotion over the dunes, and I realize I probably need to walk a bit faster. Breaking into a full sprint, I clear the boardwalk in a few seconds. This makes the second time I've had to run today, and I'm thinking when I get home to Greenville, I might join a cross-country team for adults. I'm not even sure if they exist, but if they don't, I'll start my own team.

The scene is quite dramatic. Cal is holding his head, kneeling in the sand, crying—actually crying. I swear he never cried a tear when the doctor looked at both of us to tell us I had cancer. Drew is standing off to the side watching Cal but also looking for me. I see relief wash over his face when he spots me. I'm embarrassed. A grown man—one I'm married to—is in the sand crying. Loudly, might I add. What is the deal with this little girl? Why does Cal care so much about her?

"Cal, come on." I kneel down beside him, gently taking hold of his arm with my hand. "Come on, we need to go home." My voice is gentle, soft, trying not to add chaos to the scene.

"I can't leave until we find her," he cries. "This is all my fault. I wasn't watching her. I wasn't watching her!" Cal is hysterical. His face is soaked in tears. I've never seen him like this. Ever. I'm not even sure he's registered it's me kneeling down next to him.

"Cal, she's not your child. They'll find her. They will," I say softly, but inside, I am full of rage. "We have to go now. This isn't our responsibility anymore."

"I've got to find her," he insists, wiping snot from his wet face with the back of his hand. I'm not sure I have ever seen him so unkempt. Most mornings, he wakes up looking like a men's magazine model. He's never really had to try hard to look good, but now he's a mess. This is unacceptable in every sense of the word.

"Well, you aren't going to find her in the sand like this, blubbering like an idiot!" I was trying not to cause a scene. I was trying to be gentle, trying to get my husband out of the sand. Now, I'm shouting. The gentleness didn't take long to shed. This is embarrassing, and he's making a fool of me, not to mention himself, right here on this sand.

Cal looks up at me, his eyes wide, shocked now at my shouting. "So, now I'm an idiot because I care about a little girl who is missing?"

"She's not your little girl, Cal. She's some kid you met while on vacation this week. That's it. All you're doing now is distracting them from their purpose. They can't focus on finding Lilly because you're having a nervous breakdown in the middle of the beach! We have a home. You have a wife. We have a dog!" I'm standing over Cal now, my hands on my hips. He looks up at me, still kneeling in the sand.

"A dog? A dog! We have a dog because you can't have a child! You can't give me the family we always talked about having!" Cal shouts now, but with venom in his voice.

I step back instinctively, shocked now myself. The words I've always known he felt were now out in the open, hanging there, suspended in the sea breeze and bouncing off the water, reverberating through my head like a broken record. *You can't have a child. You can't give me a family.*

I can't say anything. I'm frozen. My feet suddenly feeling like cement blocks in the sand. My breath catches in my throat, and all I can do is stare at him—my husband. A man I loved. A man I thought I was going to spend the rest of my life with. Someone I thought I knew. Someone I thought loved me despite some pretty crappy decisions he's made. This, I imagine, feels worse than if he'd had an affair. This feels worse because he hates me. I know that now. He doesn't love me anymore. He resents me. At least, men who cheat on their wives do still have some sort of love for their wives. They're generally remorseful. They make lots of promises of never cheating again; and though they sometimes fail, at least they try. Cal walked out on me years ago and just never had the balls to tell me. And I have continued to play my part because I promised I would. No more.

The emotions hit me like a wall of water. I don't feel real. I feel like my entire body is falling away from me. That's when I feel Drew's hand on my arm, pulling me back behind him. It takes me a few seconds to realize he's confronting Cal.

Drew's voice is calm, unshaken, stern. "Cal, you need to go home. There's nothing else for you to do here."

I can't be sure Cal has even registered what he's just said to me. He's gone from being hysterical to angry, and his eyes could burn a hole through Drew's head right now if those powers actually existed in the world. Angry Cal is the one I'm afraid of. Angry Cal is ruthless. He hits low and cuts deep. I've never seen Cal use his fists, but he doesn't have to. His words have the ability to hurt worse than any punch to the face could.

"You know what?" Cal begins, his venomous tone now shrouded with some sort of a manic screech. "I think it's time. Lindsey, it's time." He looks over at Lindsey, who, up until this point, has distanced herself from Cal like an embarrassed teenager hiding from her parents.

But now, Lindsey is attentive to Cal. The words *it's time* seems to have triggered a new fear in her. She wears a look on her face that denotes a silent plea to Cal to stop talking. "What are you talking about, Cal? Go home." She says this quietly but between gritted teeth and a sharp glare. If a glare could kill, Cal would be a dead man right now.

Drew looks back at me. My eyes meet his, but I am still frozen. I cannot move. I cannot speak. I'm not even sure I can breathe. There's more to this story. It's not only that he resents me. It's not only that he hates me. No, there's more, and he's about to confess it all.

"Cal, please don't do this," I hear Lindsey growl, pleading. Her voice is low, but I've got pretty decent hearing. In fact, my parents used to call me Big Ears because I heard everything they ever talked about in secret. I think I just have impeccable listening skills.

Cal stares into Lindsey's eyes. He's hesitant, weighing his options. I know this look, too. Cal is a very logical man. He thinks through circumstances before he acts. This is why he's been so successful in his career. He's a predator who knows the precise time to attack.

His eyes slowly turn back to me and then to Drew.

"Cal!" Lindsey protests again, this time louder, grabbing his arm in an effort to stop him. She knows him well, too. She knows what's happening.

"Lilly is my daughter," Cal says, ignoring Lindsey's pleading. The words come out of his mouth as though he's been rehearsing this moment for weeks. Even as the confession slides from his lips, it looks as though an invisible load he's been carrying on his shoulders is lifted. He suddenly appears taller, relieved. I do believe he's been carrying this secret for quite some time—for at least a year and nine months.

Lindsey's arms wrap around her own head, and she turns away from all of us.

Drew and I don't move. We can't move. I still can't breathe. Shouldn't one of us say something? What do we say?

Suspicion is one thing. You can suspect someone of something all day long, but it doesn't mean they're guilty. Sometimes, there is a solid explanation. But confession is another story. Confession answers all of the suspicions. Confession is confirmation. Confession is final.

The silence on the beach is nearly deafening. Even the ocean seems to have dropped its volume a few notches. It feels like everyone is staring at me. At Drew. At Cal. Lindsey, too. An entire search party has been gathered for hours at this point to hunt for a missing baby, and Cal seizes the moment to announce his infidelity. To announce this giant lie he and Lindsey have both been telling. I said he was logical. I never said he was tactful.

Drew reaches for my hand, his eyes cutting toward Lindsey, who's still turned away from us, crouched in the sand, rocking back and forth like a psychopath. I can only hope she's dying from embarrassment. "Well, I think I've had about all the fun I can handle for one day. What about you, Jess?"

I nod my head, unable to speak. My whole heart is shattering. Every memory I've ever created with Cal flashes before my eyes—the same way they say your life flashes before your eyes right before you die. My life with Cal is flashing before my eyes.

"You can't just leave," Lindsey says to Drew between her sloppy tears, stepping out of her crouch but then tripping in the sand as she moves toward Drew. "She's your daughter, too."

"I'll be back in the morning. But tonight, I'm done," Drew says to her. And then, he turns to me, taking my hand completely in his. "Let's go."

Together, we walk off the beach, Drew leading me. I can feel all of their eyes on my back, and I've never wanted to get off a beach faster. When we're out of sight and sure no one has followed us, Drew turns to me and wraps his arms around my body, holding me tighter than any man has ever held me before. I fold into him, too; and without prompting, we both begin to cry. Drew's body shakes against mine; his face is buried in that space between my neck and shoulder, his own tears rolling down my neck as they slide from his eyes.

After a few moments, Drew lifts his face from my shoulder, takes my face in his hands, and looks into my eyes. "I'm sorry." He says to me gently.

I halfway giggle between my tears, "I told you, stop apologizing for things that aren't your fault. You didn't do this. I didn't do this. *They* did this."

He sighs, taking me into his arms again. "You don't deserve this."

"You don't deserve this either, Drew," I point out between sobs. "I...I know you suspected Lilly wasn't yours, but this? Did you suspect this? They've been a whole family for over a year! I mean, I may have thought about it once this week, pondered the thought that *maybe* Lilly is Cal's. But honestly, I thought I was just being dramatic. I didn't think that was possible. I didn't think he'd do that to me."

"I've learned a lot of Lindsey over the last couple of years, Jess. I've known she was capable of quite a bit, but this..." Drew is searching for the right words, but there aren't any. This is the wrong kind of situation—on all levels.

"Lilly is my husband's daughter. I...I don't know how to wrap my mind around that. What are we going to do?"

"Well, we were probably getting divorces after this week ended, anyway," Drew points out. "I suppose Cal's little confession there on the beach just escalated things a little quicker."

"I can't be in the same house with that man."

"I can't be in the same house with Linds."

"We can get hotel rooms. It's too late to drive home tonight."

"I...I still need to help find Lilly. Regardless of the circumstances now, she's an innocent baby, and I do love her. She didn't ask for this," Drew explains with a shroud of guilt—like looking for Lilly is neglecting me. But that's not how I feel. That's not what I think. Regardless of who Lilly's real father is, Drew has raised her up to this point. He loves her. Besides, Lilly is a baby; and despite who her parents are, she doesn't deserve to be missing.

I nod my head, understanding. "I'm going to go pack. I'll be okay," I tell him. "I probably need some time to myself, anyway."

"Promise me this. Promise me you won't leave and go home, Jess," Drew begs of me. "Please don't leave here without telling me goodbye."

"I won't leave," I promise.

27
Joyce Rose

"I just found a baby sleeping in our bedroom—the same baby we babysat last night." Harold's voice comes as a surprise to me as I sit at the table playing a game of Solitaire with a deck of cards. I didn't hear him come in from wherever he had been. I stopped asking Harold what he does in his spare time without me.

"A baby?" I try to sound surprised, but of course, I'm not.

"Joyce." Harold's voice is bland and yet stern. I can feel his presence behind me, heavy and brooding.

After much hesitation, I finally look up at him. "Don't worry about it, okay?"

"Joyce, what did you do?"

"It had to be done," I say. "It's fine. I'll return her when the time is right."

"Joyce, you kidnapped a child? Do you understand what you have done?" Harold's face is red with anger, but his expression denotes fear.

"I didn't kidnap her! She came with me willingly."

"What did you bribe her with?"

"I didn't have to bribe her. She's a baby. She doesn't understand bribes," I explain. "I told you she came with me willingly. She's safe. No one is going to press charges against me because when I give her back, they'll be relieved that she was safe the whole time."

"You're a bit too confident, Joyce," Harold says to me. "You've done a lot of really crazy things in our time together, but this one takes the cake."

"Don't look at me like that, Harold. I've had the advantage of getting to know Drew and Jess this week. They don't deserve what their spouses have done. I had to do this. I had to create a situation to force them—*all* of them—to be honest."

"This isn't any of your business, Joyce. Let them go home and figure it out on their own. This isn't your battle. I've been begging you all week to stop!"

"I can't do that. I couldn't do that." I turn back to my game of Solitaire. "Trust me, Harold. Please. On this, trust me."

"I'm not helping you out of this one. You did it, not me." With that, Harold storms out the door, slamming it behind him. I wonder where he's going now.

A few seconds later, Lilly begins to cry from the bedroom. I sigh, wondering if Harold is right. This is crazy. I kidnapped a child, a baby. I'm essentially holding her hostage in this house. I mean, not really. Like I told Harold, she came with me willingly, and she's not asked to go home yet—not that she can really speak intelligibly. But I'm a mother, too. I know what they want.

I put the Solitaire game aside and head to the bedroom to get Lilly. She's lying in the middle of the queen-sized bed, eyes closed but crying softly. I go to her, lift her in my arms, and observe her soft facial expressions—her chubby cheeks, her clear complexion, her blue eyes—and the way her blonde curls seem to go everywhere and nowhere all at once.

"Are you hungry?" I ask her. I can assume so. It's been a bit since she last ate, and it is dinnertime. I stocked up on some toddler food at the grocery store yesterday when I devised this whole plan. Keeping Lilly last night while her parents went out for dinner wasn't part of the plan. No one was more surprised than I when I opened the door to see Lindsey standing there in a fit of rage holding Lilly in her arms and practically demanding I watch her for the evening. Of course, I was more than willing to watch after Lilly. I miss having little children around. They can bring so much light to people like me.

I don't have a highchair for Lilly, but I figure she can sit in my lap while I feed her some bananas. I've done this before, multiple times. It's just been a while. But Harold isn't wrong. This idea of mine was pretty stupid. It's too late to change it, though. The plan is in progress, and I can't confess to this kidnapping yet. The best thing to do now is to let it play out the way I had hoped it would. And if it backfires? *I'm an old lady. I'm confused. I didn't know what I was doing.*

28
Drew Clark

"Lindsey, stop apologizing. You think I've been in the dark this whole time? I knew! Deep down, I knew." I'm not in the mood to fight. I just want this nightmare to end so that I can get back to living my life, which is why I'm carelessly throwing my clothes into my suitcase and working very hard at getting the hell out of here as fast as I can. I'll still help find Lilly, but I won't stay here in this house with this woman anymore.

"I-I never meant to hurt you." Lindsey has been a blubbering mess for hours now, since Cal confessed to the entire beach that the child missing doesn't even belong to me.

I sigh and rub the palm of my hand over my face aggressively. "I swear if the next thing out of your mouth is, *It just happened*, I will lose it."

"What about Lilly?" Lindsey wipes the tears from her face with the back of her hand.

"What about her?"

"Are you not even going to help us look for her?"

"There's nothing else we can do tonight, Lindsey. I'll come back first thing in the morning, but we need to let the police do their job. They know more than we do. You should get some sleep."

"I don't know how you could even think about sleep."

"You can't find Lilly if you're lacking in the sleep department," I tell her. "You have to rest. It's been an exhausting and traumatizing day."

"Where are you going?" For the first time, she's noticed that I've been packing my suitcase while we've been talking.

"I'm not staying here with you."

"You can't just leave."

I glare at her. "I *can* just leave." With that, I zip my bag closed and grab my wallet and car keys. That's my car out there. She has her own at home. She can figure out how to get it.

"Drew, this isn't how this ends."

"It is, Lindsey. This is it. I've spent this entire week watching you with that man—watching you and Lilly with that man. You've practically ignored me this entire time, and now you want me to stay? I've been here! The *whole time*. I knew our marriage was on the rocks. I had suspected you hadn't been faithful, but I went into this week hoping that I could fix us. I was even willing to ignore my suspicions and try. But now, knowing you not only had an affair but that you also lied to me about Lilly, too? You made me think she was mine when you knew all along she wasn't."

Lindsey doesn't say anything, and instead, she plops down on the couch and buries her face in her hands. I can't decide if she's upset because she's remorseful or because her secret is out and she's embarrassed. The Lindsey I married would be remorseful. The Lindsey sitting here now is probably embarrassed.

My heart, heavy in my chest, has a lot of questions it wants to ask her. But logic tells me that the answer to those questions won't matter—not really. It happened—the affair. The child isn't mine. There's nothing left to say, nothing left to fix. And so, I walk out the door without even looking back.

I won't stop looking for Lilly, but I don't have to be Lindsey's husband anymore. Who would expect me to be, anyway? Just as I told Lindsey, I'll be back in the morning to continue the search because regardless of who Lilly belongs to, I have loved her every day of her life. I need to find her. I need to know she's safe. Something in my gut tells me she is safe, wherever she is. And that's the only thing that's going to allow me to get some rest tonight, so I can be bright-eyed and fully functioning by daybreak.

The motel is four blocks from the beach house we have been inhabiting over the last few days. Red neon letters spell out VACANCY on the sign. I could afford better than this, but it's the closest motel to Lindsey and wherever Lilly may be. There's a pool out front, and though it's late, there are some kids still splashing around. I assume their parents granted them one last swim for the day so they'd sleep hard tonight. When I was a kid, the best kind of sleep always came after swimming. No one can sleep harder than a boy who's been swimming all day.

A bell dings over my head as I push open the glass door to the main office, and then my heart stops when I see her standing there at the front desk. Jess. Jess and her dog, to be precise.

"What are you doing here?" She looks assuming, like we didn't just both decide to get hotel rooms for the rest of the week—like I followed her here or something. I didn't. It's obvious that great minds think alike.

"What are you doing here?" I quip.

"Did you follow me?"

"Yes, Jess. That's exactly what I did. I followed you," I reply dryly, only slightly annoyed by her accusation.

Jess halfway chuckles at my sarcasm, and the sound of that half-hearted chuckle seems to rejuvenate me to an extent. Somehow, in the last few hours, I have forgotten that her chuckles, giggles, and laughs make me happy. How one can forget that so soon, I have no idea. But in my defense, quite a bit has gone down in the last several hours.

"It was the closest one to…" Jess says, not finishing her sentence but, instead, casting her eyes sorrowfully toward the door and toward the beach where our spouses are no doubt together again.

"That's why I'm here, too. I can get back to the beach quicker in the morning from here."

"Will you two need a room together?" Suddenly, the front desk lady is talking to us. Poor woman probably works this desk all summer. I can imagine there's not a lot she hasn't seen.

"No. Not together. Separate," Jess says quickly, reaching for the key card the front desk lady had started to push across the counter.

Front Desk Lady looks at me with a question on her face like she's wondering if maybe I'm the problem.

"Listen, lady," I begin, "we both just found out our spouses were cheating on us with each other, and they produced a child together—a child I have thought was mine since the day she was born. So, yeah, we need some alone time this evening in separate rooms."

Front Desk Lady's expression changes to one of horror. She

doesn't ask any other questions verbally or with her facial expressions. She reaches for another key card, hands it to me, and then goes back to whatever it was she was doing before Jess arrived.

Jess and I walk out of the office together. I've got my key card in my hand, and she's got hers. Our footfalls echo against the cement walls of the motel corridor.

"How is Cal?" I ask, though I'm not sure why. I really couldn't care less.

"He begged me not to go," she says softly.

"Lindsey, too, to an extent." I shrug.

"And Lilly?" Jess asks.

"No news. I'll check in with Linds in the morning and rejoin the search party."

"This is my room here," Jess says, stopping in front of a yellow door with the number sixteen stamped across the top.

"Looks like I'm here." I point at the door next to hers. That damn Front Desk Lady put us in side-by-side rooms.

"No need to make this any weirder than it already is," Jess mumbles. "I'm going to bed now. See you in the morning?"

"In the morning." I smile at her. "I'm here if you need me."

She smiles back at me. "I know." With that, she slides the key card into the door and then disappears behind door number sixteen.

I stand there for a few seconds before letting myself into my own room. The door snaps closed behind me, and I flip on the lights.

It's not bad. At least the floors are tile, and the bedding looks new. It's definitely not the beach house I was living in until about an hour ago, but it's better than being under the same roof with Lindsey.

I decide I won't unpack. Instead, I dig through my bag and find my sleep pants, a clean t-shirt, and some fresh boxer-briefs. I think I need a hot shower—as hot as the motel will allow. Then, I'll try to sleep.

I doze for a little while. When I open my eyes again, it's just after midnight, and I notice a text message on my phone's screen. Jess.

You awake?

I'm hesitant to text back. What if she's asleep now? The text was sent an hour ago. I do it, anyway.

I am for now.

Immediately, she types back, *I can't sleep.*

Want to come over?
I know she'll say no, but I have to ask, anyway.
No. Call me?
Okay.
I wait two seconds before calling her.
"What's wrong?" I ask her when she answers.
Jessica laughs. "What's wrong?"
I can't help but laugh, too. It's like when someone's husband dies, and you ask them how they're doing. Unless it was a super horrible marriage, they're generally not doing well at all.
"Sorry, I'm not good at stuff like this. Of course, you aren't okay. I'm not okay either," I confess with a sigh.
"The way he spoke to both of us on the beach tonight…"
"He can talk to me anyway he likes, but not you. You don't deserve that," I tell her. "They both deserve each other."
I hear Jess crying softly in the background. She sniffs, and I can hear her pull a tissue from the motel tissue box. Tissues make a very distinct sound when pulling one from its box—a little swoosh sound that not many people pay attention to.
"I'm sorry, Jess," I say because I don't know what else to say. What can I say? My wife and her husband started a family together.
"What do we do now?" she whispers.
"Go home. Get our divorces. The same thing we were probably going to do anyway."
"I have to figure out how I'm going to get home."
"Jess, you know I can drive you home," I say gently.
"I was going to leave in the morning, and with you rejoining the search party…"
"I can't leave until we find Lilly. But as soon as we find her, we're out," I promise her. "Okay?"
"Okay."
"We should try to sleep." I don't want to get off the phone, but I also don't want to feel like death tomorrow without having any sleep. I need to be sharp.
"Stay on the phone until I fall asleep," Jess says softly.
"Okay. Goodnight, Jess."
"Goodnight, Drew."
I hear some rustling on her end of the line indicating that she's getting comfortable, and then the line is quiet. I roll over, too, putting the phone on speaker and laying it on the pillow next to

mine.

"Drew?" her voice comes softly after a few moments of quiet.

"Yeah?"

"Tell me your most favorite story that you've ever covered as a journalist."

"You want a bedtime story?"

"Something like that."

"Okay. Let me think for a moment." In my mind, I begin shuffling through every story I've ever written. Since I know Jess loves dogs, I pick a story that happened a few years ago. An entire litter of puppies had been found dumped in a ditch off the side of the interstate. They were all in very bad shape as they were really too young to be away from their mother. The community had come together and raised money for the puppies, and the puppies were given the help they needed. All ten puppies were nursed back to health and adopted. It had been a happy ending to an otherwise tragic story.

"Jess?" I whisper softly when she doesn't say anything after I tell the story. She doesn't respond, and that's when I hear her soft snoozes. I smile, knowing that Jess did, indeed, need a bedtime story. Only part of me wishes she had stayed awake to hear the entire story. Abandoned puppy stories generally don't end well, but this one did because strangers came together to save them. Sometimes, I think there is still some good left in this world. It doesn't feel like it most days, especially in journalism. It would be so easy to get caught up in all of the bad and think, *This is just how the world is now.* But maybe we just stopped looking for the good; that's why we think it's so bad.

If I've learned anything in my career, it's that most people are the same, even when they're different. Some people are resilient and strong. Some are weak. Some people want to do the right thing, always. Some want to see what they can get away with. We want friends. We want family. We want to foster abandoned animals because it makes us feel good. But the reality is, selfishness feels good, too. We're all selfish, and that's what makes us the same.

Lindsey was selfish. Cal, too. And I've probably been selfish myself. Lindsey didn't just wake up one day and decide to have an affair. Something drove her there. Of course, she never really expected me to find out about her and Cal the way I did. I believed her when she said she never meant to hurt me. When the affair began, she wasn't thinking about anything else because her selfishness told her she deserved this. She didn't think about the consequences. We never think of those things when we're after something we think we really want.

THURSDAY

People Watching

29
Jess Dawson

The morning sun wakes me. It breaks through the pulled curtains of this motel room the way darkness fills a room at night—suddenly and gradually all at the same time.

I remember falling asleep with Drew on the phone, and I'm not sure if I should be embarrassed by that. Cal tells me that I snore from time to time, and I would be absolutely humiliated if Drew had stayed on the phone long enough to hear me snore. Sweeney never seems to mind my snoring, but Cal usually had something to say about it.

Cal. My husband. My *cheating* husband. The memory of last night's event hits me like a tsunami. Anger fills my chest almost immediately. How dare that man treat me this way. How could he? I still can't even believe he has done this. I never in a million years could have expected anything like this out of him. Even when I suspected him, I still talked myself out of it—because he couldn't do that. He wouldn't do that. If anything, he would have asked for a divorce first.

If I had known Cal was this type of man, I obviously would have never married him. Of course, if we knew half of what is going to happen to us in our lifetime, we'd probably never leave the house. Still, Cal wasn't that man. He's not a cheater—or he wasn't. He wasn't the kind of man who would leave his wife to do her chemo treatments alone either, but he did. I wonder if we, as humans, can ever truly know someone inside and out. Cal and I can finish each other's sentences. I know his favorite color, his favorite food, his favorite movie, and where he'd rather spend a Friday night. I know how he takes his coffee, that he's allergic to pepper, and which country he's always dreamed of living in; but he still needed to have an affair. None of what we have been through together mattered to him. There was nothing that he loved so much about me that stopped him from doing what he's done.

I won't let his actions define who I am, though. This wasn't my fault. His adultery had nothing to do with me not being good enough. He cheated because he is a no-good, lying, selfish son-of-a-bitch. That fact has nothing to do with me and my value.

"Come on, Sweeney. Let's go potty," I say, grabbing his leash after I've tossed a sweatshirt over my pajamas.

Sweeney stands from his spot on the bed, wagging his tail—which always makes me smile—and then lunges towards me, ready for the leash. Unlike most dogs, Sweeney loves his leash. For him, it means he's about to go on an adventure—even if the adventure is just a new place to potty. I try to live vicariously through Sweeney. Dogs truly take the deepest pleasure in the simplest of activities. I think people should strive to be more like dogs. The experts say that dogs are generally very selfish, but I don't agree with that at all. Sweeney doesn't care about much else except my happiness—well, my happiness and my food that he thinks I should share with him every single time I'm eating. I wish Cal had been more like Sweeney—faithful, loyal, selfless.

As I unlock the motel door, there's a soft tap against it from the other side. I stand back, a little startled, wondering if I hadn't imagined the gentle knock. No one really expects for someone else to knock on a door you're about to open. It's an anomaly.

"Jess?" a voice comes through the door, and I recognize it as Drew's.

I open the door, relieved. I thought a serial killer had found me. Or worse, Cal. "Good morning," I say. Then Sweeney bolts, pulling the leash and my small frame with him. "You'll have to run with me. He likes morning potty time in new places." I can't help but laugh at Sweeney's enthusiasm.

Drew follows me out to the designated dog area. "Joyce texted me. Asked if I could come by this morning. I wasn't sure if you wanted to come with me?"

"Drew, let me call an Uber or something." I sigh. "There's no reason for me to stay here. Lilly doesn't belong to me. Neither does Cal."

"I am going to drive you and me home. I only need a few hours," Drew says.

"I know we agreed on that, and I'm so thankful to you for being willing to do so. You still have unfinished business here, though. I don't. As far as I'm concerned, this vacation is over."

"Please stay, Jess. With me." Drew is pleading now, and I'm not sure why. There's definitely some sort of an attraction between the two of us, but we can't be together. Not after this. Not after the way our marriages fell apart on the beach last night.

"Drew, why would I stay?" Sweeney sniffs the base of a tree and then promptly lifts his leg to pee on it.

Drew's eyes drop and then turn to me again. "Because I want you to," he says honestly. "Just until we find Lilly. And then we can go. Both of us."

"Forgive me if I'm not thinking through this situation clearly enough, but why on earth would I want to stay and help search for my husband's daughter? The one he couldn't have with me?" This comes between clenched teeth, heat rising to my cheeks as the anger resurfaces.

Drew considers me for a few seconds before saying, "You're angry today, aren't you?"

I stare at him for a long, quiet second, confused as to why he would think I could be anything but angry. "I *am* angry, Drew. Really angry. Suspecting Cal of cheating on me was one thing, but actually finding out that I wasn't imagining it is another. When I married Cal, I never imagined that any of this would happen. Cal—the Cal I married—was not this man. He was loving and caring and so full of life. We had so much fun. That damned cancer diagnosis destroyed it all—Cal, me, my marriage. Sometimes, I wish I had just died." The last part is the first time I've said that out loud to anyone. I've thought it plenty of times, but I've never said it out loud.

Drew steps toward me, his eyes dark and angry now. "It sucks. All of it. I'm a victim, too, remember? But you know what? Meeting you has quite literally turned out to be the best thing that has ever happened to me, and I mean that. I mean that more than I meant my vows when I married Lindsey. I don't know what's going to happen—well, outside of divorce. But I know that I want to be around you, that you are a light I need.

"And now that I've met you, I don't think I can pretend like it didn't happen. I think we're stuck together now, Jess. I'm not even talking romantically. I'm talking as friends—two people who found out the worse possible news together on a beach in the midst of a tragedy. So, no, you don't get to just walk out of my life either. I need you. And you know what? I think you need me, too; you're just too stubborn to think about it."

My heart is pounding. I swear I can feel the blood pulsing through my veins. I'm angry and sad and hopeful. He is right, and he is wrong; and he is everything in between. I don't want to need him. I'm perfectly capable of being my own independent and single woman. I fought cancer on my own and won. I can do life on my own and win, too.

I don't have anything to say back to him. The feminist in me sort of wants to slap him for telling me I can't do something like walk out of his life when I most certainly can. It's a free country. I can quite literally do what I want where Drew is concerned.

"Jess, I know you haven't known me but a few days, but I'm asking you to trust me. Please? I'll take care of you, and again, I'm not talking about romance. I don't know what this is. But what I do know is that now that I've met you, I can't live another day without you. And maybe selfishly, I don't want to do this alone. We're sort of in this together, whether we like it or not."

"You don't know what you're saying, Drew," I whisper. "This isn't responsible. This isn't logical. Your wife slept with my husband, and they have a child together. That's…that's the situation."

"Where does the situation with my wife and your husband leave you and me?"

"What does that even mean?" Tears are welling up in my eyes now.

"It means that I refuse to believe that there isn't a reason we were meant to meet. Don't push me away, Jess. Let's go through this together." His voice is soft now, still pleading but gentle. "Please, stay. Just for a little longer."

Sweeney sits by my right leg now, looking at me and then Drew and then back to me. I look down at him; and his big, brown eyes bore back up into mine. His tail wags slightly—not a full wag like he's about to get a treat, but that little twitchy wag that indicates it's okay, that I am capable of making any sort of decision I want. And maybe that little tail twitch means I should do something for myself—for once, anyway.

"So, what are we going to do? Find Lilly, leave this beach, and become roomies in some shabby apartment with jobs that cause neither of us to ever see each other?"

"This is not *Single White Female*," Drew jokes. "My point is we don't have to figure out any of this stuff alone."

"This is insane, Drew."

"You're the one who said you wanted to stay in touch when we left," Drew points out.

I did say that, didn't I? In my defense, I was still mostly hoping that I had imagined Cal's affair—that I was just paranoid or something. That conversation was only a couple of days ago, but I was a different person then. I'm angry now. I don't want to know anyone or anything. I want to find a hole somewhere, crawl inside, and die. I know that's dramatic, but it's how I feel. More than half of my life has been a lie and I've only now found out about it. How am I supposed to process that? Everything I thought I knew—all of the decades between meeting Cal and now—were completely destroyed in one confession on a beach.

"Fine. I'll stay." I finally sigh. "But I can't help find Lilly. I just…not now. Not with…" I really have no idea why I'm staying, other than I believed Drew as he stood here and begged me to stay. I believed everything he said. And maybe that's because there was hope in the words that fell from his mouth, and hope is the only thing I have to cling to at the moment.

"That's fine. Come with me to Joyce and Harold's house, at least. We'll figure out the rest from there."

"Fine. I have some calls to make. I'll just do that from Joyce's house while you're out searching for Lilly." I could make the calls from the motel, but then, I'm not really interested in spending my whole day inside that motel room. It's not the filthiest place I've ever slept in, but I still feel as though I should get tested for some sort of disease before we leave for home.

The ride to Joyce and Harold's is quiet. Even Sweeney sits in the backseat like a good boy and gazes out the window. He didn't even need his CBD. I find myself wishing I was sitting on the beach. The sun is absolutely perfect today. The temperature, too. I hate Cal for doing this—for taking away a perfect beach day, for ruining a vacation, for what he did. I hate him.

The smell of freshly brewed coffee meets my nose as Joyce opens the door to their beach house. The smell is intoxicating, and I remember that I haven't had my coffee today. I never begin a day without coffee. Drew and I both try to move through the doorway and into the house, which Joyce allows, but she doesn't really let us move beyond the kitchen. She's acting sort of strange. There's even an odd expression on her face that I can't quite identify.

"I made you two some fresh coffee," Joyce says, watching us while she pulls two coffee mugs from the upper cabinet over the coffeemaker.

"Thank you. I just realized I've not even had my coffee this morning," I say, taking the warm mug from Joyce's hands after she's poured my cup.

"Cream and sugar are over there." Joyce points toward a table next to the refrigerator. "It's a sort of makeshift coffee bar. I couldn't get Harold adjusted to brewing coffee over there, so that's why the coffeepot still sits here," she explains while pouring Drew his cup of coffee.

"Where is Harold?" Drew asks.

"He left last night. Went back home," she says. "Which is why I called you here."

"Why would he just leave like that? Did you have a fight?" Drew prods.

Joyce sighs. I sip my coffee. Drew waits for Joyce to spill the beans.

Just then, a cry comes from a bedroom down the hallway. A baby's cry. Not an adult. Not an animal. A human baby.

At first, I think I've imagined the cry; but then Joyce stiffens, and Drew freezes in mid-sentence. Even the color in his face has gone. I'm confused.

The silence is deafening, and the cry we all heard doesn't sound again. Did we imagine it? I don't think so. Not judging by the expressions on Joyce and Drew's faces.

Drew still doesn't speak. He continues to stare at Joyce for a few seconds longer before he turns on his heels and charges down the hall in the direction the cry had come.

"Drew, wait! I can explain everything." Joyce slides by me and runs after Drew.

"You kidnapped my baby?" Drew's voice is slightly muffled as he yells now from some place down the hall. His booming voice echoes throughout the whole of the beach house, and I decide it's time to start working at zoning out of this situation because I refuse to be a witness to an apparent kidnapping. Also, I'm not quite sure what to do. This is a new circumstance for me. Apparently, it's a new situation for Joyce, too. She's never mentioned being a professional kidnapper before.

"It wasn't a kidnapping!" Joyce says back, nearly pleading with him.

All I can hear are their voices, going back and forth at each other. Drew says one thing, Joyce says the other. From what I've been able to gather by listening to them from the kitchen is that Joyce got the idea to bring Lilly back here for a few hours—long enough for Lindsey to realize her daughter was missing—which she had hoped would then force the truth out of Cal and Lindsey. Joyce had intended all along to return Lilly by Wednesday evening. She had planned to claim that she had found the baby crawling up the street, but when the situation on the beach went down a bit more severely than she had anticipated, she knew she couldn't take Lilly back then. It would have fixed one situation, but it would have only enhanced the other.

Still shouting at each other, their voices come back up the hallway and then into the kitchen, where I pretend that I've been looking at my phone the whole time and not eavesdropping.

"Lindsey is crazy, Joyce! If she finds out about this, she'll make sure you go to jail!" Drew is holding Lilly close to his chest. She appears to be unscathed. She actually looks happier than she's looked all week with Lindsey and Cal, even in the midst of raised voices.

"It was only supposed to be for a few hours, and then I was going to take her back," Joyce repeats. "All I wanted was for the truth to come out so that you two didn't have to go home and deal with it alone."

"Oh, it came out all right! In the worst way. Do you even know what Cal said to Jess? She didn't need to hear that. This wasn't your truth to tell, Joyce. This wasn't your problem to solve."

"Funny, that's what Harold said."

"Maybe you should listen to your husband a little more!" This final statement by Drew is angry and demeaning. It surprises me.

I've not yet seen him this irate.

"I was trying to help," Joyce defends herself. "I've been watching you two all week—watching them, too. It was tearing me apart, and I...well, I couldn't sit here any longer and do nothing."

"Drew, give me the baby," I say softly. "You're too upset."

He reluctantly passes Lilly to me, and then he goes back to glaring at Joyce. "What am I supposed to tell Lindsey?" His voice is a little calmer than it has been.

"My original theory was that Lindsey would be so thrilled that Lilly is safe, she wouldn't press charges."

"You don't know Lindsey," Drew mumbles and then pushes both hands through his hair, "I'm glad she's safe, Joyce. I am. But this? How do I explain this?"

"In Harold's words, it takes the cake for the craziest thing I've ever done." She sounds slightly ashamed now, but I'm still not sure that she fully regrets taking Lilly. I actually don't disagree with what she did either. She forced the truth out, instead of Drew and I having to go home and force it out ourselves. Even still, she manipulated a situation that was only up to Drew and me to confront.

I search for a solution in my mind—one that gets Joyce off the hook and Lilly back into the arms of my husband and Lindsey.

"Drew, what if you were the one who found her," I say suddenly. They both look at me.

"Drew found Lilly. Somewhere. I don't know. Some place that we didn't look." I realize I'm not being very helpful now. It doesn't sound like a solid story that someone would believe. But then, I remember a few years ago when one of my students went missing from home. They searched for the little boy all night until his father actually found him, curled up in one of the outdoor barns on their property. Apparently, the boy had been grounded for a bad test grade, and he took it upon himself to move out of the house and into the barn. Second-grader logic.

"At this point, she's been gone for nearly twenty-four hours. Where could she have been for an entire day, alone and unscathed?" Drew asks.

"The pier? She loves the lemonade from the pier. Maybe she went there."

"Without anyone noticing?" Drew challenges me.

"Kids are weird—especially when they can't speak. She's a baby. She's small, and she can hardly walk a few feet by herself, anyway.

It's plausible that she found her way into the pavilion at the pier and then hid. She got scared and hid." The story doesn't sound half-bad as it comes from my mouth now.

"That's insane, Jess." Drew sighs. Obviously, he feels differently about my made-up story. I never claimed to be a writer.

"Well, so was Joyce kidnapping the kid, but here we are," I quip.

"Let me do this," Joyce says. "I took her. Let me do this."

Drew is tense. His brow is furrowed, but there's a mix of emotion behind his eyes.

"I don't mean this how it's going to sound," I say to Joyce, "but I think you've done enough."

Joyce does look slightly hurt when I say this, but she nods her head and agrees. "I'm sorry. Again. I...I thought I was doing the right thing. Now, Harold is gone. Everything is a mess."

"Out of curiosity, how did you think this might end?" Drew asks her.

"I don't know. I didn't think that far ahead. Really, I was just thinking that if I could force the truth out of those two instead of having to watch them do the two of you the way they have all week, then it would make everything okay. You would know the truth about your spouses, about Lilly, and... I don't know. I've seen the way the two of you have looked at each other this week. I guess I'm a bit of a romantic."

I blush and slide my glance toward Drew. He does the same to me.

"I think my story is good enough," I say. "Drew found Lilly in a storage room on the pier."

Drew and Joyce look at each other and then back at me. "It just seems so simple."

"Honestly, most missing children are simple circumstances—not kidnapped or murdered like you cover in your stories, Drew. Most children who go missing simply get scared and hide." That's one of those things they teach us when we're learning to become teachers. We're not only supposed to be well-versed in educating children, but we must also learn how to think like they do. A missing child is like looking for a frightened dog. You're to look in the most obscure places.

"She's actually not wrong about that," Drew admits. "The paper only wants us to publish the tragedies. Most of them don't end in tragedy."

"Then you've got your answer," Joyce says. "You found Lilly in a storage closet on the pier."

Drew looks over at Lilly, who sits contently in my arms. She is watching all of us as though she, too, is following along with this big lie we're concocting. I'm thankful she can hardly speak—just a few words that are mostly unintelligible.

Lilly looks at Drew now from my arms, her eyes wide, and she pokes both of her arms out toward him, squeezing her hands in and out of fists repeatedly. I'm not a mother, obviously, but this looks like a gesture of Lilly asking for Drew. His eyes drop like he's going to cry, and then he takes her from my arms and holds her tightly against his chest. Drew stands there, holding this little girl in his big arms, and he cries.

I don't know what it would feel like to have raised a baby that you believed was your own flesh and blood, only to find out they're not. Now, Drew holds her as though he'll never hold her again. And he probably won't. Drew was born to be a father.

My own heart begins to break. I wanted to be a mother. Even if Drew and I become romantically involved after this fiasco is over, I will never be able to give him a child of his own. He deserves to be a father, at least.

"I'm sorry," Drew says, wiping the back of his hand across his cheek. "It's just that I can't believe she isn't mine. She was the most beautiful baby the day she was born." He looks into Lilly's face, smiling, but tears still leak from his eyes. "I never really thought she looked like me, but that didn't matter. Not really. I wanted us to be a family—a happy family. Maybe I'm not capable of making anyone happy."

"That's not true, Drew," Joyce says, taking on the tone of a mother. "Things just got a bit awry. That doesn't mean you'll be miserable for the rest of your life. Is it going to hurt for a little while? It will. I won't lie about that. But you still have a future. You and Jess both do. If it's with each other, fine. But if it isn't, you both deserve to have a happy family. With or without children."

Drew and I glance at each other. He looks back at his daughter, and then he wipes any last resemblances of tears from his cheek. "I'll take Lilly back now," he says.

"I'll go with you," I offer.

"No, I'll go alone," he says quickly. "Before we leave, there are some things I need to say to Lindsey."

People Watching

I probably should have a few words with Cal, too. After everything that went down on the beach last night, I've ignored every one of Cal's phone calls and text messages. He's not been incredibly remorseful about the affair or Lilly in his text messages, but it does sound like he's remorseful for what he has done to me and the things he said to me on the beach. I'd still like him to roll around in that filth a bit longer before I entertain a conversation with him, but Drew is right. Before we leave, we need to have our conversations with our spouses.

"I'll have another cup of coffee with Joyce, then," I say. "And then I'll go have a conversation with Cal, too."

Drew starts toward the door with Lilly still in his arms. He pauses before reaching for the doorknob, and then he turns to look at us. "Pray before you start sipping on that second cup of coffee. Pray that story works." He checks Lilly's diaper. "And pray I'll come up with a story that explains this super clean diaper."

Joyce looks ashamed again. She's not a very good kidnapper. A real kidnapper wouldn't have changed Lilly's diaper.

Drew looks sick to his stomach as he and Lilly push on through the door and head over to Lindsey's.

Joyce and I sit across from each other at the table. We're not speaking; we just hold our coffee mugs in our hands as though we're attempting to warm our palms.

Finally, I break the silence. "You think he's okay?"

"Drew will be okay," Joyce says. "He's a strong man. Stronger than he thinks."

"How do you know?"

"Jess, when you've lived as long as I have and people-watch as much as I do, you just know these things about people." Joyce sighs. "But sometimes, it gets me into trouble. Harold has never left like this before. I messed up this time."

"You were just trying to do what you thought was right."

"Kidnapping a child is a bit much, though, don't you think?"

I laugh. "That was a bit extreme."

"What do you think will happen to you and Drew?" Joyce asks with a smirk on her tired and exhausted face.

I cast my eyes back into my coffee, watching the dissolved creamer spin in a creamy swirl among the brown liquid. "I don't know."

"You like him, don't you?"

"Joyce, I'm a married woman."

She gives me a look that says, *Nice try*.

I sigh. "I don't know. I can't think about that right now. There are so many other things to think about—divorce, a place to live, a job. Besides, the only romantic relationship I've ever really known has been with Cal. I don't know how to be with anyone else."

"Do you want to know what I think?"

"Probably not, but I bet you're going to tell me, anyway." I smile to hide the sarcasm.

"I think that life is too short for formalities." With that, she stands from the table, pours the rest of her coffee down the drain in the kitchen sink, and then sets her mug inside the sink. "Go talk to Cal," she instructs, and then she disappears. A few seconds later, I hear the shower turn on.

I text Cal first to see where he is.

He's in the beach house, getting ready to join the search party for Lilly. My stomach turns thinking about talking to him, standing in front of him, looking at him. This would be so much better if I never had to speak to him again.

I knock on the door because it's not my house anymore.

"You don't have to knock," Cal says as he opens the door. "This rental is just as much yours as it is mine."

"We both know that's not true anymore," I say. My voice shakes, which is not something that I wanted to happen. When I'm angry or have an issue to confront, I either start crying like a baby, or my voice is so shaky, I sound as though I've done something wrong. It's quite embarrassing, and these traits have never given me an upper hand in any type of argument.

Cal closes the door, and we stand in the kitchen just staring at each other for a few quiet seconds before he says, "I'm sorry. About last night. About everything."

I hide a chuckle and shake my head at him. "Apologies will not fix this one, Cal."

He nods his head. "I feel terrible. We were going to tell you. Both of you."

"The one question I keep asking myself is why you two chose our vacation to be together. Why not just disappear for a week? A work trip or something. Did you think I was that stupid? Did she think Drew is that stupid? You both have spent most of the week with each other."

"I don't know what we were thinking, Jess." He sighs. "I don't. And with Lilly missing now, I can't..."

I run my hand through my hair. "I'm going home," I tell him, "to pack my things and get out before you come home."

"Don't do that, Jess," Cal begs. "I didn't... I don't want it to end like this."

"How did you think it was going to end, Cal?" I snap at him.

"Not like this," he says. "You deserved a conversation, at least. I...I didn't want what happened last night to happen."

"Well, regardless, I'm going home. There's no reason to stay, and I'd rather not be under the same roof with you any longer than I have to be. I am done, Cal." My voice doesn't sound shaky anymore. It's confident, which takes me by surprise.

"How are you driving home? You can't have my car." One final stab to get me to stay. He had to know that wouldn't work. Even if I didn't have Drew, I'd get home one way or another.

"Drew is going to drive me home." I don't mention Lilly or the fact that she's not even missing anymore. He can figure that out on his own.

"So, are you two together now?" There is a tinge of jealousy in his voice.

"What's it to you?"

"Nothing. Absolutely nothing."

"We're not together. We're friends," I tell him. "And victims."

"Jess, I'm sorry," he says again. "I know it doesn't make anything less horrible, but I am sorry."

"I just came to say goodbye."

Cal's phone buzzes in his hand, and he glances at the screen. "It's a text from Lindsey. Hold on." He takes a second to read the text message, and then he looks up at me with wide eyes. "They found Lilly! She's okay."

I can only smile. "I'm glad she's okay. Go be with your daughter."

"Wait, Jess—"

"Cal, it's all over your face. You'd like to not be standing in this kitchen anymore because you'd like to go see your daughter. Go."

He hesitates, the decades we have spent together now between us. "Jess—"

I shake my head at him. "I'll be okay."

With that, I push the handle of the front door and slide out, walking back to Joyce's house to wait in Drew's car. I'm ready to head back to Greenville. This vacation is officially over. I do believe it will go down as the worst vacation of my entire life.

I climb into Drew's SUV to wait on him. Sweeney meets me in the front seat happy as always to see me, the fur around his face cool from having it stuck in front of the SUV's air conditioner vent.

I figure Drew can't be gone much longer, so I pull out my cell phone and begin working on the to-do list I'll need to accomplish for divorce proceedings.

30
Drew Clark

"You found her! Where did you find her? Oh, Lilly! Oh, I missed you so much. I was so worried about you!" Lindsey is hysterical as I step into the beach house with her daughter in my arms, practically assaulting me to take Lilly from my arms.

Lilly clings to my shirt at first, unsure of her mother's hysterics, but then she lunges forward into Lindsey after a few seconds. It briefly hurts my feelings. I find the kid, and she still loves her mother more. I pass the rest of Lilly to Lindsey and then step back, digging my hands into the pockets of my khaki shorts.

"I know how she loves the ice cream at the pier, so I thought I'd search for her there. I don't know how she made it up the steps and into the pavilion of the pier without anyone noticing or without getting hurt, but somehow, she ended up in a storage closet." I explain the story, calm and collected as though it were true. I won't throw Joyce under the bus for what she did, though. She doesn't deserve that. I'm also hoping Lindsey doesn't notice the clean diaper because for the life of me, I could not come up with a lie to cover that up during my walk over.

"The pier?" Lindsey is kissing Lilly's cheeks and forehead and hair. She squeezes the little girl so tightly, I think Lilly might pop.

"She's okay," I assure her. "Just a little hungry maybe."

Tears stream down Lindsey's face, and remarkably, they don't make me feel any certain way. I don't feel compassion, but then, I don't exactly feel compassionless either. Her tears do at least me tell me she is human. She does have some sort of a heart. There is still a little bit of the Lindsey I married in there…somewhere.

Lindsey looks at me, bouncing Lilly on her hip "I'm sorry, Drew. For everything. I didn't… I can't believe he just said it out there on the beach like that last night. It wasn't supposed to happen that way."

"If I'm being honest, I wasn't blindsided. I knew something was going on. And then the way you three have hung out together this week… I'm not stupid." I shrug. "And we were probably going to go home and get a divorce, anyway—well, not probably. We were."

"It's been that bad?"

"Are you serious?"

She doesn't answer me. Her eyes take in Lilly's face as though she's inspecting her, making sure she's not cracked or broken.

"Anyway, I'm going home today. To get my stuff out before you and Cal get back."

"Don't do that, Drew," Lindsey says sadly.

"This vacation is most definitely over," I tell her.

"I'm sorry, Drew," she says softly before kissing Lilly's cheek again. "I never wanted this to happen."

"Then why did you do it?"

Lindsey looks at Lilly, not me. Her eyes are sad. "I don't know."

"Do you love him?" I didn't want to ask this question. In fact, I'm quite sure I really don't want to know the answer. Still, the words slipped from my mouth before I could stop them.

Lindsey turns her eyes toward mine. She gazes at me for a few seconds, and then her lips part. "I…"

It's all I need. She does love him. She loves another woman's husband and not her own. All I can do is nod my head. A person can't force another person to love them. Love is organic. Lindsey doesn't love me anymore. Maybe she never loved me. I loved her, though—at one time.

"Drew, you can't just leave." Lindsey catches my arm as I turn toward the door.

I spin on my heels and face her. "What would you have me do then? Continue to sit here the rest of the week while watching you three have a vacation together? Do you understand how sick and demented it was what you and Cal did this week? No one does that. Ever. So yes, Lindsey, I *can* just leave."

"What about Jessica?"

I grit my teeth, feeling fury build in my chest because I never want to hear Jess' name come out of Lindsey's mouth again. "You don't get to ask about her." I seethe.

"For the record, Cal has never had anything negative to say about Jessica."

"Why would he?"

"He just couldn't figure out to help her when she had cancer. He didn't know what to do, and so he just..." She shrugs as though Cal's actions were okay.

I look at Lindsey in disbelief. "Well, let's hope you don't end up with cancer in the future. He'll abandon you the way he did Jess." With that, I walk out the door.

Jess is sitting in my car when I return to Joyce's house. She's scrolling through her phone and startles when I tap on the glass. "Sorry, didn't mean to scare you!" I say through the window. I can't help but laugh, though. Why is it always a bit comical when one succeeds at startling another?

"Ready to go home," she says to me through the glass.

"Let me at least say goodbye to Joyce—thank her for everything. Well, except for the kidnapping."

Jess giggles. "I'll go with you."

I open the car door for her, and she jumps out of the SUV. Jess looks up at me before we walk back up to Joyce's front door. "Are you okay?"

I gaze down into her eyes for a moment, and then I smile. "I will be."

"And Lindsey?"

"Something tells me they'll all live happily ever after."

Joyce still hasn't found her pep in the half hour we've been away. But how could she? Her husband left her on vacation for doing something that had only really helped Jess and me. I can't be angry at her for it because I know she took Lilly with no intention of harming her. I still want to be angry at her for it, though, because it made Cal and Linds' confessions a bit hasher than it might have been in a civil conversation. There's no point in shaming her for the kidnapping anymore. She knows exactly what she did, and I am willing to bet she'll never do it again.

"We're headed home," I tell Joyce as we step inside her beach house. "Lilly has been delivered safely to her mother. We've had our conversations with our almost ex-spouses. It's time to go."

Joyce smiles at both of us with tears in her eyes, and then she hugs Jess and me individually before speaking again. "I'm sorry for what I did. I am. I don't—"

"Joyce, it's okay," I interrupt her. "Truly. Though a heads-up would have been nice," I joke. It's not really a joke. I really would have appreciated a heads-up.

"I think the greatest tragedy of this entire week would be if you two went home and never saw each other again," Joyce says to us. Her eyes bounce between Jess and me.

"We'll be in touch," Jess promises. "At this point, I'm not sure we have a choice."

"I've never met anyone like you, Joyce. I'd like to keep you," I add with a smile.

"I think I'd like that," Joyce replies. "I am sorry your vacation is ending so soon, though. You two deserved a whole week."

"Maybe we'll have another." Jess smiles.

"We should probably get going," I say. "We have quite the drive ahead of us."

"Please be safe, both of you," Joyce says like a typical mother, except that we aren't her children.

There's something about driving away from the coast that has never really set well in my soul. I always imagine the distance between the coast and me, stretching like a rubber band the further I get. I've always said that a very large chunk of my heart resides on the coast, and it does. I can physically feel the pull when the distance is great.

I'm grateful to be going home, though. And I'm grateful to be going home with Jess. It's funny—I arrived here with one woman, and I'm leaving with a different one. I could laugh about it if the whole thing wasn't so tragic. Maybe one day, we'll be able to laugh about it. Maybe next week. Not today, though. Today, the emotions are wild. I can't really pick one and stick with it. The emotions vary with every passing minute.

I glance at Jess in the passenger seat. She's got the window down, gazing out across the flatlands of the South Carolina Lowcountry. The Lowcountry is beautiful. It's a scene I'm certain I could live in for the rest of my life. Of course, Jess only adds to the beauty of the scene. Her thick, dark hair floats on the breeze coming through the rolled-down window. Her eyes, hidden behind her sunglasses, closed. Her face is turned into the sun. I wonder what she's thinking about. I can only imagine. She's a woman, so I imagine she's likely going down a list of things she has to do when she gets home. Or maybe she's reliving her memories with Cal. She could be doing both at the same time. She might not be thinking about anything at all.

I've always admired women. It started with my mother. Their ability to multitask and think about a thousand different things all at one time has never ceased to amaze me. I'm such a single-minded man. The only thing I'm thinking of right now is how beautiful Jess is.

It's impossible to explain, but I do believe I have fallen into something with Jess. Too soon to call it love, I think, but it's something. We need time and space right now, though, and we'll both need a friend. And just because I'm angry with and hurt by my wife doesn't mean that I won't have to reconcile our relationship eventually. I'm that sort of person.

For now, though, I think we have to start processing what exactly has happened. It really goes beyond infidelity. Jess can't have a child, so Cal created one without her. Lindsey lied about who Lilly belonged to. Somehow, I think I could have dealt with the affair. Jess could have, too. It would have hurt, but we could have dealt with that.

I've believed Lilly was my daughter ever since the day Linds told me she was pregnant. I've loved her like she was my own flesh and blood. I used to sit and stare at her, trying to find something in her that looked like me. That was really the only thing about being her father that freaked me out. The kid has never looked like me. Not a nose or a dimple or even in the way her eyebrows arch when she's upset. Nothing about Lilly resembles me.

In a lot of ways, Linds and I divorced a long time ago. There hasn't been much love between us for quite some time, but still, we remained together because it was easy. Divorce is messy. It throws your whole life in shambles. It costs a lot of money, too. If Linds and I both had to admit to something, I think we would admit that we stayed together because it was cheaper that way. And convenient. Neither of us willing to mess up the routines and schedules we've established.

I can't answer why Jess and Cal remained together. I've not had that conversation with her yet, but I can't really fathom why Jess stayed with him after she was cancer-free. His neglect through that process alone was enough to file for divorce. And yet she didn't.

Still, as I drive us home with Jess in the seat next to me, Sweeney in the backseat, and the sun warm through the windshield, I can't help but feel happy. I *am* happy, despite the pain in my heart, despite it all.

On the horizon is a road sign that reads, *Greenville 200 miles*.

Jess turns her head toward me, pulling back her hair. She smiles wide and says with excitement, "What if we don't go home? What if we never go home?"

31
Jess Dawson

It was out of my mouth before I could stop it. I'm not sure what came over me, but all I could think about as Drew drove us further from the coast was how bad I don't want to go home. I can't really explain all of the reasons I don't want to go home, but I'd confess to one of them being that I really just don't feel like packing up my life with Cal. I'm not ready to face our home, our things, our life.

"We certainly do not have to go home today," Drew says after a bit of silent shock at my suggestion. He begins to veer off onto the exit for a rest area. "Before I go any further, though, let's figure this out."

"It's crazy. I shouldn't have said it," I say quickly. "We must go home. We have to pack up our things up before they come home."

"Why should they get to enjoy the rest of their vacation?" Drew asks me. "Seriously? We both know they'll live out the rest of their vacation together. They're not going home early either. So, why should we?"

"Don't you think the week is pretty much ruined? How do we keep going, knowing what we're facing?"

"It can be ruined, or we can make the best of it. I'm in favor of the latter. We don't have to go back to Edisto, but there's a thousand beaches along South Carolina's coast. We could go anywhere you want to go."

"Anywhere?" I think about this for a few minutes. I've always loved Edisto Island, but we do have at least a hundred beaches (a thousand is a bit dramatic) we could consider.

"Jess, for you, I'll go anywhere," Drew says to me.

"But isn't this weird? I mean, we hardly know each other. Again, how can I be sure you're not a serial killer?" I'm only halfway joking.

"It's only weird if we make it weird, and I swear, I'm not a serial killer. Stalker, maybe. Not a murderer, though."

I smack his arm in a playful manner, laughing at his stalker joke. He does have stalker tendencies (thinking back to the text message from him the other night while we were out for ice cream), but I really don't think he has a mean bone in his body. When I look at Drew, I don't feel threatened or afraid. I feel safe and warm. I'd know if he were bad, and he's good. I'm willing to bet he's a better human than I am, and I feel like I'm a pretty decent human. Still, one look into Drew's eyes and you just know—he's good.

"What about Folly Beach? It's not far," Drew suggests.

Folly is a cute, little beach town, but it's generally pretty crowded, even in the off-season. But then I think about this really good Mexican restaurant on Folly's pier. I really can't recall if the restaurant was really that good or if it's because I had a taco on a pier at the beach on Cinco de Mayo.

"I had a really good burger on Sullivan's Island one time." Drew breaks into my thoughts.

"Are we picking a beach based on restaurants or good beach sitting?" I ask. Strange that I was thinking about tacos on Folly, while Drew was apparently thinking about burgers on Sullivan's Island.

"I think both are pretty important attributes to consider."

He's not wrong. They are important. A good beach has amazing restaurants and stress-free beach-sitting. Some of South Carolina's beaches have gotten so crowded, one would need to sleep on the beach to secure a spot for sitting the next day.

"You said you had a good burger on Sullivan's?" I mean, the tacos on Folly were amazing, but I really can't ever pass up a good burger.

"Probably the best I've ever had—Poe's Tavern. I remember the menu had Edgar Allan Poe's face as a backdrop." I can visibly see Drew visiting this restaurant again in his head. "There were signs and photos all over the restaurant of Edgar Allan Poe and his work. It was a cool place."

I think about it a few more minutes and then decide, "Sullivan's Island it is! And if that burger isn't the best burger I've ever had, I'll be sorely disappointed in your burger tastes."

"That's just not fair. What if they're having an off night when we go, and everything is horrible, right down to the service?"

I shrug. "If they're as amazing as you say they are, they shouldn't have an off night." I point out.

"I've worked in the restaurant industry. It's not that simple."

"I've worked in the restaurant industry as well, and it is. Just depends on how you run your ship."

"Okay, we can argue about this later." Drew puts the SUV in reverse to back out of the parking spot he had pulled into. "Sullivan's Island for the rest of the week!"

"Sounds like a lot of time, but it's not."

"You're sort of a pessimist, aren't you?"

"I'd like to think of it as being logical."

Drew laughs. "I guess that makes sense, too. You're a realist."

"I'm very much a realist," I agree. "Cal used to call me Debbie Downer, but it's not negativity. Not all the time."

"I get it." Drew pulls out onto the interstate again, but this time, we're heading back in the direction of the coast and Sullivan's Island. "I'm more of a dreamer myself, but we need people like you to keep us grounded."

"If we all acted and thought and spoke the same, this world would be quite boring."

Perhaps this is also why I enjoy people-watching. Observing others is sort of a hobby of mine. I like to note their differences, especially if I'm observing a couple or a group of friends.

We all have a role in this world, and if we all worked together, the world would run like a well-oiled machine. The problem is that humans aren't always that great at working with each other. We like to take full credit for discoveries and inventions, even if someone else helped us get there.

Somewhere, somehow, we forgot how to work together. We became divided in our own communities, and selfish motives took over. It's always a treat when I witness a human helping another human, but really, should it be a treat? Shouldn't we see these things daily? It's not hard to stand out when being kind because people just really aren't all that nice anymore. Generally speaking, of course. There are still thousands, if not millions, of beautiful and kind people walking the globe.

Maybe that's what changed Cal—selfish ambition. He climbed the socioeconomic ladder rather quickly, and I climbed it with him. But now that I think back on his success, the higher he climbed the ladder, the further we grew apart. He sacrificed things to get to where he is now in his career. He's not as valiant as he sounds, though. He sacrificed things like morals, ethics, honesty—good, basic human values. That's what he sacrificed. He had gotten so good at lying at work, he became a pro at home. Even when I knew he was lying, his story was so convincing, accusing him of lying wasn't an option.

It's been less than twenty-four hours since Cal's confession on the beach, and in a lot of ways, I'm having a hard time believing this has even happened. I've not really been able to wrap my mind around it, and I don't really know how I should feel, anyway. Broken, angry, relieved, confused, optimistic. There's an entire catalog of emotions I'm currently feeling, and I can't land on just one. It's like they're all mushed together, and I'm unable to tell one from the other.

But one question I keep coming back to is why didn't I say something? Confront him? I knew. I knew, and yet I told myself I was crazy.

I guess I was afraid. I didn't want to accept the truth. So, I sacrificed every ounce of my being just to pretend to be happy. Maybe I pretended for too long because now I can't even connect with myself long enough to filter through the mushy emotions. I realize now that I've survived the last few years by dividing myself into two different people. Oblivious Jess was obviously a coping mechanism so that I didn't have to truly face what I knew was going on, but Aware Jess did a little pretending, too. I pretended things would go back to normal. I pretended that time would heal it all.

Perhaps that's how I feel—like I deserved this. I did let him keep going, pretending he wasn't doing anything wrong at all. Now, I can see how I was selfish, too. The narratives I made up in my mind protected me, for the time being, but eventually it hurt not only myself but Drew, too. He's lived the last year or so believing he had a daughter.

What if I had said something when I first figured out that Cal was having an affair? When I knew his red-stained lips weren't caused from red wine? When his car smelled of women's perfume? If I had done something then, maybe that would have changed things now.

Granted, the affair would still be there, but the lies wouldn't. Not all of them, anyway.

That's the other thing about life. There are so many paths we can take in making one simple decision. There aren't a whole lot of signs telling us which road to take, so we take the roads that feel comfortable to us, even if it doesn't seem right.

I knew that I needed to confront Cal a long time ago. I didn't. And now an entire vacation has blown up in my face, affecting not only myself, but also Drew, Joyce, Harold, and an innocent baby. My one decision to do nothing led to a much larger issue.

In my defense, how could I have known that this is how it would end? I'm not a psychic or a prophet. I'm just a thirty-something female trying to make the best of this life she's been given, trying to believe the best in people. Trying to survive.

32
Drew Clark

I had not expected Jess to suggest we not go home. I had assumed it's all she wanted. This is why I was bit a shocked when she looked at me with those big, beautiful eyes of hers and asked what would happen if we never went home.

I'm still figuring Jess out, but so far, I'm enjoying the person I am getting to know. She's sort of a loose cannon, and I like that. Lindsey is a loose cannon, too, but in a dysfunctional manner. Jess is logical. She's real. She's blunt. Jess isn't afraid to change the narrative. What if we didn't go home? Who said we had to? Everyone who cares knows we're on vacation this week. Even with the original vacation ruined, we don't have to miss out on the last few days. We can save this vacation!

"There aren't any hotels on Sullivan's Island." Jess is staring at the screen of her phone, scrolling, searching for us a place to stay.

"It's sort of a fancy, little island," I tell her. "We'll probably have to find a small cottage."

Jess turns her head slowly in my direction. "Drew Clark, we are absolutely not sharing a bed."

"Who said anything about sharing a bed? We'll get a two-bedroom cottage."

I see her shake her head at me from the corner of my eye, and then she goes back to scrolling.

People Watching

"Listen, I'm not trying to get in your pants." I say this rather bluntly. I suppose Jess is rubbing off on me a little, but I figure it's best to clear the air now. "I've not had sex in quite some time, so very honestly, it's the furthest thing from my mind. I'm not even sure if it works anymore." I'm mostly joking now. Well, at least about the part about whether or not it still works. It works. I think.

"I really could have gone the rest of my life without knowing the second part of that statement—the second *and* third part. I don't need to know how long it's been and whether you can get it up or not."

I can't help but laugh, which triggers her to laugh, too.

"I wonder if every day is like this with you." It was a thought in my mind that somehow made its way to my tongue and then out into the open.

Jess looks at me, wiping her tears from laughter. "Like what?"

I shrug my shoulders, keeping my eyes on the road. "You're not like any girl I've ever met."

"Well, I'm not a girl," she says. "I'm a woman."

"Obviously. You know what I'm saying, Jess. You're different—good different. Like a breath of fresh air. You just say what you want to say, regardless of how it may sound. I like that."

"That may be true, except that I didn't say what I wanted to say to my husband a few years ago, and now look what's happened," she says dryly.

"I had a cousin once," Jess says, beginning a story. "We were quite close when I was a kid; but when he went to middle school, he started getting into trouble with drugs and such, and we drifted.

"I was a senior in high school when he and my grandmother got into an altercation. It ended with her in the hospital and a brain bleed. She survived, but she was never the same again. She never walked again. I didn't think I could ever forgive him. He changed her entire life.

"A few years later, enough time had passed; and I realized that somewhere along the way, I had forgiven him. At that point, my grandmother had died, and there was really no reason for me to continue harboring this anger I had toward him. I had typed out a letter to send to him on social media, but I just couldn't send it—not because I had changed my mind on forgiving him but because I was afraid of how he might feel when he read my message.

"Two days after I had written the letter, my cousin died in a car wreck. I was devastated. I was angry at myself for not sending him the letter—not that I believe he died waiting on my forgiveness, but what if I had sent it before he died? What if he read it, and my words had prevented him from getting in the car that night to go to a club?" Jess shrugs her shoulders. She's quiet for a few seconds.

"What if I had called Cal out as soon as I realized he was having an affair? None of what happened this week would have gone down. You would have never had to believe Lilly was your daughter. Instead, I knew something was up, and I just let it grow."

"Jess, you can't shoulder things like that. You had no way of knowing your cousin was going to pass away in a car accident, and you definitely had no idea that the affair our spouses are having with each other was going to become what it has."

"I don't think I blame myself. I just don't want to bite my tongue anymore," she says to me.

I understand that, too. Biting my tongue only made me a recluse. I thought I bit my tongue for peace—and maybe that was some of it—but mostly, I kept my mouth shut because it was easier. If I kept my mouth closed, then I could just exist. It's laziness, really. That's it. I didn't feel like fighting, so I didn't start a fight. I just took it.

Sullivan's Island is a small barrier island near the entrance of Charleston Harbor in South Carolina. It's only about a couple of miles long and has a population of less than three thousand. By that measure, it doesn't sound like much of an island at all, but I remember it giving me that town of Amity vibe from the movie, *Jaws*. As long as there aren't any great whites waiting to gobble us up, I think we'll have a couple of good days here.

Sullivan's Island reminds me, in many ways, of Tybee Island in Georgia. I've only been once, but the restaurants and shops along the main road on Sullivan's Island give me that same vintage feel of Tybee. So many beaches are now riddled with high-rises and ridiculous-sized restaurants, but not Sullivan's Island. Not Tybee. Not even Edisto. I think that's where the bulk of the charm of these little islands come from—the vintage feel.

"Poe's Tavern is coming up on the right," I tell Jess as I drive us down Middle Street. The shops and restaurants sit in a rainbow-colored row. Poe's has a white picket fence around the property, which just adds to its character.

Jess is gazing out the window. "It's such a cute, little island."

I smile, satisfied that she's happy. I've already spotted at least three different things that Lindsey would have snarled at. "It's got charm."

"Drew, I would not think any less of you if you, too, agreed that this place was cute." Jess looks at me now.

I glance at her for a second and feel a smile break across my face. "Fine, it's cute."

"See, that wasn't so hard." She smiles, satisfied now.

"A buddy of mine has a small house here that he doesn't rent out. It's for him, really. I'm going to give him a call and see if we can't stay. I don't think he'll say no, and besides, he owes me one."

"Ahh, a man who is owed something." Jess smirks.

"I broke a story on his behalf about a scandal going on among a few high school sports teams. It's not what I typically write about, but he asked me to do him a favor. He owes me a couple of nights in his Sullivan's Island cottage," I explain.

I pull into a public parking lot just off the beach to make my call. Jess unbuckles her seatbelt. "Sweeney and I are going to check out the beach while you call your connection." She winks at me before bouncing off to the beach with the dog following along happily by her side.

I dial my buddy, hoping this works out because if his home isn't available, I'm not sure what we'll do. Sullivan's Island isn't the cheapest place in the world to stay a night or two.

"Hey, Matt, it's Drew."

"Drew, you're supposed to be on vacation. What are you calling me for?" Matt generally cuts straight to the chase. He's not one for small talk, which makes sense because he's in sales.

"Well, that's a really long story, but to shorten it up a bit, I'm with a girl that's not my wife. We both discovered our spouses were cheating on us with each other, and so we're finishing off our vacation on Sullivan's Island. I was hoping your house wasn't occupied."

"Wait, back up. I think I need the longer version of the story."

"Matt, you'll get the longer version later. For now, can we use your house for a few nights? We'll be out by Saturday."

"I told you the house is always open to you," Matt says. "And it's available, so have at it. Just make sure you clean up before you leave."

"Of course," I oblige. "Thank you. I wasn't sure what we were going to do without your help. I sold Sullivan's Island to her on a good burger but then realized I might not have a whole lot left to offer."

"Are you going to tell me more about the girl?"

I laugh. "Her name is Jess. She's pretty amazing. Situation is complicated."

"Worst vacation ever?"

"In a sense, but then, it could end up being one of the best vacations. We'll see. For now, I just wanted to buy her a good burger from Poe's and provide her with a nice place to stay."

"Happy to help. Door code is 1987. Make yourself at home. We were just there last week, so it should be suitable."

"Thank you, Matt. You have no idea how thankful I am."

"Just know that you owe me the longer version of the story."

"As soon as I roll into Greenville on Saturday, I'll make you my first stop," I reply sarcastically.

Sweeney and Jess appear back over the dunes, and I find myself at a loss as I watch Jess come toward me. The breeze catches her hair perfectly; I feel like I'm watching her move toward me in slow motion. Somewhere in my imagination, a soft tune is playing. The moment is ruined when Sweeney forces her to stop so he can lift his leg and pee on the smokers' station sitting just off the sidewalk.

"We're all set!" I proclaim as she meets me at the SUV. "The cottage is just a few streets that way. I have the door code and everything."

Jess smiles at me. "Look at you. A man with means."

"I've always got means." I smile back.

I help Jess back into the SUV as she holds Sweeney in her arms, and then we start to the cottage.

"Your friend was cool with us staying a couple of nights?"

"He was. I thought he might be," I tell her. "He's a good guy. He just talks fast, and he's always to the point. He can be quite exhausting, actually. It's sort of like being around a ferret. He's usually everywhere all at once."

"Sounds like a few students I've had." Jess laughs. "But isn't that better than listening to ever minute detail of a story? I'd rather get the highlights. I don't need the details."

"But as a writer, the details are important. They make the story."

"True. I suppose details have their time and place."

The cottage appears on our right with its stately front porch. The white paint of the house only accentuates the orange front door, which screams Clemson University. Matt and his wife are lifetime Clemson Tiger fans. There's an American flag on one porch column and Clemson Tiger flag on the other. Both greet guests as they ascend the front porch steps. The porch itself has two swings hanging at either side and then a couple of sets of rocking chairs.

"This is beautiful!" Jess exclaims as I pull into the cobblestoned driveway. "I love that orange front door."

"Matt would be proud to hear you say that. It's a beautiful place. Lindsey never liked it here really. It's a bit too sleepy of a beach town for her. She always wants action—like water parks and miniature golf and Ferris wheels. I enjoy the laidback quiet of Sullivan's Island."

"We should stay here for a whole week," Jess says excitedly as she pushes the car door open and hops out, holding Sweeney.

"Maybe one day, we will." I say this before I understand what I'm suggesting.

I punch in the door code and swing that orange door open. The house smells clean as though it's not been closed up for a week or so. Jess and Sweeney walk in first, and I watch as Jess's eyes are wide, observing the interior of the house. It is charming. Matt and his wife are very good, very clean people. They have a meticulous eye for design, but then, they should. Matt's wife is an interior decorator. Some of her clients have been celebrities purchasing their own beach houses on Sullivan's Island and surrounding areas. Lindsey always assumed I had a crush on Matt's wife, but I don't. She's not really my type, but I've always appreciated her eye for artistic design.

"What do you have to do for a living to afford a house like this?" Jess is standing in the middle of the living room now, turning in a circle and taking in all of the unique features this old cottage home has. From the beadboard walls to the planked ceilings and the beautiful pine floors, it is exquisite.

"Two things you'll need to understand about Matt and his wife. One, Matt is a pretty swanky salesman for pharmaceuticals; and two, his wife, Gloria, is a professional interior decorator. They're not hurting for money, and Gloria knows how to decorate. It's sort of a win-win for both of them."

Jess looks at me, a smirk on her face. Her eyes have grown soft. "I'm glad I stayed with you. This place is a much better ending to our vacation. We deserve this."

"I definitely do not believe we deserved to cut our vacation short. We didn't do anything wrong."

"And we should take advantage of every second of the last day or so of vacation. Throw caution to the wind. Eat good food. Oooh, do they have sunset cruises? We could take a sunset cruise!"

Her excitement sends me into a bout of laughter. In a lot of ways, she reminds of a deprived child being taken into a candy store for the first time. It's pure and innocent joy. I don't meet too many people like Jess anymore. She's a treat.

"We still have a good burger to eat before we hop on a sunset cruise," I tell her.

"I need to calm down," she admits. "I just didn't expect this. I've never been to Sullivan's Island before, so I didn't have anything to expect, I suppose. But if I had had expectations, they have certainly been exceeded."

"I'm happy that you're happy."

"What does that mean?"

"Exactly what I said. It makes me happy to see you so happy. It's been a while since I've made a woman happy. So, forgive me if I feel a little prideful about it."

"You know what we should stop doing? At least for the remainder of the week?"

"What?"

"I won't compare you to Cal, and you don't compare me to Lindsey."

"We haven't been doing that, have we?"

Jess's face sort of crinkles. "Yeah, a little bit, if you think about it."

She's not wrong. I did just compare Jess's happiness with Lindsey's unhappiness.

"Okay, how about this? No mention of Lindsey and no mention of Cal for the rest of the week. It's just you and me and this fancy island."

"And supposedly, the best burger you've ever had," Jess adds.

"Yes, that too. Speaking of which, are you hungry?"

"I thought you'd never ask! I'm famished."

"Maybe we aim for Poe's for lunch? It's a bit harder to get into at night."

"I could definitely go for a big burger for lunch. Let's go. I'll leave Sweeney here to rest a bit. He's not always a social doggy."

Sweeney is already curled up on the couch, his eyes heavy, giving his official approval of the cottage. It's definitely a few steps up from

People Watching

the motel we slept in last night.

33
Joyce Rose

Harold is the kind of man who will leave his wife at the beach, drive all the way home just to prove a point, and then realize that he can't just leave his wife elsewhere, so he has to turn around and drive all the way back. I knew he wouldn't leave me here forever, but I wasn't exactly disappointed to call Edisto home either. Regardless, our vacation is over, so I've packed our things and am waiting on Harold to return.

Maybe I should give my people-watching habits a break. I crossed the line this time, and I see that. Poor Harold thought I was going to jail. I can only assume his fear was rooted in flashbacks from the first and only time he's ever had to be bail me out of jail. Still, he's never actually left me like that, and perhaps that shook me more than anything.

Now, Drew and Jess have left, and I've had to watch the two homewreckers with their daughter enjoy the last bit of their vacation together. I know they've practically spent the whole week with each other, anyway; but now they've set up their spot on the beach together, and if you ask me, they look too smug sitting there like that. I've decided I will confront them. I know, I said I was done people-watching for a while; but I need to tell them this one thing, and then I'll go home and never think about either of those two people ever again. Of course, I don't expect the one thing I need to tell them to make any difference, but I must try.

Harold is about thirty minutes out from Edisto Island, so I decide now is the time to confront Cal and Lindsey. I can't imagine the confrontation will take thirty minutes, but I need an escape plan in case things go awry. That's why I needed to wait until Harold was closer to Edisto before I could get the last word in.

Cal is the first one to notice me as I approach. His facial expression falls, and he doesn't stand from his chair. He knows exactly who I am, even though we've yet to officially meet this week.

"Hi." I smile wide as I stand in front of both of them, obscuring their view of the ocean. I peek at Lilly curled up in her beach tent, sleeping soundly.

Lindsey and Cal both stare at me, regarding me and wondering what on earth I'm doing here, I suppose.

"I just wanted to say a few things to you before I leave."

Cal says, "There's nothing left to say."

"Oh, but I think there is." I keep my smile. "You need to understand exactly what you've done to two of the best people I've ever had the privilege of meeting."

"That's not necessary, Joyce. We are both *very* well aware of how we've hurt our spouses." Lindsey speaks now.

"Well, I'm going to tell you, anyway." I plop down in the sand right in front of them, ready to tell them my story—the reason I had to get involved in their lives this week and could not turn a blind eye.

"Joyce, this really isn't necessary. Just like Linds said. And honestly, it's really none of your business. None of us knew who you were before this week began, so your opinion really doesn't matter," Cal says, annoyance creeping into his tone.

I think about driving a seashell through his right eye, but instead, I continue to smile and then begin my story. Cal rolls his eyes.

"Harold is not my first husband. And I know you probably don't know who Harold is, but he was the grumpy-looking man walking around this week. Anyway, that's not important. Before Harold and I married, I was married to his best friend. I was head over heels for that man. He was in the United States Army and very handsome—and he loved me. I felt so very lucky.

"Three months after we were married, he was deployed overseas. We wrote letters constantly until he was eight months into his deployment. That's when the letters stopped. Of course, I had worried that he had been killed. I knew the letters could stop or delay if combat was intense or if they were moving and unable to write, but after three weeks of no letters, I finally called his mother.

"She acted like she didn't even remember having a son, like she didn't even remember me. It was so odd, but I immediately knew something else was going on, something no one was telling me. It definitely felt like his mother was keeping something from me."

Lindsey interrupts. "And what made you think that?"

"Well, for one, when I called and asked if she had heard from Freddie, she promptly responded with 'Freddie? Freddie, who?'"

Lindsey glances at Cal and then back to me.

"I called Harold. He was my last resort. I didn't know him all that well, but we had spent a little time together in the past. I thought he'd tell me the truth, even if I didn't really know what the truth was. All I knew was my husband had stopped writing me, and my mother-in-law apparently had amnesia.

"At first, Harold didn't want to tell me anything. I think it had more to do with him not wanting to tell me the truth over the phone because he asked if we could meet somewhere in person. At this suggestion, I knew that I wasn't going crazy. Something really was going on. So, Harold took a train into Atlanta, where I was living at the time, and we had dinner together. That's when he told me my husband had met someone in Vietnam. Freddie had written Harold to tell him and then to ask him if he'd break the news to me. Harold had been sitting on that letter for two weeks, unable to figure out how he was supposed to tell me my husband had fallen in love with someone else."

I look at Cal and Lindsey, drop the smile on my face, and say, "There are a lot of things that can go through your mind when you find out you've been cheated on—when you've found out that your spouse, the one who promised forever, actually didn't mean forever at all. Now, Freddie and I were only married a few months, but you two? You both had more than a decade with them."

I look at Lindsey now. "You made him think Lilly was his daughter." And then to Cal, I say, "And you? You made her think she was crazy, so she wouldn't ask so many questions." Now, I look at both of them. "But I'll tell you both one thing right now—those two people knew exactly what was going on and had talked themselves into not believing it and not confronting it. Why? Because they had hope. They loved you. Lindsey, Drew loved you more than the man sitting next to you ever will."

Cal seems to choke on his tongue, trying to speak.

"I'm not done yet," I tell him, putting my index finger in the air to hush him up.

"Cal, your wife was nearly eaten alive by cancer, and you left her to fight that battle all by herself while you were out and about starting this affair."

"We never meant to hurt them," Lindsey says again.

"How did you think it was going to make them feel when the truth came out?"

Cal and Lindsey swap glances.

"In my defense, I wanted to tell them as soon as Lindsey found out she was pregnant," Cal chimes in, seemingly throwing Lindsey under the bus now.

Lindsey's mouth falls open, and she glares at Cal now. "That's not even true!"

"It is true if you'll remember it correctly. I told you we had to tell them, and you insisted on waiting. I missed her first birthday, Linds."

I stare at Cal, incredulously. He really does think he's a victim. I recognize his innate ability to force someone to question themselves. I can physically see Lindsey recalling that conversation in her head, and it doesn't appear that her memory is lining up with Cal's. But she won't say anything because that's how men like Cal control people. They force others to believe their truth because anything outside of that didn't happen. It's manipulation. It's something I grew up in and something I can spot so clearly now.

I stand up from the sand. "I'll say one last thing—don't make this difficult for either of them. You know what you did."

Cal's mouth opens again, but nothing comes out. Lindsey casts her eyes away from me. I give them one final look before I turn and leave.

My heart is racing from the confrontation, but I feel better, too. I couldn't leave this island without telling them my story and trying to make them understand what they have done to Drew and Jess. Humans walk around every day making decisions that they think won't affect anyone but them. That isn't true. It's not true for the drug addict or the alcoholic or the abuser or the cheater. Every decision we make affects others, regardless of what the decision is. All decisions, good and bad, have a chain reaction of circumstances that follow, good and bad.

When Harold pulls up, I'm sitting on the steps of our home with our luggage in front of me. He gets out of the car as quickly as he can and comes to me first, wrapping his arms around my body and then kissing my lips. It feels good to have his arms around me again. I missed him last night.

"Are you okay?" he asks me.

I smile up at him. "I'm just fine. And you'll be glad to know I've decided to take a break from people-watching."

"Oh, thank goodness!" he exhales a breath of relief. "I'm an old man, Joyce. I can't take much more of your teenage antics."

I laugh at my husband. "How did you survive our kids and me?" Our kids did take after me mostly. They were always into something as they were growing up—nothing we couldn't handle, but I did find myself craving quiet Friday nights for once. Our Friday nights were never quiet once the kids got into middle and high school.

"I've got a strong ticker." He claims, tapping his chest, "And it helps that I love you and our children."

"I'm sorry for what I did, Harold."

He smiles at me. "I know you are. I'm sorry for leaving you. Guess that didn't make me any better than the offenders in this year's people-watching extravaganza, did it?"

"You've done a lot of things, but you'll never be him. And for that, I'm thankful." I kiss my husband. "Let's go home."

34
Jess Dawson

It's not that I doubted Drew could find us a nice place on Sullivan's Island. I just had no idea he had these types of connections. What I've learned about Drew this week is that he's very unassuming. He's quiet. He's caring, but he also doesn't say everything that he wants to say. He bites his tongue more than he should. I think the real Drew is still there somewhere, but his wife, undoubtedly, has spent their marriage making sure Drew was where she needed him to be.

I'm not sure what forced me to decide that I wasn't ready to go home yet. A lot of it was that I don't think I should have to end my vacation early because of what Cal did. I would have been fine with a fleabag motel on some shabby beach on the coast, but Drew's connection for the cottage on Sullivan's Island beats everything—even the house back on Edisto we rented for the week.

Of course, if we never had to go home and I could stay here in this cottage with Drew and my dog for the rest of my life, I think I'd be satisfied. That's not an option, though, so I've decided I will enjoy every second of the rest of this vacation with Drew—as friends, obviously. But I have found myself growing increasingly enamored with him. He's incredibly attractive—that much is obvious—but he is also unfolding into a man of many wonders. My first impression of him—besides his incredibly handsome attributes—was that he is a passive man. But I think that couldn't be further from the truth.

Drew's not passive. He became passive to survive. He does know a lot of things. He has feelings, too—something I think Lindsey would be shocked to find out about her husband. I wish I had known Drew my whole life, but there is something about him that makes me feel as though I have.

"Are you sure you want to leave Sweeney behind?" Drew asks me as we gather our things before heading out the door for Poe's Tavern. We decided to walk, since it's not far and the temperature outside is perfect.

I glance over at my sweet boy curled up on the couch. He appears content. "I think he'll be okay. He's tired."

"How can you tell?"

"He's lying down."

"I guess that makes sense."

"When was the last time you had a dog of your own?"

Drew thinks for a few seconds and then replies, "Not since my black lab died. Before I went to college. Lindsey—"

"We are not talking about Lindsey anymore!" I cut him off, but I have to. I don't want to hear Lindsey's name anymore, and I don't want to say Cal's. Heck, I don't even want to think about them. Either of them.

Drew smacks his face. "I've not had a dog since my lab died," he says, leaving Lindsey out of the answer this time.

"I'm getting you a dog for your birthday," I say as I walk to the front door.

"You don't even know when my birthday is." Drew opens the front door for me.

I step out onto the porch. "You feel like a summer birthday. I bet you were born in June. Oh, and when we get back, I want to sit on this porch and have ice cream. It looks like a front porch conducive for eating ice cream."

"How did you do that?"

"Do what?"

"How did you guess my birthday is in June?" Drew appears slightly freaked out by my fortune-telling abilities. But it's not sorcery. I'm an empath. I just know these things.

"Oh, I was right?" I try to act shocked because I forget that sometimes my empathic abilities do scare others. I think they think I've got a voodoo doll or something on hand.

"What day do you think I was born?"

"Hold on, I have to look at you for this." So, we stop walking, and I look him over. He appears uncomfortable, his green eyes scanning me as I evaluate him. "Hmm, I think you were probably born sometime between June fifteenth and June twenty-fifth."

His eyes widen. "June twenty-third."

I smile proudly. "See? This is what a lifelong hobby of people-watching gets you—the ability to know personal details about a person without them having to tell you."

"It's creepy."

"No, creepy would be if I could guess what color underwear you're wearing."

Drew laughs at this. "I bet you can't guess what color underwear I'm wearing."

"I'm not guessing your underwear color, Drew Clark."

"Fair enough." He may be blushing slightly.

Poe's Tavern sticks out among its other peers along Middle Street. The building itself is surrounded by a white picket fence, and a wooden sign baring Edgar Allan Poe's face and the words "Poe's Tavern" hangs at the entrance. The restaurant looks like an old house that was converted into a restaurant. There's patio seating, deck seating, and then more seating inside the building.

"You want to eat outside?" Drew asks, pointing to a vacant picnic table with a big, blue umbrella shading it.

"Always outside, unless it's winter." I smile.

We order our burgers and a couple of cocktails; and then, for no reason at all, we can both be visibly seen, relaxing into our seats as though we've just come out of combat. In a lot of ways, it feels like we've just survived a battle. This may be the first moment in this entire week that I feel I've been able to finally take a breath. Cal had been weird since we left the house on Saturday morning, and I don't think I ever fully unraveled on Edisto. I feel like I've been tense and alert. On vacation, one should be soft and oblivious.

"I'm so mad," I hear myself say. It was more of a thought, but I guess the thought slipped right on through my lips.

"What's wrong?"

"This is so nice, and it's just a restaurant; but it's the nicest I have felt all week."

"You're drinking alcohol. I'm sure it helps."

"I'm being serious, Drew." I kick him lightly under the table. "I can breathe."

Drew thinks on this for a few quiet moments, and then he agrees with me. "I did just realize that I'm not consciously living in fear of the next time she says my name."

"We're not supposed to be talking about them," I remind him.

"I didn't say a name. Besides, in a roundabout way, you're talking about them."

I guess he's not wrong. "Well, how do we enjoy this without thinking about them?"

"I think once the burger arrives, you'll never think of either of them ever again," Drew says. "I'm telling you, it's so good, you'll get amnesia."

At this, I laugh. "This drink is pretty good, too."

"Better than the Long Island on the pier back at Edisto?"

"Dare I say, maybe?" I take another sip of my drink. "It's pretty good."

Soon, our burgers are laid out in front of us. I got the Annabel Lee, and Drew got the Pit & Pendulum. There's only a small part of me that's fearful of eating burgers named from Edger Allan Poe's poetry collection.

"Oh, my goodness." I never talk when my mouth is full, but this burger requires an exception. "This is amazing." I cover my mouth as I speak, trying to hold in its contents. I don't want to waste a single bite of this burger.

"I told you," Drew says proudly. "Best burger you'll ever put in your mouth. Oh, and try those fries. Those fries are something else!"

"You should be one of those food bloggers for your news site. You could travel around, trying all the burgers, and then write about your favorite ones."

Drew laughs. "I can't stand food bloggers!"

"Seriously?"

"Seriously. You'd have to know these people. I mean, some of them are decent people; but they tend to be some of the pickiest, rudest, and most high-maintenance people you'll ever meet."

"If they're rude, why would you want to dine with them, anyway?"

"Well, they do have pretty good taste in restaurants, and they usually get the food for free."

"So, basically, you take advantage of your food-blogging friends—not because you like them but because they could get you free, high-priced food."

Drew shrugs. "When you put it that way, it makes me sound like a horrible person."

"You think 'horrible,' but I find it intelligent—selfish intelligence maybe, but when it comes to food, you're allowed to be so."

"I feel like you should be an eight-hundred-pound woman."

"Because I like food?"

"I bought your breakfast yesterday morning," Drew reminds me. "I've never seen a woman eat that much food first thing in the morning."

"I told you, I wake up in the morning completely starved. I can't help it."

"I like it. Most women are scared to eat in front of other people. You have no fear."

"I've never understood women afraid to eat in front of others. We all have to eat to live. It's not like it's a secret. I mean, I guess if you're standing over a buffet shoving fistfuls of mashed potatoes in your mouth, that could be a problem. But in general, it's perfectly normal to eat."

"If I could stand over a buffet and eat anything I wanted with zero regard to my appearance, I would be shoving fistfuls of macaroni and cheese in my mouth," Drew says right before he shoves in about six fries.

"I think I'd go for the dessert buffet. Cookie after cookie. Maybe a few slices of lemon pie. Definitely the brownies."

"Why are we talking about food like we've been living in famine? We're adults. We could literally stand over the dessert buffet and shove our faces with whatever we want, and no one is going to say anything."

"That's not completely true. I got my family kicked out of a buffet once when I was a kid," I confide.

"How do you get a whole family kicked out of a buffet?"

"I was standing under the chocolate fountain with my mouth wide open, catching it all. I was proud that the chocolate never landed anywhere else but my mouth. Not even a drizzle of chocolate in my hair or my shirt. It was perfection. I couldn't understand why the staff at that buffet couldn't appreciate the talent."

"Probably had something to do with sanitation laws," Drew points out sarcastically.

"Oh, please! It's a buffet. We won't even talk about the metal tongs that *everyone* in the buffet line touches to grab their chicken tenders."

"I've not been to a buffet in many years for that very reason."

"Same," I agree. "Sometimes, I miss being a kid, unphased by germs. I'm a bit of a germophobe now." At least, I can admit to it. I use hand sanitizer before and after I pump gasoline into my car. I also apply hand sanitizer before and after I have to touch the handle of a buggy in a grocery store.

Anyway, the thing that gets most people about me is that I absolutely will not drink after anyone else. I never drank after Cal. I don't know if it's trauma from all the backwash my little brother would leave in my afterschool Dr. Pepper treat or what. Regardless, I have to be close to dying from dehydration before I will drink after someone. And by close, I would have already needed to lose consciousness because even if drinking after someone else is the only thing that's going to save my life, I would never agree to it.

It's midafternoon now. Our stomachs are full from lunch, but we take the walk back to the cottage and decide to hit the beach for a couple of hours. A sunny day on the beach should never go unappreciated.

Drew carries my beach chair on his back while holding his own in his left hand. We packed a cooler with some water bottles that we found in the refrigerator at the cottage. Drew assured me that Matt would not miss the waters. He'd actually be angrier if he visited his home and found water bottles in the refrigerator. Matt, too, is a bit of a clean freak, which explains the quality of the cottage. I've been afraid to even wear my shoes across those hardwood floors. It's all so immaculate.

"I'm glad we didn't go home," I tell Drew as we pad across the sand in our bare feet. The sand is pretty hot, but there's no sense in being a sissy about it. Hot sand burning the bottoms of one's feet is guaranteed to make one a bit more resilient. Resilient against what, I'm not sure.

Drew cocks his head to the left and grins. "I am, too."

"If we had kept driving, we'd already be home. It would be quiet, lonely. This is better. You and me, Sullivan's Island, and a belly full of the best burgers we've ever had." I look back out in front of me, spotting a place for our chairs.

"It is 2023. We never have to go home if we don't want to. We can get divorced virtually. We can hire movers to pack our things and bring them to us. If you don't want to, we never have to go home."

"You forget a few things. While your job goes wherever you go, I actually need a job. I've got a little money for myself stowed away that should get me by until Cal starts paying out my half. But we should handle this like two grown adults. And then, when it's over, we can still call the movers to pack our things and bring them to wherever we end up."

"I noticed there was a lot of *we's* in that statement," Drew points out.

He doesn't miss a single thing.

"Hypothetically."

Drew stops in the exact place in the sand that I had spotted just moments before and sets up our chairs. Then he pulls out the umbrella and gets it situated correctly the first try. He remembered how to use the twisty thingy. We both nestle into our chairs, and then I hear us sigh, together, as the weight of the last twenty-four hours is shrugged from our shoulders.

Give it to the breeze. That's what my mom used to tell me when I was having a hard time as a kid. Today, I'm giving it to the ocean breeze.

"I could take a nap," Drew says after we sit there quietly for a few minutes.

The sun is warm and enveloping. I could take a nap, too. Why can't we take a nap? I turn my head to Drew. "We can take a nap."

"All I can think about is John Candy in *Summer Rental* falling asleep in the sun and then looking like a lobster for the rest of his vacation." Drew grimaces.

"I love that movie!" I've never met anyone else my age who actually knows what the movie *Summer Rental* is, much less who John Candy was. It is one of my favorite movies. Sometimes, I watch it in winter to make myself feel better.

"Well, then you understand my hesitations with falling asleep on the beach like this—especially with the kind of meal we've just eaten. We're liable to sleep for days."

I laugh at him. "You're so paranoid. One of us would have to wake up. It's not like we've been drugged."

"Do you not feel drugged?"

I think about the heavy feeling in my stomach and in my limbs. I suppose I do feel drugged, but I also just ate my weight in french fries and a giant burger. I would consider this feeling normal after being a glutton.

Drew lays his head back in the beach chair, settling in a bit more, prepping himself for his beach nap. His eyes close; we grow quiet; and then a few minutes later, as he begins to fall into his food-induced coma, I hear him say, "I think I might love you, Jess Dawson."

35
Drew Clark

I have no idea why it came out of my mouth. Well, that's a partial lie. I do know why I said it, but it wasn't meant to come out of my mouth. I actually wasn't sure that it had, but when I awoke from my beach nap, Jess was staring at me. It was as though she had been staring at me the entire time I was sleeping, which, by my watch, was about thirty minutes.

She didn't say anything at first. Her face was long and maybe even sad. I thought something terrible had happened until I remembered the last words out of my mouth before I succumbed to the burgers, fries, and summer sun.

Now, we're quietly walking back to the cottage. I plan to discuss my mishap once we're inside, but I'm not sure what I'll say. I think I do love her. Yeah, I know, we just met, but it's how I feel. And I know our marriages just ended less than twenty-four hours ago, but my marriage has been pretty loveless for a few years. In a lot of ways, I think I may have moved on, at least mentally. And now that I've met Jess, there's this feeling in my chest that cannot be understated. I'm not proud of it, and I can't help it either.

It's not like I've been daydreaming of Jess since the day we met. My mind has actually been very preoccupied with my cheating spouse and the daughter I just found out wasn't mine. Still, meeting and then getting to know her over the course of this week has churned up something inside of me that I thought had dried up a long time ago. It's light. It's fresh. It's air. I can't apologize for that, can I?

"I think I'm going to shower," Jess says to me as we enter the cottage. Sweeney hops off the couch and comes to each of us for greetings. Jess picks up the dog and gives him cuddles before putting his four legs back on the ground.

"Jess, wait, before you go—"

She turns to me. "Yeah?"

"The beach, earlier, before I fell into my coma…"

Her expression goes soft again. "We don't have to talk about it."

"We should, though. I don't want that to…change things. I'm having fun with you, and I hope you are with me. I won't apologize for what I said, but I…I'm sorry I said it out loud." I feel like that's an apology without apologizing for telling her that I think I love her.

"It's just very confusing, Drew. Everything. Not just you. All of it. I have feelings, too—feelings I haven't grasped yet. But…"

"But we need to handle what's happening right now first." I finish the sentence for her because I know she's not wrong.

She nods her head. "And that's going to come with its own set of feelings and emotions—for both of us. I know we both have felt that our marriages were over for a while, but they weren't officially over until last night. We have things to deal with, Drew, and I don't think complicating things is smart."

"I agree," I tell her softly.

She smiles at me and walks back toward me. "For the record, I am very happy that we met. I'm also very certain that we're going to know each other for the rest of our lives. I'm just not sure what that looks like yet."

I stare down into her beautiful, brown eyes, and all I want to do is lift her in my arms and kiss those perfect, pale pink lips of hers. I want to touch her hair, her skin. Gazing at her, my heart beats a little quicker; my lungs breathe a little easier; and if I couldn't feel the hardwood floors beneath my bare feet, I'd think I was levitating. Maybe I've been falling for her all week, or maybe it just hit me that I'm attracted to her. More than attracted to her. I feel connected to her in a way I've never felt with anyone else. It's like now that I know her, I can't be without her.

Jess' eyes are locked on mine, even as she says those words to me. She's strong, and I know now that I lack the power to persuade her one way or the other, which is something else that instantly attracts me to her—her confidence in the things she believes in.

"I'll wait," I tell her, and I find that it's the safest and easiest thing I can tell her right now. I can't promise not to fall deeply in love with her. But I can tell her that I can wait—on her, our circumstances, the right time. Whatever *wait* means, I can do it.

She smirks at me. "Okay."

I watch her turn away from me and pad down the hallway to the bathroom. Sweeney watches after her until she disappears into the bathroom, and then he looks at me like he expects me to entertain him now. I suppose I could. He's been stuck in this cottage while we were gorging ourselves with beef and potatoes and napping on the beach. Well, I was napping.

"What shall we do while your master bathes?" I smile at the little dog, squatting down to ruffle his little head. I've missed having a dog.

While he doesn't answer me, I think he looks like the kind of dog that is happy with a warm body sitting next to him on the couch and rubbing his belly. So, I collapse on the couch. Sweeney hops up next to me, and I turn on the television.

I can't believe how long this day has felt. I woke up on Edisto this morning, and I'm on Sullivan's Island this afternoon. It feels like the scene on the beach last night happened months ago. While I relax into the couch, flashes of the events of the last twenty-four hours pop into my mind. The picnic with Jess. Lindsey hanging from my body on the beach with Lilly still missing. Cal's confession. Divorce officially imminent. I'm exhausted, even after that nap on the beach earlier.

And then, of course, there's Jess—a girl I never knew existed until this week, a girl I can't believe I've lived my entire life without, a girl I told I would wait. A girl I think I love.

It's impossible to wrap my mind around what's happened with Lindsey and how I feel about Jess. I have feelings around both situations, but one tends to override the other. If I'm thinking of Jess, I somehow end up reminding myself that my wife cheated on me. And if I think about my wife cheating on me, then I think about Jess. It's driving me insane.

There's a part of me that wishes I could forget not only Lindsey, but also Lilly. My family, in reality, wasn't real at all. They didn't belong to me. I mean, Lindsey did legally, but ultimately, the realization is that they were never mine. Lilly was definitely never mine. And how is that supposed to make a man feel? There are memories—good memories—even with Lilly, that I don't want to forget; and I suppose that's why this entire situation is not only confusing but also painful.

Do people get married believing one day they'll divorce? I certainly didn't. When Lindsey and I married, I wanted her and nothing else for the rest of my life. I had felt like that for most of our marriage. I think I could still feel that way for my wife, but something *did* change between us even before Lilly—something irreparable. Not to mention the whole affair thing.

Honestly, I've not really felt like myself for a while. I've spent so much of the last couple of years focused on what Lindsey wants and then what Lilly wants. But when was the last time I did something I wanted to do? When was the last thing I did something for me? When was the last football game? Baseball game? Golf? I don't even like golf, but now I think I kind of would like to play. When was the last time I watched a movie that I wanted to watch? Or a T.V. show?

And as I think of all these things I've taken from myself for no reason whatsoever, I begin to grow angry. With whom, I'm not sure. The easy person to be angry with is Lindsey. She didn't promise me this life. She promised me forever, too—in good times and in bad. And then, she broke her promise.

Maybe I'm angry with myself mostly. I allowed the degeneration of myself to happen. Spending today with Jess showed me that I'm still in there somewhere. I'm not dead yet. She is drawing me out, slowly but surely. I feel like she's recharging my batteries, refueling my tank. Jess is unlike anyone I've ever met. Not even Lindsey could fulfill those parts of me when we first met. Jess is fire and water and everything in between. She makes me want to be better, and that I can't really explain either. She makes me see differently.

"Do you want to go out tonight?" Jess is asking me as she comes back down the hallway with a head full of damp, curly hair. The smell of Jess' bodywash sends my olfactory senses into overdrive; the scent is like an early spring morning. Intoxicating.

"What about pizza and a movie? I sat down, and I'm not sure I can get back up." This is the truth. I'm very much an old man, despite my age.

Jess laughs at me. "Maybe pizza and a movie is a good idea

considering the last twenty-four hours," she agrees. "But I still want to do that sunset cruise tomorrow night. I've never been able to do one of those things. Cal hates the sea salt."

Jess plops down on the couch on the other side of Sweeney and instinctively begins stroking his belly, same as me. We sit there together, rubbing this dang dog's belly, and all I can think is how spoiled this dog really is.

"I'll take you on the sunset cruise tomorrow," I promise her. "It'll be a pretty good finish to this very odd vacation."

Jess lays her head back against the seat and turns her eyes toward me. "This house is very nice. Thank you for bringing me here."

"I'm glad we came," I tell her.

Both of our eyes divert back to the television, our fingers stroking Sweeney's belly and exhausted silence floating between us.

The sun that wakes me, which is completely unexpected because I thought it was night. Regardless, it takes me a few seconds to collect myself. I realize it must be morning, and I remember where I am—on Sullivan's Island with Jess in Matt's cottage. I must have fallen asleep on the couch because it feels like my head is positioned on something soft, warm, and squishy. I'm a little afraid to open my eyes the rest of the way. What am I lying on?

People Watching

FRIDAY

People Watching

36
Jess Dawson

It's the sound of Drew screaming that wakes me. I jump straight up, my heart racing, ready to attack an intruder. Instead, I find Drew doing some strange dance in the middle of the floor while rubbing a pillow vigorously across one side of his face as though he were trying to wipe off something. Something gross. I hesitate before asking what's happened because the sight in front of me is quite a thing to behold. I'm not sure I've ever seen a grown man dance a jig and shout the way Drew is.

Finally, when I'm not sure he's not going to hurt himself in his self-imposed fit, I ask, "What in the world is wrong with you?"

Drew's green eyes, wide and horrified, fly to my own. "Sweeney's…his…his thingy…" Drew is hardly speaking in complete sentences.

"What thingy?"

"The thingy he pees with!"

"His penis?" I'm stifling a laugh. When I was teaching, I had gotten rather good at not laughing at one of my students when they said something inappropriate. It's harder than you think.

"Yes! That! I slept on that thing all night. There's a permanent imprint of it on my face!"

And now, I laugh. I laugh so hard, it doesn't take long to start crying, and poor Sweeney is just sitting there like an innocent doggy completely confused by the commotion.

"This is not funny," Drew says sternly.

"At least his thingy is clean!" I laugh through tears.

"That's not the point, Jess." Drew finally drops the pillow and looks at me helplessly. Then, he, too, begins to laugh.

I wrap my arms around Sweeney and assure him that he's done nothing wrong. To this gesture, he promptly wags his little stump of a tail and licks my nose.

"Worst way to wake up," Drew finally says after he's stopped laughing at himself. "I was scared to open my eyes. I could tell I was lying on something that wasn't a pillow."

"What was your first clue?" I'm laughing again.

"It was warm and squishy."

I'm rolling again.

"Would you stop laughing at me?"

"You laughed at yourself, too."

"I did but still." Drew is trying to appear serious again, but I can't ignore his flared nostrils and how they seem to inflate when he's trying not to smile or laugh.

"Okay, I'm sorry. For laughing. But no, I'm not. That was the hardest I've laughed in ages!"

"Well, I'm glad I could be a source of entertainment for you."

"Can we talk about the fact that we slept all night on the couch?" I roll my neck around, suddenly very aware of the stiffness residing there.

"Believe me, my first surprise this morning was that it was morning. The second surprise…well…"

I giggle and kiss Sweeney's head. "Come on, sweet boy. Let's go outside to potty."

"Oh, so he's the sweet boy?"

I turn to him just before I open the front door. "He's always the sweet boy."

Drew turns his eyes to Sweeney, who is already trotting out the front door. "I've got stronger competition than I previously thought." This time, he smiles.

"No one will ever beat Sweeney. Ever." I wink and then close the door behind me.

The air is humid and warm—my favorite kind of morning air. The island is quiet, not quite alive yet. As Sweeney explores the yard, I listen to the breeze rustle between the fingers of the palm leaves.

In the distance, I can hear the low rumble of the ocean as its waves roll in and out. Gulls fly overhead, squawking their coastal song.

Morning at the beach is always a peaceful time. It's the kind of moment I wish I could bottle up and keep forever. But I suppose that's what makes vacations so special—mornings that are different from your typical mornings.

Mornings at home aren't nearly as peaceful. Cal is generally rushing around the house trying to decide on which socks to wear or what tie to put on. He's generally cursing the dog hair that clings to his clothes, but he would always kiss me goodbye before he left.

Now, mornings at home will be quite different, I suppose. No more Cal. Just Sweeney and me. Kind of the way it is this morning. I suppose, though, Drew may become part of my daily routine at some point. I'm attracted to the man. I wouldn't lie about that. But I was attracted to Cal, too. I married him, remember? I never would have imagined our marriage ending the way it is, so what would make any other relationship I try to pursue different?

I would kind of like to know whether the relationship is forever or if he'll get bored eventually. I know there's no way to know what the future holds; but I think if I get married again, I'd like to know he's not going to cheat on me, too. I don't want to end up in this place again.

I've not even allowed myself to wrap my mind around the events that have happened this week. I don't think I can—not until I'm somewhere without distractions. Not that Drew is a distraction, but I think the two of us need this last day of vacation to pretend our worlds didn't just collapse. We'll deal with the debris when we get home tomorrow.

Once Sweeney is finished with his morning business, we find ourselves back in the house. Sweeney's nose and my own go berserk when the smell of sausage cooking hits us as we walk in the house.

I have two thoughts: Drew apparently cooks; and where in the world did he get sausage?

I round the corner to the kitchen and find Drew standing over the stove, the sausage sizzling perfectly. There's a carton of eggs on the counter next to him, and coffee is brewing.

"I have a lot of questions, but first, where did this food come from?" I startle him as I begin to speak, but he smirks when he realizes it's only me. Sweeney has already made his way to Drew's feet to beg for sausage.

"Don't worry. It's not old," he says, turning back to the stove, his back to me again, "Matt was just here a couple of weeks ago. His wife called while you were outside to let me know she had hidden some food in the storage building's refrigerator. Matt hates leaving things in the fridge when no one is home, so she has to hide it. Anyway, it's all within date—barely—but it's fine."

"Why wouldn't she have just taken the food home?"

"You'd have to know Matt, really. Maybe you will one day. He's a great guy, but the dude has some quirks. You know how most people feel pretty good about themselves when their fridge is full? It gives Matt anxiety. He's worried they won't eat it all and be forced to throw it out, which, in his head, is money that he might as well have lit on fire."

"Sounds like a stickler."

"In some respects. He's quite wealthy, though. I'd say it's served him well." Drew lays a couple of cooked sausage patties on a plate next to the stovetop. "You like your eggs scrambled, right?"

"Always scrambled." I smile at him, surprised that he remembered this from our breakfast on the pier the other morning.

I move toward the coffee put to pour myself a cup.

"What are your other questions?" Drew asks me.

"What?"

"When you came in, you said you had lots of questions, but you wanted to make sure the food wasn't stolen or something first, right?"

I laugh. "I didn't think it was stolen! I just didn't know where it came from. Forgive me for wanting to know these things."

"What other questions did you have?"

"I guess it just surprised me to see you in here cooking—sausage, of all things. Especially considering that you woke up on Sweeney's sau—"

"Okay! I had just forgotten about that."

I giggle. "But seriously, you cook?"

Drew shrugs his shoulders. "I used to cook a lot. Not so much anymore."

"Do you enjoy it?"

Drew scoops some scrambled eggs onto my plate, reaches into the toaster and pulls out a bagel, and then turns to present me with the most beautiful homemade breakfast. "For the right people." He smiles.

"This looks delicious," I tell him. "Thank you."

"Oh, wait! Cream cheese for the bagel. There's a bit of that in the refrigerator." Drew swings open the refrigerator door and pulls out a neatly folded tinfoil of cream cheese.

We have our breakfast together at a small table nestled inside the cottage's bay window. It's nearly perfect, really, with the way the morning sun comes through the window and casts itself across the breakfast table. Drew seems to be catching up on news and events on his cell phone while I catch up on social media. My social media is pretty bland, but I use it to keep up with my relatives across the country. I've got relatives as far west as California, and I do enjoy getting to see their happenings on the other side of the country.

Drew finally looks up at me from his phone. "What's going on?"

"Well, not a whole lot really," I tell him, briefly looking up. "Nothing important, at least." Some days, my family have a lot to talk about. Some days, it's only funny memes and news articles. "You?"

Drew shakes his head. "Not a whole lot here either. It seems we've not missed out on too much."

I shrug my shoulders, my mind shifting to Cal. I sort of can't believe he's not called or at least sent a text since we left Edisto yesterday. Perhaps our relationship was a lot more over than I had previously thought. "Have you heard from Lindsey?" I ask Drew, but then I wish I hadn't. We weren't supposed to talk about Cal or Lindsey anymore.

Drew looks at me for a long moment, his mouth partially hanging open with bits of bagel visible between his parted lips. "Why?"

"I'm sorry. I know we're not supposed to talk about them. I guess I thought Cal would have at least sent a text or something."

"What is there left to say, Jess?"

This question surprises me—mostly because I thought he'd understand why I'm a little distraught that Cal's not even called. I mean, one would think, even in the midst of divorce, that the offending partner would at least try to make some sort of contact after she left him.

"I'm sorry. I didn't mean to say it like that," Drew apologizes quickly. "We're not supposed to talk about them."

I nod my head. "I know. I'm sorry. I guess I expected a text message at least. Something like *I'm sorry*. Or *I can't believe how bad I messed this up*. But nothing since we left Edisto yesterday." I keep having to save my mind from imagining what our spouses are doing on that island together now that we're gone."

Drew sits back in his chair and looks at me softly. "I don't know if it was this way for Cal, but Lindsey checked out a long time ago. She's not going to text me. Does she feel bad about what happened? I mean, she's a witch, but she's not completely heartless. I don't need her to text me to tell me that she feels bad. I know she does. But it's still not enough guilt to change anything, and even if it were, would it *really* change what they did?"

I cast my eyes to the table. There's a dull ache in my chest. I recognize it as sadness. Maybe I am sad. I have a right to be sad. My husband cheated on me *and* made another human with her.

"Jess." Drew's voice is soft and sincere, his face straight and serene. "I don't really think that you know how truly special you are. I've never met anyone like you. You're caring. You love. You think and speak in a way that I've never met in another person. You are better than he is. You are better than any man walking this earth."

"Even you?" I'm smirking because it's a joke, and I'm grasping at anything just to break this sudden strange tension.

Drew's expression doesn't change at my attempt to joke, though. "Even me." His green eyes glisten as though tears could be building inside of them.

"Drew, you don't have to say those things." It's clear that this is now a very serious conversation. "You don't know me. We just met a few days ago. You know nothing of my past. You can't speak honestly about me without knowing me."

"I don't have to know those things to know who I'm looking at, Jess," he says. "Everything I just said is what I already know about you. It's what I've discovered since the day we first said hello."

"I said hello first," I point out.

"You did, but only because you weren't watching where you were going and bumped into me."

"You should warn a person before you sneak up behind them." I shrug and attempt a smirk again, trying to thin out whatever the air is made of at this moment.

"It almost makes me angry."

"What does?"

"The fact that you don't see yourself the way I see you."

"Drew, I didn't... I wasn't trying to—"

"I'm not angry, Jess. I'm sorry. I got serious quickly." He takes a deep breath as though he is attempting to calm himself down. "You didn't deserve what Cal did to you, and it's everything inside of me not to pound his face in—not because he slept with *my* wife but because he cheated on you." Drew stands suddenly from the table and slides his hand through his hair. "I can't stand it, Jess. And the more I get to know you, the more I can't stand it."

I stand now, too, to take up for myself. I feel like he is viewing me as a weak woman. I'm not a weak woman. I'm logical. "I'm not some feeble woman who was cheated on by her husband." My voice is strong but calm. "I knew what he was doing. I'm not stupid. I just chose to believe differently. But now that I know for sure, I am angry. I'm angry that he left me not once, but twice. I'm also angry that after everything we have been through together, this is how it ends. Just like this. What a cruel thing to do to someone. How could he do that to me?"

At some point in the rant, I started shouting; and now I stand before Drew, next to the beautiful breakfast nook with its yummy breakfast that Drew prepared, and I'm crying like a lunatic. I am full-on ugly crying. Half of me is thinking that this is really embarrassing, while the other half of me is thinking that I really don't care. I want to cry because I have not really cried yet. But now, it pours out of me as though a dam has been broken. It's not just tears for Cal and Lindsey, but also everything else. My cancer. His neglect. My inability to become a mother. The loss of the life I had dreamed for myself.

Drew wraps his arms around me, his chin on my head. I melt into him involuntarily, but I relax into him all the same. My tears soak through his t-shirt, and my body shakes. But Drew continues to hold me, tightly. I find, as we stand there together in the kitchen like this, my sadness becomes subdued, and my tears begin to subside. Through my sniffling and heavy exhalations, I hear his heart beating against my ear. It's a calm, strong beat. Gentle. Transfixing.

Finally, I pull away a little and look up at him. "I'm sorry for that. I don't want you to see me like that."

"What, like a human?" He smirks, and then his palm is holding my cheek. "If I'm being honest, I was sort of waiting on it. And I didn't help matters."

As I gaze up into his eyes, there's a feeling of forever. I can't explain it because I've never really felt that before. I can't recall a time I ever looked into Cal's eyes, even when things were really good, where I felt that *forever* feeling. With Cal, when I think about it now, the feeling was always *until*. I didn't know what "until" meant, but I guess I do now.

Drew's hand moves into my hair, and I find myself moving my face closer to his. His eyes are heavy as he leans down; and though I've not had a first kiss in quite some time, I believe this is how it starts. I want to pull away from him. I don't want to dive into Drew this quickly. It's not the right thing to do—not yet, anyway—but I can't seem to stop the progression of this moment.

My thoughts hang in the silence between our lips. He hesitates, and I do, too. The tension is building, and I know that one of us must pull away from the other soon or else…

He pulls away first, and for that, I'm thankful.

"We better get out on the beach if we want time in the sun today. We have a sunset cruise to get ready for this afternoon." Drew smiles as he turns away from me, clearing the table of our mostly eaten breakfast. "It's our last day. We should make the most of it."

Last day—that's always a sad notion. Even with this trip having gone as bad as it has, I really don't want to leave Sullivan's Island. I'm not ready to face what waits for me at home.

37
Drew Clark

As soon as Jess is out of sight, getting dressed for our day on the beach, I find myself collapsing in a squatted heap right there in the middle of the kitchen floor. I'm mostly horrified. I almost kissed her. I almost did a lot more than kiss her. And I can't be sure that she would have done a whole lot to stop me. This girl makes me weak in the knees, and I don't know how I'm going to remember to breathe around her today. I can't stop the trajectory in which my heart is going, but I have to put a delay on it, at least.

I'm in trouble. I've allowed my heart and mind to join forces, and all either of them wants is Jess. Not Lindsey. Not Lilly. Not even the life I left behind to go on vacation. Everything, for me, has changed completely.

Sweeney stands in the doorway of the kitchen. He looks up at me. I wonder what he thinks about the situation. Surely, a man shouldn't be reduced to a childish knee-hugging squat in the middle of a kitchen floor over a girl. I gather myself and slowly stand, turning back to the sink to finish cleaning up the breakfast dishes.

"Okay, this is not what it looks like. It's just the only clean swimsuit I have left." Jess's voice arrives in the living room before she does, but when I look up at her, I decide that she's just torturing me now.

Jess stands before me in a big straw hat (which I could do without, but it looks nice on her) and a black bikini. It would be considered a modest bikini on anyone else, but on Jess, it accentuates everything. I want to reach out and touch her the way one would reach out to touch a famous sculpture or a beautiful flower. She's been wearing once-piece swimsuits all week, which I didn't mind either. I've got an imagination, but the mystery of what's underneath it all makes the entire situation very intriguing.

"I don't see a problem, but if you'd like us to stop by one of the shops on the walk to the beach for one of those skirts Joyce was wearing over her swimsuit, we can."

Jess throws a couch pillow at me, laughing. "After what happened in the kitchen, I'm not trying to make a difficult situation even more difficult. I'm not trying to show you my body; it's just all I have left."

"There are women on the beach in thong bikinis," I point out.

"This is fine. I'd prefer it, actually."

"What about you? You've basically been wearing a t-shirt all week on the beach."

"That's not true. I have a tan." I push up my t-shirt sleeve to show her.

"Oh please. I've never seen you completely topless. You either have your t-shirt wrapped around your chest or on."

"Woman, what are you trying to do to me?"

"Let me see your chest." She crosses her arms and taps her foot like she's impatiently waiting on something.

"Right now?"

She doesn't say anything. She just stands there, staring, arms crossed, foot tapping, trying not to laugh.

"No, not right now. I promise to remove my t-shirt once we're on the beach," I tell her. "I don't undress on demand."

Jess laughs, and I melt. That laugh—there's something in her laugh. I feel certain that there's nothing I wouldn't do just to hear her laugh. I always struggled to make Lindsey laugh. She never thought my jokes were funny, and she definitely didn't appreciate my sarcasm.

We make sure Sweeney is all set before we head out to the beach. I carry our chairs, and Jess insists on carrying the cooler. I'd much rather carry it all for her; but she insisted, and when Jess insists, there's no arguing. There's not a lot to say as we walk. I watch her out of the corner of my eye, admiring everything about her—the way her hair moves under that big straw hat, hiding her eyes but highlighting the sharp angles of her jawline. She doesn't know I'm watching her. No, she's too busy admiring the birds as they fly above or rest in trees and bushes. I catch her watching the birds more often than none, and I've found that I also love that about her. Sometimes, I forget to watch the birds.

I set our chairs in the sand and lift the umbrella, and Jess settles the cooler between our two chairs. She doesn't waste a lot of time to sit in her chair, but she's waiting on my shirt-removal. I can see it in her eyes, on her face, the way she's watching me. On the walk to the beach, she was all about the birds. Now, she just wants to see me with my shirt off.

"I feel so objectified," I joke.

"What?" She tries to appear innocent, like she's not waiting on the arrival of my bare chest.

I smile and look away from her. I think I'm embarrassed. This is worse than having sex for the first time.

"Oh, just take it off!" She laughs at me as I do everything else *but* take off my shirt—like grab a beer from the cooler and spread my towel over my chair.

I roll my eyes at her, and then, without any further hesitation—mainly because I'm pretty over the buildup she's created in her mind to this whole thing—I rip off the shirt. Not like the Hulk or anything. I just lift the t-shirt right over my head and then let my arms fall by my side once it's off.

I stand there in the same way the *David* statue that Michelangelo sculpted stands in the Accademia Gallery of Florence—not naked, of course, but I might as well be. Jess' eyes observe my stomach and chest, running all the way up my neck and then to my face. She smiles. She may even be blushing, even though I'm trying hard not to look at her face.

"Wow."

"Wow what? Good wow or bad wow?" Now, I'm sort of panicking. I feel like a pubescent, sixteen-year-old boy wondering if my body is shaping up the way it's supposed to.

Jess doesn't answer that question. She turns in her chair to face the ocean as it rolls in toward us and then proceeds to pull a book from her bag.

"Jess, you can't just make a spectacle out of me and then stop

People Watching

talking about it." I'm still standing, just like *David* in Florence.

"I'm just a little intimated, okay?" she says, and I catch her eyes cut toward me.

"Intimidated?"

"You obviously enjoy your salads and lean meats, while I'm a big fan of huge breakfast meals and greasy burgers."

"Oh please! Look at you." I decide to take a seat in my beach chair. I don't want to be David anymore.

"I don't have abs, Drew."

"Neither do I—" I look down at my stomach, though, and it would appear that I do have abs. I was actually hoping the burger from yesterday had bloated me enough to hide them, but to no avail. I don't spend a lot of time looking at my body, and the only reason I really go to the gym is to get some time away from Lindsey and Lilly. If I'm being completely honest, I'd go to the gym after work just to delay getting home. I'm not proud of that, but when one is in survival mode, one does what they have to do to survive.

When I look back up at Jess from my stomach, she's giving me a look.

"Okay, fine. I go to the gym. Daily. Not because I'm some fitness freak. It was just something to do before I went home to Lindsey and Lilly."

"Drew, it's okay. It's just not what I expected to be under that t-shirt."

"What'd you expect? A dad bod?"

She shrugs with a giggle. "Maybe. I don't know."

I still feel self-conscious, but I do feel better about things. Jess thought I might be all soft and pudgy, but no, I take care of myself. Maybe not for the right reasons, but that's not the point.

Jess picks up her book again, and we both relax in our beach chairs. I'm not much interested in a nap, even though I've got a crick in my neck from sleeping on that dang dog's belly and his…thingy. Regardless, the beach is full of families today, and I find myself people-watching.

To our left is a young couple. They're younger than Jess and I. They've got two little boys with them; both seem to be happy and content, playing with their sand buckets and beach toys. In front of us is an older couple. They remind me of Harold and Joyce, which makes me think of Joyce. I should probably check on her. The way we left things on Edisto was a disaster.

To Jess' right is a family a bit older than us. They've got a teenage girl who looks as though she wishes she were anywhere except at the beach with her parents. They also have a teenage boy who can't keep his eyes off the other females on the beach. I caught him catch a glimpse of Jess a few minutes ago. He stared for a while until he decided she's probably a bit too old for him. That's right, young man, she is too old for you.

I think of Joyce again and pull out my phone to send her a text message.

Me: *How are things?*
Joyce: *Back home with Harold. Everything is fine. Where are you?*
Me: *Sullivan's Island.*
Joyce: *With Jess??????*
I note the extra question marks.
Me: *Yes, I'm with Jess. We decided at the last minute not to go home yet.*
Joyce: *So, how is that going?*
Me: *I woke up on the dog's thingy this morning.*
Joyce: *His thingy?*
Me: *Seriously?*
Joyce: *I just want to see you type it.*
Me: *Fine, I woke up on the dog's penis this morning.*
Joyce sends some laughing emojis, and I roll my eyes.
Me: *I was checking on you. This is not a check-up on me.*
Joyce: *Fine. How are you?*
Me: *I think I've fallen in love with a married woman. But I told her I would wait on her—whatever that means. Joyce, I don't know what I'm doing.*
Joyce: *Keep being you, Drew.*
I think about that for a few seconds, and then I type back: *Outside of my mother, you may be the only woman in the world who has ever thought I was good.*
Joyce: *You are good. Better than good.*
Me: *Thank you.*
Joyce: *Now stop texting my old, saggy butt and start talking to Jess!*
Me: *Aye-aye!*

Jess lays her book page-side down on her legs and looks over at me. "Who have you been texting?"

"So, this is where we are in our relationship? You need to know who I'm texting?" I'm joking, of course.

"Fine, keep your secrets." She shrugs and goes to pick her book up again.

"It's Joyce. I was just thinking about her," I tell her. "I wanted to be sure she and Harold were okay."

"Well, are they?"

"They're home and fine." I leave out the rest of our text conversation.

"You really took to Joyce, didn't you?"

"I don't know what it is about her, but she reminds me of my mother," I tell her. "I miss my mom. I've always missed her."

"I'm sorry you lost her."

"It was so long ago, sometimes I forget her. I wish...I wish I didn't." I thought there was something wrong with me. I live months, sometimes years, and I never remember my mom. She died when I was so young; it feels like I've lived a million years since. Still, shouldn't a son remember his mother always?

"I don't think you've forgotten her," Jess tells me. "I think you live in such a way that remembers her."

"How could you say that when you don't even really know me?" Jess shrugs. "I suppose I sense it."

"For the longest time after Mom died, my dad wanted me to remember her. We left her chair at the dinner table open, and no one ever sat in her chair in the living room. My dad left obvious vacancies everywhere she should be. I don't know that it was helpful. It evoked fear in me more than anything. If someone sat in her chair, would she be gone forever? I mean, I know she was already gone, but the way my dad protected the places she inhabited in life felt like if it were disturbed, she'd be gone forever."

Jess sits in her chair, her head turned toward me but resting against the back of the chair. She instinctively reaches out to take my hand, and I take it without thinking.

"So, when I met Joyce, it was the first time I had ever encountered someone who reminded me of my mom. She helped me on the beach that first day. Lindsey basically packed Lilly's entire playroom for the beach, and I didn't know what to do with any of it. She helped me. And then Lindsey was rude to her. I've never hit a woman, but I wanted to knock her back a few paces."

"Joyce reminds me of my mom, too," Jess tells me.

"Your mom is still living?"

Jess nods. "She's basically my best friend. She never liked Cal.

People Watching

She'll probably take me out for manicures and drinks when we get home and I tell her everything that happened."

"Sounds like a woman I'd like."

"Oh, she'd love you," Jess says. "I mean that."

"What about your dad?"

"He's still around, too. He didn't care for Cal either, but my dad would never say anything like that. He only advises when he feels it necessary. Other than that, he's more of a 'that'll teach him' kind of person without ever saying anything about it."

"Do you have siblings?"

"I have a brother."

"I was an only child," I tell her.

"That sounds lonely."

"Yeah. No one to fight with or steal things from. No one to help you rob a convenience store."

"You've got a list of convenience stores to rob?"

"No. But when I was a kid, playing video games designed to teach one how to steal a car, it was all I could think about doing. The only reason I never stole a car—besides the fact that I have a conscience—is I didn't have a brother to help me."

"You are ridiculous. You would have never robbed a convenience store or stolen a car!"

"I'll never know. I didn't have any siblings."

She laughs again, and I sit in that laughter for as long as it lasts.

We're quiet for a few moments, and then Jess looks at me again. "What's going to happen when we go home tomorrow?"

I speak confidently, so she knows I'm not going anywhere. "We have to find lawyers first, but we file for that divorce as soon as we can."

"Yeah, but then what am I supposed to do? I don't have a job. I've got a little of my own money stashed away, but how will I live? Where will I live? I don't...I don't know what to do."

"We'll figure it out, Jess. And you won't do it alone. We'll go through this together, but I'm not about to ruin my last day of vacation with this type of discussion. That's not what today is for."

She smiles a little. "You're right."

"Always."

Jess goes back to her book, and I return to people-watching. It really is the best type of entertainment while sitting anywhere in a public location, but especially the beach.

38
Jess Dawson

    Well, I was not expecting a perfectly carved six pack of abs when Drew removed his shirt. Why in the world has he been hiding that all week? Cal used to have abs, but he's certainly gotten soft over the years. Drew over here, though, is cut. I suspected that he may have been. I caught a peek at a bicep one day earlier this week, and it was impressive. I can't get wrapped up in Drew's chiseled chest, though. No, it's a distraction. I shouldn't think about what happens when we get home either. I should enjoy this day.
    When I was a kid, in the summer, we'd get afternoon thunderstorms a good bit. Most days, I had a hard time believing the storms would happen because the day was so beautiful. Blue skies, the sun high in the sky, and no sign of a cloud anywhere. But as the afternoon crept on and the humidity of the day peaked, those storm clouds would begin to build. Summer afternoon thunderstorms in South Carolina leave you with little time to seek shelter. There's time, but not a lot of it.
    I think about this in comparison with my relationship with Cal and how it ends. I wonder if maybe I should have done something when I noticed the clouds begin to build. I also wonder if it would have made a difference if I had. I'd like to think I've got power, but I don't think it was up to me to save my marriage. And maybe that's where my mind is. Maybe I've been subconsciously punishing myself

for not trying to save Cal and me. But who am I to think I could have done that all on my own? Relationships are two-sided. Even if I had noticed the clouds beginning to build, even if I had acted quickly, the storm would have still come.

I don't want to, but I like Drew; and if I were actually being honest, I more than like him. And that's not just because I finally saw him shirtless (although that may have solidified a few things within me). He listens. He cares. He loves. I think he even loves Sweeney, despite their sleeping arrangement last night. Drew is intelligent and meticulous. And I can't forget how it felt in his arms this morning when he held me as I cried. I've never felt that in my life.

Every time I allow myself to slide into these thoughts about Drew, Cal's big, stupid head pops up in my brain and ruins the whole thing. It's like he pops up to remind me that I have to get rid of him first, which then sends my mind down a rabbit hole of all the things I must do when I get home tomorrow. First things first, I have to pack all of my things. I have to pack all thirty-five years of my life into a box and find somewhere else to live. I know I can stay with my parents, but what thirty-five-year-old woman who's had a career and beaten cancer wants to move back in with her parents? It's embarrassing.

Why do I have to move, anyway? Why can't I stay in the house and Cal move? Why am I just now thinking of this? It's my house, too, and Cal is the one who cheated. I'll be damned if he moves Lindsey and Lilly into *my* house.

My chest grows tight as I realize that I was about to just roll over and let Cal have it all. Why would I be passive about this?

"Oh my gosh!" I sit straight up in my beach chair, scaring Drew in the process.

Drew jumps out of his chair in a panic like I had just screamed that a shark had walked up on shore. "What's wrong?"

"Why were you just going to let me give the house to Cal?" I'm yelling, but not necessarily at him.

"What? What in the world? What are you talking about? Holy crap, Jess. I thought something terrible had happened." Drew sighs with his palm over his face, and then he collapses back in his chair.

"Why does Cal get the house?"

"He shouldn't," Drew says. "And you know he'll just move Lindsey and Lilly in there."

"I can't let that happen! That's my house, too."

"We're not supposed to be talking about this."

"Drew, as a woman, I need to know where I'm going to be sleeping tomorrow night. I can't stop thinking about it."

"You found a solution?"

"Cal can move in with Lindsey and Lilly."

"What am I supposed to do then? I was really looking forward to watching Lindsey walk out of my house with suitcases."

"I have a guesthouse. It's by the pool. You can live there!"

"Oh, so you're basically rich?"

"Well, I mean, Cal is a CFO. He makes a lot of money—money that he now has to give at least half of to me."

"Then why are you worried about where you're going to go? You have the upper hand."

"I'm not worried, Drew. I was just approaching the situation wrong. I was planning on living somewhere else, but why do I concede? I didn't do the cheating. He did."

Drew laughs. "I feel certain you could make him homeless if you wanted."

"I don't want to do that to him, but I'm serious. You can move into my guesthouse—a.k.a. the pool house. He can move in with Lindsey and Lilly."

"I like my house, though."

I give him a look.

"Fine. You're right. I like the house, but I'm certain Lindsey's voice is permanently ingrained into the walls. Even with her gone, I'd probably still hear her calling to me in the middle of the night. I'd probably become an insomniac."

"Great. So, it's settled then. We have places to live when we get home."

"I feel like I've been downsized."

"You've not even seen the pool house, Drew."

He considers this. "I hope it's fancy."

I smile at him. "Oh, it's fancy." It's really a studio apartment, but it's open and wide and has walls made of windows. I spent a lot of nights in the pool house when I was going through chemotherapy. I developed a case of insomnia during my cancer battle. The doctors tried to medicate me with just about everything under the sun. Nothing worked. So, especially on treatment days, I had to "sleep" in the pool house so that I didn't disturb Cal. Now that I think back on it, though, why didn't Cal move to the pool house? Why was I the one who had to vacate my bedroom and my bed?

I suspect there was a lot of neglecting myself for Cal's needs in our time together. Only now am I beginning to realize that our relationship may very well have been one-sided—things like my having to sleep in the pool house while I was fighting for my life just so Cal would be comfortable.

"Where did you go?" Drew's voice is breaking through my thoughts as he waves his hands to catch my attention.

I shake my head, snapping out of it. "Sorry, I was lost in a thought."

"A Cal thought?"

"How did you know?"

"The expression on your face changed from angelic to demonic."

I laugh. "I've never been accused of looking demonic, so thanks for that."

"It's a compliment!"

I shake my head at him, still giggling, and pick up my book. "I need to retreat from my thoughts again."

"You should people-watch. It's helpful to mentally scrutinize other families. Makes you feel less incompetent."

"I people-watched enough this week. Granted, it did lead me to you, but I don't think I can stomach any more people-watching. You go ahead. I'll read this fictional novel with its fictional love story and forget about my reality."

"What are you reading, anyway?"

I hold up the book. "It's a love story that takes place in Auschwitz."

"Well, that's not depressing." Drew looks at me, horrified.

"It's sweet, actually. And besides, I think they'll make it out together. I've not gotten that far yet, though."

"I've never understood the fascination women have with World War II fiction. That was a horrible time in the history of the world."

"I learn a lot reading historical fiction. It's not a bad thing! Besides, it's not all horrible either. Even in the midst of tragedy, there can be good. Sometimes, the good is the only thing that helps anyone survive."

39
Drew Clark

    We have to drive into Charleston for our sunset cruise, which neither of us minded because Charleston is a very beautiful place—old oaks; lots of Spanish moss; beautiful, old homes; and scenery like one only sees in movies. It's pretty spectacular. I've never really had to wonder why Hollywood likes to film here. It's obvious.
    Charleston has a lot of history, and it's evident as we drive through to get to our sunset cruise. I suppose Charleston, South Carolina, is most famous for its Battery. Charleston's Battery is a defensive seawall and promenade. South Carolina hasn't had to fight any wars recently, but the Battery has taken the brunt of a lot of hurricanes over the years. Still, she stands strong. A few years back, it was decided the seawall and basic structure of the Battery needed to be restored. If another major hurricane came into South Carolina's coast, the Battery might not hold any longer. Thousands visit Charleston each year, and all of them visit the Battery at least once. It does provide some amazing views of Charleston Harbor.
    Tonight, though, we're visiting Charleston Harbor for a sunset cruise. I picked the nicest cruise with the best reviews. This is our final night on vacation, and we both need this night to be unforgettable.
    Jess hasn't really stopped talking since we left the cottage on Sullivan's Island. I usually mind a lot of chatter, but with Jess, it's

different. It's not just chatter; it's a whole conversation where I can be involved, and no one makes me out to be stupid.

I thought I had gotten bored with conversation because I was getting older. I've probably covered every topic there is to talk about in my thirty-something years of life, but as it turns out, Jess is made up of a plethora of conversation topics that I have never even considered.

"How do you know a little bit about everything?" I ask her incredulously.

I see her shoulders shrug from the passenger seat. "I watch a lot of *Jeopardy*."

"Even after Alex Trebek died?"

"Well, yeah. I mean, it's obviously not the same without Alex, but it's a great show to learn a lot of random facts. Random facts are good to have when you're trying to get a classroom of elementary-aged kids to settle down. So, you just start with something random to get them quiet. Like, did you know that the human heart creates enough pressure to squirt blood thirty feet?"

"The human heart could really squirt blood thirty feet?"

Jess laughs. "Yes, it's true!"

"Fascinating." It *is* fascinating. I like random facts, but I'm not sure I've heard that one. "Did you know that Diet Coke wasn't even invented until 1982?"

"I did know that!" she says excitedly. "We're almost as old as Diet Coke!"

Now I laugh with her. "I've never understood diet sodas. Why can't folks just drink water?"

"You're a water-drinker?"

"I was in ninth grade and randomly decided one day that I'd give up sweet tea and soda. No reason, really—just decided to do it. Best decision I ever made."

"I did the same thing, only I was a little older and had a prom dress I needed to fit into." She smiles. "Cal took me to that prom."

The car falls quiet for a few moments as that last statement sort of floats in the air between us. It's easy to distract yourself from life's pain, but the pain always inevitably finds you again at the most inopportune times. Sometimes, it feels like pain is impatient, like it has somewhere else to be. It demands to be dealt with so that it can go on living in someone else's heart elsewhere.

"I lost ten pounds," Jess adds, breaking the silence.

"I doubt you even needed to lose ten pounds."

"Why do men get nervous when women start talking about losing weight? It's so frustrating. If I feel like I need to lose a few pounds, I need to lose a few pounds. Cal would always argue with me about it. I'm not saying he needed to agree with me, but regardless of what he thought, arguing with me in the moment only frustrated me more."

"So, next time you say something self-deprecating, I'm not meant to argue with you, but I shouldn't agree either?"

"Absolutely."

"What should I say then?"

She thinks about this for a few seconds. "It's probably just one of those things you shouldn't respond to at all. Pretend you never even heard me."

"Oh, come on. In movies and television shows, the female lead is always demanding her man argue the fact that she thinks she's fat."

"Exactly! They're wrong. Don't argue with me. It makes me angrier."

I laugh. "Okay, got it. No arguing any of Jess' statements when she hates her body."

"Perfect."

"Glad we got that conversation out of the way." I smirk and glance at her. She's beautiful, gazing back at me with a smile on her face.

"Oh, your turn is coming up in five hundred feet."

I hit the brake a little harder than I normally would, but five hundred feet happens quickly. "Worst navigator ever," I mumble.

"Sorry. I got distracted." She's looking at her phone again as the map app shows her exactly where I should turn.

I complain a lot about technology, but you'll never catch me complaining about the navigation systems they've placed in our vehicles and mobile phones. It's much better than reading a map or, worse, ten pages of printed directions that were downloaded from the internet.

I park the car in the designated area and present our sunset cruise tickets to the lady at the gate, and then we board a small, double decker boat. The temperature is perfect this evening. It's warm with an even warmer breeze. So, once the boat begins to move, I don't suspect Jess will get chilly. Just in case, I've brought a light jacket for her to put on.

People Watching

We find our table on the boat, where our dinner will be served, and take a seat. A server approaches nearly immediately to see if we'd like anything to drink before dinner. We both accept his offer and order a bottle of wine.

"This is exciting." Jess smiles from across the table. "I've never been on a sunset cruise before."

"Well, I don't imagine it'll be like a cruise to Jamaica or anything like that," I tell her, "But I suspect the views will be breathtaking."

"And dinner sounds amazing." Jess is gazing at the hardback menu that was placed elegantly at each seat on deck.

I take a look at the menu, too. A Charleston sunset cruise complete with dinner was a requirement as I looked into several different cruise companies along the Charleston coastline. This particular company claimed to serve the best wine and the best food. Reading the menu now, it doesn't look like they lied. For the more expensive meals, they've listed roasted duck. I've had duck before, and it's a little heavy for my liking. So, I look at the other menu items and land on a roasted chicken with an arugula salad, toasted bread, and steamed asparagus. There aren't too many men that will admit to liking asparagus. I like it. Even if it can make my pee smell funny after I've enjoyed a few asparagus stalks.

"I think I'll have the steak," Jess says, "with steamed asparagus and a baked potato. That sounds amazing."

The steak does sound amazing, but then so does my roasted chicken.

At precisely 7:30 p.m., the boat toots its horn and begins to set sail. Most of the tables on the deck are now filled with people. Mostly couples are on board, but there are a few families with children sitting on the other end of the deck. I'm thankful for that. I've always wondered why parents think their children would enjoy something like this. It feels intimate and romantic—not a place to bring the kids. Lilly would be absolutely miserable. Lindsey would have probably forced me to ask the captain to turn the boat back to shore. And I would have tried.

The harbor begins to grow a little smaller on the horizon the further out we go, and it is quite beautiful. To view land from sea is an alternate perspective that no one really thinks about. Well, unless they're a fisherman or in the U.S. Navy. Other than that, most of us walk on this earth without any regard as to what it looks like from above or from the sea. For me, it's always been a reminder of how small I actually am.

The sky is a mix of orange and purple as the sun begins its descent into the sea. The lights of Charleston city define the coastline a bit more than I had noticed before we set sail, and ahead of us is nothing but the Atlantic Ocean, deep and rich in color. I look across the table at Jess. Her hair catches in the breeze, and she smiles into the slowly setting sun. She's beautiful—absolutely stunning. And I'm not sure I've ever seen an expression as peaceful as hers. I hate Cal for what he did to her. If Jess had been my wife, I would have made her feel like she was the only woman in the world. She never would have ever had to feel less than anyone.

"Why are you looking at me?" Jess asks me this while her eyes are still closed, her face pointed toward the sun.

"I'm not looking at you." I feign ignorance.

"I can feel your green eyes burning into my skin," she says with her eyes still closed.

"Okay, fine. I was admiring you," I confess. "You're beautiful, sitting there like that—your face in the setting sun, your eyes closed, the way your hair catches the breeze. I've just never seen anyone more beautiful."

Jess' eyes open, and she turns her face toward me now. Her face is still relaxed and at peace. The corners of her mouth curve into a slight smirk. "Why are you obsessed with me?"

I know it's a joke, but the truth is, I *am* obsessed with her. I've been obsessed with her since she first introduced herself at the pier on Edisto, and I'm beginning to really understand that now. "I can't help it, Jess. You've got a pull or something. The more I resist it, the stronger it gets."

Jess doesn't say anything. She just gazes back into my face the same way I'm gazing into hers, and I now notice the shine in her brown eyes. The lighter brown specks that dot the darkest brown of her iris seem to ignite as though electricity were running through them.

"Why me?" she asks quietly. I almost don't hear her at all.

I can't answer that question. I have no idea why. Every time I think about it, all I can come up with is that she consumes me—my heart, mind, and soul—in a way that I can't explain.

"I don't know," I tell her. "I really can't explain it."

"You don't know me," she reminds me again.

"Oh, but I do, Jess. I've come to know you in what is probably second to the most devastating thing that has ever happened to you, and I've never seen anyone handle anything so gracefully while still remaining beautiful. You could have gone a thousand different ways on the beach Wednesday night when Cal confessed it all. You didn't, though. You're graceful, Jess. You're kind. You have a heart like nothing I've ever seen in another human."

Jess shakes her head slightly and then casts her eyes back out to the sea. The sky is changing quickly as the sun continues to dip lower and lower into the sea. Swirls of pink and orange cover the sky, but in its highest places, where the heavens seep into the atmosphere, the sky is a deep blue, exposing a few stars. I'm not sure we could have picked a more perfect night for a sunset cruise.

A musician sits not too far from us, playing a soft acoustic tune on his guitar. The boat is mostly quiet chatter, and for that reason, I forget that there are more people on this cruise than us. But that's what Jess does to me. She looks at me, and suddenly, we're the only two people in the world. Nothing else matters to me.

"I'm afraid, Drew," she says to me. "I feel things for you, too—things I've never even felt for Cal. But it's only been two days since I found out for sure that my own husband had not only cheated on me but had also started his own family. It would be so stupid to jump from one relationship to another. Not to mention the psychological implications. We both need to feel and heal from what our spouses did to us. We can't do that together because we didn't share that life together."

"I told you I would wait for you," I remind her.

"But what does that mean?"

"It means that when you're ready, I'll be ready. I'm not going to push you, Jess. You don't deserve that."

She's quiet for a few minutes, and then she looks at me again, her eyes soft. "Will you dance with me?"

"Wait, what?"

She giggles. "I love this song that he's playing. Dance with me."

I look around nervously. I don't dance—especially if I'm the only one dancing. But it surprises me to find other couples dancing with each other as well. I hadn't really paid attention to the tune the musician was playing; but now that I am, I can tell that he's playing "Love Me Do" by the Beatles. It makes for a beautiful acoustic tune. And I just found out something new about Jess—she loves the Beatles.

I stand from my chair and walk to her side, holding out my hand to dance with her.

Jess looks up at me, a smile on her face. She hesitates for a few seconds; but then I feel her soft fingers land in the palm of my hand, and my heart is suddenly on fire.

It's awkward at first. I can't remember the last time I danced with a woman. Lindsey wouldn't even dance with me at our wedding. Something about her shoes killing her feet. I don't know.

Jess moves in close to me, our hands clasped together, and I can smell the shampoo in her curls as they float in the breeze around us. We don't talk; we're too busy looking into the other's eyes—thinking, dreaming, wishing. I can't really pinpoint where my thoughts are except that I know I never want this moment to end. I remember how I wanted moments like these with Lindsey. As I said, I don't dance, but I used to dream of post-dinner dancing sessions with Lindsey. Fast or slow, the beat mattered none. I've only ever seen things like that in movies, and I've always thought it looked nice. Romantic. Intimate without getting naked.

This moment with Jess is everything I have ever dreamed a dinner dance would be.

The song begins to near its end, but my heart is pounding hard in my chest. There's electricity between our hands and a magnetic pull between our bodies. I want to kiss her. I want to put my hands in her hair, pull her as close to me as physics will allow, and kiss her. Instead, I work to remain content holding her gaze in mine and feeling her skin against mine.

Our faces, naturally, instinctively, gradually move closer to each other. Our lips are mere centimeters apart. Her eyelids drop a little as her eyes shift to focus on my mouth. Heat builds in my body, and it's all I have inside of me not to take her right here on this boat deck. I decide to put my focus on self-control and not how badly I want her now, in this moment. But this invisible pull between us is almost too much.

40
Jess Dawson

I remember the first kiss Cal and I ever shared together. It was quick and sloppy, and I actually debated on whether or not I ever wanted to kiss him again. He did redeem himself eventually and blamed his sloppiness on nerves. Even though Cal was a pretty good kisser, I've never in my life ever felt like I was on fire because of it. I always assumed something was wrong with me when I would read romance novels and the author would write about the electricity between romantic couples.

We were so close. I was ready to throw caution to the wind and allow myself to fully melt into him. But Drew pulled away first, just as he did in the kitchen this morning. I respect him for that.

To prevent either of us from changing our minds, I rest my cheek against his chest. The music still plays in the background. Couples still dance. Our bodies are together, hands clasped, and we sway slowly to the music, both of our hearts beating harder than they've ever beat before.

"Jess—" I hear him whisper.

"Shh..." I stop him "Don't talk. Just be here with me, like this."

Drew's hand moves through my hair, and then he pulls me a little closer. I tilt my head back slightly and gaze into those green eyes of his. I want to settle here in his eyes, in this moment. It feels comfortable, safe. It's peaceful here. Calm. Loving.

I fight against my logic. Things like this don't happen. They just don't. It's not real life. They happen in movies and television and even books but never in real life.

I thought I knew what I had with Cal. I thought I understood our relationship, our marriage, to be made of true love, which is why I know I can't act on anything with Drew in this moment or any moments after until I come to terms with what my marriage to Cal actually was. I'm still so angry. All of that time with Cal and for what? What even did I accomplish in being married to him? Nothing. Absolutely nothing.

I want my job back. I want my life back. I want to find myself again. Maybe then, I'll be ready.

"I was just going to say, look at the sunset," Drew says. His voice is almost a whisper.

The sunset. I forgot all about the sunset.

I turn my head to face the water, and it is the most beautiful sunset I've ever seen. Every shade of orange fills the sky, highlighting the edges of the few clouds that hang suspended like fluffy pillows against the colorful backdrop, while other clouds resemble the hottest lick of a flame. The last of the blue sky from the day is being completely taken by the fading light; and I know that in just a few minutes, the entire scene will look quite different. It'll be mostly dark with the remaining orange flames fading away.

Drew puts an arm around my shoulder as we watch the sun gradually sink into the water before us. I sort of curl into him as the night air begins to cool, and then, when the sun is gone, Drew turns me into him. He watches me at first as I look up into his eyes; and then he grazes my hair and my cheek with the back of his fingers. "I'm glad we went on a sunset cruise."

The cottage is waiting for us when we return home from the sunset cruise. We're laughing as we come through the cottage door, and Sweeney wags his tail as though surprised to see us so giddy. Drew opens his arms wide like he's going to take my little doggy up in them, but Sweeney stares back at both of us with large eyes that denote suspicion.

I have to assure Sweeney that all is well before he lets Drew take him outside to use the potty, but when they go, I take the opportunity to head to the bedroom and change into my sweatpants. The cottage is quiet, giving me a moment to feel sad, despite the evening I've had. Our vacation ends bright and early tomorrow morning, and I don't want it to for obvious reasons. The last two days with Drew have been more like a break from reality, but I've not really had time to digest the life change that will rise with the sun. Tomorrow, I don't go home to Cal. In fact, I'll never live with Cal ever again. I'll never again follow the cologne trail from our bedroom to the kitchen on work mornings or straighten his tie. There won't be any more corporate Christmas parties or company-wide Easter egg hunts. He'll never know another Thanksgiving with my family, and I'll never know another holiday with his.

The finality of it all is a bit hard to take. It's hard to fathom how nearly two decades of knowing and loving someone can abruptly end. But it has. It is. And it's not like he's dead. No, it's over because he chose to end our relationship. This could probably be easier if he was dead. At least then, I wouldn't have to know what it feels like to simply be discarded by my own husband.

But I also have to choose to keep moving, to look for the good in this big, horrible mess. So, I am looking forward to Drew moving into the pool house—to have him close. I had been thinking how strange going home was going to be without Drew. You don't get to go through something like we have this week and remain strangers. I don't think I want to know a world without Drew now. Even if nothing becomes of us, I need him, and I'm not sure I've ever needed anyone.

But why do I need him? That's the real question. I've never really needed anyone my whole life. I've always been independent. But tonight, standing there on the deck of that boat with him, I decided I need the calm he provides, the safety he emits, the comfortability of Drew himself.

"What do you say we finish off this vacation with a movie?" Drew shouts to me as he walks back inside with Sweeney.

"What sort of movie?" I call back from the bedroom as I pull a hoodie over my head.

"I don't know. Whatever is on." Drew sort of mumbles this, and then I hear him land on the leather couch with a sigh.

I meet Sweeney halfway down the hallway. He wags his tail and throws his head in such a way that motions me to Drew. Sweeney would like a movie night, too.

"We just can't fall asleep on the couch again," I tell Drew as I plop down on one end of the couch. Sweeney hops up between the two of us.

Drew eyes Sweeney. "Definitely not sleeping with the dog again."

I laugh and pull Sweeney into a cuddle. "He's so soft, though. Perfect sleep buddy."

"Unless you're using his underside as a pillow."

"Sweeney likes you. I don't know that he ever quite warmed up to Cal."

"They—whomever they are—say that dogs know who is good and who is bad. I must be a good one."

Drew flips through the channels, hunting for a movie. In the age of streaming movies and T.V., the possibilities are endless.

"We have to go home tomorrow," I tell Drew as he continues to search for something to watch.

"We do," he replies without looking away from the television. "But we go home together. That's better than alone."

"Do you think they'll try to fight us or just let us go?"

"I don't think I really care, Jess. They did what they did. Not us."

"Cal is not going to like you staying in the pool house."

"You're already backing out?"

"I didn't say that" I say quickly. "It might not be easy is all."

"I think we'll figure out," he says confidently.

"And what about tonight? On the cruise?"

"What about it?" He smirks.

"We can't get that close again. There was something in that, and it scared me."

"I agree," Drew replies nonchalantly.

"Aren't you a little afraid?"

"Only of messing it up." Drew is looking at me now. "However, whether we end up together or just friends, I think you're stuck with me."

I've caught him reading my mind a few times this week, and it weirds me out. How is it that I was thinking on this same thing a few minutes ago, and now, here he is confessing to feeling the same way. "How do you mean?

"Sometimes, people who experience a trauma together as we have this week, end up lifelong friends. Stuff like that can connect two people in more ways than one. It's an unbreakable bond."

Something in his explanation reminds me of why I need him. He's confident, sure.

Over the years, I've thought about how horrible it would be if I actually had to date again. Every married person probably thinks about it at least once. Dating was hard enough as a teenager. Awkward silences, acne—dating is quite horrible. And maybe it's because I really don't even know how to date.

I never had any boyfriends outside of Cal. It's like all the guys at school knew I belonged to Cal, even when we were just friends. Then, Cal and I finally started dating in high school, and that was it. However, we never really went out together, just the two of us, on a date. We went to movies with friends and things like that—never one on one. I used to think that maybe Cal was afraid of being alone with me. Now, I'm thinking maybe that thought wasn't completely off base. He couldn't be content just he and I. He needed a child, a family.

I am proud to have had the idea of Drew living in the pool house and my keeping my house. I can't fathom why I was so willing to walk away from it all as though I had done something wrong. My home may not be my dream home, but it's still my home. Still, I have no idea if Cal will pitch a fit over the house. I don't know why he should. All he did was buy it. I did everything else in that house. I even hired our landscapers. So, no, I don't think Cal should keep the house. It's my house.

People Watching

SATURDAY

People Watching

41
Drew Clark

I awoke earlier than I would have liked, but I'm not exactly sure how this day is going to end. So, I figured a head start was better than a late start. I won't wake Jess, though. I checked on her, and she's still sleeping soundly in one of the bedrooms. Sweeney follows me around the cottage as I tidy up the space. We didn't make a huge mess, but I like to leave things that I've borrowed in better condition than how I found them—which would be hard to do here. The cottage is basically perfect.

I wouldn't tell Jess this, but I am nervous. Before the day is done, I will probably have had to see Lindsey again. I likely will have had to see *my* family with Cal. It doesn't matter what happened between Jess and me yesterday; this still sucks. It hurts. I can pretend not to be angry. I can pretend not to care. But the fact is that I do care. I *am* angry.

I left my house a week ago to set out on a family vacation—a vacation that I had thought could put Lindsey and me back together. I had thought I'd try. She didn't let me try. And okay, maybe I didn't try to love Lindsey as much as I could have when the vacation began, but how does one dish out those lovey-dovey feelings when the other is throwing fireballs? Now I know that I was fooling myself. We were already over.

I've thought a lot about my mom this past week, too. I've

wondered what she would think about all this. Did I let her down? Most of the decisions I've made in my adult life were for my mom. I didn't want to turn out like my dad—so dependent on a woman that I couldn't even tie my shoes without her. I think, for the most part, I've succeeded at that. Sure, I let Lindsey shred away every part of me that was truly me, but I can get those things back. I still know who I am underneath. She didn't kill me. She hurt me. There's a difference.

It's already getting hot outside. The humidity is thicker this morning, and sweat rolls down my forehead as I put the last of my luggage back into the car. As I close the trunk, I look up at the cottage and see Jess standing there, smiling at me. She's beautiful this morning. Her hair is long and loose, trailing down her shoulders. She's got a thin throw blanket around her shoulders, and she leans against one of the columns on the porch with a cup of coffee in her hands. What is it with women and throw blankets? It's a hot and humid July morning, and here she stands with a blanket around her shoulders.

I can't help but smile back at her as Sweeney stands next to her, looking back at me. "Good morning, sleepyhead."

"You let me sleep late."

"I couldn't wake you. You were sleeping too well."

"Do we really have to go home?" she asks me.

I nod my head. We really do have to go home. "You're beautiful," I tell her with a smile.

"I didn't take you for a morning person," she says to me, ignoring the compliment. "But I kind of like you being a morning person."

"Oh? Like it enough to start joining me for a six a.m. jog?"

Jess laughs. "I would never intentionally go for a jog at six o'clock in the morning."

"Not a morning runner?"

"I can't believe people actually run on purpose first thing in the morning. That's like an afternoon activity."

I open the front door for her. "Whatever happens today...when we get home..."

"We'll be okay," she assures me. "We've got this."

Sweeney trots inside behind us. "We should probably leave soon to beat the traffic," I tell her. "I don't want to go, but we..."

"We have to," she finishes my sentence. "I guess I'll call Cal. Let him know what our living arrangements will be."

"Do you think he'll fight you on it?"

"I don't know. It could go either way, I suppose." She shrugs. "But the house is mine. It's the least he can do."

"It is the very least," I tell her, and then I take her coffee mug from her hands, set it on the table, and pull her into me, wrapping my arms around her small body. "You know what I think? I think we should imagine ourselves a year from now. Maybe we'll be right back here in this little cottage, toasting to our divorces, toasting to a new life. We'll laugh about all of it."

"I hope we'll be able to laugh about this in a year," she whispers against my chest.

"A lot can happen in a year." I let her go and turn to the dog. "Besides, the victims who end up with the dog in the end, are always the winners in the movies." I give Sweeney's head a pat, and he wags his tail.

"This is true," she says. "One of my favorite parts of *Legally Blonde* is when Elle helps Paulette get her dog back."

"That is a very good scene," I agree. "And that's all I'll say about *Legally Blonde*."

"Drew Clark, I think you like chick flicks."

"I do no such thing."

"Admit it!"

"No. I'm not admitting to anything that isn't true."

"There's nothing wrong with liking chick flicks."

"There's a lot wrong with enjoying a chick flick."

"Name one thing."

"For starters, real life never works out that way. Ever."

Jess is staring at me, arms folded across her chest, tapping her foot at me, and trying not to smirk at this silly conversation. This look, even this look from her, steals my breath away.

This woman. She gets under my skin in the very best of ways. "Okay, I'm not going to stand here and argue over chick flicks. We have our own drama to get home to."

"You're such a buzzkill," Jess mumbles, picking up her coffee from the table. "I'll wash this when I'm done."

"You're not the first person who has ever accused me of being a buzzkill," I point out.

"Oh good, then you're aware." She gives me a sarcastic smirk before disappearing into the kitchen. I laugh at her silently. I don't mind friendly banter. Actually, I prefer it. It's fun. Lindsey wasn't capable of friendly banter. The moment she felt like she was being backed into a corner, she hit low, and she hit hard. Every time. Our friendly banters always ended in a fight.

We don't really chat as we drive away from Sullivan's Island. The stretch of road that leads from the island to the mainland is depressing, at best—nothing but trees and marsh and a reminder of what is being left behind.

I think we did a pretty good job on our last couple of days of vacation, ignoring what today would feel like. It's every bit as horrible as I thought it would be, and by the look on Jess' face, I think she's feeling the same as me. Sweeney is curled up in the backseat, oblivious.

I've envied many dogs in my lifetime. It started when I was a kid and had my black lab puppy. I always envied him. Dad would be shouting for me to cut the grass, and I'd look over at my lab. He never once looked anxious to help me with household chores, which made no sense to me. He slept in our house. He ate food that we provided for him. He required baths and naps and sleep and basically everything a human requires. So, why was he allowed to be lazy, and I couldn't?

That's child logic, I know, and in my defense, I *was* a child. But I find myself envying Sweeney right now. I'd like to be oblivious. I wouldn't mind a time machine either. We could flash forward into the future, skip all this, and get on with the rest of our lives. But life isn't a movie or a television show or even a novel. This is reality, and like reality, it must be dealt with moment by moment until there is resolve.

I resolve that a year from now, on this exact date, Jess, Sweeney, Joyce, Harold, and me will gather together to celebrate the one-year anniversary of the worst vacation ever. I'm still not sure we can classify this past week as the worst vacation ever. A lot of really bad things went down; but I'm sitting next to Jess in this current moment, and that feels like the best thing that has ever happened to me.

Hardly a word has passed between us since we left, but now, Jess reaches her hand over to mine and rests it there. She doesn't look at me as she does so, and I don't look her as I open my hand and hold hers tightly.

42
Jess Dawson

I think we did a pretty good job on our last two days of vacation, not anticipating today and how it might feel. But as the coast descends behind us and we inch closer to home, the reality of what has happened to me and Drew is more than just setting in. It's overwhelming my soul—the sadness of it all, the end of Cal and me.

I've allowed myself to be taken back to that Wednesday night on the beach more times than I should—the way I felt in the moment that Cal confessed everything. You know, there was a small part of me that felt sort of victorious after his confession. Maybe *victorious* isn't the right word. Perhaps the word I'm looking for is *validated*.

Even though Cal confessed more than just infidelity, the entire confession validated what I had suspected all along. It made me feel better knowing that I already knew, even though I didn't really know. I felt a little less crazy, but I guess that's because Cal has been forcing me to feel crazy since we've been together. I see it now, how he could manipulate anything to make him out to be the wise one. Even before he had cancer to blame everything on, he was a professional at making me believe a lie. He was so convincing in telling me why I was wrong. I believed him. I even believed myself to be less intelligent than he. Maybe he really could remember things better than I could. But that's not true, is it? That man has mentally abused me for years, and I'm just now realizing it.

That's not to say I have been oblivious to his antics. I knew something wasn't right. I knew my mind and my heart were trying to convince each other of two completely different things. Yet when a person is being manipulated by a master manipulator, it's not always obvious. They may know something is off, but they don't know enough to win the fight. And so, they don't say anything. They don't fight. They take it. Because maybe they really are a bit crazy. Their parents always told them they *were* dramatic. Maybe they are. Maybe there is something wrong with them, and the abusive husband is the only one who will ever love them.

I'm not crazy, though. I know that now. Cal has been manipulating my mind for nearly two decades now, and that thought alone leaves me feeling even angrier.

This is why the house is mine. It doesn't belong to him. For everything he did to me, he doesn't deserve it. I sent Cal a text message a little while ago informing him of the new living arrangements. He's called me ten times since I sent that text, but I can't bring myself to answer the phone. I don't want to speak to him. I just want to get home, watch him carry his stuff out of our home, and move on with my life.

Now, my hand rests cradled in Drew's hand, and it's as close to peace as I think I can come to feeling right now. We're heading home to drama and who knows what kind of trouble. I hope that Cal will do the right thing. I hope that he gracefully removes his belongings from *my* home, and he leaves without a fuss. But I know Cal, and he doesn't always operate that way—especially when he feels he's being cheated out of something he rightfully earned.

And I guess I could see his point. Cal was the breadwinner for us. He did work hard, climbing the ladder and finally reaching the top. He didn't get to where he is now in his career without being a shark about it, and that's what he is—a shark. But the thing about sharks is they are strong and fearless, and they will literally eat anything just to see if it can be digested. However, one bop on a shark's nose, and you've confused the hell out of them long enough to get yourself ahead. This is what my kicking Cal out of our house is—a bop on the nose—because I know he expected me to roll over and go back to living with my parents.

Cal has missed one very important thing about me—cancer made me stronger, not weaker. Of course, he wouldn't know that because he checked out a couple of weeks into my illness and never checked back in when I was better.

"You okay over there?" Drew's voice breaks through my thoughts, a welcome distraction.

"Just thinking," I tell him.

"I'm not going to let anything happen to you, Jess. Or your house. I don't want you to worry." I believe him, but I'm also not worried.

Cal was only ever able to protect me with money. That was his solution to everything. *I'll just pay them a few thousand dollars, and they'll go away.* He thought he could solve any act of injustice done toward me with money. Drew is different. He'd protect me with something a bit more viable than money—logic, for one, or maybe his fists.

"I know," I tell him. "I want him to be civilized is all. He can be difficult when he wants to be."

"We can't control his actions, but we can control ourselves. Maybe we focus on what we can do and say instead."

"Should I go with you to get your things from your house?"

"I don't think so, but let's not make any plans just yet. We need to assess the situation first," Drew says. "What if we plan for the wrong reactions?"

"So, you're suggesting we just play it by ear? I don't like play-it-by-ear situations. Anything could happen."

"Sometimes, you have to, Jess."

"I'm not a very spontaneous person," I tell him. "Like at all. It sort of freaks me out."

Drew laughs. "But it's sort of exciting, too, right? The thrill of the unknown can be fun."

"Not in this situation, Drew. I don't want any more surprises. I just want it to be over. And once it is, I never want to see Cal Dawson ever again."

"We've got at least an hour and a half before we have to face either of them. So, let's just enjoy the rest of this trip home. Like Sweeney."

"He's sleeping."

"Sleeping is a very joyous activity," Drew points out.

"I suppose." I can't disagree with that. I do like sleeping.

We're thirty minutes away from home now. So far, the only plan is that Drew will take Sweeney and me home first. He'll stick around in case Cal is there. If Cal isn't there, then he'll go pack his things from his house. I suppose it's an okay plan. It's the only thing Drew would allow me to work out in my head.

My stomach is in knots; my heart is pounding; and I've not felt anxiety like this since my first chemo treatment. Even Sweeney, sensing this anxiety, has awakened from his slumber and moved into the front seat to sit with me. Why couldn't we have just stayed on Sullivan's Island forever?

My phone continues to buzz in my lap. It's Cal still trying to reach me after I informed him of what our living situation will be. I've ignored the calls, obviously, but I don't think I can ignore them anymore.

Drew glances at me. "You have to answer it eventually, Jess."

"Why?"

"Because you're a grown-up and you are capable of handling grown-up situations." He talks to me now as though I were Lilly. He's not poking fun at me, though, because he can't. He's been ignoring Lindsey's calls, too.

"I'll handle my grown-up situation when you handle yours."

"Lindsey can wait."

"So can Cal."

"Jess…"

"Fine." I sigh and pick up the vibrating cell phone out of my lap. Cal's name, flashing across the screen, does nothing but make me want to puke.

"I'll talk to him," Drew offers.

An escape! I hand him the phone.

"I was mostly joking." Now, he looks terrified.

"It's only Cal," I say sweetly with a sleezy kind of grin on my face. I do weird things like this when I'm anxious. I get a little goofy and make funny faces.

Drew reluctantly takes my phone, which is still vibrating because now Cal has resigned himself to the back-to-back calling. As soon as my voicemail kicks in, he ends the call and starts a new one. It's been quite obnoxious, and I have considered turning off the phone completely. I haven't, though, because I know I have to talk to him.

"Hi, Cal, it's Drew." His voice is smooth and confident. Drew pokes the *speaker* option on the phone screen so that I can hear what Cal has to say as well.

"I was beginning to think you had murdered my wife. She's not answering any of my calls." Cal does sound angry but mostly annoyed.

"She's not your wife anymore, Cal," Drew reminds him. "And there's not much to say. We're not far from her house; and my hope is that when we arrive, your stuff is out."

"See? This is why she needed to answer my call. That's my house. She doesn't get my house. Lindsey, Lilly, and I get *my* house."

Drew's facial expression changes slightly. I think it's an expression of hurt. The thing about this whole situation is that both of us forget, in our efforts to comfort the other, that we're in this together. Lindsey stabbed Drew in the back, too.

As for me, my face has grown hot as the anger has begun to build, replacing the anxiety I was feeling. I want to say something, but I don't. I let Drew handle this conversation.

"You don't deserve that house, Cal. You deserve *my* house with *my* wife." I notice that Drew doesn't say anything about Lilly being his daughter. She's not.

"She's not your wife anymore." Cal uses Drew's line against him. "I guess we'll have to let the courts decide who gets what," Cal says strongly.

"You don't have a leg to stand on," Drew tells him. "You cheated and created a human with Lindsey. No court will ever side with you—especially given Jess' bout with cancer and how she had to fight that alone. So, you do what you think is right, and we'll do what we think is right. But I'm telling you, it won't go in your favor. Save yourself the time and money. All Jess wants is the house."

"And his money!" I add, mouthing the words silently but furiously.

"You'll owe her a pretty big payout, too," Drew adds, cutting his eyes to me to make sure he said that part right. I nod.

Cal is silent on the other side of the phone. I can't hear anything except his breathing, which is really only because he's that upset. Cal sort of breathes through his nose like a dragon when he's angry.

Finally, he says, "We'll discuss this at another time when we're all calm. For now, she can have the house."

"You're damn right she can. And not just for now. For as long as she wants it."

"Like I said, we'll discuss these matters at a later date when we're all calm enough to discuss it without fighting," Cal repeats himself. "Where are you two now?"

"About fifteen minutes out," Drew says. "And we're sort of

hoping you won't be there when we arrive."

"Well, you're in luck. We got home last night. I packed some stuff then and slept over at your house last night. I'll go ahead and set myself up here with *your* wife." Cal's voice is vicious, seething with venom. I've never heard him to talk anyone like this, except for bad clients and colleagues who have tried to screw him over in the past.

Drew's jaw tightens. He's fighting his own anger; I can see that in his body language. I feel guilty. I should have talked to Cal, not Drew.

"Then, can I ask you and Linds a favor? Please go find something to do while I'm there packing my belongings." Drew's voice is even.

"I think we can accommodate that request," Cal replies. "We're heading out now for a few hours, anyway. Have at it. Just don't touch my stuff."

I stifle a laugh at that childish last sentence.

"Cal, you're the one that has an issue touching *my* stuff," Drew says, and then he ends the call. Abruptly, angrily. I mean, as abruptly and angrily as you can be when poking that bright red circle on the phone's screen that ends the phone call.

"I'm sorry," I tell him almost immediately. "I should have talked to him."

"No, I'm glad you didn't," Drew says, pushing his hand through his hair and adjusting his body in the driver's seat. This must be something he does when he's frustrated and constrained by a seatbelt.

"I'm a grown-up," I remind him softly. "I'm sorry."

"How did you marry that guy?" Drew's tone is exasperated.

"He wasn't always like that," I say sadly, turning in my seat to force my eyes to gaze out the window. I'm not even offended by the question because I've asked myself that same question many times over the last few years.

We are home now. I recognize it all—the grocery store, Target, my favorite McDonald's. Yes, I like McDonald's. I suppose it's a guilty pleasure, but if one ever tells another that they love McDonald's, the other always acts like it's a horribly unhealthy sin. But if that many people were truly disgusted by McDonald's, would the drive-thru always be so busy? More people enjoy McDonald's than will admit to it, I think.

"Once Cal became successful, he changed. He thought he was

above a lot of things, including sitting with me at the hospital."

"Lindsey wasn't always a slut either," Drew says, his voice not as frustrated this time.

"You shouldn't call women sluts," I correct him, only halfway joking. There is a piece of me that hates hearing men call women sluts and whores, no matter how slutty or how whorish the woman in question is.

"Fine, Lindsey wasn't always… Jess, there's not a word to describe her that isn't going to offend you."

"That's fine. I've met her. I don't need a description."

"I guess we both married people who turned out to be two totally different people after a while," Drew resigns.

"I guess that's a polite way to put it."

As my driveway and house come into view, I do feel a sense of relief. Home is home, regardless, and I'll never not be happy to be home.

43
Drew Clark

I am immediately intimidated as I pull into the circular driveway of Jess' home. I had no idea what to expect. I knew they had money, but even the mention of my living in a pool house didn't formulate an image of a home this grand in my head. No wonder we never ran into each other in Greenville. We're in different tax brackets. We don't go to the same places or even know the same people.

I know it's the right house because Jess doesn't try to correct me, and as soon as I put the car in park, she's unbuckling her seatbelt and hopping out of the SUV with Sweeney in her arms.

"I'll get our luggage," I tell her, but the only question rolling around in my head is whether this house is paid off. Also, does it come with a bellhop?

I'm just a journalist—an editor. I've never made anywhere near six figures. What if the relationship between Jess and me evolves into something serious? What if we do end up together? If this house isn't paid off, then how can I support Jess and keep her here in this home she loves so much?

Fear and doubt run through me as I carry our things through the very large double front doors. I can't help but look up as I pass under the threshold at the height of the doors. If one of these ever need new hinges, I'd have to hire someone to do that. There's no way I could manage this massive door on my own. They remind me of the front doors on the Biltmore Estate in Asheville, North Carolina. But the Biltmore is allowed to have doors like that because it belongs to the freaking Vanderbilts!

Jess is a schoolteacher—not that being a schoolteacher isn't as important as being a Vanderbilt. It's the most important job there is outside of police, doctors, firemen, etc. Anyway, the point is, schoolteachers don't live in homes like these.

"I'll show you to the pool house." Jess' voice echoes against the hardwood floors of the interior of the house. The entire home is open concept, which makes it look even larger on the inside than it does from the outside. I know that sounds hard to believe, but I'm telling you the truth.

As I follow Jess through the living area toward the glass French doors on the far wall, I take it all in, mesmerized. I can't understand why Jess was so taken by the little cottage on Sullivan's Island when this is her home. Why were she and Cal staying in that beach house with basic amenities and not staying in the house down the street with a pool and an elevator? None of this makes sense to me.

"Are you okay?" she asks me as we cross through the French doors to the outdoors and into the most magnificent private backyard I've ever seen in my life. The grass doesn't even look real. The pool glistens as though it were full of glass marbles, and the pool house is like something from a magazine.

"You really should have told me that you live in a mansion. I was not expecting this," I tell her.

"It's not a mansion. Well, I guess I don't see it that way. This house was my fortress when I had cancer. I know it's big, but I found solace in the spaces of the home. A lot of times, I'd sit here all by myself, days on end, and I…I found a way to make it a castle! Every day was a new adventure." Jess smiles as she reflects; then she shrugs her shoulders. "The walls know me. They know Sweeney. The floors know us, too. The pool, the grass—it's home."

"I'm not wealthy, Jess." I think we should go ahead and get that out in the open. I'm not poor either, but I've never known a wealth that could provide a home like this.

Jess turns to me. Her eyes grow serious, and her expression falls. "Do you think that changes anything, Drew?"

I search her eyes for a few moments, my heart breaking as I do. "You deserve whatever you want, and I can't… If these are the things you want, I can't provide this."

Jess steps closer to me, taking one of my hands, and then she whispers, "First, you don't have to provide for me. Second, this house is paid for, Drew."

I ignore the part about where she says I don't have to provide for her. "But the taxes alone…"

"That's what Cal's money is for. And maintenance. Everything else I can make work on my salary." Jess corrects herself. "Well, I don't have a salary yet. But next week, I've made an appointment to renew my teaching license. It shouldn't take long to find a school. Then, I'll have a job."

Jess, still holding my hand, leads me to the pool house. Not that I needed directions. This pool house probably has its own address. She types a code into the keypad by the door and then pushes open the glass doors.

We step inside, and Jess was right. It's not your basic pool house. People pay top dollar to live in studio homes like this. It's immaculate! There's a large, open living area with a platform king-sized bed, seemingly sitting in the center of the room itself. But the room is so large, it serves as the divider between the living area and kitchen.

"The bathroom is through that door there," Jess says after I've done a full 360-spin of the entire pool house.

"Jess, are you sure about this?"

"You don't like it?"

"I love it. That's the problem. I don't deserve this."

"Stop it. But I am curious—the way you've carried on about this house… Is your home a dump? I'm sort of hoping so. I'd like Cal to live in a dump."

At that, I laugh. "No, it's not a dump. But it's not this either. Just…mediocre, I guess. Average."

"This is ours now," Jess tells me. "This pool house, the pool, the house itself—it's ours. Not officially, obviously." She smiles at me; and in her smile lives hope for us, and I can't dismiss that.

"What are we doing, Jess?" I move closer to her.

"I don't know yet, but I think…I think it's going to turn out just fine." She beams.

"I have to get my stuff from my dump now."

"I thought it wasn't a dump," she says.

"Next to this, Cal definitely downsized." I smirk.

"Hurry back."

"Believe me, I won't delay."

Just as Cal said, Lindsey, Lilly, and he are gone when I arrive to pick up my things. I sit in our driveway for a few seconds, staring up at my modest two-story home. It's nothing spectacular—just your average home in the sort of neighborhood where every other house looks like a duplicate. I remember when we bought this house. It was our first home, and it was a happy day. I had carried Lindsey through the front door the way superstitions tell you to for good luck. But I suppose that act is just a superstition. Luck never found us.

As I walk through the front door, the familiar scent of home fills my nostrils. I expect to feel a tinge of sadness, and maybe I do a little. But honestly, part of me is expecting Lindsey to appear at the top of the stairs screaming orders at me. But she won't because no one is here. The house is quiet. The only audible sound is the air coming through the vents from the air condition unit.

I don't have a lot of stuff I'd like to keep. Most of my keepsakes are in a storage building, but I would like my clothing. Lindsey made this home mostly hers, but I do have a closet with clothes in it. I want my clothes.

It doesn't take me long to clean it out all out. I find some yard bags in the garage which can hold hundreds of pounds of yard debris and, turns out, a few hundred pounds of clothes and shoes, too. I look around our bedroom, allowing myself to remember the good things that happened here—like our first night after we bought the house. We made it a point to make love in every room of the house. I think about that now, and I'm not sure why that was so exhilarating. I guess because we were newly married and had our own home. We were young, still in love, and high on the hopes of life. It's almost scary now to think of how quickly our marriage changed, how quickly our whole lives changed.

Before I leave with my bags full of clothes, I find myself standing in Lilly's room. It smells like baby powder and lotion, a sweet smell that I've always loved about Lilly. There's something strangely comforting about that scenty combo.

My eyes dance across Lilly's crib, her toy box, the shelves of books and stuffed animals. The framed birth announcement that I wrote and published in our local newspaper. I smile because I really love that kid. Standing here now fills my heart with something like sadness. It hurts knowing how much I love Lilly, and she's not even my own flesh and blood. All of the plans I had for her, the memories I thought we'd make together—none of that was real. None of what I dreamed up in my head can even happen now. I am not a father. I only played one for a little while.

I sit in the driveway for just a few minutes longer before backing out for what I hope will be the last time. I gaze up at our house. It's nothing like the house Jess and Cal shared, but it was our house. I worked hard for this house, worked hard to keep Lindsey and Lilly happy in it.

I can still remember what the big, pink wreath looked like on the front door when we brought Lilly home. We had good memories, fun times—things I'll cherish forever, I guess. And maybe that's why leaving my home feels a little harder than I expected. It *is* my home—my memories, my life—time that I'll never get back. And I don't think that I would try to get it back, even if I could. Regardless of what Lindsey and Cal did to me and to Jess, Linds and I were happy once upon a time. We did have a wonderful life. Some people never even get a chance at that—a chance at having at least one moment in their life when they were absolutely, positively happy.

I'm happy now. Relieved, too, I think. Still, it feels like I'm mourning this life that I had as I look up at my house that my wife will now share with another man. I'm mourning my happy memories with a family that used to be mine.

It doesn't feel right or fair. It makes me angry. It hurts, too. I wonder if I'll ever stop asking where it all went sideways. Despite it all, I'm looking forward to the future. With Jess. With whatever is next. It is time for a new chapter.

44
Jess Dawson

When Drew left to pack his things from his house, I gave Joyce a call. I thought she might like to know that we are home now, and I kind of missed her, too. I was also thinking that maybe it would do Drew some good to see Joyce again, since when we left, things were quite tense. So, I invited Joyce and Harold over for a little afternoon drink, and I hoped they'd arrive before Drew did.

As I had hoped, Joyce and Harold arrived only a few moments before Drew did, so he was both delighted and absolutely surprised when he walked into the house and found both Joyce and Harold sitting at the kitchen table with me.

After hugs are exchanged between Joyce and Drew, we all sit at the kitchen table. The guys are sipping on beer while Joyce and I sip on our wine. We make small talk but avoid the topic of vacation.

I admire Joyce and Harold. I was a bit worried about them when we left Edisto on Thursday. Joyce's normal dose of cheer and happiness was in short supply that morning, and though she would have never admitted it, she was sorry for taking Lilly and for putting Harold in such a situation. That much was obvious in her facial expressions Thursday morning.

"I'm just glad to see you forgave Joyce, Harold," Drew says from across the table finally confronting what has happened over the last week.

"I really didn't have any other choice. She threatened to cash out my life insurance." Harold cuts his eyes at Joyce.

I giggle, but Drew points out, "You're not dead."

"Yet," Harold replies.

At that, we all laugh. Joyce reaches over and places her hand in Harold's, and this simple act seems to warm him a bit. Joyce and Harold give me hope. Love that lasts *does* exist. They're living proof of it.

"Well, Drew, I'm not sure what kind of house you came from, but I'm willing to bet that you definitely upgraded," Joyce says, admiring my house.

My kitchen is my favorite, and I don't even really like cooking. I just really love how it turned out—white marble countertops, refurbished hardwood floors, modern-style cabinets.

Drew laughs. "I thought Jess had taken me to the wrong house."

"I don't mean offense by this, Jess, but you don't look like you're made of money," Joyce says to me.

I try not to take offense by this statement, but I can't help but feel as though she just accused me of appearing poor. I don't dress horribly. But I am humble. I didn't grow up with money. Heck, I didn't even get married with money. Cal made the money. Now, it's my money.

"Well, I didn't come from money, so I guess, I never let it get to my head. This was always Cal's money. But now that he's done what he's done, his money is my money. To be honest, my dream home is on a coastal farm somewhere. It could be falling apart. I don't care. This house isn't me, but I'll be damned if I let Cal and Lindsey live the rest of their lives here. So, I'm taking it."

"You are an amazing woman, Jess," Joyce says to me. "I knew it the moment I saw you, but I know it for sure now."

"What did you two do with the last couple of days of your vacation, anyway?" Harold asks, speaking up in a gruffy sort of voice.

"I've got a friend who owns a little cottage on Sullivan's Island," Drew says. "We almost came home, but then we both realized, we didn't want to. So, we spent two good days on Sullivan's Island."

"I'd say the last couple of days were the highlight of our vacation," I add.

"What's next?" Joyce asks, a smirk on her face as her eyes dart between Drew and me.

Drew and I look at each other.

"I'm not sure. I think we're going to take it one day at a time." Drew smiles at me.

I smile back, but I feel desperately like I want to change the subject. "How is it that we all have lived in the same town for many years, and yet our paths have never crossed?"

"It is a big city," Drew says.

"Not New York-big, though," I retort.

"Who's to say we didn't cross paths at one time or another?" Joyce counters. "We wouldn't have known. We wouldn't have been looking for each other."

"I still think I would remember crossing paths with Jess," Drew says, and I feel my cheeks warm.

Joyce is still smiling at both of us, dreaming up who-knows-what in her mind about Drew and me, and then Harold clears his throat, signaling something to Joyce.

Joyce seems to recognize the meaning behind the throat clearing because she nods her head. "We do need to head. Meeting our oldest son for dinner." She smiles as she stands from her chair, Harold following suit. "We did want to see you two, so I was grateful Jess called."

"It was good to see you both—especially with how we left things," Drew says as he gives Joyce a side hug.

Drew shakes Harold's hand, and then we both walk them to the door.

Joyce is looking my front doors up and down again, just like she did when they arrived. It makes me feel a little uncomfortable. I know it's a big house. But aren't people capable of acting like they've never seen a large house before? I don't go over to small houses and start talking about how tiny it is. I love Joyce, but she's just like my mother was when I first brought her over to our new house—like I had committed some cardinal sin by living in a home this size. I don't even think my house is as big as people make me feel it is.

"It bothers you when people talk about the size of this house, doesn't it?" Drew asks me after I've closed the front doors. It's like he can read my mind. Or maybe he's already able to read my body language.

"It does. It's just that this house doesn't define me. Just because it's big and expensive doesn't mean I'm expensive or have expensive tastes. This house is just something that happened because of Cal's success," I explain. "And it is home. I've lived here for years now. It doesn't even feel that big to me anymore."

Drew wraps his arms around me. "I won't make fun of your giant house anymore."

I can't help but laugh into his chest. "Thank you." And then I pull back slightly and look up at him. "Are you okay? After having to pack your own things from your own house?"

"I'll be okay," he tells me. "I realized I really didn't have a whole lot of things I wanted from the house except for my clothes. I've got a storage facility with the real treasures in it."

"Ooooh, treasures?"

"My treasures. You wouldn't care anything about it." He smirks.

"Who says? You don't know what sort of treasure I like."

"I don't, do I?" He smiles wide. "We are brand new."

"So new, we still have that new car smell."

He laughs. "What does that even mean?"

"I have no idea. It just sounded good."

Night has fallen. The clock has just ticked past midnight, and I'm finally crawling into my own bed for the first time in a week. I want to sleep. I'm exhausted, but as I lie there staring up at the ceiling, watching the ceiling fan blades spin in the faint moonlight coming through the bedroom window, I can't discount exactly how long the last seven days have felt.

I left this house a week ago with one man and came home with another. I left this house with my husband and came home with a soon-to-be ex-husband. The last time I slept in this bed, my husband was next to me. Tonight, I'm alone—well, apart from Sweeney. He is next to me, curled up on Cal's side of the bed.

I know that all I would have to do is call Drew, and he'd vacate that pool house in a second to sit with me. But I won't do that. I know how to be alone. I've done it before. I've been alone while married. It's not hard. It's frustrating. When you're married, when you have a partner, you don't expect the loneliness. But it comes, and one must learn how to deal with such things without going insane. I learned. I started reading, binge-watching Netflix, shopping online—basically anything that brought me joy. That's how I learned to keep myself company. It also helps to have a dog.

Sweeney lies next to me now, his little snores filling the room gently. He was quite surprised when I told him he could sleep with me. Cal never let him in the bedroom at all. As far as I'm concerned, Sweeney can go into all the rooms of the house. He can roll his body all over the sheets and the floors and the couch. Cal always hated how badly I spoiled him, but guess who is still here and who had to leave?

Dogs really do make life a bit happier. And they're always happy to see us, even if it is only because they live for belly rubs. We love their personalities and how they look to us from day to day. We love their cuddles and snores and licks and paws.

When Sweeney is hungry and his bowl is empty, he'll sit right in front of me and just stare right into my eyes as though he could cause me to spontaneously combust at any moment. I'm not sure he blinks—just sits and stares. I can't even ignore the stare, it's so hard. It's mostly obnoxious because a part of me would rather him bark to tell me what he needs. Staring can get weird after a while.

But then there are times when Sweeney is sad. This is usually if I don't take him on his morning walk or if it's a rainy day. He hates rainy days. But I've not yet decided if he hates the rain because we can't walk when it rains or if he hates the rain because he loves the sun that much. Regardless, I've had dogs my entire life, and each of them has left a special place in my heart when they've left this world. Sweeney will be no different.

There's an old phrase about being a parent to young kids: the days are long, but the years are short. I wouldn't reserve this phrase for only parents to young kids. This phrase applies to everyone living and breathing. I had a whole life before Cal. I had parents and doggies and friends. With Cal, I had all of that and then some. Now, I've got Sweeney and Drew and this big house and a divorce on the horizon. How many lives do we truly live in one lifetime?

When my paternal grandmother died, I had a really hard time coping with her death. She was the victim of nursing home neglect, and I was angry she died the way she did. The entire situation was out of my hands, but still, I somehow made it my fault. There had to have been something I could have done. The truth is that there's nothing I could have done to save her.

Thankfully, my grandmother had written a memoir of sorts a few years before she had to be moved into an assisted living facility. Her mind was mostly clear then, and I think it says something about who she was as a person to recognize that she needed to leave her family with something, and she needed to do it soon because the days are long, but the years are short.

About a month after her death, I read her memoir. I needed to. I didn't know what I would find in it that would bring me solace, but it was what I had—all I had, really. Turns out, it was exactly what I needed. My grandmother lived a thousand lives before I was even born—lives I had never even heard about. I read her memoirs and realized that I only knew one part of my grandmother—not the whole part of her. No one can really ever know the whole piece of someone. We really only know what we've seen of them.

When I finished reading her memoir, I realized that the way my grandmother died was inhumane and nearly murderous, but she lived a whole life. At ninety-four years old, she had seen it all. She had even been to France!

The point is, we live many lives in the amount of time we're here on this earth. Some live more than others, but one thing we all do consistently is completely lose it when we're in the midst of really terrible circumstances. We think, *This is it! This is how I go. This is how the rest of my life is going to play out. This is a horrible life.*

Life goes on. As long as the world keeps spinning, so shall we. If we stop, we die.

People Watching

ONE WEEK LATER
Monday

People Watching

45
Drew Clark

Linds and I both showed up at the same lawyer's office on the same day at the same hour to file for divorce. The whole thing was a little strange, but I did breathe a heavy sigh of relief when I walked out of the lawyer's office. The paperwork had been filed, and now all we had to do was wait on a hearing.

It was recommended that we talk civilly through some things before a hearing. They encouraged us to divide our assets without fighting. Lindsey texted me the morning we went to file for divorce with five simple words: *I just want the house.*

I obviously screenshot that text message because I don't trust her completely. Maybe that is all she wants, in which case, she can have it. But I'm not a fool. I'm not taking her word for it. I'll keep this screenshot on my phone and backed up in every photo storage app that exists just so I won't lose it. Then I'll have that text message as proof that I don't pay her a single penny. I might even print the screenshot out, frame it, and hang it on the wall in the pool house until this whole thing is over.

Tonight, I'm cooking Jess dinner. She's been testing to renew her teaching license all day, and I want to surprise her with dinner. Of course, this entire gesture will go completely sideways if she didn't pass the tests required to renew her license; but somehow, I've got a lot more faith in her than I do myself. I know she'll get her license renewed, and I'm willing to bet she'll have a job by the end of the week.

Sweeney sits patiently by my feet, waiting for me to drop some sort of scrap of food for him. I've discovered that this dog will do anything for cheese. I'm pretty sure I could get him to dress up in a coat and top hat and dance a little jig for some cheese, but I've not tested that theory yet.

I've just put Jess' plate on the table with a glass of wine at its side when she walks through the door. The front door hasn't even shut completely before I hear her shout, "I did it!"

I smile to myself as I hear the patter of her feet running toward the kitchen where I'm now placing my plate on the table. I refuse to eat in the dining room. It's too big, and we're too small. As soon as her feet hit the floor of the kitchen, she makes one jump right into my arms and squeals with joy.

"I knew you would!" I tell her.

"I can be a teacher again!" She's nearly singing.

"I think you'll have a job by Friday."

"You *would* think that."

"If I'm right, you can take me out to dinner on Friday night." I set her feet back on the ground, and then she sees that I've prepared dinner.

"What's this?" she asks with wide eyes and sweet smile.

"Dinner."

"You didn't have to cook dinner, Drew."

"I know I didn't have to. I wanted to surprise you so we could celebrate the renewal of your teaching license. Besides, I really wanted an opportunity at cooking in this giant—I mean, very small and mediocre kitchen."

She rolls her eyes. "What if I had failed?"

"I would have immediately thrown all this food in the garbage, and we would have gone to a bar and gotten trashed."

Jess laughs. "You're a good man."

"All right, all right, sit down. I'm hungry." I instruct, only kind of trying to push her away from me. I could totally skip dinner and go for the sheets, but that's not how this relationship is going to work. I'm hoping I can at least court the woman, but who knows what's going to happen? Still, my feelings for Jess seem to continue to grow with each passing day.

"This smells so good. Did Sweeney get some cheese?" she asks me as she slides into her chair and picks up her fork.

Sweeney and I look at each other. I think about lying, but somehow, I think he'd tell on me. So, I answer honestly instead, "He did not get cheese."

"Drew!" Jess scolds. "Sweeney always get cheese." She slides out of her chair again, walks to the refrigerator, and pulls out a bag of shredded cheese. It takes Sweeney all of about half a second to slide across the floor to her where he happily gobbles up his cheese in one breath.

"I wouldn't side with Cal on hardly anything, but you have spoiled that dog," I tell her.

"Dogs are meant to be spoiled," she informs me as she sits back in her chair to finally eat.

"Not everyone feels that way about dogs, you know. Some think they're there for hunting. Others think they're just there for the aesthetics."

"Well, those people are wrong."

I agree. Those people are wrong. I still miss my old lab.

"I saw Lindsey and Lilly today," I tell her.

The fork and pasta hang in midair between Jess' plate and her mouth. "Like, you went over to their house?" She shoves her pasta into her mouth.

"More like I was minding my own business at the grocery store, and bam! There they were. She doesn't even shop at that grocery store. It costs too much." It bothered me, seeing her and Lilly there. Now that she's with Cal, she can afford to do her grocery shopping at this particular grocery store. I was there for the produce because that's all I could afford, but still.

"Did you talk to them?" she asks me after sipping her wine.

"Started to. But then Cal popped up when I was en route, and I made a last-minute U-turn."

"Did they see you?"

"I don't think so."

We're quiet for a few minutes, and then Jess asks, "Did they look happy?" Her big, brown eyes look at me now, hoping that I say they looked miserable.

I hesitate before answering, "They did look happy." I can't lie to Jess. I won't. Not even to spare her feelings.

Jess picks up her wine glass and takes a bigger sip. "We're happy, too, aren't we?"

I smile at her. "I'm happy. I really am. I feel lighter, more hopeful. I'm happy."

Jess thinks about this; and then I watch as her lips curve upward in a tiny smile, and she nods her head. "I am, too—not just because you said you are, but I… I feel like I've got my whole life ahead of me again. A clean slate. I like it."

"I feel less like a prisoner."

"I guess I never felt like a prisoner. More like an object. Just something he kept somewhere and only took it out when he needed it."

I understand that, too.

I lift my wine glass to Jess, and she does the same. "To new beginnings."

"New beginnings." She smiles. We tap our glasses together and sip our wine.

I like our night routine these days. We have dinner together, retire to our separate quarters for showers and pajamas, and then reunite in the living room for some television viewing. Sometimes, we meet in the pool house; sometimes, we meet in Jess' living room. Regardless, at ten p.m., the television goes off; we say goodnight; and then we depart. It's sort of like being in college again with a college girlfriend who lives in a dorm separate from mine. We don't really have any responsibilities outside of ourselves. I have a job. She'll have a job. We have Sweeney. It's simple. I hadn't realized how much I craved simplicity.

After Lilly was born, nothing was ever simple again. Nighttime feedings and early morning wake-up calls, diapers, baby formula, toys—it all became so loud. But because I thought Lilly was mine, I was happy to experience it all because that's what being a parent is about.

I had no clue how depleted I was until my marriage was officially over, and it was over the night Cal stood on that beach and confessed everything. It was actually over long before that, but that confession was the nail in the coffin. It was the finality of our marriage, our relationship, and the life we had built together.

It's been a couple of weeks since that night, and I'm just not sure I've still fully grasped the entire situation. I'm a dude. We aren't really taught how to work through these things. In the South, men are taught to bottle up feelings and keep charging forward. If one ignores their feelings, then they go away. This teaching is why there are so many bitter and angry elderly men in nursing homes. They never resolved the bad things that happened to them—the cheating wives or girlfriends, combat and war, loss of children, or even loss of a spouse.

I'm not a therapist, but I think if we forget to confront and make peace with the trauma from our past, it comes out of us in other ways. For most people, they just get angry. These are the people who have no qualms with cussing out a teenage cashier for not hearing them correctly or for giving them the wrong order. These are the men who end up alcoholics or drug addicts. They find coping mechanisms for the traumas that still haunt them.

I don't want to be that man. I want my mind to be clear and pure. I want my heart to be at peace and full of love. I want to be exactly who my mother wanted me to be—a good man, a kind man—one who dies without any regrets, a happy family, and some sort of a legacy. Jess makes me want to be that man.

Have I failed as a husband? Should I have fought harder for Lindsey? Even before she had the affair, things were falling apart. What if I had stepped in? Tried to keep them from falling apart? I don't think I wanted to. What does that mean?

Maybe it's not that I failed. Maybe it's that I made a mistake, and those two things are not the same. Are they related? I suppose they can be, but perhaps Lindsey and I should never have married in the first place. If I'm being honest with myself, I suppose there were red flags. I wonder if she had them, too. But I thought I loved her. She was so vibrant and full of life. Lindsey was like a drug without having to take a narcotic. She made me high on life—until she didn't.

Lindsey grew up a little quicker than I did. I stopped doing the "immature" things she hated like going to college football games or going out after work with a couple of male colleagues for a drink. But instead of finding something we mutually enjoyed doing together, I let her pick everything. I let her have control. We didn't share it. She ran our marriage, our household, and our calendar. And I did absolutely nothing to contribute.

Let me be clear, though—it wasn't out of laziness. It was out of fear—of Lindsey, yes, but also of losing her.

Of course, over the last couple of years, the fear of losing Lindsey began to sound more like a dream, but then the fear of Lindsey herself actually grew, too. I sort of feel bad for Cal now. He really has his work cut out for him, but somehow, I feel like they will make it. They're both just crooked enough to make each other incredibly happy. I suppose I should feel bad for Lilly. Or maybe I should feel sorry for her future spouse. There's no telling what kind of woman that kid is going to grow into with Lindsey as her mother and Cal as her father. But that's not really my problem now, is it?

FRIDAY

People Watching

46
Jess Dawson

I hadn't realized how much I miss the smell of an elementary school. It's an indescribable smell. It's like a mixture of old crayons, construction paper, and chicken nuggets with a hint of sanitizer. I don't remember ever picking up on this smell when I was an elementary school student, but it's prevalent now.

This particular elementary school is an older one on the rougher side of town. I don't mind. Despite popular belief, some of the best students I've ever had were the ones who didn't come from wealthy families—not to say there weren't some wealthy children I've taught in the past that turned out to be some of my favorite students, but my heart tends to gravitate toward the kids who probably don't get to go home and eat a warm meal for dinner.

The leather of the chair in which I'm sitting in the lobby of the office is peeling, but the rest of the school's office seems to be clean and upkept. The secretary keeps glancing at me from over the counter, probably being nosy, wondering why I'm here. She thinks I haven't noticed the sneak peeks over the rim of her thick, black-framed glasses, but I have. Part of me wants to ask her why she keeps looking at me, but I don't. If I am hired at this school, I don't want to get off on the wrong foot with the secretary. Still, it bothers me.

"Mrs. Dawson?" Another woman appears in the doorway that leads into the back offices, her voice startling me in the near-silence of the school's office.

"Yes?" I stand.

"Mr. Waters will see you now." She smiles at me and continues to hold the door open as I gather my things and meet her.

Mr. Waters is sitting behind his desk when the woman shows me in. He looks up at me slowly and then smiles. "You must be Jess Dawson." He stands behind his desk, holding his hand out for me to shake.

Nervously, I extend my arm across the desk and give his hand a firm shake—just the way my daddy taught me. Firm handshakes mean something to bosses—and potential bosses, I assume. "It's very nice to meet you," I tell him.

"Sit down. Tell me a little bit about yourself." Mr. Waters sits down in his desk chair just as I sit in mine.

I look across the desk at Mr. Waters. He's probably just a few years older than I am with kind, blue eyes and graying hair. He could stand to lose a couple of pounds, but I've seen chubbier men. If one were to look up the word "principal" in the dictionary, there would be a photo of Mr. Waters next to the definition. He's the image of principals across the country—slightly overweight, graying hair, bags under the eyes. A lot of teachers go back to school for their master's degree, so they, too, can one day be the principal of a school. I've never been interested in that. I don't want to gray. I don't want to be exhausted—well, not any more than a teacher already is. And I spend too much money on eye cream to accept that bags under the eyes is part of the job description.

"My name is Jess—that much is obvious." I giggle nervously. "I've been teaching elementary school kids for a few years now, but a couple of years ago, I had cancer and was forced to step back. The chemo I underwent took more out of me than I had expected, and I was doing an injustice to my students. For the last couple of years, I've been a housewife as I healed."

I stop for a few seconds, wondering if I should reveal that I'm in the process of a divorce, too. I decide against it. "I've been getting a little anxious around the house, and I realized I was ready to head back to the classroom. Which is why I'm here." And then I smile because that's what you do after you tell someone about yourself, don't you?

Mr. Waters flips through some papers on his desk—my application and my resumé resting at his fingertips. "It looks like you're most experienced with first graders?"

I nod. "Mostly. My first year, I did teach a second-grade class."

"The position you've applied for is third grade," he points out.

"That's correct. I feel more than qualified to take on a class of third graders." My palms are sweating from the anxiety in my chest. I'm not normally a nervous person, but job interviews never really get any easier, no matter how many I've sat through.

"Mrs. Dawson, I have to ask, why do you want to teach here? Of all places? If I'm being honest, we lose teachers the way first graders lose teeth. There are some very good kids here, but there are also some challenging ones—kids with only one parent, kids living in the foster system, kids who wear the same clothes to school every day because it's all they have."

"I don't have any qualms about poverty or unfortunate circumstances. If you'll notice, the last school I was in was at the bottom of the list in rankings of best elementary schools for that district; and I've got to tell you, it was my favorite school to teach in. Leaving those kids, rich and poor, was the hardest thing I've ever had to do." Apart from having to stand on a beach and hear my husband confess his adulterous affair that resulted in a child.

Mr. Waters considers this response, and then he replies, "Well, you're certainly qualified."

I nod.

His blue eyes meet mine. "I really don't want to do this because you seem like a very nice lady..."

My heart sinks in my chest. How do I fail a job interview at an impoverished elementary school? They usually give these jobs away to the first teacher who shows.

"And I hope you understand what exactly you're getting into," Mr. Waters continues. "The job is yours if you want it."

"Wait, what?" I am sure I misheard him. The way he started that statement sounded like a rejection.

Mr. Waters chuckles. "As long as you understand what you're getting into, the job is yours."

"I do! I understand completely! I have a job?" Now, I'm standing, nearly screaming with excitement; and I realize this is probably the most unprofessional I've ever been on a job interview. But he would just have to understand what my life has been like over the last few weeks. I need this. He doesn't know I need this, but I do.

He laughs at my excitement. "I might also have you lead a workshop to get the rest of our teachers as excited about this school as you are right now."

"I'll do it!"

"It was a joke. Mostly. I don't know. It's actually not a bad idea. Anyway, don't worry about that right now. Go home and get ready for your first day of school. I'll see you bright and early on Monday morning."

I shake Mr. Waters' hand again, fighting the urge to hug him, and then I proceed to thank him profusely.

The heat coming off the asphalt of the school's parking lot is nearly unbearable as I head toward my car, digging in my purse for my phone. July and August tend to be the hottest and most humid months of our summers here in South Carolina. I'm conditioned for it because I've lived here my whole life, but there is something uncomfortable about feeling the heat rise from the hot asphalt. There's a smell—a whole feeling, really. And it's not pleasant.

I step into my car, turn on the ignition, and then crank up the air. While I wait for the car to cool, I dial Drew, smiling when he answers on the first ring.

"I got the job!" I scream into the phone.

Through the phone, Drew lets out some sort of excited man shrill. I can't even describe the sound, nor have I ever heard it come from any man's mouth; but I guess there really is a first time for everything.

"I thought he was about to turn me down. My heart sank and everything," I tell him. "I can't believe it. But, Drew, this school is really sad. It's so run down. It's clean, and it smells good; but there were lightbulbs out and cracks in the wall. Maybe we can do something. You know, schools don't really have the ability to make improvements themselves. They have to wait to be funded."

"What can we do? You've not even taught your first class, and you're already thinking of ways to make the school better."

"It's what I do, Drew. I make things better."

"That's true. You've definitely improved my life." He flirts now, but I can admit that I walked right into that one.

"You're making me blush."

"I like when you blush."

I laugh. "Back to what I was saying, how can we help the school?"

Drew is quiet for a few seconds, and then he responds, "We can have a fundraiser. I'll write about it, put it in the papers and magazines. We can do an interview with the principal and see if we can't pull the community together to fix up the place."

I like the idea. "You would do that for me?"

"Baby, I'll do anything for you," he says smoothly.

My heart does that fluttering thing again when he uses this tone of voice. The addition of *baby* in the sentence also doesn't help matters. His cheesy pick-up lines actually turn me on a bit. They're silly, yes, but it's the way he says them—like some sleezy bartender. It's sort of sexy. No, I don't have a thing for sleezy bartenders. Well, only if they look like Drew. I'm still fighting against the current that Drew is—especially since we've officially spent every day of the last two weeks together. The current is strong, and some days, I picture myself letting go and allowing myself to sink into him.

"I start work on Monday morning. I'll give the place a good evaluation, and then we can get a plan in motion."

"Our first project together." I can hear him beaming through the phone.

"It's really our second."

"What was our first?"

"Getting the hell out of Edisto and still making the best of the two remaining days we had left of our vacation."

"Ah, that's true. That was quite the task."

"But it worked out beautifully," I point out.

"Indeed."

"Okay, I'm picking up a bottle of champagne to celebrate, and then I'll be home! We'll take a swim and enjoy my last weekend as an unemployed woman."

"Sounds like a plan. Jess?"

"Yeah?"

"I love you." He says this so gently, so simply. Like he actually means it. And you know what? I think he does.

My heart stops at the confession. It's the first time he's said these words to me when he wasn't in a cheeseburger-induced coma. As I mentioned, the attraction is obviously there. It's not even to a point that I can still deny. If I hadn't had Drew these past couple of weeks as we settled into a new life, I can't say I would have handled it as well as I feel I have. I renewed my teaching license, got a job—two major things that I'm not sure I would have been motivated to do so soon if it weren't for the way Drew makes me feel about life, about him, about the future. Maybe it's the prospect of happiness again. Or maybe it's knowing that all is not lost. My first marriage may be over, but it doesn't mean there's no time or space for a second and (hopefully) final marriage. My first round of love ended, but that doesn't mean there's not room for more.

But I can't say those words to him yet—not because I don't mean them because I think I do love Drew. I think I can love him more the closer we become. I think I could definitely see myself growing old with this man. However, I can't give in yet. It's not the right time. Not for us anyway. Not yet.

"I'll see you when I get home," I tell him, and then I hang up before he can say anything else.

MONDAY

People Watching

47

I picked out my first-day-of-school outfit last night just as I've always done. Drew laughed at me, of course, because he just doesn't understand. A teacher's outfit is important. First impressions are important. I don't want my students to think I'm some fashion flunky or something. I know the trends; I dress the trends. But even still, that first outfit must be thought out thoroughly.

I'm nervous—beyond nervous, actually. I haven't been a teacher in quite a few years. What if I've forgotten? Stupid cancer. I had figured the whole teaching thing out. What worked and what didn't. How to communicate with the students who are abused at home and how to talk the wealthier kids into helping the less fortunate ones. Every year, I had to redesign the whole process; but it worked, and I had very successful school years.

Mr. Waters is waiting for me at the door as I walk up the parking lot toward the school. He smiles boldly at me, his blue eyes bright in the morning sun. "Good morning, Mrs. Dawson."

"Good morning, Mr. Waters." I smile back at him. "It's going to be a wonderful day!"

"I sure hope so." He turns in behind me as we enter the school. "Your classroom is just up the hall here." Mr. Waters falls in step beside me, guiding me with his arms. "You may want to decorate differently. The last teacher sort of left rather quickly, and she didn't take anything with her. It's all yours to keep, or you're more than welcome to do your own thing."

"Thank you," I tell him.

Mr. Waters stops in front of a closed door. The nameplate next to the door reads, "Mrs. Stock." He slips a key in the door and then pushes the knob down. "We'll get your name on the nameplate soon. The printer is down."

The door opens, and he flips on the light switch. Only two of the fluorescent light fixtures come alive. The rest are burned out. The darkness of the room surprises me. How can someone teach these students in a room as dark as this? They'll fall asleep. *I'll* fall asleep.

"We've been trying to get someone out to replace the lightbulbs for weeks. There are other schools more important than ours, I suppose." His blue eyes sadden for a bit. "Most schools at least have a PTA. We can't get anyone to volunteer. Half these kids don't even have parents."

"Mr. Waters?" I decide now is the time to tell him about the plan Drew and I have conjured up to get this place fixed up. "My friend is a journalist, and after my interview on Friday, we thought we could help get this place fixed up a bit. We sort of hatched a plan."

Mr. Waters shifts his weight onto his left leg and crosses his arms over his chest. "What does his being a journalist have to do with anything?"

"Well, the awareness factor. He can write about a fundraiser to give the school a makeover and post it in newspapers, the internet. We'll get volunteers to donate for our cause, and then we'll have a beautification day. We all show up here at the school, repaint, fix the lightbulbs—the whole thing."

"And this won't cost anything?"

"It shouldn't—not if we position the fundraiser correctly and petition the right people."

He stares at me with his arms still crossed. I have no idea what he's thinking. Finally, he speaks. "I'll think about it."

"That's all I ask."

"Well, I'll leave you to your new classroom," Mr. Waters tells me. "If you need anything, you can hit this speaker button here. It rings the office, and they'll respond through the speaker."

"Thank you, Mr. Waters. I've been in a classroom before." I

smile, only being slightly sarcastic.

"None like this one, I assure you."

When Mr. Waters leaves, I glance at the clock. I have roughly thirty minutes before my students should begin arriving. What can I do in thirty minutes to make this room a bit brighter?

There is one solid wall made of nothing but windows; but there are yellow vinyl shades that have been pulled, and they're blocking the sunshine. That's a start. I go to pull up the first of seven vinyl shades, but as soon as I tug the roll, the entire thing falls off the wall. All seven shades come crashing down to the floor. I freeze for a few minutes, waiting to see if someone comes running in to make sure I hadn't already died on the job. The noise had been extremely loud; but the quiet has taken over again, and no one comes.

Well, that's nice to know. No one comes running when there's a loud, hazardous noise in this school. But the room is finally bright. Someone who had never been in this room before would never know that the lightbulbs are burned out—unless they looked up, of course.

I gather the shades from the floor, rolling them up neatly, and then I place them in the room's storage closet, which then provokes me to make a mental note to stay after school and clean out this closet.

There aren't any pictures on the walls—not even a cursive handwriting chart or a banner of the ABCs trailing across the top of the chalkboard. It's not even a whiteboard. It's an old-fashioned chalkboard. Well, I will miss my dry erase markers, but chalk is fun, too.

From my bag, I pull out a few rolled diagrams and pictures from my last classroom. They're not necessarily age-appropriate, but they'll do for now until I discover the personality of this classroom. I hang them in different spots with tape.

Then I notice that all of the desks are lined up vertically in rows like a high school classroom. I think elementary school kids benefit from group settings. So, I decide I have enough time to rearrange the desks into groups of four.

I'm just getting the last cluster of four desks together when the first student walks into the classroom. I notice her as she stands in the doorway, unsure if she should come in or not. She's got strawberry blonde hair and bright blue eyes. She wears two different types of shoes; dirty, white shorts; and a t-shirt that is a bit too big

People Watching

for her. I make another mental note to see about finding this girl some clothes that fit, match, and are clean.

"Hi, my name is Mrs. Dawson. I'm your new teacher."

The girl is bashful. She chews on the end of her thumb. She doesn't say anything.

I keep a smile on my face but lower myself to her level so that we can see eye to eye. "What's your name?"

"Olive," she says in an almost-whisper.

"Well, it's very nice to meet you, Olive," I tell her. "Can I shake your hand?"

Olive is hesitant; but then, she reaches out the hand she wasn't chewing on, and I take it in mine, giving her a firm handshake.

"My daddy always taught me that when you shake someone's hand, you give them a firm squeeze," I tell her gently.

"Why?"

"To show you're confident," I tell her because that's what she needs to hear right now. "I'll tell you a secret—your handshake was pretty firm."

She smiles at me, her blue eyes lifting, and my heart fills with warmth. I hadn't forgotten, but now I remember exactly why I wanted this job with these kids.

Olive finds her seat, and soon, more kids begin to fill the room. I greet them all at the door, showing them to their seats; and then, as the bell rings, I take my place in front of the classroom.

"Good morning," I tell them all. Most of them echo the phrase back to me. I smile. "My name is Mrs. Dawson, and I am your new teacher."

One of the boys raises their hand. "Mrs. Dawson, why the room so bright?"

"The correct way to ask that question would be, 'Mrs. Dawson, why *is* the room so bright?'" I correct him, and then I follow it up with an answer. "Well, if you want to hear a secret, I sort of broke the shades that were on the windows. I didn't mean to, of course. I'll clear it up with Mr. Waters after school."

They all giggle, which was my intention. I really don't think Mr. Waters will care about some broken yellow vinyl shades that had clearly been hanging over those windows since the 1970s. They were bound to go sooner or later—if not by force, then certainly by themselves.

"Today, I want to tell you a little bit about me, and then I'll go around the room and get you to tell me a little bit about you. You don't have to share anything personal, and if all you want to do is tell me what your favorite color is, that works, too."

They all seem willing to participate, so I go into a little spiel about myself. I even tell them about Drew. They were all very delighted to hear about Sweeney, and they've even asked if I can bring him to school with me one day. I'll definitely have to clear that one with Mr. Waters.

As each of the students go around the room telling me about themselves, I do feel a wave of sadness for each one of them. They're not all poor, but most of them are; and if they're not, they tell me things, like their parents are divorced or their father died in the military. Everyone really does have a story—even kids.

The school day flies by. When the bell rings at 2:30 and they all file out into the hallways, I find myself sitting at my desk nearly exhausted—not physically, emotionally. I certainly signed up for a project. Mr. Waters tried to tell me, and even now, he couldn't tell me any differently. I'm here to help these children. That's my purpose here. They need help. The school needs help. I can help. First things first, I have to fix up this classroom.

I text Drew: *I'm staying late at the school. I've got a lot of work to do.*
Drew: *How late? Need dinner?*
Me: *I broke the vinyl shades that have been hanging out in this room since at least the '70s, and there's a closet that needs emptying. It's a whole thing. This place is a mess.*
Drew: *Dinner?*
Me: *I'll pick up something on the way home. Don't wait on me.*

I haven't forgotten about Drew's confession of love, but I've done a great job at keeping myself distracted so that I wouldn't have to think too much about it. That's why I'm standing in front of this storage closet now, thrilled to find that this is definitely going to be another distraction to keep me from having to think about "I love you."

The closet is filled to the ceiling with everything—baseball bats, balls of all shapes and sizes, books, movies, even a T.V. There are stacks of paper, folders, and years of miscellaneous garbage accumulated in this little closet.

I start by sorting through everything. I make stacks of books, folders, papers, outdoor toys, etc. By the time the closet is empty, the entire classroom looks like a junk store exploded. I stand in the middle of it all, overwhelmed but determined.

I'm hidden behind a wall of books when I hear the classroom door swing open. "Um, Mrs. Dawson?"

"Over here!"

It's Mr. Waters. "What is going on in here?" He appears in my line of sight, his hands on his hips, a bewildered expression on his face.

"All of this was in that closet," I tell him. "Oh, and I broke the shades."

"The shades have been there since the '70s." He shrugs. "They were coming down eventually."

Those poor shades. And it's a good thing they didn't fall on any of the kids.

"What are you going to do with all this stuff?" he asks me, turning in a circle, clearly overwhelmed by the mess.

"There's a dumpster out back, right?"

"Yeah."

"Most of it goes there—with the exception of the books. Oh, and the baseball bats and balls can be donated to the P.E. classroom."

"Mrs. Dawson?" Mr. Waters asks after a few moments of silence. I had looked up once to make sure he hadn't stroked out. "Something tells me you're going to do great things here. We've not had a teacher like you since...well, me."

I smile. "I hope I do."

Then there's a knock at the door. We both look up, and it's Drew, standing there with a strange look on his face and a box of pizza in his hands.

"Drew? What are you doing here?" I'm excited to see him as I bound over the wall of books to greet him, even if I may subconsciously be avoiding any deep conversations with him right now.

"Bringing you dinner. What happened in here?"

"My thoughts exactly," Mr. Waters replies, stepping toward Drew with an extended hand. "Zach Waters, principal of this fine school." He smiles sarcastically.

"Drew Clark, the journalist," he replies, eyeing Mr. Waters a little too long. Drew would have to notice that Mr. Waters is not my type.

"Nice to meet you, Drew Clark," Mr. Waters repeats. "I just finished telling Mrs. Dawson that I think she's going to do really great things here."

"Doesn't look like she's off to a great start." Drew sets the pizza down on my desk.

"It's all going to the dumpster. Well, with the exception of the books and the P.E. equipment," I tell him.

"Jess, you shouldn't be in here doing this by yourself," Drew says. "This is too much for one person. You pulled all of this out of the closet without any help?"

This is the one thing I need Drew to let go of. I *was* a cancer patient. I'm not one anymore. I'm not helpless. I'm not weak. He didn't even know me then, and still, he insists on trying to prevent me from doing any heavy-lifting. "Drew, it's fine. I scooted most of it out. I didn't have to lift anything."

"If I had known, I'd have helped," Mr. Waters interjects.

"Thanks," Drew replies. "She's hardheaded. You have to watch her."

"I'm not hardheaded. I'm determined." I smile.

"Care for any pizza?" Drew opens the lid of the box, looking at both Mr. Waters and me. The smell of the hot pepperoni pizza fills the classroom quickly, and suddenly, I realize just how hungry I am.

Mr. Waters looks as though he's salivating, too. "If you don't mind."

The three of us shove pizza down our throats like our lives depend on it, and then, thankfully, the men decide they'll carry everything out to the dumpster for me. I'm not weak. I can do manly things. But if someone is offering to carry a bunch of garbage out to the dumpster for you, you let them do it.

I spend the time, instead, filling a nearly empty bookshelf that already existed in the classroom with the books I found in the closet. Tomorrow, I'll bring the rest of my books from home. I love children's books, and I've spent many years collecting them. I'll pick up some from thrift stores and yard sales. Others I'll buy on sale. I don't believe in having too many books.

By the time it's all done, it's nearly nine p.m. Drew and Mr. Waters come in from the last trip to the dumpster, and the classroom is back to normal—well, better than normal. It's dark out now, and the room is back to being dim; but it feels better, fresher.

"Maybe I'll have you redo all the classrooms over fall break in

September. This whole place could use a facelift," Mr. Waters says to us as we walk across the dark parking lot together toward our cars.

"Consider what I told you this morning about the fundraiser and Drew," I tell him. "We can make it happen. We don't need the district's money."

"We'll talk about it. Tomorrow," he says. "Go home. Get some sleep. You've done a lot today."

Drew slides his arm around me. "Thank you for letting Jess do what she needed to do."

"I think she's really going to turn this place around—if not with aesthetics, then definitely with her attitude. She's already changed mine." He smiles, and then he steps into his car and disappears from the parking lot.

Drew looks at me. "You never stop surprising me."

"What does that mean?"

"Everything."

3 MONTHS LATER

People Watching

48
Drew Clark

I really don't understand why these things are necessary. If two people want to get a divorce, I don't know why they can't just get one. Why do we need a hearing?

Outside of the legal expenses, this whole process has been pretty simple. I've heard horror stories of how these things go down, so I feel pretty grateful that Lindsey isn't being difficult and we can settle this today with civility. It's been three months since Edisto happened. We've not had to talk to each other a lot, and I wonder how much of that has to do with Cal. Regardless, we agreed on a clean break. She keeps the house; I'm a free man.

Of course, Lindsey is late for the hearing. Cal has not changed this part about her. Lindsey will likely be late for her own funeral. I can imagine it now—Lindsey running through the doors of the church in high heels and a too-tight dress, frazzled to the max, and then elegantly climbing into her own casket, waving at everyone before she closes the lid.

It's exactly how she's just arrived at the lawyer's office. Only, there's no casket for her to slip into. She practically falls into the chair across from me at the extra-long conference room table. I can't help but crack a smile. I did always have a thing for Lindsey's spontaneity. It made her messy and forgetful and late for appointments, but somehow, that was okay with me. It was part of her charm.

"Sorry I'm late." She's out of breath. "The sitter was late to arrive this morning."

Her eyes fall on me, and for just a second, she takes my breath away. It's only a second, and maybe it's more of a memory than a moment. This condition that she's presently in isn't that different from the day we met.

She was running late for something that day, too, and we collided with each other as we both tried to exit a shopping center at the same time. She laughed, and I did, too, as I helped her pick up the papers she had dropped during the collision. As I stood to face her, she immediately took my breath away. Lindsey, at that time, had been the most beautiful woman I'd ever laid eyes on. It was a movie moment—the kind of moment where time stood still around us, and some sort of breeze from some unknown source was blowing through her hair. There was probably even music in the background. Lindsey became the beat of my heart, my adrenaline rush, the very air that I breathed. But what goes up must come down, right?

I've spent the last three months trying to figure out exactly when our marriage went down the toilet. I don't know that there was a defining moment—well, outside of the whole adultery thing. Anyway, we just…changed. I think that's all there is to it. We changed, and we went in opposite directions. That's what happened to us—that and Cal.

"Andrew, do you have any final comments?" The lawyer's voice breaks through my thoughts, nearly startling me. I realize I've been zoned out during this entire hearing.

I look at Lindsey across from me. Her eyes glisten with tears, and I realize that this hurts her, too. It's always going to hurt when a relationship ends, whether it's romantic or not; but I think one of the most important things we can do for each other is to know when to walk away. We should have walked away from each other before either of us had the opportunity to hurt each other.

"I don't think so, no," I reply. "Except, well, Lindsey, I sincerely wish you a happy life." I'm not being sarcastic or unkind. If Jess has taught me anything over the last few months, it's how to forgive and forget, how to keep moving. She may be struggling with the forgiveness piece with Cal, but she's kept moving. I admire that.

She wipes a tear from her cheek and nods her head. "Thank you." It's more of a whisper, but it's genuine.

Without any further comments, complaints, or arguments, we are officially dismissed as two divorced people. It was that easy. People spend years planning their weddings only to have the entire marriage end in a couple of hours in a room with a long table and more legal people than is necessary.

As I trek across the parking lot toward the SUV, I send Jess a text letting her know it's done. She's currently sitting in her own divorce hearing, and I hope it's going as well as this one did.

"Andrew!" Lindsey's voice catches my attention from a few feet away. "Andrew, wait!"

I stop at the driver's door of my SUV and wait for her.

"Hey," she says, out of breath now from the slight jog she took to the car.

"Hi," I say blandly but also with a hint of a question.

"I...I felt like we should say something to each other."

"I did. I wished you a happy life."

"No, that's not what I mean. We were married, Drew. For years. This isn't...this can't be it completely."

"Linds, this is it. I-I'm moving forward," I tell her gently. I don't want to be mean—not anymore, at least.

"What about you and Jess?"

"What about us?"

"Are you happy, Drew?" she asks softly.

"Linds, we're both going to be okay." Then, I do something I don't expect—I pull the woman into a full body hug. My arms wrap around her slender self one more time. I feel her cry into my shirt, and her body trembles the way it always did when I would hold her as she cried.

"I'm so sorry," she cries softly. "I am. I really am. I've been so ashamed of myself—of how I made you think Lilly was yours. I'm just so...sorry."

I pull back from her slightly, tilting her face toward mine. "We both did and said some really horrible things to each other. So, how about I forgive you as long as you can forgive me, too?"

Her face cracks with a weak smile. "You were always too good for me, anyway."

"For what it's worth, I'll always love you—my first serious girlfriend, my first fiancée, my first wife. You're pretty special, Linds. Not a lot of women can lay claim to all of those things."

She giggles. "Maybe I'll see you around?"

"I'm sure we will," I tell her. "But let's please try not to vacation together next year, okay?"

"Definitely not. It's my year to pick the mountains, anyway."

"Ahh yes. Well, I hope Cal is a bigger fan of the mountains than I am."

"Not really, but he'll adjust." Then Lindsey takes a few seconds to take me in. "I'll see you around then?"

"Sure."

Lindsey nods her head and turns to walk to her car but not before turning back to look at me one more time. I stand by my SUV, waving at Lindsey as she exits the parking lot, and then I climb into my own vehicle.

I take my first drive as a divorced man around Greenville. The sun is exceptionally bright today, the temperature perfect; and I'm not sure how most people feel after a divorce is finalized, but I feel ready for whatever life is going to bring me. For the first time in my life, I don't want to make plans. I can make goals—and I have—but in this new season of my life, I think I just want to see what will happen.

49
Jess Dawson

Cal is already waiting for me when I arrive at the appointed time for our divorce hearing. He's always on time. I'm never late for anything, but I prefer to be right on time. "On time" for Cal is arriving at least twenty minutes beforehand.

"Good morning," Cal greets me at the elevator. He smiles at me as though I don't hate his guts.

"I suppose so," I reply, trying not to notice how extremely dapper he looks today. Despite his betrayal, I can admit he's still a pretty attractive man.

"Everything will be fine. I plan to sign off on everything we have agreed to," Cal tells me. "The house, half of the money earned while married."

"I would appreciate that, Cal. It's not like I'm the one who started a family with someone else." I realize there's still venom in my tone toward him. I don't know how Drew has been able to forgive Lindsey so easily while I've struggled to even say Cal's name.

"Yes, well, we're all very aware of what I did," he mumbles.

"I just want it to be over." I sigh and then push past him as the elevator door opens. I start down the hall to our conference room without him.

I hear him following behind me, keeping his distance. I

appreciate that. Being near him makes me sick to my stomach.

When we enter the conference room, we take our seats opposite each other. The long conference room table is intimidating to me. I've seen these in movies portraying divorce hearings, and they're always full of different types of people required to be present for the hearing. But today, it's just Cal, his lawyer, my lawyer, and me. I can't think of a single reason why we need this giant table. I don't even know why we need this hearing. Just sign some papers and be done with it.

I speak. Cal speaks. No one argues. Papers are signed. The whole process moves rather quickly, and before the hour is out, Cal and I are officially divorced. I'm thankful for the ease of it all; but I find it odd that I spent the better half of two years planning our wedding, and the whole marriage was undone with a few signatures on some paper.

I try to hang back and let Cal depart before I do, but I find him waiting for me by my car when I assumed the coast was clear. I'm instantly annoyed, rolling my eyes at him as I approach.

"I just wanted to talk, Jess," he explains, reacting to my rolling eyes with surrendering hands.

"There's nothing left to talk about, Cal. I don't want to rehash everything. I'm just now beginning to forget about it—everything, not just the affair." I make it clear that my feelings for him run much deeper than the adultery he committed. There's the whole cancer journey and how I was forced to handle that on my own. And I really can't forget his shouting about my inability to provide him with a child on the beach that night in the midst of his adulterous confession.

"I think there's plenty to talk about. It would be a shame to end this way," Cal argues. "I just want to—"

"No, Cal. You don't get to clear your conscience." I push past him, opening my car door, forcing him to move.

"Are you serious?" He looks shocked.

"Serious," I tell him. "Cal, you have to live with what you did to me—the way you left me while I was fighting for my life, the way you found her in the midst of it all, the way you stood on that beach and shouted at me like I had done something wrong, acting like you weren't up to no good. You're ridiculous. You are not the man I thought I knew. I thought I loved an honest, loving, and caring man, who would do anything for his wife. Instead, I married a liar, a cheater, and a narcissist. You are scum."

Cal stares back at me, his eyes burning holes into my skull. "Feel better?"

"No, I have more." I take a deep breath. "But I'm not going to give you the satisfaction. I hope I never see you again, Cal Dawson. Ever."

With that, I slide into my car, start the engine, and pull out of the parking space, hoping I run over his damn toes in the process. He's intelligent enough to step back.

I don't like being angry. I don't like living like this and feeling the bitterness greet me in the morning like a hot cup of coffee. I've figured out how to tuck it away, distracting myself with other things like my students and Drew. But the bitterness is still there, hiding beneath the distractions, ready to ruin my day at any moment.

I need therapy, I know. I have a therapist. I went to a few sessions after cancer, but oddly, the topic of Cal neglecting me during that time never came up. What exactly did I share with that woman?

I probably need a new therapist. I'll add that to my to-do list.

Instead of heading home, I go to the elementary school. Mr. Waters brought in a substitute teacher to take care of my class for the day, but I don't like the idea of someone else teaching those kids. I've fallen in love with every single one of my students, and now, my heart tugs toward them—especially Olive. There's something special about that girl, and I wish I could take her in as my own. She doesn't have any parents; both died by drug overdose. Her grandmother is raising her, but her health is failing, too. It won't be long before Olive finds herself in the foster home system, and it breaks my heart. All children deserve a loving mother and father. They shouldn't have to navigate this part of their lives on their own.

"Mrs. Dawson, I thought you were handling some private business today." Mr. Waters is shocked to see me as I enter the office. He knew what my private business was, but for the sake of everyone else in this office, he keeps it discreet. I appreciate that.

"It's all done, and I didn't want to go home. Can I send the substitute home?"

"Mrs. Dawson, I think you should take care of yourself today," he says carefully. "Your students will be okay. You left the substitute with everything she needs. If you go in there, you'll disrupt the class."

I feel like crying—not because Mr. Waters won't let me teach my class today, but because he's right. I know he's right. Cal was right. Still, confronting these feelings within myself is not something I feel like doing. I'd rather just move sideways and ignore the whole thing.

"Mrs. Dawson?"

"Please stop calling me that," I hear myself whisper. "I'm Jess. Call me Jess. Or Jessica. I really don't care."

"Then call me Zach," he says after a few quiet seconds. "Go home, Jess. Or take a drive. Go to the park or the zoo. Whatever you need to do, do it."

I've been defeated. My shoulders fall. I nod my head and turn to exit the school. My feet feel heavy as they cross the parking lot, and as soon as I'm back in the safety of my car, I cry. It begins to flow so naturally. Oh, but the pain in my chest as the tears stream down my face is nearly unbearable.

I'm not sure what all I'm sobbing over—an ended marriage, yes, but more, too—a life I thought I'd have forever. Maybe I'm even mourning what cancer took from me—my husband, my reproductive system, my students, and my classroom. It took time away from me—time I'll never get back.

And then my marriage—a marriage I had believed would last a lifetime—is now gone. Again, time spent with someone who doesn't even matter anymore. Those memories don't mean anything anymore either. I don't want to remember Cal. I don't want to remember our marriage.

When I'm sure I've cried the last of the tears I have left, I put the car in reverse and drive away from the only place I really care to be. Where I'll go, I have no idea.

OCTOBER

People Watching

50

Today, the sky is gray. A gentle rain falls to the earth. There's a distinct smell when rain hits asphalt, especially when the air is still humid. It's late October, and we're all gearing up for Halloween; but in Greenville, October is also the month we experience our second summer. We don't get to slide into our sweaters and boots for the fall season as early as other places. I've never minded this. The longer it stays warm, the happier I am.

I had planned a science lesson outside today, but we'll have to move those activities indoors. I spent the better part of the early morning stalking frogs in my backyard. Drew thought I had officially lost my mind. He awoke to the sight of me crawling through the grass in leggings and a raincoat. I can't blame him for thinking I had lost my sanity. I'm sure it was quite the sight. But I found one—a frog. Well, it's a toad actually, but the class will still love him. We'll examine his spots and then set him free.

As my students drag in, sleepy from the rain, I decide they need some music this morning to get the blood flowing. In the past, especially in fall and winter, I'd put on some peppy music and make all of my students get up and dance. The rule is that we must dance for the entire duration of the song, and they can dance however they'd like as long as it's appropriate.

"All right, class, it looks like you all need a dance-off this morning. Come on, let's go. Everybody up and assume your positions.

Only a few of the students groan at the thought of any type of physical activity first thing in the morning, but mostly, they're all excited to begin the day like this. I walk over to the old boombox that miraculously still works and push play on "Twist and Shout" by the Beatles.

My dance-it-out-trick works like a charm, and soon, all of my students are wide awake and ready to learn. We start with a little reading because I'm admittedly waiting for the rain to let up so we can go outside for our science lesson. But even though the kids are ready to learn, I can't help but notice their glances toward the playground through the windows. It's like they are expecting something, and I can't figure out what because I've not yet told them about the frog.

"Okay, everyone, why do you keep looking out the window?" I can't take the distraction anymore.

Their eyes all dart back to mine, and I can see that they're stifling a giggle.

Now, I'm curious. It reminds of the scene from *A Christmas Story* when the kid got his tongue stuck to the pole and the whole class kept it from the teacher.

"What are you all hiding?" I ask them with my hands on my hips like a teacher who means business.

Olive raises her hand bashfully.

"Yes, Olive?"

She points out the window again. "On top of the slide."

I walk over to the windows for a closer look at the playground. As my eyes scan the perimeter to the slide, they finally land on what has been distracting the class for the last few minutes. My eyes grow wide, and I realize it's not a *what* they've been distracted by but a *who*.

"What in the world?"

"He's got a sign!" one of the boys in the classroom calls out.

I stare harder at the person on the slide, realizing they are indeed holding a sign. I squint my eyes to read it because I am mostly blind, even with contacts.

The sign reads, *Will you marry me?*

Drew Clark is wearing a suit, sitting atop the slide, smiling like a moron as he proudly holds his cardboard sign in his hands.

I look back at my students again, eyes wide. "You knew about this?"

Olive nods. "He told us it was a secret."

"When?"

"Last week when he came for career day to tell us about journalism. It was when you went to the potty," Olive replies.

I look again at Drew, who is still sitting in the same position, still holding his sign, still smiling.

"Well, I guess I should go out there and give him an answer."

All of the kids begin to cheer.

"You have no idea what my answer will be. What if I go out there and tell him no?" I smile at them.

"But you won't," Olive says.

I shrug. "I guess we'll just have to see. Come on, line up; it's time for recess." I'll get the frog later, I decide. There's more important business to handle.

I don't have to beg. Every single student, even the one kid I have who argues with everything I say, lines up quicker than I've ever seen. I lead them outside, expecting them to sort of take off in all directions the way they normally do at recess. Instead, they stay in a single-file line right behind me the entire trek to the slide.

I stare up at Drew on the slide, folding my arms across my chest. I'm trying to hide a smile and the pounding in my chest, trying to appear cool and calm.

"So, what'd you say?" Drew beams.

"I can't believe you rallied my students into this shenanigan of yours."

"They were all very excited."

I turn to my students. "And I can't believe you all kept a secret from me. We've talked about keeping secrets from teachers. You shouldn't."

Their eyes drop a bit, unsure if I'm actually scolding them or not.

I turn back to Drew. "Why?"

"Because I love you."

"How do you know that?"

Drew looks at all the hopeful students behind me, his expression a little nervous now and maybe not as confident as he first appeared. "I…because…because I do."

"Forever and ever?"

Drew relaxes slightly, and a small smirk spreads across his beautiful face. "Forever and ever, babe."

I let silence hang on that playground for a little while longer. I think about the current that Drew is, the pull I've been feeling since the day I met him.

Having been a beachgoer my entire life, I've had the procedure for when one gets caught in a rip current drilled into my head since I was two years old. If you're ever caught in a rip current, you're not supposed to fight it. You're supposed to float on the water and wait it out. Fighting to get out of the current will only leave you exhausted, which ultimately leads to drowning. Fighting is futile.

I've been floating too long, floating on the idea of Drew since this summer— occasionally fighting it, but mostly, floating. Perhaps it is time to stop floating.

"Okay," I say.

Drew doesn't react immediately. I watch him as my one simple word, settles on his heart. His face lights up; he throws the sign behind him and slides right down at my feet. He doesn't hesitate. He doesn't even ask me if it's okay. He lifts me up in those strong arms of his and kisses me. Our first kiss and it's on a playground. But I'm not sure I could have picked a more perfect scene.

All of my students cheer behind us, and when we turn to them, we notice Mr. Waters and several other teachers and students standing at the door, clapping. Something tells me this whole school knew about Drew's very brave marriage proposal. I can't decide if I'm embarrassed.

"This is humiliating," I mumble to Drew.

"It's perfect."

I look at him. "I love you."

His green eyes grow bright because this is the first time I've told him that. Even after he said those words to me a few months ago, we never talked about it after. I wanted to forget about it, and I guess he didn't want to push it. But now, I can say it. Because I do love Drew. I probably loved him the moment I met him, but it's been these last few months that have forced me to understand that Drew is not Cal. Drew will never be Cal.

I can't float on this rip current forever. I can't fight it either. It's time.

A FEW MONTHS LATER

People Watching

51
Jess Clark

"I can't tell you; it's a surprise," Drew tells me. He blindfolded me before helping me into the SUV and driving off to some undisclosed location.

"I can't see anything!" I groan.

"That's the point," Drew says to me. "I don't want you peeking."

"Can you at least give me a hint? We've been riding for three hours. Toward the coast, might I add. And I know this because this is not what the mountains smell like."

"How can you smell the coast?" Drew asks me.

"I'm technically blind at the moment, so my sense of smell is heightened."

I hear a gentle chuckle from the driver's seat. "You'll find out soon enough."

The SUV is quiet for only a few moments.

"But how much longer?" I ask, breaking the silence.

"Geez, woman!"

I laugh. "You can't blindfold a woman and expect her not to have questions."

"Ten minutes—we have ten minutes before you can take the blindfold off," Drew announces. "Okay?"

Fine. I'll trust him. Ten minutes and then I can take off the blindfold.

I feel the SUV turn off the main road and onto a path that is a bit more of a rougher ride than the pavement of the highway. There's a part of me hoping that Drew hasn't somehow snapped and is bringing me out here to murder me. I still don't think he has a murderous bone in his body, but after the things I've been through in my thirty-something years of life, I can't be too sure. Anything can happen.

Finally, I hear the words I've been dying to hear since he made me put on the blindfold. "All right, take off the blindfold."

I don't waste a single second. My eyes look out in front of us from the SUV, and I feel my heart do a little flip inside my chest at the scene before us. "Where are we?"

Drew looks at me. His green eyes are bright, his smile wide. He says, "Home."

"Home? What are you talking about—home?" I've never been more confused in all of my life. From where I'm sitting, all I can see is the cutest little white cottage with fields as far as the eye can see stretched out beyond it. This is definitely not the city or anything close to what we're accustomed to. This is a farm with a cute house that's not nearly as large as mine, which is fine—less rooms to clean. But still.

"I bought this place."

I look out the windshield again. "What do you mean, you bought this place?"

"You once told me that you dream of living on a farm with enough room to foster as many doggies as you want," Drew explains.

"Yeah?"

"I think the kennel could go over there…" Drew points off to the left of the cottage. "I can build it. I think there's enough space for at least fifteen dogs."

"Wait a minute. I don't…I don't understand."

"We're home," Drew says to me again. "I mean, I hope we're home. I put my whole life savings into this place."

"I still don't understand… What about our house? Your pool house?"

Drew looks a little disappointed now. "I thought this is what you wanted. I thought this would make you happy."

"I'm just…we haven't even had our wedding yet, and now you've bought this beautiful land with its beautiful house and all the space in the world to foster as many dogs as I want." I'm crying now.

"Jess, this is for us. All three of us. Sweeney included. It's what you've always dreamed about, and I couldn't... Well, I saw this place for sale on the drive into Edisto last summer. I had kind of forgotten about it until a few weeks ago. I checked into it, and lo and behold, it was still for sale. And since it had been on the market so long, I got a good deal. I actually bought us something I can afford to keep."

"But it's so far from home."

"But exactly where we want to be," Drew counters.

And I know he's not wrong.

"Come on, let's get out! Check it out." Drew remains enthusiastic, despite my pushback. I really do wish he had consulted me before buying a freaking house.

Sweeney is the first one out of the SUV. He and Drew make a run for the front porch, excited to have a look inside. I keep my enthusiasm at a minimum because I'm still a little angry that he bought this house and this land and made all of these plans without even talking to me about it. A person can't make decisions like this based on a conversation had on a vacation where our prior marriages were falling apart. I didn't know what I was saying. I was upset. I was confused.

But was I really?

I have always dreamed of living on a lot of land with a small house and all the dogs in the world to foster and care for. I told Drew that, and he never forgot it. Can I really be angry with him over this?

Drew comes to me, Sweeney trotting along next to him. "Jess..."

The tears begin to flow before I can even begin to speak.

Drew pulls me into him, only halfway laughing at me. "I should have talked with you first. I just wanted to surprise you."

"I... I never expected you to remember that about me," I tell him.

"I remember everything about you. But there is one more thing I should tell you before we go any further."

"What did you do?" This man and his unpredictability may be the death of me.

"We're getting married tonight." He smiles wide at the confession.

"What in the world are you talking about now?"

"In thirty-minutes, Matt—my friend who owns the cottage on

Sullivan's Island? He's going to arrive to marry us."

"You can't have random dudes marrying you. It has to be official."

"He's actually a wedding officiant. Long story, but he agreed to come and marry us."

"You are insane! My parents aren't even here."

"I figure we'll get married tonight and have a big party later," Drew says. "Both of us have already done the whole 'walking-down-the-aisle' thing. Let's do something different."

He's not wrong. And I have been putting off wedding dress shopping for a few weeks now. I've actually put the whole wedding planning process on hold because I really just don't want to. It's exhausting. I spent two years planning my wedding to Cal, and we saw how well that worked out.

"You're crazy, Drew."

"Only because I'm in love with you." Drew, smiling at me, his eyes so green and calm, says, "Want to be Jess Clark before the night is over?"

I look at Sweeney, who is now standing on the front porch of our new house, his tail doing the little twitchy wag it does sometimes when he's urging me to make a decision.

I look at Drew, standing right in front of me, his green eyes big and hopeful. I think about what my life was a year ago, and I imagine what life can be a year from now.

"I'm not getting divorced again," I tell Drew.

"Of course not."

"And you're stuck with us. Both of us!" I point at Sweeney.

"That's fine." He smiles.

"My mother is going to kill me," I mumble.

"I doubt it. She's sixty-five years old. She's tired of being upset over things," Drew jokes.

"I'll let her know you said she was too old to care."

"I mean, we can just leave that between the two of us."

I laugh. "Drew Clark, I will marry you tonight."

"You will?"

"I will."

And so, we were married. Matt showed up when he was supposed to and married Drew and me out there on the cottage's back patio, overlooking acres of green fields that seemed to go on for miles. The sunset was perfect, and honestly, I'm not sure I could have planned a better wedding or a better evening. It was small, intimate, and so very personal—simple. Best of all, our makeshift wedding didn't cost any money; we didn't have to hire any caterers; and Drew gets to sleep in my bed tonight as my husband. My new husband. A husband I feel certain will stick around forever this time.

People Watching

EPILOGUE

People Watching

In the days and weeks that followed, we moved into our new place. I was able to foster five dogs right from the beginning. The money I made from selling my home in Greenville allowed us to build several kennels for my foster dogs.

I took a teaching position at an elementary school near our new home; and somehow, the three of us fell into the most perfect rhythm.

I could never say that I am glad my husband cheated on me with Drew's wife. That's a pain, a betrayal, that I wouldn't wish on anyone. But the fact is, it happened. Drew and I could have reacted a thousand different ways. We could have fallen apart. And maybe we would have fallen apart without each other. I'm glad I'll never know what might have happened if we hadn't had each other.

Of course, it really all leads back to Joyce. Without her, none of this would have ever happened. I would never have met Drew, which means there certainly would have never even been a Drew and me. There would have been no confession on the beach. Maybe Lilly would have lived her whole life believing Drew was her father. One thing is for sure, with or without Joyce, Cal and I would have divorced—if not after that vacation, soon after. That part was always inevitable in hindsight.

Most people want to frown at people-watching. *Mind your own business. Stop watching strangers.* But if Joyce hadn't been participating in a little people-watching that first day on Edisto Island, we would have never known her either.

Sure, I believe in privacy. It's our right as humans. But people-watching has saved a lot of people in the past, too. It has saved the abused wife or child. It has saved neighbors from being robbed by strangers. It has been the witness to a hit-and-run car accident. It has a saved a child from being kidnapped.

What are we doing with our lives if we can't open our eyes and look for ways to help others in theirs? Sure, not everyone needs rescuing, but some do. I'm glad Joyce didn't ignore a silent plea for help.

Admittedly, Joyce kidnapping Lilly was a bit extreme, but you have to respect a woman like Joyce—a woman who is willing to go to such measures just to save two strangers. She saved our lives.

Ten years have passed since the Summer Vacation of 2023. Sweeney, my sweet boy, lived a very long and happy life. He loved working in the kennels with us when we would get a new round of foster dogs. He played with the dogs who were scared, and he slept next to the ones who cried at night. There will never be a dog like my Sweeney. When he passed away last year, I wasn't sure how to keep moving without him. He'd been by my side through so much. Living without him just didn't feel right. But Sweeney lived in such a way that even with him gone now, I still feel him everywhere I go. I choose to believe he still sleeps in the kennels with the dogs who cry at night, and he still plays with the puppies, too. Sometimes, I still feel him sitting next to me, his body warm against the side of my left leg.

We lost Joyce and Harold two years ago. Harold passed away first, but Joyce joined him a few days later. It was mostly unexpected. Harold had been sick off and on, and Joyce had suffered a minor stroke. For the most part, they had been doing okay. We would drive into Greenville to visit them once a month, which is why we were shocked and devastated when we learned of Harold's death. We rushed to get to Joyce as soon as we heard, but she was mostly gone when we arrived. I was glad they went together. Joyce would have wanted that. Harold, too.

Cal and Lindsey eventually married and had two more children together before Cal had a heart attack and passed away nearly eight years to the day of that fateful vacation to Edisto Island. Lindsey and her children moved out of state not long after but not before surprising us at our home to tell us goodbye.

I remember gazing at the children my ex-husband and Lindsey had created together and not feeling a single morsel of regret. Lilly had grown into a beautiful girl, and she looked so much like Cal, it was almost like meeting a ghost. But perhaps the saddest part of seeing them again is that Lilly couldn't remember Drew. Drew had kept a photo of the two of them together that he showed her, and it still didn't help to ring any bells. She looked at this man who had played the role of her father for over a year like she was meeting him for the first time. That hurt Drew, but he understood, too. Lilly had only been a year old back then and had no reason to remember him. What were Lindsey and Cal supposed to do? Keep reminding her about the man her mother had cheated on and lied to?

I never expected my life to take the twists and turns that it did. When I met Cal, fell in love with him, and married him, I didn't think

there was anything else. I thought that was it. *Till death do us part.*
That wasn't it.

But it wasn't the end either.

There's a great, big, ol' world out there that has yet to be discovered. There are days we haven't lived yet, people we don't know yet. This life isn't over until it's over. We'll write a thousand chapters before we close our book for good.

People Watching

DISCUSSION QUESTIONS

1. Jess has battled cancer and endured her husband's neglect and infidelity. How do you think that has shaped who Jess has become? Do you think she would have allowed her husband to continue to be unfaithful if she hadn't fought cancer?

2. The reader is left to wonder about how Lindsey and Cal met. What do you think could have pulled them together? Do you think they deserve each other?

3. Would you have been able to watch your partner/spouse with someone else and choose not to say anything? Do anything?

4. Joyce is sort of a comic relief to the story. Do you think that she was right in meddling into Jess and Drew's lives? How did her people-watching help others?

5. Would you have taken the measures Joyce did to help a stranger discover the truth?

6. Obviously, Lilly, as a baby, was innocent in the chaos. Do you think anyone else was completely innocent? Did Jess and/or Drew have any burden to bear in their marriages falling apart?

7. At the end of the book, the author says that people-watching has saved people in different ways. Do you think that's true? What are some ways you have seen people-watching save someone?

8. Which character(s) did you relate to the most and why?

9. The concept of others finding humor in the midst of terrible circumstances isn't new, yet some still feel it's a bit uncouth.

Would you agree? How do you react to bad circumstances and tragedy?

10. Would you agree with Joyce in that some relationships are worth fighting for, while others simply are not?

11. If you were Jess or Drew, how would you have reacted to Cal's confession on the beach? Would you have stayed to search for Lilly or would you have left?

ABOUT THE AUTHOR

Samantha Lauren was born and raised in Greenville, South Carolina, where she still resides. Samantha married her college sweetheart in 2007, and together, they have a teenage daughter, Bree. When Samantha isn't writing or reading, she can be found watching a good movie or television series, heading to the beach, or simply enjoying time in her backyard.

www.authorsamanthalauren.com